W9-CHS-854

THE UNFORSAKEN

The Unforsaken

BY

CHRISTIAN MURCIAUX

Translated from the French by
PETER WILES

Pantheon Books *New York*

A DIVISION OF RANDOM HOUSE

FIRST PUBLISHED IN THE UNITED STATES IN 1964

 Published in New York by Pantheon Books, a division of Random House, Inc., and simultaneously in Toronto, Canada, by Random House of Canada, Limited. Manufactured in the United States of America.

Library of Congress catalog card number: 63-15371

Originally published in French under the title *Notre-Dame des Désemparés* © 1958 Librairie Plon

Author's Note

THE CHARACTERS AND SITUATIONS described in this book are imaginary. The author has not been so ambitious as to try to mirror the successive phases of the Spanish Civil War in the incidents of a novel, nor so presumptuous as to attempt an evaluation. He has endeavoured to recreate the fierce climate in which the destinies of a few human beings took shape. His one concern was to establish a close link between, on the one hand, the adventures, experiences and revelations surrounding these few and, on the other, the paroxysm of courage and cruelty, of clearsightedness and blindness, that tore a people in two. His aim has been to transport his readers into a different place and time, as he has previously sought to do in his portrayal of Italy at the time of the Renaissance, of Russia in the grasp of the Nihilists, and of America soon after the landing of the Pilgrim Fathers.

The only truth that a novelist can arrive at goes by the modest name of verisimilitude: it is hard to define, but every reader can feel it in his bones. It springs, not only from the way in which characters behave, but from the profound complicity that exists between the author and each and every one of them. It implies a scrupulous adherence to eyewitness accounts, but it calls for more than even the most intensive research. All references to historical events are accurate, then, whether in regard to the identity of a unit participating in the battle of the Ebro, to the failure of the Republican conspiracy at Jaca, or to the last words of the Falangist leader. To the open-minded, it may seem that José Antonio's and Firmin Galan's words have the same ring to them: there is only one Spain.

The Madonna of the Forsaken, from whom this book derives its title, has held sway over Valencia for centuries past, and the Civil War did not rob the city of its palladium. The art critics regard her statue as the work of Vicente de San Vicente, a present from Pope Pedro de Luna, in the early years of the fifteenth century, to the confraternity entrusted with the care of the Forsaken, the Insane and the Innocent. But the people of Valencia believe that this Madonna, enveloping in her cloak the infants fleeing from Herod's soldiers, was sculpted by a mysterious traveller, as company for the bodies of executed criminals. The author has not attempted to resolve this problem, or to explain the strangely huddled attitude of this Virgin, who seems to invite confidences, anticipate confessions and ferret out secrets. He has merely tried to evoke her with the innocent fervour of a child of the *huerta* and to see her through his eyes . . .

Notes on political and military personalities in the text

Azaña, Manuel—Republican leader. President of the Republic, 1936.

Calvo Sotelo, José—Monarchist politician whose assassination, 13th July 1936, sparked off the Civil War.

Casado López, Segismundo—Republican, led coup against Negrín.

Franco, General Francisco—Exiled 1936. Gained control of Morocco, then landed in Spain. Nationalist 'Caudillo' Victor of Civil War. Present Head of State.

Goded, General—Nationalist. Was exiled, returned to Barcelona, was captured and executed.

Largo Caballero, Francisco—Socialist Premier, 1939. Held responsible for extreme leftward trend of Republican Government.

Lorca, Garcia—A great Spanish poet, famous in the thirties. Was executed by the Nationalists.

Miaja, José—Outstanding Republican General.

Mola, General Emilio—Leader of Nationalist Resistance prior to Franco's invasion of the mainland.

Negrín, Juan—Republican, succeeded Largo Caballero as Premier.

Nin, Andrés—Co-founder of Marxist Workers' Party (P.O.U.M.), executed by communists for Trotskyist 'heresy'.

'La Pasionaria', Dolores Ibarruri—Popular communist orator and politician.

Primo de Rivera, José Antonio—Founder of Falange. Son of Alfonso XIII's Dictator-Premier. Executed by Republicans.

Segura, Cardinal—Primate of Spain. Opposed both Republic and Falange. Exiled, returned at end of war.

Tomás, Belarmino—Socialist deputy, led Asturias miners' revolt, 1934.

PART ONE

The Huerta

I

IT WAS SO HOT that the flies adhering to the votive offerings had given up buzzing. In the village church the children were having a job to keep their eyes open for all the priest's description of the wrath of God smiting the first man. His thin voice, which alone seemed to fill the worn soutane, was describing the jealous fury of the Everlasting. But this first family quarrel left the plaster statues unaffected. A bee strayed among the altar flowers, which had lost their smell, immersed in the cavernlike clamminess of the thick walls. Staring down at his scarred knees, Juanito Sanchez sat pondering Parde Enrique's words.

'In the sweat of thy face shalt thou eat bread . . .' Such a punishment held no fears for a peasant boy. Was not the Eden from which Adam and Eve were sent forth the Valencian *huerta*, where rice, vegetables, fruit and flowers grew all the year round? Men barely had time to gather in the crops, sheave the corn and sort the fruit before other harvests were upon them. Agile hands reached out to gather and sow, to heap the light baskets with oranges and lemons, to water the flowers and plant out the rice. The Earthly Paradise could not have been richer than the Valencian plain. Why waste tears on the men living in the big, white, deep-roofed farms? Covered with a supple green or golden fleece, the *huerta* repaid their toil a hundredfold every season.

Juanito's neighbour had fallen asleep. Padre Enrique was dwelling on Adam's remorse and Eve's tears. In the weeks when nothing grew the *huerta* was not drab, Juanito was thinking. In winter, water glistened in the furrows. Wild duck swooped down on to the fields, with discordant cries; they continued their unwieldy flying, their graceless somersaulting, among the reeds on the Albufera lake. Shooting parties came out from the city. There were long, gay, fireside evenings in the farmhouses. God must have passed it over in his anger . . .

The priest noticed that Juanito, in turn, was giving way.

'I'll teach you to look at your knees! You will sweep out the church before Mass tomorrow.'

Juanito blushed. The priest's punishment was ineffectual too. Before running to the fields, he would quickly swill the uneven stone flags and place a bunch of fleshy roses in a blue vase at the foot of the Virgin's altar.

The priest retired to the sacristy, sighing to himself. Juanito hung back. He loved the shadowiness of the church, the Father's sonorous, despondent voice and the flies, now starting to buzz again as though Sunday school were over for them too. As he made for the door he thought back to the *huerta* in wintertime, when the peasants flooded their fields and leased them out to the shooting parties. There was something strangely fascinating about that fluttering of wings, those raucous cries, those men of a different species suddenly appearing with their fur garments, their costly guns, their horses, their sports cars: a whole sumptuous, refined world. The poorest of these mighty lords owned several palaces, huge tracts of land, more stables than the village had houses, more servants than the village had inhabitants. These men, all-powerful under the sun, whose whims—as unpredictable as drought or wet weather—affected countless lives, shared the king's meals, his duties and his recreations. Hence, no doubt, their jaunty and imperious manner. They talked and laughed louder than the peasants. Their voices carried far in the limpid darkness and were enough to give them away when they were hiding behind trees, keeping look-out for game.

In the middle of the lake the beaters kindled huge resinous torches, whereupon fiery caverns opened in the watery depths. Lured by these unfamiliar lights, these suns pulsating level with the earth's surface and apparently sinking underground, the ducks started wheeling. They supposed that they were warming their numbed wings on the first flames of dawn. But shots would ring out on the shore; more than one startled bird would scorch its wings on these torches driven into the ice like stakes.

The huntsmen derived little joy from this victory. Behind them they left piles of grey wings and smashed birds'-legs. And the peasants could taste silt and gunpowder in the fowl's flesh.

These cruel games intrigued Juanito. Was this some kind of obligation the rich were under, to lose sleep when there was no need, to kill without pleasure? These arduous diversions, like the joys and sorrows of the mighty, made up a strange ritual. Juanito was inclined to pity those who were subject to it from birth. One day he had glimpsed this world in which exertions turned into fun and danger into a ruse for escaping boredom. It was his ninth birthday. Uncle Manuel announced that the land abutting on the pond had been leased out.

For a single day's shooting the great noble, who had named his own price, would pay more than was yielded by the annual maize crop. The news was greeted with a tremor of incredulity, but no one could find any objection to the Duke of Villahermosa's liberality.

Juanito's mother stroked the boy's head and smiled. 'It's a lot of money,' she said, 'but the Duke of Villahermosa is not as rich as I am, for his son cannot hold a candle to my Juanito.' Juanito's mother had a reputation as a wag; in her girlhood there had been no lovelier pair of eyes and no warmer-hued complexion in the whole of the Valencian plain. She had transferred to her son the pride that she dared not take in her own beauty.

Uncle Manuel flung an irritated glance in her direction, but a flawless face disarms anger. For appearances' sake, Manuel pointed out that it was wrong to make such flattering remarks about one's own children.

The birthday marked by this profitable transaction was a joyful occasion. The whims of the rich benefit the poor, the peasants and the priests who, as a result, will occasionally come by a chalice, a chasuble or a crucifix. Everyone started talking about a wonderful float that the Duke of Medinacelli had just presented to one of the confraternities in Seville because the float that usually bore the Cristo del Gran Poder had shown signs of giving way in the last procession.

At the crack of dawn the Duke of Villahermosa arrived amid a great hullabaloo, compounded of creaking carriages, whinnying horses, oaths and barking dogs. Waking with a start, Juanito realized what was happening and dashed out of the farmhouse just as the Duchess was arriving. She was Scottish by birth and prided herself on being able to sit a horse like a man and spend a night stalking game without getting tired. Sybil was bold and beautiful, with over-red lips and light-coloured hair. Was it this peculiarity that kept all these men buzzing attentively about her, or fascination with the happiness that emanates from any young married couple? The vehicles were promptly unharnessed. Juanito admired the padded collars, the reins, the glittering metalwork. He helped a footman to let down the folding steps of one of the coaches. The lacquered door opened. It was a coach out of some fairy tale, lined inside with a light, almost snowy leather. A small human frame imparted barely a tremor to the steps. Juanito, not daring to look up, saw a small bare hand resting on a fur jacket, and then a face that wholly proclaimed zest for life. From a fur toque spilled hair of unreal goldenness.

'Do you live here?' asked this stranger.

The boy was bowled over by the question. He could not understand this fabulous creature's concerning herself with his existence. Already, making her way into the main room, she was admiring the pans, gridirons and strainers whose superbly wrought designs stood out bold and black against the lime-white walls. She stooped, intrigued, to examine the *paella* ingredients, the rice in which the tender chicken, the hashed octopus and the shellfish, still with their sea smell, would be blended with sweetened green peas, pimento and saffron.

Juanito's mother was laughing unrestrainedly. 'In the *huerta*, men are as good at cooking *paella* as women are.' All the time she was showing the foreigner round the *barraca* she was hugging her son to her. The Duchess asked what his name was.

'Juanito.'

The young woman turned to her husband, whose jealousy amused her.

'Before I married you, I pictured all Spaniards as being like this child, with those blue-grey eyes and that grave expression.'

'Really,' said the Duke, somewhat stung.

But now Sybil had ears only for the young Marquis of Silva,

who was giving a colourful account of hunting trips up the Zambezi.

Juanito, his waist neatly pinched in by his belt, went off reluctantly to the orchard; he was helping Uncle Manuel graft the orange trees. But, carrying the ladder out, he wondered what the young woman was up to in the main room of the *barraca*. A series of reports announced that the shoot was under way . . .

At nightfall Juanito saw Sybil again, sitting surrounded by the sportsmen, who were laughing very loudly, stimulated by the fragrance of the food and fortified by the full-bodied Rioja wine. To the boy she looked tired and even more beautiful than in the morning. Her companions' bragging was getting on her nerves. She ridiculed the young Marquis of Silva when he tried to repeat his tales of buffaloes and rhinoceroses. Shooting game was a romantic pleasure, and one swiftly exhausted, like going to Venice, being presented at Court or attending one's first ball. Within a few hours one's eagerness and curiosity were sapped; novelty and unpredictability had lost their bloom . . . It had become merely a dull topic of conversation.

The only thing that pleased her was the incredible dignity of Juanito, who was asking if he might pour some more wine into her glass. He was charming, with his strongly defined features and his eyes of turbid blue, like those lakes rimmed with pale heathland that Sybil loved so much. In the rather clipped Spanish that she had learned at school, she said to him: 'We have not had time to make friends.'

Juanito blushed violently, but he replied at once: 'You will be back next year.'

'What's that you are saying?' the Duke asked uneasily. He disliked Sybil's private utterances to strangers on trains, the servants at home, or even her neighbours at official dinners.

'I'm making plans for next year!' said Sybil. She gave Juanito a fond, quizzical smile that threw the boy's mind into a turmoil.

She refused to journey back in the sumptuous coupé. One returned from a day's shooting on horseback, she said. When the thoroughbred's stirrup proved too high, Juanito made a step for her with his hand.

Up on the animal's back, Sybil wondered what she could give Juanito without hurting his feelings. Her husband was always telling her that she must avoid hurting the feelings of the poor. If the poor had such delicate feelings, Sybil had asked on her arrival in Madrid, what did that leave for the rich?

Balthazar had pondered this for a long time, then answered: 'The rich have pride.'

Sybil had told herself that life among these particular rich and poor would not be easy, but that anywhere else it would be tame.

In the pocket of her fur jacket she found nothing but some small change and a packet of cigarettes that she had already started on. She handed the packet to Juanito.

'Perhaps these will do till Christmas?'

Juanito bowed gravely: 'They will do till you come back.' He was taking her at her word. Sybil smiled at him.

When the party moved off, Juanito slipped the packet under his shirt, right next his heart.

In the world of the rich, opulence is a curse afflicting the idle, obliging them to concoct elaborate duties, ingenious pastimes, futile woes; but sumptuousness is also a tribute paid to God. That is why the grandest buildings, the rarest jewels, the golden monstrances and ciboria and the silver or enamel crucifixes were His by right. And to approach Him the priests robed themselves in silk, fine linen and lace. Smells of flowers and incense mingled in the churches' cool shade. Voices formed other flower beds, exhaling the sweetness of fresh-blown roses and lilies. Each screened-off private chapel was a favourite's antechamber for petitioners to wait in. On the way up to the high altar one had to secure the saints' backing. Like superb chamberlains, these half-naked, haloed creatures, gold-clad or silver-armoured, conducted Juanito and his mother towards the Madonna.

Under many names and guises, the Mother of God reigned over Valencia. Her favourite palace was connected to the cathedral by a strange passageway in mid-air; the Madonna was thus able to visit her Son, unobserved, at any hour of the day or night. To the many-doored rotunda where she held court came an incessant flow of worshippers. Men and women of every class flung themselves down before Our Lady of the Forsaken, the Virgin of the Distressed. These sinners, each prostrated by his or her own weakness, were oblivious to one another. They would fling out their arms and give vent to soundless cries of anguish. This chorus of entreaties surrounded the Virgin as surely as the rows of blazing candles; but these calls for help, these unreasoning fits of despair, these silent frenzies, these effusive lamentations did not trouble the peacefulness of her grave countenance. They all wailed over the same fears and the same desires. They craved access to another human body, that to them seemed glorious. In order to live, they demanded illusion, not truth. They mumbled about mercy and renunciation and purity, but tight about their shivering souls they drew the old rags of their sins; only the recollection of their joys, their lusts and their squalid moments of indulgence kept them from shaking in their shoes.

Just as priests grow used to the routine of remorse and forgiveness, so the Virgin accorded a rather weary attention to their admissions, their evasions and their lies. Out of pity she pretended to believe in these faltering displays of ardour, these pathetic entreaties, these reckless vows. For centuries, she had been watching hearts bleed. But, amazed at the supreme power of her silence, she gazed sadly upon the incurable wounds of the spirit and the flesh. For the Virgin of the Forsaken knew that men's hopes were as futile as their regrets and that every living creature was free only to suffer and cause suffering.

On certain days, the chapel was a mass of white flowers. The statue of the Madonna towered in the midst of a bed of lilies.

Juanito's mother loved the glitter of these weddings, at which human happiness and celestial joy were artlessly mingled. Squeezed against a pillar by the crowd, Juanito would glance nervously up at the altar. Forgetting the young couple whom the priest was blessing, he imagined that he was witnessing the Virgin's marriage to the people of Valencia; and there on the altar, under a heavy diadem, the loveliest of brides was smiling at him from out of the depths of the remotest ages . . .

But one had also to seek spiritual improvement by going to

look at holy remains. A shiver would run down Juanito's spine when the sacristan in the Archbishop's palace drew back a garnet-red cloth more imposing than the curtain in front of a stage. The leaves of a huge cupboard swung slowly open. Instinctively the crowd recoiled. Beyond the thick pane of glass, on velvet-lined shelves, stood rows of ornamented reliquaries. These thickets of gold and quartz, to which rubies, topazes and pearls clung like dewdrops, at once shielded and in part revealed brittle coils of hair, the swaddling clothes in which the Virgin had wrapped the babe, a piece of the sponge with which Our Lord's thirst was slaked with vinegar. Juanito's mother never tired of gazing at these overwhelming religious proofs which seemed to draw her closer to the Virgin, for the swaddling clothes of the Infant Jesus looked as though they had been made from the crudest material and were faded from use and laundering.

Juanito preferred the reliquaries that reproduced a saint's head in gold and silver, with its gaping sockets; or those long gleaming arms, complete with the wrist-joint and the drab yellow humerus, like a bone found neglected in some graveyard; or those hands, imitating the slightest folds of skin and hiding from view a phalanx or a fingernail. At night Juanito dreamed of saints resembling huge articulated dolls whose arms and legs were made of precious metals. This glittering company shared both the repose of the Creator and the toil of his creatures.

The rarest relics were displayed only on certain feast days. On such occasions the saints who had returned to earth listened to people's entreaties. Then they plunged, laden with messages, into the deep blue of the Valencian sky.

But the custodians were afraid lest the fervour of the onlookers' stares should wear out these all but transparent pieces of fabric that still bore faint traces of blood spilled centuries ago . . . The sacristan would jealously draw the brocade curtain over the sinister jawbone that had once been covered by a girl saint's lovely lips, or over some martyr's kneecap that looked like a battered pebble. An acolyte would step forward and rattle some coins in an offertory plate.

Juanito would feel disappointed. He pictured saints as being armour-clad in light, brandishing swords that were sharper than earthly swords, swords capable of running people through without drawing blood. His mother would whisk him off to the cathedral, where the chalice used at the Last Supper was displayed for veneration. This was a stout reddish shell perched insecurely on its mount. But the chapter room contained other treasures brought back from the East by the Crusaders. Curled up in its glass coffin, like a monstrous tadpole, lay the now grimy body of one of the Holy Innocents. One day the sacristan lifted Juanito up so that he might feast his eyes on this Lamb who had been set upon by Herod's ruffians. The warriors fully harnessed for the good fight, the naked athletes tortured with red-hot pincers or broken on the cross, had merely been imitating the first martyr. Today the Holy Innocent had joined the Infant Jesus and was fluttering close to the Virgin.

Juanito was amazed that he should have left this outer covering behind, so like the silkworm cocoons that the old women out at the village unravelled in wintertime. The ivory caskets, the crystal pyxes, the missal-covers encrusted with enormous blue and red cabochons, the plated ciboria in which saints had transformed bread and wine into the body and blood of Our Lord, the silver candelabra brought back from the Indies by the conquistadors—in vain did these shine out beneath the stained-glass windows. Their glitter could not take Juanito's mind off the hideous goldfish bowl in which the Holy Innocent lay convulsed for all eternity.

Every Friday a miracle was worked in the Archbishop's chapel. A husky old clock would strike eleven. In the shadowy chancel a row of candles would flicker. The altarpiece would noiselessly disappear. The mechanism was so good that angels could not have rolled it away more quickly. In its place appeared a spread-eagled Christ. He had just uttered his last cry and his head drooped on to his shoulder, while his arms and legs sagged forward, trying to free themselves from the cross. Even though he had witnessed the ceremony several times, Juanito would shake from head to foot when the canvas slid along the grooves, vanishing like a wraith before the terrifying reality of this Christ bleeding, unseen, in the midst of human indifference, the prayers of the unctuous and the flutter of fans beating out a rhythm to the local gossip.

On leaving the dark churches, where the saints seemed to be perpetuating their wounds, Juanito would duck under the stalls in the flower market. The stallkeepers, who all came from the *huerta*, would recognize his mother; they would contend for Juanito, as though he were going to buy up their whole stock. The least lovely of these strapping, radiant women was worthy of comparison with the basketfuls of flowers clustering on her stall. The pinks, flimsily bundled together by thin lengths of bass, the huge bunches of roses with their bruised petals, the sheaves of jasmine and narcissi—it was as though they were all competing in an effort to cover the market-place with an aromatic cloud, in which the smells of blood and fire, of brimstone and pepper would capriciously give way to the fragrance of orange blossom and the cool savour of mint . . .

Back at the farm, Juanito would keep himself to himself, so as to recall all the things that he had seen. His mother, on the other hand, would describe the stained-glass windows, speak wonderingly of how an altar had been decorated, and artlessly intersperse the account of her devotions with a list of cravings aroused by a shawl, a pair of shoes or a mantilla displayed in a shop window near the Lonja monument.

2

THESE OUTINGS served as landmarks between harvests: hemp would be followed by corn, maize by beans. Sweet potatoes would have to be planted quickly on the banks of loose earth dividing the fields. The rice, which grows quickly in the warm mud, would need pricking out. Juanito would learn how to pick flowers while they were still just buds, how to sort oranges. In the morning twilight he would help load the carts with fruit and vegetables that were still damp from the dawn mist, then he would go out into the fields with the men.

Meanwhile the women would be squeezing the sickly-sweet juice out of the hoary sedge-roots and scenting it with almonds; or cutting sheets of broadcloth into sashes for Juanito's uncles to wear round their waists; or weaving esparto soles for the boy himself and adding brightly ribboned bows to those light shoes that give Valencians their springy, dance-like walk.

In spring the farmhouse walls had to be gone over with limewash so that the *barraca* should retain that shrill whiteness secretly tinged with blue upon which the balcony balustrades, the wrought-iron tracery and the shaft of a lamp seemed to have been picked out with a deft brush.

When there was a dispute over water rights Juanito's father would go into the city on Thursday, dressed as though it were a feast day. The Water Tribunal held its deliberations beneath the left-hand portal of the cathedral. There was only a wrought-iron screen between onlookers and judges, each of whom sat in an old carved chair bearing the name of one of the seven main canals that irrigate the Valencian plain. The saints and apostles followed the debate from their niches.

Juanito's father would lay his complaint before the Tribunal just as though he were talking to neighbours. The judges would listen attentively. Some would frown, and their deeply lined faces were as good to gaze upon as well-ploughed fields. The others would follow the litigant's account deep in his eyes; they would weigh his hesitations and expressions of repentance, breaking in briefly if he was contradicting himself or straying from the point. Then they would glance inquiringly at one another. There would be a swift consultation, centred round the oldest member, who would rise majestically from his old chair—its imitation leather mildewed by the dampness of the sacristy—to pronounce judgment. When he said: 'We', the plural referred not only to the seven water lords in their black clothes and espadrilles, who for ten centuries had been dispensing prompt and unerring justice. His pronouncement was issued in the name of all the peasants of the *huerta*. If the convicted party protested, his fine was doubled on the spot. The loser would walk sheepishly away, with gibes ringing in his ears . . .

Meted out in the presence of these stone brows and staring eyes, the justice of the Water Tribunal was final and irrevocable, like God's: the saints and apostles were there to endorse it. After the hearing, judges and plaintiffs would meet in the inn over a glass of *anis* or white wine. They would all praise Juanito for being as self-possessed as a grown man, even though he was only nine. He had learned to read all by himself, his father would say proudly, and yet he knew how to drive a plough and look after the animals. Another few years, and at harvest time he would be able to work all day and dance all night like a true Valencian. He would be a good Christian, but also a lusty Spaniard dwelling under the cloudless sky of the Levante: dashing, genial, jocular and full of character, Joaquin was already seeing himself in his youngest son . . .

In spring, Valencia became a scene of gay turmoil. Far too many cartloads of flowers were driven through the gates that the Moors had never been able to force. All the good humour and laughter, all the joy pent up throughout the winter and singing accumulated under the frost of silence and dancing repressed during the months of toil seemed to burst out, sweeping the men and women of Valencia along in a whirl of pleasure. For three days and three nights they did honour to St Joseph, the workman saint. He was treated to a procession of giant figures conjuring up both the fight against the Moors and present-day happenings. Blue, green and red stars streaked the night sky. The sight of the long tails of the nebulae unfurling drew cries of terror and enchantment from the crowd. Satan's pomp and the splendours of Paradise went hand in hand. The Moorish Kings were confused with the Demon Kings and the Three Kings at the Nativity. Pulling their beards was an act of piety. Juanito would overcome his fear. The tussling of these absurd giants ended in a firework display. Their brass, wood and paper carcases burnt joyously at the Virgin's feet. And the crackers of the street urchins exploding on the pavement, and even in doorways, completed the task of turning the procession into a riot.

Juanito would ride home with his big brothers Domingo and Federico, the three of them squatting on the plough-wheels, harnesses and sacks of manure with which the cart was cluttered. Processions and 'battles of the flowers' were never more than an interlude between sowings or reapings. Juanito would stare out at the countryside from under the flap of the awning. The curling evening light lingered on the ears of corn, the young maize stalks. A golden blur, a tremulous dust, hovered close to the ground. Above the sulphated vines the sky was turning rust-coloured. Vague yearnings were stirring in Juanito's heart. What was the point of these festivities, which so upset the rhythm of work? For three whole days the men had been eating, drinking, singing. The soil went on producing in silence. Unaffected by griefs and rejoicings, it asked nothing of the peasants of the *huerta* except to be kept fertile. And doubtless its only joy was to be impoverished and devastated at their hands.

Next day, at first light, the voice of the city bell-tower dedicated to St Michael would summon Juanito to the fields. The chimes of the Miguelete would scatter over the *huerta* like a flight of large, silver-winged birds; the men would hurry out of bed and run to the well for a splash, laughing and calling one another names. They were all so eager to start digging. The sounds seemed to produce concentric ripples in the clear sky. The sun moved higher. The men toiled bent-backed in the rice fields. Despite their wide-brimmed straw hats, sweat poured down their tanned faces. The midday angelus brought the men back to the farmhouse where, with their arms flung over their faces, they slept through the hours in which earth and sky caught fire. This was everyday life, life indispensable, whose flavour—like the flavour of bread and water—never lost its edge. Juanito desired no other.

When he danced in the village square on Sundays, there was not a fifteen-year-old boy in the whole *huerta* who performed with more flair and vigour. After the fast and furious *jota*, the girls would crowd round Juanito as he stood recovering his breath. They would shower him with compliments and bantering remarks. But he had chosen Soledad because she was the most reserved. At night they would stroll through the fields, without speaking. If their bodies brushed against each other, it was without their willing it. One August evening when they were sitting in the shade of the trees, Juanito clasped Soledad hotly to him and bit her; she sighed with pleasure.

3

IN VALENCIA, Juanito and his cousins would rush off to the cinema near the flower market, without even looking to see what was on. This helter-skelter succession of images made his head swim. The passions that activated these all too beautiful beings, with their all too expressive features, remained more of a mystery to him than the cities of the New World, the countries of Scandinavia and the resplendent alien surroundings in which these peculiar feelings blossomed out into unrestrained actions and searing words. Men and women of quite a different species would smile, cry, quarrel or make it up for reasons unintelligible to Juanito. Was, then, the life of the *huerta* not the only possible life? A revelation stole into Juanito's artless mind as a result of this momentary uprooting. Yes, he could have been born in Montmartre, he could have walked assertively into a New York night club wearing a jacket with black silk facings. He could have been a gangster, a Bohemian or a multi-millionaire. Other women would have approached him with Soledad's smiles and kisses on their lips . . . When they left the cinema, his companions would debate the actress's charms as they would have debated those of some local girl. Juanito would come away with the slight lurching feeling that persists even on dry land at the end of a voyage. But, for his companions, memory of one pleasure was effaced by anticipation of the next. They would race to the café and Juanito would follow them, feeling lost, as though part of him were still back there in the dark auditorium, in front of the magic screen.

One Sunday in April, Juanito's companions put their heads together. At the far end of a long, dark passageway lined with houses that all looked unlived-in, Alfonso gave a resolute tug to a bell beside an iron gate. They made their way into a small patio where, by fits and starts, a fountain was distributing an illusion of coolness; but the evergreens were wilting on the side of the basin, which was rimmed with red and yellow tiles. Alfonso ventured under the balcony at the side of the patio and returned with a buxom gipsy with regular features and the bronze colouring of a Hindu idol. Señora Martinez had been the number one dancer in Cadiz, a fact that she brought to light as she took her place among the boys. Shutters banged open along the first-floor gallery. A row of sleepy faces appeared, and Señora Martinez complained that the girls on her staff had no thought for anything but sleep. Her gaze lingered approvingly on Juanito.

'It is a sin to sleep alone,' she said. 'Sweet dreams do not come to a woman unless she is in a man's arms.'

Juanito blushed. This preamble was giving him the same peculiar feeling as certain films. How was he to gain a footing in this world so close to and so different from his own? The señora did not have time to enlarge on her opinion. Conchita, Mercedes and Pepita appeared. They were still pinning up their hair and smoothing down their skirts. As they took their places at the table they called for drinks.

'Nowadays they need nannies to hold their hands,' Mercedes said.

She clapped the castanets that dangled from her wrist; the cicada-like whir spoke to Juanito in a familiar tongue. He asked Mercedes whether she danced. She said with a laugh: 'When the weather isn't so hot and I've nothing better to do!'

She had tucked a pair of speckled pinks between her breasts;

when she leaned forward to speak to Juanito the scent from them did not mask the smell of warm, moist skin.

'It's nicer up in my room,' said the girl. Señora Martinez shrugged at this unseemly directness. Juanito followed Mercedes. A short flight of stairs led up to a dark, cool room in which a dressing table and a rumpled bed could be dimly made out.

'I keep the shutters closed,' said the girl, 'on account of the sun. You'll manage.' Naked already, she lay down on the bed. Juanito joined her. In the poor light his inexperience might pass for momentary clumsiness and his fumbling for impatience.

'How old are you?' Mercedes asked between kisses.

'Twenty,' said Juanito, calmly putting three years on his age.

'Have you had many women?' Mercedes asked casually.

To evade the question, he nibbled her lip.

While he was dressing, she switched on a small bedside lamp with a pink shade. The room exhibited its untidiness. A divan with torn sheets, a battered chair and an enamel bowl: these sufficed for making love with chance acquaintances. To the peeling wallpaper she had affixed a coloured picture of Nuestra Señora de las Angustias, patroness of Granada. Mercedes surveyed this scene of squalor while Juanito knotted his tie.

'I'll come and see you again,' said Juanito. For this woman lying prostrate on the bed he felt a mingling of unsatisfied desire and revulsion. The pink light fell on the bare shoulder, the full breasts; it glanced off the shameless belly.

'Have you said that to many women?' Mercedes asked sceptically.

'None,' said Juanito. 'That was the first time . . .'

When she had unbuttoned the front of her dress Mercedes had laid the two pinks beside the lamp. Their scent filled the room, drowning the smell of violet soap and cheap eau-de-Cologne. The sight of the youth's body was ridding her mind of the memory of other caresses. Juanito held his peace. Stooping over the mirror, which was surrounded by picture postcards, he was carefully combing his hair. His silence was obliterating the sighing and rasping, the confiding and rhapsodizing that follow in the wake of the act of love . . .

She refused Juanito's money.

'Some other time . . . what's your name?'

She kept saying his Christian name as though Juanito were the only person in the world to bear it, as though it could not conceivably go with any but his round face, any but his strangely velvety blue-grey eyes. She wanted to crush her lips against those pupils that were the colour of the sea; she gave him a kiss on the cheek.

'*Adiós*, Juanito!'

She let him go back to the patio by himself. She switched off the lamp. He was a fine-looking boy, like a good many others in Valencia; but he was more open-hearted than those others because he was from the country. Mercedes lay in the shadows, wondering what seam of undeserved happiness she had struck.

His companions greeted Juanito with quiet respect. Alfonso and the madam were talking about a girl called Lola, whom a client had run off with and married. Since she had risen in the world, her workmates had seen neither hide nor hair of her, which just went to show what poor stuff she was made of.

Juanito had the same feeling of being transplanted that his visits to the cinema gave him. This time he had stepped through the screen. A few gestures, a few words, and he had penetrated the disconcerting world of pleasure, in which body and soul swapped their secrets and pooled their raptures.

A month later, Juanito returned to the señora's—alone. He order an *anis*, and Mercedes came to his table as though he could not conceivably wish for any other woman.

'I knew you would come back,' she said.

He blushed slightly. Up in her room, Mercedes was content to yield to his desire. After the caresses in the dark she slid her hands over his muscular frame and firm thighs. His was a body fashioned by toil, moulded by the seasons like fruit and flowers, and his very skin smelt of the rain-drenched or sun-baked soil.

'What a lovely-looking boy you are! What a lovely-looking boy . . .!' To cut short this carnal litany, Juanito clasped her to him again. Mercedes groaned, overjoyed at having so swiftly initiated a young lover.

The week after was Holy Week. Like everyone else in the village, Juanito went to confession. He was not so much remorseful as disturbed at the hours spent at Señora Martinez's subject to Mercedes's admiring eyes and greedy hands. Even when they were sitting in the patio she found it necessary to sleek down his hair or marvel at his ears, which were as small and shapely as a woman's. She wanted to treat him to ties and bottles of scent. Juanito refused these presents. He insisted on paying for Mercedes's love and for the bottle of Manzanilla that they drank under the tender-hearted gaze of Señora Martinez.

At confession, Juanito charged himself with yielding to the sinful desires of the body. The Padre did not know of the youthful tendency to confuse lust with a perilous curiosity about another human being. He reassured Juanito: gratification was sinful only when found in the arms of a woman of ill-repute; husbands and wives coming together within the sight of God were experiencing the bliss of Adam and Eve in the garden of Eden.

4

LIFE WENT ON, punctuated by the trips to Valencia, the purchase of a horse that reared dangerously first time out, the sale of the rice crop at a very high figure and the unexpected departure of the king. In Spain, kings come and go every few years. During their absence, somebody looks after their furniture and their gardens for them. The change of constitution is of smaller consequence to a peasant living and working in the *huerta* than drought, floods or the embargo on the export of oranges to Britain or France.

In the Cortes, the right-wing majority was being replaced by a left-wing majority. This word 'majority' was bringing another word, 'coalition', to the politicians' lips; but in a coalition the minority determines the majority. All this would leave Juanito thoroughly confused . . .

For him, Spain was simply the towns where his friends and relatives lived. In Toledo, one of his mother's cousins was a sacristan at a monastery hidden away in the heart of a tottery maze of synagogues, churches and palaces that seemed about to spill over into the ravines below. This holy town, still laden with the memory of the Moors and the smell of the ghettos, the latter the colour of stale gingerbread, was a black-and-gold hive deserted by its bees, an ex-voto discoloured by the smoke of incense and candles, a jewel as brittle and indestructible as the steel tempered in the waters of the Tajo.

In Madrid, one of Juanito's uncles worked at the Ministry of Commerce. This small, puny man was thereby invested with the magic of one who exercised control, held discretionary powers and was privy to state secrets. Juanito, on seeing him for the first time, was amazed that he did not wear uniform. But Juanito's mother was always talking about Salamanca, where the richest of her sisters lived in a house built of that honey-coloured marble which with the passage of years turns saffron yellow. At sunset this pink and copper town rising from the river paraded its tiers of monasteries, churches and palaces, many of them bristling with gargoyles, roofed with shells or studded like those old chests that used to contain brides' dowries.

In the evenings the crowd would flock into the Plaza Mayor, framed by tall houses and surrounded with arcades. The women out on the balconies would flutter their fans and make eyes, and every man in the square below would feel as though he were in the theatre, and the target of the stares and laughter and gibes raining down from the boxes. This was reminiscent of the stands that are put up in the heart of Seville to afford the prettiest women in town, and their attendant admirers, a view of the Good Friday procession. On these occasions, the attention of onlookers tends to be divided between the white faces, fluttering eyelashes and glittering jewellery of these women—the jewellery enhanced by the black velvet of their dresses—and the flagellants brandishing their candles and rattling their chains.

In the eyes of Juanito's uncles, Seville was the only town that anyone could possibly prefer to Valencia. The palaces of the rich deployed their summerhouses amid sweet-smelling flowerbeds; and the public gardens with their green arbours and secret pools and fountains and huge underground baths, once used by royal favourites, were the palaces of the poor.

When his family reeled off the sensuous names of unknown towns, Juanito would picture Granada and the sparkle of its spring waters, Malaga heavy with the intoxicating smell of wine-harvesting, and Murcia whose sturdy palms sprang up amid the mulberries and orange-trees, but no stretch of country was as manifestly chosen by God as the *huerta* round Valencia. The fruits and the flowers bore witness not only to human toil, but to the earth's richness, the sky's blessing and the bountiful gift of water. And this harmonizing of the elements rose to the greater glory of the Creator.

For the Valencians, thanksgiving burst out in the middle of spring, on the second Sunday in May. On this day the peasants' gratitude for the fertile soil and their devotion to the Virgin would combine in a single upsurge of feeling. At the Madonna's feet, deft hands would fashion a mystical garden, mingling colours and scents. The bride from the Song of Songs trod a bed of jasmines, roses and pinks. On the basilica walls, tapestries woven from petals revived familiar scenes: St Vincent Ferrer in the fervour of one of his sermons, the Madonna surrounded by kneeling saints. And along the roads the trampled buds gave off a sweet, pungent, intoxicating smell.

Inside her palace, the Madonna received her courtiers, bemused as a princess whom the envoys of some foreign king were about to snatch from the bosom of her family. Never had the flowers, the candles, the prayers poured out a fierier hymn of praise to this surrounded captive. The carpenters would be hammering away at the stands that were being erected by the basilica doors.

The Virgin, still protected from the roars of the crowd and from the blinding sky stretched taut above the narrow streets of Valencia, was a bride-to-be wavering now that the moment had come for her to leave her childhood surroundings. Juanito would feel even greater love for this defenceless woman whose face was soon to be put on show. When, next day, she was tugged from her chapel, she would be unsteady on her feet like an invalid risen from her sickbed; but sturdy arms would guide her safely through the eddyings of her people, amid all the cheering and shooting—for the smell of gunpowder gave the procession the exhilaration of a rodeo and the intense excitement of a kidnapping.

From a window, Theresa would watch this ceremony, which had all the breathtaking inevitability, all the tragic suspensefulness of a bullfight. She would hug Juanito to her bosom, and when the statue approached she would order: 'Quick! Down on your knees!'

The bearers would fight for the honour of protecting this frail captive: every year the Madonna would look more beautiful and more bejewelled. On the corner of the Calle del Miguelete the statue would slew round in their grasp; a patch of sunlight would invest the crown and ear-rings with a visionary halo, then spill on to her throat and breast with their array of necklaces and pendants. A celestial being enveloped with incandescent stones, the Virgin would loom larger and larger, and it was as though the onlookers' stares were setting this sacred bush ablaze. The spokes of her crown would turn her little face into the heart of a sun. Theresa would clasp her boy to her: 'Juanito, the Madonna is looking at you!'

Caught in a downpour of petals, deafened by the outcry from every side, the Virgin of the Forsaken would give Theresa a fond, lingering, rather weary look. But the impatient bearers would hustle the statue away. All that Theresa would be able to see of the Madonna, now, was her flowing hair. She would rise to her feet, bewildered by this mark of favour that others might have envied her. Her hand would tremble on the window-ledge, covered every year with a strip of red brocade. She would throw her arms round Juanito. Mother and son would stand there in silence, to extract the utmost rapture from this sign of predilection, and the others would chatter away—perhaps to spare their blushes.

5

IN THE SPRING, a few days before the Feast of the Blessed Virgin, Juanito's father was forced to take to his bed. Coming right in the middle of the season, this illness seemed a bad omen. To stop sowing, driving the plough, gathering in the harvest was, in itself, to turn one's back on life. The doctor spoke of blood-poisoning, then of an inner growth: the diagnosis made Juanito's father feel guilty. His illness had neither name nor cause. It was like deserting in the midst of battle. This discordant event shattered the rhythm of work, violated the tacit agreement between man and soil. The young rice-shoots were sprouting thick and fast, and their avid greenness called to mind the even grass of a well-kept lawn. Now was the time for them to be planted out in the wet furrows, but Juanito alone had the strength to turn the big manly frame over in bed without risk: the weight was too much for Theresa. Nursing his father gave Juanito much the same feeling as missing Sunday school. His chums would hail him from the roadway. He would hear the girls laughing very loudly in the orchards. As they came by with their heaped basketfuls of early fruit, they would make a point of pausing for breath outside the *barraca*.

They would mildly poke fun at him for being got up as a nurse, and then—catching sight of the bearded man gazing unseeingly at them from his bed—take to their heels. He would be left to himself, listening to his father's noisy breathing and feeling, somewhere at the back of his mind, that he was playing truant.

With the approach of evening, the bowl of the sky would deepen above the plain. The canals would multiply the blaze of the setting sun. But his father would wake up. He would gaze at Juanito in astonishment, as though he had taken advantage of this hour of troubled, fevered sleep to turn into another man. He would say sadly: 'It's your turn now, Juanito. How tall you are! How strong you are! You will have to look after your mother and your brothers. And when you have a son of your own, and he is old enough to get about on his own two feet, you will take him along to the Water Tribunal . . . and afterwards you will go to the inn for a drink, and the men from Alcira or Ruzafa will say to you: "That's a fine, strapping youngster you've got there!" and then it will be your turn to laugh for joy . . .'

Theresa would come and relieve her son at the sick man's bedside. She would insist on his going out for a walk; at nightfall Juanito would roam the empty fields for a while, feeling utterly at a loss. At the farmyard gates the kilns thrust up their strange cement cupolas. Each *barraca*—with its outhouses, where the animals were dozing off—looked like a Noah's ark setting sail for the night with a pair of every form of living beast on board. In the doorway of the farmhouse a figure could be dimly made out, rocking back and forth in a wicker chair. It was a neighbour, hailing Juanito for news.

Juanito would answer with embarrassed politeness. His father's illness was upsetting the world in which he had lived till then, the dispensation whereby plant and man could only grow bigger and stronger, whereby fruits and human bodies merely acquired richer sap with the passage of days and nights. Juanito would wander from field to field, avoiding the sodden furrows by keeping to the narrow strips of banked-up earth. He would come out on to the Perello road. Labourers would be cycling home from work, each with a dog perched obediently in the basket attached to his handle-bars. They would stop and chat to Juanito. It was going to be a fine year for oranges; on the big estates in Carcagente and Alcira there were rows and rows of orange trees, and beneath their sturdy, green-glazed, ever-darkening leaves the fruit hung heavy even now. In the minds of these men, the living essence of the *huerta* was indistinguishable from this glorious pulp, swollen with a blood that was lighter and richer than man's.

On the Albufera lake, punts glided along, showing black against the glow of the setting sun. The men propelled these craft with a leisurely action, resting their weight on the pole. Their shouts and exchanges echoed on and on through the dark-invested countryside, where only the canals blazed, like the boundaries of an impenetrable kingdom.

Despite the anguish gnawing at his heart, Juanito could not but relish this warm, lingering evening, this smell of herbs that had slowly infused in the sunshine, a fresh, sweet smell which the evening breeze took pleasure in spreading far and wide. His companions would leave him. As the stars took up their places in the sky, the frogs hiding under the yellow irises would start to croak. The *huerta* did not belong to human beings any longer, but to the delightful, discordant voices of spring. Juanito was ashamed at being happy.

For the Feast of the Blessed Virgin, Theresa decided that her son should go into Valencia by himself. The Madonna responded appreciatively to tokens of homage. He would take her a cartful of tightly bunched pinks and roses.

On the eve of the procession Juanito deposited the flowers in the crypt of the basilica; they had been cut at dawn and were still dripping with dew. Then he strolled in the square in front of the cathedral, amid the cry of lottery numbers and the pealing of bells. The male-voice choirs that had come to Valencia for the big event were having an early shot at an aubade. As the carpenters erecting the stands in the Plaza de la Virgen banged home their nails, they hummed Neapolitan songs brimming over with moonlight and heartbreak. All this hubbub made everyone cheerful and entertained the saints, who pricked up their ears in the shadowy seclusion of their side-chapels. Juanito listened, till he could stand no more of it, to this joyous medley of laughing and singing and joking which took its rhythm from the hammer-blows. He went back and knelt down in front of the statue. On her face, as familiar to him as his own mother's, light and shade were playing in a new way, as though the Madonna were at once dreading and crying out for her deliverance. Dazzled, Juanito weighed up with his eye the gold chains restraining the Virgin, the primitive stone necklaces intertwining on her throat and shielding her like a breastplate, the rings burdening her taut fingers, the sceptre that her hand was on the point of letting fall. Her diadem was fitted very low on her forehead and three pearls glittered between her eyebrows.

'How lovely you are, Mother of God!' sighed the simple Juanito. 'How frail you are and how precious your body and blood! Tomorrow your jewels will put the sun to shame; even the best-looking girls will pale into insignificance beside your eyes and mouth. Tomorrow you will go out and mingle with your people, unescorted. The women will kiss the hem of your dress as you pass by, and the men will make up songs for you, just as they would for their fiancées . . .'

From daybreak onwards, long lines of vehicles blocked the bridges over the Turia and the old embattled gateways, amid a pandemonium of whipcracking, swearing, threatening and laughing. But the compact Plaza de la Virgen, the pulsating heart of Valencia, was absorbing the hottest and liveliest blood in town: young men and youths were already thronging round the fountain. Several Masses had been said from the platform in the small hours. But as they tossed their beautiful flowers at the Madonna's feet, the men of the *huerta* were extolling the source of all abundance, the fertility of the soil, the hidden basis of their strength. If it were not for her, the *huerta*—where rice and corn ripened, fruit and vegetables, the vine and the orange trees—would remain barren. In fêting the guardian spirit of their race the Valencians were glorifying the blazing sun and inexhaustible supply of water that brought forth the crops. People were heralding this consecration by ringing tiny clay and china bells. Their widespread jingle announced that an incarnation was at hand. At the centre of all the flower-throwing and hymn-singing lay an offering, and the whole of Valencia was participating in this mystery. The crowd was coming to a standstill on the pavements, invading the roadway, overloading every available balcony. And in every pair of eyes there shone the same curiosity, the same fever, the same devout impatience.

When four horsemen appeared, clad in full regalia and mounted on prancing steeds, there was a frenzied outburst of applause. The groomsmen were moving forward to escort the Madonna. She was emerging, pale and nervous, from the gloom of the basilica. Juanito, who was directly under the platform, recoiled. A roar mounted from the square, a single cry of fervour and ecstasy. The men seemed to be drunk; the children were flinging crackers under the horses' hooves. The Virgin was preening and displaying her plumage of jewels like a peacock spreading its tail in the sunshine.

Valencia was acknowledging itself in this thin face surrounded by its huge halo. This rather weary Infanta was betrothed to every man there. They were making a dash for the shafts that supported her statue. The youths were jogging one another furiously to get to her. In their grasp, the Virgin of the Forsaken was swaying like a ship in a high sea. A bunch of flowers at her feet was quickly torn to pieces by greedy hands. The statue was progressing by fits and starts and seemed, at times, to be covering the same ground twice. The Madonna was advancing on Juanito, tottering under the weight of her halo, which rose at the back of her head like a shield of gold. The open air and the cheering were going to the head of this recluse.

'Your turn! Hurry up!'

Juanito recognized a boy from his village who was offering him his place. The statue was heavy. Juanito was in the front group of bearers, and the Madonna's gaze caressed his sunburnt neck.

The other bearers were all heaving furiously in different directions. The Madonna, caught up in an eddying movement, was sloping forwards. The smooth black covering of her hair, edged with thick braid, was tilting too. A cry of fear arose: the Virgin was going to fall flat on her face. Using all the strength in their hardened muscles, Juanito and the men round about him gave an upward heave to straighten the statue. The tumult died away. The Madonna recovered her balance; the crowd applauded, as though it had been witnessing a feat of acrobatics.

The procession was turning into an abduction. It was becoming a brazen struggle for possession of a panting prey, with the collusion of a whole city. One member of the crowd, perching on his neighbours' shoulders, directed a brief madrigal at the Madonna: no woman's kiss, no love-bite could compare with a single smile from her closed lips. There was a burst of applause. Quickly unseated, the man disappeared from view; but already other, even bolder invocations were being poured out. The Madonna was not offended by these artless compliments, these immodest declarations, these uncouth advances that would have brought a blush to the cheeks of a mere woman.

Uncontrollable currents were at work in the square. The statue was suddenly swept along in a brisk semi-circular movement. Juanito had to leave go of the shaft. He was flung back and pinned against the wall at the top of the narrow street leading to the cathedral. The Madonna was pitching violently again. The procession was turning into a brawl. The ferocity with which the men were clashing, like young bulls leaving the pen, induced an exquisite feeling of panic in the hearts of the women looking on. But the Madonna, inclining gently towards the crowd, was still the prize for which the males were jousting so fiercely.

She was reeling slightly from all the laughing and shouting, from the praises and the handfuls of petals that were being flung at her. She was groping in the midst of this frenzy of adoration. At long last she managed to find her way into the Calle del Miguelete, the only channel left free in this solid mass of spectators, many of them standing on chairs or clinging to railings. Obeying some unfathomable impulse, the statue swerved violently to the right. The Virgin was breaking her journey to go up to Juanito. At this, an unprecedented strength invaded his every fibre. He shot forward and made room for himself among the bearers. He lost his footing in the pulpy remains of trampled flowers. Already, other buds and petals were raining down from the next house, blinding him, intoxicating him. The whole street was giving vent to a single cry of adoration. Valencia was fêting herself in the shape of this age-old figure, at once talisman and hostage. God would never forsake Valencia, since He would never forsake His mother. The Virgin was held in pledge. Valencia was acclaiming the Purissima, borne aloft not by puny priests but by the toughest men the *huerta* could provide. Juanito, too, was quivering with pride. This other-worldly being was more surely his than any woman. Sweat was streaming down his forehead. The shaft was cutting into his shoulder. Juanito was getting out of breath; but, elated by this fiery conquest, he was putting the joys, the hard work, the whole life of the *huerta* behind him and crossing a threshold, undergoing an initiation: he was becoming the slave and master of this radiant figure.

Within a few yards of this hurly-burly, the priests from the basilica and the cathedral were—together with the leading local officials, headed by the Alcade and the General—trying hard to preserve their dignity. The crowd was ignoring them and rejecting them. It was an embarrassment for them to witness this display without taking part in it. From the top of the gallery connecting the cathedral to the basilica, a canon tried to signal instructions to the bearers. But nobody paid any attention to him . . . This abduction, carried out in a stench of gunpowder to an accompaniment of whoops of joy, was gratifying a hidden yearning which the Valencians had inherited from the Moors. Perhaps this procession was a rite dating back to the beginning of time. And the Virgin was joyfully accepting this horseplay, this snowstorm of flowers, these explosions, these passionate outpourings as the attestation of an age-old fidelity.

At the entrance to the cathedral, under the baroque porch, Juanito had to let go. For some minutes he rested against the cathedral door, feeling weak at the knees; he was exhausted and glowing with happiness. The Virgin would rest beneath the cool vaults till the afternoon procession. She would slowly make the rounds of her kingdom, along the narrow streets of the old town, amid a fluttering array of banners, to the lulling sound of hymn singing. The joyless palaces of the rich would open their shutters a few inches; reluctantly, heads would protrude to pay their respects to the Madonna of the Forsaken as she made her official visit.

But the Madonna took no pleasure in this sedate procession,

however much it might appeal to seminarists and old women. All she cared for was the bridal cortège which, one Sunday in May, plucked her from the gloom of her chapel and pitched her into an exhilarating rumpus that lasted all the way to the cathedral. And back in the darkness of her basilica she would spend the next twelve months remembering this epithalamium from the mouths of twenty-year-olds . . .

It was after dark when Juanito got home. Theresa was waiting for him in the silent house. They sat down in the kitchen, but Juanito pushed away his plate.

'Did you carry the Madonna?' asked Theresa.

'Yes,' said Juanito. 'Twice, and the second time the whole length of the Calle del Miguelete.'

She suddenly saw her son as through the eyes of a stranger. The Madonna must have taken to him. Her fingertips caressed his firm, handsome jaw.

'You are a fine-looking boy, my son.'

Had Juanito gone into a seminary, she would have had to share him only with the Madonna. Theresa was upset: one day a stranger would take him away from her. Yet he, like her, would hide the intensity of his feelings. The world belongs to those who burn in silence. To conceal her thoughts, Theresa said: 'It is almost as though your father were getting some of his strength back.'

It was not strength, but an ominous gentleness that was invading this splendid man who had always been so easily roused, so colourful, so gay. He had forgotten the fighting and quarrelling, the bragging and wagering of his early days. He could recall only the shy fiancé he had been. His nature seemed to have softened in some peculiar way. All that he talked about now was Cadiz, where he had done his military service, a town kept constantly aired by the breezes sweeping in from sea and ocean. In the evenings he imagined that he could feel the balm of its touch. He wanted to escort Theresa along the sea front on those rambling walks that young couples, innocently entwined, like to take under the trees in big cities. Of this rather tame pleasure he would remain cheated. His experience would be confined to hard work and to the satisfaction of bringing in the harvest and selling the crops at a good price.

'Juan, when you are grown-up, don't forget to be happy!'

Theresa would shrug resignedly. She had no hope left.

6

GIVE THE SLIGHTEST SHAKE to the trees, with their gnarled trunks, twisted branches and metallic leaves, and the sturdy olives would bounce upon the grass or fill the baskets in no time at all. It was going to be a fine year for olive oil, the women were claiming, as though every year the presses of the *huerta* did not squeeze out the liquid gold that would be the hidden source of wealth of the poorest villages in Estremadura or Castile. Bringing in the olives was a game played with a good deal of laughter and rivalry.

A boy from the village came dashing into the orchard, puffing hard.

'Your father is very ill. Hurry home!' The boy was so embarrassed that he began to cry. Juanito guessed that his father was dead.

Back at the house, the shutters were closed and the neighbours were intoning prayers and responses. Theresa was staring silently down at this partner who, lying alone in the big double bed, seemed to be prolonging the midday siesta.

Juanito knelt down, lifted his father's cold hand and kissed it. Then he went off to inform the Padre, called in at the post office and even thought to forewarn the grave-diggers. When his uncles came in from the fields they found Juanito giving the Latin responses to the Padre's prayers for the dead. And, for all her grief, Theresa thanked heaven for the gift of this steadfast, bright-eyed, true-hearted son, upon whom she would lean from now on.

During the vigil, some men came back from the city, full of talk of Calvo Sotelo. People pricked up their ears. This Galician, Governor of Valencia at twenty-eight, did not yield to threats. La Pasionaria, the renowned communist leader, had prophesied that he 'would not die with his boots on'. The circumstances in which he *had* died were obscure. He had been arrested in the middle of the night by an unidentified gang. The bloodstained lorry in which he had been executed had only just been found. But even before any inquiry had been instituted, men were taking sides: this was the beginning of civil war, the moderates were murmuring, while the parties of the left were claiming that the death of Calvo Sotelo would be enough to direct people's minds towards peace again.

The door of the farmhouse was still wide open, and beyond it lay the silent countryside. The July night was a warm one. At the dead man's bedside, voices were rising. This killing was exacerbating the old political quarrels. The king by his selfishness, Primo de Rivera by his indiscriminate lust for power and the trade unionists by their incitement to violence, had brought matters to an impasse. Grudges were being vented at last. The Republic had failed in its task by turning the Asturian uprising into a bloodbath. The stringing-up of priests on butchers' stalls beside notices reading: 'Pork for sale', had met with its answer: firing squads . . .

Everyone was drawing up an impassioned indictment, in condemnation or justification of this murder. Several times the Padre pointed out that they were supposed to be watching over a corpse. Aghast, Juanito stood gazing at his father, so silent and withdrawn. He alone seemed aloof from the quarrel. The whole of Spain was keeping vigil over a dead man but the dead man was Calvo Sotelo.

At midnight a few of the neighbours went home, while those who stayed on were given cups of coffee. The Padre fell asleep. The women were saying the rosary, and this made a very gentle sound, a domestic noise, a buzzing of bees round the hive. But out in the kitchen, the men's argument had revived. The whispered exchanges were growing even more heated than before. Theories were bandied back and forth: what would the right do to avenge this outrage? Wouldn't the communists seize power? The death of Calvo Sotelo would surely result in an attempt on the part of the right-wing or left-wing extremists to impose their order, or disorder, on the country. The peasants of the *huerta* were all in favour of order, but nervous of the generals' ambitiousness and the soldiers' looting. They were all in favour of freedom, but wary of its defenders—the glib and cynical politicians.

Juanito's mother let slip her shiny boxwood rosary. Juanito was the only one to notice that she was asleep, overcome with exhaustion, in the attitude of prayer. The men were now trying to determine which towns would rally to the army and which would support the communists, and which provinces would endeavour to win back their independence. They would argue in the same way, on Sundays, as to which matador would come off best in Barcelona or Pamplona. And, in their eyes, Spain was turning into a huge ring, where there would be no barrier to protect the spectators from the maddened bulls.

The day after the funeral, the whole family was out in the fields again. Death, like a bolt from the blue, had shorn a bough from the family tree. The sap was still rising in the trunk. Theresa and her son paid little heed to the embroiled news from Madrid. The burial of Calvo Sotelo was an excuse for both sides to indulge in a show of strength. The Falangists' demonstration outside the cemetery, broken up by the police, ended in bloodshed. Each faction was voicing its rival's arguments and borrowing its rival's terminology. It was to avoid further killings, further demonstrations, further riots, that the parties of the left and right were feverishly preparing for civil war.

When the circumstances of Calvo Sotelo's death were brought to light, his assassination was still an act of justice in the eyes of the left, and an act of provocation in the eyes of the Catholic Action party. The revelations, speeches and threats merely strengthened both in their convictions.

A few days later the insurrection was in full swing: Juanito heard tell, for the first time, of a certain general recently banished to faraway islands. The uprising was spreading right through Spanish Morocco. Suddenly Spain itself was ablaze: Andalusia and Navarre, Castile and Catalonia were steeped in blood by rival manifestos. In this perilous game that was being played in every town, anything—the support of the police, a neat stratagem on the part of the insurgents, a telephone call—was enough to tilt the balance.

General Goded had given orders for the regiments garrisoned on the outskirts of Barcelona to converge on the city centre at dawn, but the factory sirens had called out the workers in the small hours, while in the Via Layetana the women were holding off the storm troopers and the Civil Guards . . . The Plaza de Cataluña was being transformed into a battlefield. Police were machine-gunning the insurgents from the rooftops. The Hotel Colon, the Maison Dorée and the civil governor's palace, which were on the edge of the square, and the University, right beside it, were turning into fortresses, packed tight with the troops who were now prisoners of the city that they had aimed to occupy.

Juanito listened breathlessly to the account of these events, an account to which everyone added some detail of his own invention, embroidering it with a deed of valour or an act of cruelty. At noon the troops from the Montjuich fortress had tried to rescue the beleaguered units. At this, the men and women of Barcelona, advancing in serried ranks and linking arms as though for a fiesta, had gone to head them off. The troops had been unable to get past this solid, stirring mass of human bodies and faces; their machine-guns had slipped from their grasp: how could they fire into this sea—wave after wave after wave of them? The troops had fallen back . . .

Juanito, who had gone to Barcelona with his father on one occasion, recalled the broad boulevards with their tree-lined walks. Down those Ramblas where flower-sellers daily displayed their bunches of pinks and roses a procession was advancing, a procession in which the wax figures of Holy Week had been replaced by defenceless men and women. Many of them were singing and laughing as they walked to their deaths. The cortège continued in Juanito's dreams: rows and rows of faces, glimpsed as though through a thick pane of glass, going to oblivion. Their shining eyes and their mouths, wide open in a shout or in song, were all appealing to Juanito. He would wake up in a sweat, no longer knowing what these strangers required of him.

Other stories added to his perplexity. In these hours of tragic confusion, how could you tell friend from foe? In whose favour did divine judgment decide? Pity swayed the women's hearts when there was talk of the vanquished. General Goded had admitted his failure, on the radio, in a curiously calm voice. It was not the voice of a self-seeker whose pride has been crushed, but the voice of a man who has lost everything. During the final assault, a bullet had hit his wife, who was standing beside him. When the soldiers burst into his office, they found him kneeling by her body, mourning her amid the chatter of machine-guns and the roar of artillery.

And there were further reports that gave rise to uneasiness: the dope-peddlers and other habitual criminals who frequented the dens down by the port and the low dives of the Barrio Chino were taking advantage of the prevailing riotousness to burn down houses and despoil churches. In the heart of the old town, Santa Maria del Mar had been gutted. This sanctuary of the Virgin dated back to the times when the Catalans had been rulers of the Mediterranean. It was an act of faith and munificence dedicated to the Madonna by those God-fearing privateers. And the dead who had built those great arches, those delicately curving vaults and deep porches would not forgive the sacrilegious for turning her church into this old hulk, this charred and battered wreck.

To Juanito, the war seemed an insoluble conflict between earth and heaven, the living and the dead. In this fratricidal struggle, the troops no longer knew which army they belonged to. And the judges of the Water Tribunal no longer assembled beneath the porchway of the apostles. Recruited from the convicts newly released from the prisons of Valencia, the anarchists were clamouring for weapons but refusing to use them; they were saving their bullets, they said, for the great reckoning that lay ahead . . . The first engagements resulted in the rout of these battalions, whose battle cry was '*Viva la muerte!*' but whose troops were contemptuous of any form of discipline. The communists despised the peasants of the *huerta*, regarding them as insects clinging to their clods of earth, and were calling for the collectivization of the land. They proved that no form of ownership was sacred by pillaging a banker's luxury villa, between drinking bouts, or plundering a shop, in the heart of Valencia, that was doing too good a trade.

These disturbances, atrocities and waves of terror awakened in people's minds those obscure memories that lie dormant in the subconscious of a people, those scenes of riot, hanging and burning that, like certain childhood nightmares, return to plague the adult on a night of feverishness or unrest.

Supply trucks were carrying out veritable forays throughout the length and breadth of the *huerta*. The troops stowed wheat, rice, maize, fruit and vegetables, poultry and livestock higgledy-piggledy into their vehicles, in exchange for slips of yellow paper covered with the mauve impressions of a rubber stamp. And the plainsmen would stare gloomily after this rich yield of the soil, which had taken time, patience and hard work. In the evenings they would sit in their doorways, grumbling about big-city madness, the greed of politicians and the destructive urge of the military.

This war was purely the concern of the ministers and the generals. The men of the *huerta* watched it drawing nearer like those big black clouds that burst before the harvest is in.

7

MADRID, BARCELONA AND VALENCIA were still in Republican hands, but the cities of Old Castile were going over to the Nationalists.

In a fit of wishful thinking, the unions called a general strike to paralyse the rebellion. The Republicans were the only ones to suffer, for in the towns that they controlled Franco's supporters used force to end the stoppage in the factories. The men of the *huerta* shook their heads. Danger is not averted by feigning death. In Navarre the Carlists, who had immediately thrown in their lot with Franco, had emerged from their sheepfolds with their red berets and their ancient rifles. This improvised army was already holding the mountain passes. Once it joined up with the units from Aragon, it would be threatening Barcelona. Entrenched in their fortress of peaks and precipitous drops, where forbidding defiles served as parapet walks, these mountain folk were defending themselves with the same courage as the rebels sheltering in the Alcazar, in Toledo. Day and night the besieged troops pricked up their ears to keep track, in the gloom, of the sounds of the Asturian miners burrowing beneath the fortress. The excavators were making the old walls vibrate, and the muffled roar of the drills must have been mentally and physically harrowing to the women and the elderly. Yet this stubborn band was refusing to evacuate the citadel, and the newsreel cameramen were hurriedly taking up their positions in the surrounding hills to capture the moment when the Alcazar, and perhaps the whole of Toledo, would be blown sky-high.

War, thought Juanito, serves only to squander the gifts of the soil and to rob even the simplest words of their meaning. Henceforth each side had its martyrs, its heroes . . . Who was the Enemy, the Infidel, in this crusade? The Moors, who had a badge of the

Sacred Heart pinned to their greatcoats, or the anarchists who set fire to churches and crossed themselves in front of the altars? The factories were working flat out to arm the defenders of the Republic. In the Sagunto arsenals, women were turning out bullets and cartridge cases and learning to produce shells, in place of the men needed in the fighting line.

One of Juanito's uncles had been called up by the Navy. His brother Domingo, who was just twenty-three, was in one of the regiments that had been hastily summoned to Madrid. He wrote that the government was issuing rifles to those who wanted to fight and, in exchange, calling in all revolvers. This was restoring law and order in the capital. With rifles, said Domingo, you could fire at aircraft. There was a shortage of uniforms, but add a cartridge belt to a pair of dungarees and a factory hand became a soldier. The supply position was excellent. He and his companions were fitting out their trenches with equipment removed from buildings in the grounds of the University City: central-heating pipes made a fine floor to keep out the damp, and by wedging doors in the mud walls you prevented the chance of a cave-in. Domingo was positive that Franco's troops would never enter Madrid. As though it were some pious invocation, he always ended his letters with the slogan that sustained the city's inhabitants in the midst of its shortages and bombardments: '*No pasaran.*'

Theresa was worried about Federico. Posted to the area in the Balearics where the Nationalists had established themselves, he had taken part in the recapture of Ibiza; but, since then, there had been no news of him . . . Finally she learned that he was on his way to Almeria.

With the arrival of autumn, a strange torpor came over the *huerta*. The beginning of this war was like a malaise. Able-bodied men were disappearing from the scene. *Barracas* were closing down. The *huerta* was acquiring a strange abandoned quality, whereas the towns were becoming scenes of frenzied activity. Soledad's mother moved to Valencia with her daughter. Her brother-in-law had just been called up to serve with the army of the North. Juanito escorted the two women into town and helped them hoist their wicker boxes to the top floor of an old house near the Turia. The windows looked straight out on to the pebbly, dried-up river bed. Juanito felt overcome with sadness. These two women transplanted into this gloomy house seemed like a pair of victims. Soledad's mother thanked Juanito and kissed him on both cheeks, calling him her son.

In the afternoon Juanito went to a cinema, but he left before the end of the film. He could not be bothered with these vicarious adventures now that his own life was becoming rich, embroiled and all-absorbing.

Wandering about to kill time, he happened upon the little turning that led to Señora Martinez's. It was Mercedes's day off. Juanito refused to accept another girl in her place. The señora was insistent. Juanito agreed, for the sake of politeness, that all the girls in her establishment were equally beautiful and skilled. He ordered a glass of *anis*, and when the señora invited him to wait for Mercedes in her private quarters, in which only her staunchest customers ever set foot, he declined this mark of her friendship. The señora shooed away the girls who had gathered round Juanito like wasps on a bunch of grapes. And, subsiding into a cane chair, she opened her heart to him. This war was sheer madness: '*Qué barbaridad!*' sighed the señora. As though life were not harsh enough already! She looked to this serious-minded boy to witness to the uphill struggle that faces a dancer once the first bloom of youth has faded. In the eyes of the audience, talent is not enough . . . Men of distinction were finding a small measure of enjoyment and carefreeness in the home of an artiste, a small means of escape . . . The señora gave a wave of the hand: the patio, despite its dowdy plants and hiccoughing fountain, became an enchanted garden.

'All wars are lost: does anyone win the day in a fire, an earthquake or a flood? War destroys everything: refinement, gracious living, propriety, restraint, morality . . . In wartime, respectable women act like courtesans and men behave as though a uniform will excuse anything.'

The señora broke off this recital of her professional grievances to dart a horrified look at this eighteen-year-old already exposed to the threat of bullets. She said: 'Boys like you shouldn't go to war. If their eyes are closed for ever, women have nothing to live for.'

She began to shed real tears, which ruined her powder and mascara, ravaged her features and effaced even the memory of her beauty. And as her wrinkles appeared, the corners of her mouth trembled like an old woman's. At this point the señora treated Juanito to another *anis*, dabbing at her swollen eyes with a fine embroidered handkerchief.

Work on the farm took up the whole day, leaving no room for daydreams or melancholy. Juanito no more had time to think of Soledad than to regret the disappearance of dancing and bull-fighting. For there were no bull-fights now: the ranches were near Seville or up on the Castilian plateaus, and both areas were in Franco's hands. In the early days of the uprising the Nationalists had arranged an afternoon's fighting: the Salamanca ring had been packed to capacity. The roar of a plane overhead had been shrugged off by the *aficionados*, who were following every movement of the cape with baited breath: no one would dare disturb the time-honoured ritual of the bullfight. Just as the matador was thrusting home his sword between the horns of the first bull, an enormous flash had filled the ring. Bull and matador had vanished without trace. The spectators had taken refuge in the bull pen. The President, alone in his box, had called off the other killings; the bulls had been spared . . . Valencians laughed at this unfinished bullfight. But that arena, in which both protagonists had found annihilation, was symbolic of the whole of Spain. The señora's words came back to Juanito. Nobody won the day. Yes, that bullfight fought out under the helpless gaze of one man, that combat in which every rule had gone by the board, that pointless and distasteful slaughter in which actors and spectators alike had vanished in a puff of smoke—that was civil war.

In the *huerta*, *barracas* with bolted doors and boarded-up windows stood beside neglected rice-fields: war was wreaking the same havoc as an epidemic, having the same stupefying effect on persons and objects. But the soil, ironically, was yielding more now that there were fewer pairs of hands to sow and reap. Neighbours were helping each other out like members of one family. And this rich produce did not linger in the barns for long, for wheat, maize and vegetables had to be delivered to Valencia at set times, to keep the army fed.

Juanito would carefully align the tomatoes, with their thick satiny skins, in their boxes and then stand looking straight ahead of him, as though waiting for somebody. At night he would stroll along the narrow path that ran parallel with the canal. The sound of the running water was like the sound of whispering and kissing. The *huerta* was gripped by an extraordinary silence. Sometimes he thought he heard a laugh. At mealtimes Theresa would try to make out what was going on behind the faraway look on her son's face.

'You're not eating, these days,' she would say, as though Juanito's listlessness were due to loss of appetite.

One morning, as she was clearing the table, she said with a sigh: 'You ought to go into Valencia and see something of your friends: it's a mistake to rely on the papers for news . . . While you are there, you can buy some seed and get the harness repaired.'

A feeling of childish happiness went coursing through Juanito.

'I'll have finished bringing in the fruit tomorrow. I'll take it to market.'

Juanito's mother smiled.

'You're a slyboots, Juanito, but there is no harm in you. The moment anyone mentions Valencia, your thoughts turn to the market.'

'Yes, mother,' Juanito admitted, 'I'd love to see Soledad. It's nearly a month since she left the *huerta*.'

They fell silent. Juanito's mother opened the door on to the countryside, which still glowed from its hours in the sunshine. The sun had gone down now, but darkness had yet to come: the earth was restoring not only the warmth of autumn but a little of its light. This simple and perfect moment was a delight in itself, like a draught of spring-water. Juanito and his mother sat down on the wooden seat that ran along the front of the low farmhouse. The roof hung down to the windows. The toads tuned up, like musicians, then attacked their joint theme.

Theresa scanned her son's features in the fading light. There was not a boy in the whole *huerta* with a more honest face or a finer physique. But the pride that swelled Theresa's breast was growing painful and acutely sensitive. For she knew that death prowls like a brazen courtesan round the most attractive men . . .

Juanito asked: 'Do you want anything in Valencia?'

She considered, and remembered the long hours that she and he used to spend looking round chapels and sacristies. Were the holy relics, those yellowed bones, those enigmatic fragments of wood, cork or stone, still exposed to the fervent gaze of the faithful in their gold and crystal reliquaries?

'Go in and see the Virgin of the Forsaken . . . All over the country, the Holy Statues are being hidden away. Of course, the Madonna will still be in her niche, with all her jewels and finery, when all the rest have gone. The Madonna knows everything that is going on in heaven—but tell her, Juanito, that it is best that matters should be set right here on earth . . .'

8

IN VALENCIA, the flower market was like a crypt hollowed out beneath the main square and lit by a sort of shaft. Viewed from below, the people peering interestedly over the balustrade garlanded this circle of clear blue sky with a wreath of severed heads. Soledad, with her mother and her cousin Pablo, was standing behind a stall that was like a flowerbed bristling with pinks and roses. Pablo, who was a combatant, as his motley attire bore witness, was complacently eyeing his small, shapely feet in their civilian shoes. His exceptionally broad belt conjured up scenes from films about Mexican gauchos, but he was drumming his fingers on the revolver in his holster with the easy assurance of an American policeman.

Juanito wandered shyly up to the group. Soledad had altered and grown thinner; she was doing up a bunch of flowers. Pablo broke off for barely a moment when the introductions were performed. He was describing the battle at the gates of Madrid: General Mola had got as far as Getafe aerodrome, four miles from the capital. With some daring, the Nationalists were cutting the road to Valencia. The civilian evacuation of Madrid would have been impossible. Yes, Pablo repeated, it had been a narrow squeak.

The Nationalists held bridgeheads along the Manzanares. That narrow thread of water would not halt them . . . Soledad and her mother were bubbling over with questions about people back at the village. Their eagerness rather nettled Pablo. He gave a quick shine to the buckle of the belt round his waist. The situation in Madrid was still critical, he resumed, despite the efforts of the Defence Council under General Miaja. Only able-bodied men were left in the city. It was strange, he said with a fighting man's objectivity, to see a fashionable square, a bus stop or a public garden in the suburbs becoming disputed military objectives. In this city transformed into a battlefield, everyday life went on as before. Shots rang out from the flat rooftops, where the washing still hung to dry. Arms were stored in lofts, among the huge strings of onions. If only all Spaniards would pull their weight as the people of Madrid were pulling theirs, the rebels would be finished.

Juanito blushed. He was only eighteen. His brother Domingo was fighting amid the ruins of the University City. Pablo was prepared to regard this as an extenuating circumstance. He started rhapsodizing about the heroic deeds of some of the volunteers. They were children who had answered the call from all over Europe, travelling on the running boards of trains, prodigal sons who had come forward to help man the barricades . . . All the time he was talking, Pablo was straightening his tie and inspecting the shine on his shoes.

Failing to stem Pablo's firebrand eloquence, the women invited Juanito to dinner. Pablo was starting back to Madrid that afternoon. Soledad and her mother kept exchanging conniving glances behind his back, as though in the presence of a tyrannical father or husband. Juanito let himself be borne along by the crowd. The face of Valencia had changed. Shops that had run out of supplies had put up their shutters; others had changed to a new line of business, for a different type of customer. Vegetables were being sold in a jeweller's. The people in the streets were in a hurry, full of a forced gaiety that swiftly degenerated into squabbling and abuse.

Inside the cathedral, all the side-chapels were closed and their railings padlocked. The gleam of the bare marble altars could be made out beyond the bars, and the saints were sheltering in their dark niches like soldiers in their sentry-boxes.

But in her circular basilica the Madonna of the Forsaken continued to receive all comers, still wearing her diadem and her stately mantle. Just as a great lady will keep her diamonds for her visits to the poor, so the Virgin wore her habitual pale smile, unostentatiously, among her jewels. This eternal young bride retained the same loving expression in good times and bad. Compline was being said. The congregation was taking up the verses of the litanies with subdued violence: Tower of David, House of Gold, Ark of the Covenant . . . The candlelight was flickering on the priest's figured chasuble. All that could now be seen through the incense was a small anxious face borne up by a swirl of lace. 'I entrust Soledad to thy keeping,' prayed Juanito. But the Virgin no longer had time to attend to the entreaties of all the sinners who came to her.

At a table outside a café, Juanito's friends who had already joined up were proudly displaying their odds and ends of old clothing. Alfonso was sporting an army shirt with a pair of grey pin-striped trousers. Jesús's trousers, on the other hand, were of a cut reminiscent of the Cuban war. They looked as though they had shared out the items of a single uniform. The group had precisely one rifle between them. Soon they would be sent to the front, but meanwhile they spent their time playing cards on an old, battered palliasse. They grumbled at the frequency of roll-calls, however. Such chores and irritations took the pleasure out of war, which might otherwise have been a delicious mixture of idleness and adventure. Having nothing to do took more out of them than threshing corn all day long. 'You don't know how lucky you are, Juanito,' sighed Alfonso.

It was dark by this time. Juanito left them sitting over a carafe of *horchata*, dubiously sipping the insipid, almond-flavoured milk.

Dinner was very awkward. The women avoided all mention of Pablo. To them, the future seemed to hold even worse in store than the present. It was inadvisable to lay any plans in wartime, they said. As soon as the meal was over, Soledad's mother reminded her daughter that they were due to go and visit a sick neighbour. Juanito stood up. Soledad walked to the door with him through the bare rooms in which wicker boxes took the place of furniture. Soledad dwelt on the unsettling effect of their life in Valencia. She said in a vague way: 'Juanito, everything has changed so quickly; everything has changed so much.'

Yet the dull glow of the lamp gave Soledad a hectic beauty, gave her that little-girl-lost look which Juanito loved. He imagined that she was talking about her conscripted uncle, about the difficulties that confront women lost in the heart of a great city.

'What a pity Pablo is so far away,' he replied artlessly.

On the landing, a draught blew the lamp out. Whereupon Juanito clasped Soledad to him and their lips met.

'You mustn't be angry with me!' said Soledad in the dark. She shut the door between them. It had been more like the brief apparition of a ghost than the leave-taking of a living girl. And there had been a strange flavour of effacement, tears and betrayal to Soledad's final words.

For Theresa, Juanito brought good news. In Madrid, General Miaja's measures were already bearing fruit. Discipline was returning, together with law and order. There was talk of the first shipments of foreign arms. On the farm, Juanito pitched into his share of the autumn work like a man in a dream. As soon as the table was cleared he would sprawl on his bed and stare up at the spotless ceiling; he barely so much as heard his mother discussing the latest Nationalist advances. Like all the other peasants of the *huerta*, he distrusted the alliance between the army chiefs and the priests. These generals who claimed to be sons of the Church were bringing the Moors back to Spain on the pretext of defending Christ. But the Arabs had come to Spain centuries ago in response to the appeal of a few ambitious princes. Juanito's old uncles recalled how the whole of Spain had united against Bonaparte, whereas now guerrillas were threatening the rear of every army. There were irregulars, snipers—*pacos*, as they were called in the Riff War—hiding out on the rooftops of Madrid. They were biding their time till Franco reached the capital, when they would embark on a wave of killing as ferocious as the slaughter that had followed the capture of the Montana barracks. Juanito remembered the newspapers: the square had been strewn with bodies, lying all higgledy-piggledy. Nobody had bothered to line them up.

The men of the *huerta* shook their heads: murders and reprisals, human beings gunned down wholesale like game: there was a terrible reckoning in store for Spain.

Juanito would listen, not knowing what to make of it all. How could one take sides? The war was a family affair that fed on old grudges and irreconcilable grievances. His mother was hoping that heaven would bring peace between these warring kinsmen before Juanito was called up. He would be nineteen next spring. Theresa prayed to the Madonna more fervently for Juanito than for Federico or Domingo, even though they were more exposed to danger. As long as he drew breath beside her, Theresa would shield her son from death.

November was so hot that after the midday meal the men fell asleep from exhaustion. They lay on their beds, disarticulated puppets with leaden arms and legs. Juanito shut his eyes. Theresa, sitting at his bedside in a straw-bottomed chair, delayed talking to him until he stirred.

'You've had something on your mind since your trip to Valencia.'

She thought it likely that some new passion was ousting Juanito's earlier attachment from his heart. He was at an age when the sight of a face is enough to set you loving, when you think it easy to die for another human being because you are only just starting to live. Theresa was gently trying to tease her son about this new fancy.

'What will Soledad say?'

'It's nothing to do with her,' Juanito said in an offhand tone; but he could feel himself blushing.

Theresa stole out. Lying there with his eyes shut, motionless on his bed, Juanito was wondering why people secretly change and let you down without your even being able to reproach them for doing so.

'You mustn't be angry with me,' Soledad had said. This entreaty made him feel more forsaken than ever. Why did people retain their outward appearance and acquire a new nature? In these siesta hours he would try to fathom the slow, relentless deterioration, the corruption that embeds itself in a human heart like a grub in a fruit. He was beginning to sense a hidden connection between the disease afflicting the blood and body of Spain and the doubt gnawing at his love and destroying his innocent joy at being alive.

After bitter fighting the University City fell to the Nationalist forces. The residential quarter of Madrid was now threatened. The government had taken refuge in the Lonja de la Seda, in Valencia. The clustered columns that had in the old days witnessed the peaceful transactions of the silk dealers were now the scene of fierce, embroiled debates: another contingent must be called up. Juanito gave no hint of what his feelings were. He was to join the colours in Valencia. He would find out what lay behind Soledad's silences and effusions, her meek excuses and shamefaced looks.

It looked like being a hard winter. Nobody went out shooting any longer. A solitary fisherman still tarried in one of the inlets on the Albufera lake. It was on a bright cold day that the Duchess of Villahermosa had suddenly appeared; her escort had been more fanciful than the procession of the Three Wise Men . . .

'Don't be sad, Juanito,' Theresa would implore.

He would give a pinched little smile that carried his mother's thoughts right back into the past.

'Remember how we used to go into Valencia and feast our eyes on the relics? In those days I thought you would train to be a priest.'

Juanito had not forgotten.

'Some of the relics used to scare me.'

Theresa would tuck a straying lock of hair into her kerchief.

'I don't miss the relics, Juanito, but I can't bear the thought of going into the Virgin's church and finding the niche above the altar empty.'

Juanito would protest. The statue was out of harm's way: it had been hidden in a crypt. As soon as the war was over, the Madonna would be back. The Grail, too, had gone from the Lady chapel. But the cables from Marseilles harbour still hung from the walls, reminding the people of Valencia of an ancient victory over foreigners.

Theresa would ponder and then answer: 'When lightning strikes, or the river bursts its banks, the Madonna or the saint should be at their places in church, to hear our prayers and transmit them straight to God.'

Juanito had been one of the last to see the statue. For safety's sake, the government had ordered the closing of churches. Services and processions had been giving rise to incidents. *Agents provocateurs* had been urging the bolder elements to set fire to churches and desecrate altars, so that the Republicans should appear sacrilegious rabble in the eyes of the nation.

Strange tendencies were coming to light among the common people. Here was a golden opportunity for them to break free of these powers by which they had been held too long in thrall, with never a word of complaint; for them to get their own back on these saints who were so stingy in their distribution of favours and miracles. Because they believed in these masters, with their gold tunics and enamel eyes, the poor were getting a diabolical pleasure out of defying them, smashing their likenesses, plundering their treasures, breaking their stained-glass windows and battering down the doors of their palaces.

9

IN JANUARY, Theresa was taken ill. Juanito and his uncles shared out the housework just as they shared out the work in the fields. When it was his turn to be cook, Juanito would gravely stir a huge cauldronful of golden rice, with its mixture of pimentos, peas, octopus and shellfish. He was as good at making *paella* as his mother; he would regale the invalid with a dish of beans or a smoked eel. Theresa could not conceal her pride at having such a clever son. She would say the rosary over and over again under the bedclothes, and each time she came to the end of a decade she would add: 'Holy Mary, let the war be over before Juanito has to go.'

Francisco, the blacksmith's son, was home on sick-leave after being wounded on the Aragon front. He often came to the farmhouse, and Juanito questioned him about life in the trenches. Francisco, his elder by two years, was much gratified at being treated like an old soldier.

It was during these freezing winter days that the Italians bombed El Grao harbour and caused a number of casualties in the newly built hospital. A sombre fury went coursing through the men of the *huerta*. The Civil War was becoming a war against the outside world. Foreigners were threatening the people of Valencia in their fields and farmhouses. Francisco no longer got any pleasure out of relating his exploits. When the time came for him to go back to the front, he seemed sick of this bloody sport.

'Take Jesús, now,' Francisco said. 'Jesús copped it before he had time to wake up to the fact that he was in Guadalajara. The very first bullet had his name written on it. He hadn't even opened his kitbag. He'd just put it down to admire the view, like a tourist. In the village Jesús is already the one-who-fell-at-Guadalajara.' Francisco had brought home the boy's papers, a wallet which he had handed to the parents and an unfinished letter which he lacked the courage either to post or to destroy. It was addressed to a girl whom Francisco knew. Should he carry out an errand with which no one had entrusted him? Juanito and Francisco were equally embarrassed at having stumbled on this secret.

Juanito could no longer keep from asking the question that was burning on his lips.

'Have you seen anything of Soledad?'

'Yes,' said Francisco, 'she has just got engaged . . .'

Juanito was scraping his nail on the red-and-white check oilcloth on the table.

'. . . to her cousin Pablo,' Francisco continued, 'a bit of a show-off who carries dispatches between Valencia and Madrid H.Q.'

'I know him,' said Juanito.

'They're getting married soon,' concluded Francisco. 'Just as well, with the child coming.'

Theresa's voice rang out. There were a number of things she wanted to get Francisco to do for her in town. Juanito was left by himself, stooping over the red-and-white checks. Yes, it was just as well. And Juanito knew everything. 'You mustn't be angry with me, Juanito.' A door was banging shut in the darkness; and in his mind, too, a door was banging shut. This was his first experience of heartache. It was making his head swim, as though he had knocked back a stiff drink too hurriedly.

Francisco started talking about the Asturias, where the miners were making a heroic stand. The Navarrese brigades would never finish off Belarmino Tomás—bullets seemed to avoid him. Francisco was growing impassioned, as though he were extolling the prowess of some legendary hero, like the Cid whose dead body mounted on his charger still struck terror in the hearts of the Moors.

The miners had succeeded in overrunning Oviedo; they were defending their soil, both from the German planes and from the Italian warships bombarding them from off shore. Francisco would have loved to be fighting with them. They must be reinforced. If more rebel units were diverted northwards the pressure would be taken off Madrid, which the International Brigades were now defending; men of all nations were advancing shoulder to shoulder, like the citizens of Barcelona going out to meet the troops from Montjuich fortress. But these were no unarmed heroes forming a human barricade. Francisco was enumerating the modern equipment, the splendid rifles being shipped over from Mexico in their thousands, the planes capable of lightning speeds. Naturally, a number of old 'kites' were still being used for training purposes, while some of the artillery dated from the 1914 war and had already seen service against the Riffs. Anything would do for fighting the rebels. The communists of the 5th Brigade were also clamouring for arms. Franco would never succeed in cutting Valencia off from the capital. The working-class districts of Madrid would stop him in his tracks more effectively than a fortress. The men of the Cuatro Caminos and of Las Ventas were all but fighting in their own homes. Between attacks, the children would play on the sandbags. To strengthen a barricade, the local inhabitants were throwing their mattresses out of the windows. The Madrid of the Dos de Mayo,[1] which had triumphed over Bonaparte's Mamelukes, was being born again. Juanito grew flushed as he listened to Francisco's stumbling words. When his companion had finished, he said slowly, as though betting on the victory of a particular matador: 'I would rather they were sending me to Madrid.'

He was ashamed that he should suffer from a woman's fickleness.

But soon the surrender of Malaga showed Francisco's high hopes

[1]On 2nd May 1808 Spain rose against Napoleon. The insurrection started in Madrid.

to be without foundation. The Republican fleet made a vain attempt to save the town, but the militia had run out of ammunition. A secret dread was awakened in the hearts of even the bravest, for at the start of the Civil War Malaga had been the scene of atrocities in which the desire to desecrate had played a far bigger part than the urge to kill. Priests had been burnt alive in their churches, and the bones of disinterred nuns thrown to the four winds. The passive witnesses of these crimes poured towards Valencia and the Levante. They were carrying their fears and remorse about with them, like germs of a contagious disease. At the thought of having, one day, to atone for the outrages perpetrated before their eyes, they took to making excuses for these acts of butchery, to standing up for the ringleaders and even—lest they themselves should be brought to trial as accomplices—to declaring them innocent.

Some of them made new homes in this village of Santa Creus. Listening to their admissions, Juanito discovered that in a civil war there is no clear dividing line between innocent and guilty, between determined martyr and luckless victim. The perturbing ease with which a crime can be committed turns each and every man into a possible murderer, a likely hostage or tomorrow's corpse.

In Valencia, the idle thronged to the tables outside the cafés. Whenever a woman walked past, they would let fly a stream of daring compliments. Restrictions were aggravating people's craving for luxury, making their lives more hectic, stimulating their desire for a good time. It no longer took a religious procession to attract a crowd or give rise to merriment. Now, Valencia had no other saints to do honour to than her own tragicomic citizens, drunk with pride of race. The soldiers marching past on their way to Madrid with their brand-new weapons prompted the same hum of admiration and fervour as the statues in Holy Week.

It was simply a matter of keeping the Nationalists away from the Portuguese frontier and denying them access to the Mediterranean. Soon they would be driven back into the towns of Old Castile, where they would be caught like rats in a trap. Russia was calling for the dismissal of Largo Caballero; his bold plans for going over to the offensive were upsetting the calculations of an ally all too adept at perpetuating the Spanish nation's wounds. In the *huerta*, these court intrigues had no effect on the rhythm of life. Even though no services were held in the cathedral nowadays —it had been turned into a powder-magazine—the Miguelete still summoned the peasants to their work. At noon, Juanito would straighten up when its peals came scattering over the peaceful countryside where the corn was already beginning to sprout. The iron ring which he used for measuring the oranges would drop to the ground beside him . . .

As she listened to the Angelus in the dark streets of old Valencia, near the Torres de Serraños, was Soledad picturing the plain shimmering under the midday sun, and the steam rising from the canals, and the houses with their surrounding hedges of ragged robin? Coming to, Juanito would ask himself the age-old question of the spurned lover: 'Why has she changed? Why haven't I changed?' There is no answer to such fundamental questions. You can forget them, you can mislay them as though they were something tangible. Their edges are just as sharp when you find them again. The war provided the only distraction. Bilbao had just surrendered. There seemed no hope for Saragossa. Juanito would slowly digest his meal while a neighbour passed on the latest news. He would be gripped by an urge to fly in the face of the facts, an urge to seize fate by the horns, to do violence to his fellow men or to God.

He would fling down his fork and say: 'Perhaps these will be the last Nationalist gains. The Brigades are with us now. They are still holding out in Guadalajara.' Juanito had condemned foreign intervention as an intrusion upon domestic affairs when it had taken the form of German cruisers or Italian planes; today he was praying for it. Russia meant nothing to him. Like all the other peasants, he knew only the Levante; like them, he loved only this bountiful soil which he had trodden, sown, impoverished and enriched times without number. 'Yes,' he would repeat defiantly, 'we have the Brigades now. We have planes, tanks, artillery . . .'

'Planes, tanks . . .' Anselmo would say after him. Anselmo was his father's half-brother, born thirty years before him of a different marriage, and nowadays he seemed a patriarchal figure to all the men gathered beneath the roof of the *barraca*. His wife and his own children were dead. He never spoke of them, and perhaps he had forgotten them, as you forget the casual acquaintances with whom you have shared a day's march in the course of a long journey, but he loved to think back to his early days, to the time when he had stowed away in Cadiz on his way to join the Expeditionary Force in Mexico.

'I was the same age as you, Juanito. I had to falsify my date of birth when I enlisted.' To him, war was an adventure in which bullets were less to be feared than bouts of fever. You fought in an endeavour to conquer an imaginary empire on the other side of the world. But this poor Maximilian had been born under an unlucky star . . . The Civil War had struck Anselmo, from the outset, as being as inexplicable as a tidal wave, as unwarrantable as a flood. Stung by the old man's disbelief, Juanito would experience that patricidal fury which at times impels a son to raise his hand against his father.

'Yes,' he went on, 'we have technicians for the tanks now, pilots for the planes . . . And the Italians have been put to flight at Guadalajara, and Belarmino Tomás is still holding out in the Asturias!'

Juanito's eyes brightened up like the Albufera lake at the approach of winter. He tossed his head, ruffling his brown hair, in which there were occasional glints of gold, as though it had been bleached by the sun. The miners were defending their rugged mountains, which were quite barren except for the coal that they extracted from the pits. He, Juanito, would defend the shimmering plain in which a cloudless spring sky already lay reflected.

Enfolded in the darkness of the warm May night, Juanito sat up late by his attic window. The *huerta* stretched away into the distance, as mysterious and reassuring as a slumbering body. This region, through which water flowed freely and rapidly like the blood irrigating the human frame, had not yet been torn asunder by man's violence. If you listened hard, you caught the rustle of a dress: the water was still glutting the rice-fields and filling the large holes scooped out at the foot of the fruit trees. Was that thudding the sound of Ramon's or Javier's pick trying to divert a little of this wealth? All thought of the fierce disputes that arose over this scrupulously shared-out water faded in the darkness, which was made for serenading and the plucking of guitars and was punctuated by the light of a lamp, or a shooting star, or a girl's laughter . . . The day's weariness was dropping from Juanito's powerful body like the clothes that he had just flung off so that he might more fully enjoy the faceless, head-to-toe embrace of the darkness.

Despite the preoccupations of his daily routine, Juanito was feeling dismal and at a loose end. The war had robbed him of even the smallest pleasures, of going out after birds with lime-coated sticks, of the processions and fiestas in Valencia, of those mornings when the barbers down by the Turia shaved their customers outdoors in the sunshine. The innocent trips into town, the carefree strolling about the streets—all these simple delights had vanished. Juanito was not to experience the leisurely moonlight walks, the snatched meetings in the early morning when the girls on their way to work in the city's spinning mills and cigar factories slow down to cull the day's first compliment from the boy already stooping over the soil . . .

His childhood had flown, his adolescence was slipping by. Yet Juanito was deriving enjoyment from his loneliness. Running his lips along his arm gave him intense satisfaction. Exercising his firm, responsive body—inured to every burden and hardened to toil, as to the rigours of dancing—was a sensual pleasure . . . 'I'm nineteen,' Juanito said aloud, a second time. From the *huerta* came no answer but sounds that resembled the ramblings of someone talking in his sleep. The villages, too, had broken adrift. The houses were sailing along with their farmyards and gardens, each displaying a light in the heavy thatched roof that fitted like a hat several sizes too big. Somewhere, perhaps, a girl was sitting up late, just as Juanito was doing in this whitewashed attic with its trestle bed and solitary chair.

Juanito wanted this darkness, this peacefulness, to explode suddenly into singing and dancing and light; he wanted the *huerta* to rise like the opaque curtain concealing a gorgeous scene in the theatre. All at once, the moonlight made a newly roughcast wall glint like snow. A cock crowed, as though to prolong this false sunrise. Juanito wanted to be talking to another human being, to be biting a shoulder, to be making someone groan from the pressure of his body . . . Was the craving that he felt simply the craving of his body? Into his mind came the *copla* that he had heard at the inn a few days before the death of his father:

At one o'clock,
The crow of the cock.
At two, the nightingale's song.
At three, the coo of the turtledove.
And, all night long,
Your love.

Again he felt infinitely sad and on the brink of great happiness. Was it life, was it love, that was calling him? Who could explain this vaguer and more insidious summons? Despite the war, was he not still on the side-line? He had something better to do than be a soldier. All the same, it would be nice to have a good rifle and use it.

But how was he to expend the energy that coursed through his eager body? That would have called for boisterous days and for nights of hectic singing and talking above the quiver of guitars, nights heady with laughing and kissing and prancing in the dark, nights whose very silence might be a serenade . . .

Shall I have time to live? he wondered uneasily. He kissed his arm at the crook of the elbow. A *copla* was still going round and round in his head. He recited it quietly, as a prayer and as an exorcism:

Tomorrow the golden boys leave the farms,
Tomorrow they answer the call to arms.
How soon will the girls consolation find
With the men whom the war has left behind?

And, flinging himself on to the bed, he fell asleep.

10

THE *huerta* was blossoming forth in the May sunshine, at the start of a new day. A slight haze hugged the soil. From this golden mist, which seemed to be melting into sunbeams, emerged the sturdy vine-plants, the broad leaves stained with sulphate sheltering the grain which had already grown to full size. And the earth's promise rose in the serried corn-stalks and swelled the hefty ears of the maize.

Juanito, who had been up since dawn, was relishing the silent hour in which the cool of night blends with the early morning mist. He whistled as he clipped the fig-tree. Afterwards he would water the roses before the heat set in. In the tiny garden surrounding the farmhouse, every bush was fully aflower. The eye was beset by an explosion of petals, a riot of bursting corollas. Every path looked as though it had been festooned for some unaccountable visit. Yet strange suspicions haunted Juanito's troubled mind, vague fears, anxieties that he dared neither face up to nor dismiss. Nin, the Trotskyist leader, had vanished from the scene just as Calvo Sotelo, the Monarchist leader, had vanished a few months earlier. The same pattern of events—first the ordinary police operations, then the furtive shifting from prison to prison, and finally a kidnapping perpetrated through countless intermediaries, double agents and agents-provocateurs—had resulted in the same gruesome mystery: someone had stumbled upon a bloated and disfigured body. Politics had been reduced to a shady squaring of accounts between naughty boys. The Valencia newspapers were treating the surrender of La Cabeza as a strategic victory: in this place of pilgrimage, which they had turned into a minor fort, a handful of men had just capitulated after a stand lasting several months. The peasants were astounded that these fanatics, meagrely provisioned by air and linked with the outside world only by occasional flights of carrier pigeons, should have held out so long against the incessant pounding of artillery and aircraft. Was violating the right of sanctuary anything to shout about?

This feat of arms, or act of sacrilege, did nothing to dispel the shadow that Moscow was casting over the war's future. The Soviets were demanding bullion in return for poor-quality rifles and unserviceable planes and tanks. The government would be better off without these grasping allies. Juanito called to mind how the Republican forces, ill-equipped and ill-led, had gone over to the attack at Brunete and broken the enemy's stranglehold on Madrid.

All that Spain needed was a few knights-errant; a sprinkling of students from the northern countries, of foreign journalists, of American artisans turned pilot, of British sailors, of Danish fishermen, of adventurers from every part of the globe, would tilt the balance in favour of freedom. This small enlightened band had fought fiercely in defence of Teruel. But the communists were plotting Largo Caballero's fall, just as they had determined Nin's death. Their machinations were paralysing the administration. The same gangrene was at work within the army, for plots and ceremonial parades were taking the place of military operations. While motions were being greeted with rapturous cries amid the general hurly-burly of political meetings, German cruisers were brazenly exhibiting themselves in the Palma roadsteads. When Republican aircraft dared to attack its warships, the German government invoked international law to hold out the threat of bombarding defenceless ports.

The evening before, word had gone round that Almeria had been the victim of savage reprisals. By nightfall the news had spread to every farmhouse in the *huerta*. Theresa hardly changed colour at dinnertime when old Anselmo had alluded to it. By then the dishes had been cleared away, and they sat silent, resting their elbows on the table, in the warm dusk. To have expressed fear or hope would have been to give shape to the calamity.

Astride the tree, Juanito lopped off one last twig; then he

leapt down. Francisco was leaning on the garden gate, recovering his breath. Juanito ran up to him.

'Juanito, Luis got back from Almeria last night. He was on the same ship as your brother Federico. It's beyond belief . . .'

Francisco started to shake as though physically afraid. In the young man's eyes, Juanito saw Almeria harbour with its sheer cliffs and deep-set bay. It was midday. Men lay asleep in the shade of the rigging. Warehouse doors were ajar, affording a glimpse of the coolness within and of the barrels in which grapes were piled high between protective layers of sawdust. Juanito had once smelt this peculiar mixture of fruit and wood. On the horizon, some cruisers were drifting slowly by—no doubt one of the Non-Intervention Committee's naval patrols idling along the coast of the Levante. The ships were getting closer. The shore-batteries protested with a few warning salvoes. Suddenly the air was full of roaring and the terrified screeching of birds. Whole flights of them were wheeling in the sky, swept along by a tornado. The sea was getting up, and gigantic waves were sweeping across the flat stonework of the quays. The warships under repair, as peaceable as the feluccas that surrounded them, were lifted up in a swirl of foam, like fish struggling to free themselves from the unseen hook tearing into them. The first ship to be hit had been Federico's cruiser . . . The crew were running about the deck in panic. The ship was capsizing, and one of her funnels buckling. The sailors were jumping into the water, most of them swimming desperately to avoid being sucked down. People were urging them on from the quayside.

Broad smooth patches lay on the heaving waters: it was the oil gushing out of the burst tanks. Blasts of scalding water were shooting up from the choking boilers. Huge oily blisters were bursting on the surface. And, in full view of his companions, Federico was swimming for all he was worth, suffocated by smoke, exhausting himself with every stroke that he took in this glutinous mass.

'They saw him go under . . . Nobody could make out what he was diving for . . . The ship was slowly sinking . . .' Francisco paused for breath, then continued: 'There were mates of his down in the stokeholds and engine-rooms . . . They are all gone.'

Juanito felt as though he himself were struggling among the shrieking, terrified sailors. From the quayside came life-buoys, hurled by the fishermen. The wind was playing havoc with the thick palls of smoke. Shells were still raining down and setting the wreckage ablaze. The survivors were clinging to ropes and planks of wood: they were screaming abuse at the rescuers for being too slow. With mingled oaths and prayers, they were calling on the Virgin to help them, and blaspheming. Fishing smacks were sinking right inside the harbour, to the sound of rending sails and shattering hulls. Buildings were collapsing. The ships' funnels were pitching in time with the horizon . . . Even the largest vessels, losing all sense of balance, were swaying above the waterline and then toppling over like toys blown down by a gust of wind. And it was as though these apocalyptic monsters were being drawn down to the seabed, impaled by giant harpoons. With its buildings in ruins and its craft dashed to pieces on invisible reefs, Almeria harbour looked as though it were in the grip of the world's final convulsions. Lurid craters were opening in the abyss. Sparks and mud were spurting out of the sea, shedding light on these erupting volcanoes.

Stooping over Juanito, Francisco was jerking out his description of the scene. All night long he had been reliving it; in his still rawly sensitive convalescent's body, with his wounded campaigner's nerves, he had been experiencing the bite of the flames and the sticky embrace of that scalding, oil-flavoured sea.

'Hell, Juanito! Luis kept saying it was Hell. And yet he managed to come out of it alive.'

In the end the smoke invaded the harbour, enveloping the boats and smothering the bodies of those who had not only drowned, but been burnt alive. Through the inferno came the outraged cries of men who had not had time to defend themselves, cries of the damned.

'Yes,' said Juanito, 'Federico must have been trying to save Pedro . . .' They had vowed that they would return to the village together. The same wave must have swept them away, the same eddy pulled them under. The two friends had been sucked down into the depths like a pair of straws, and now they were floating among the brand-new flotsam that was all that remained of the Republic's cruisers . . .

A silence followed. In the farmhouse, no one stirred; the *huerta* lay gently steaming in the sunshine. The blow had fallen. Disaster had selected its household, chosen its roof. The bombardment of Almeria was no longer a news item; the event was implanting itself in Juanito's mind and body, and in the lives of those about him, so that from now on bread and air would have a different flavour.

The German battle-squadron had retired contentedly, having cheaply avenged the slur on its honour. One day, Federico—drowned, covered with seaweed, nibbled by jellyfish—would be washed up in the underwater caves near Grao, where every child of the *huerta* has played, in those secret bights rimmed with fine sand, where in the old days the pirates had concealed their ships.

Francisco broke off. His cheeks were red, as though he had been overexerting himself.

'Come into the kitchen and rest,' Juanito said. 'I'll tell my uncles when they return for their coffee.'

Francisco followed him. Above the *huerta*, the morning air was calm. A bird started singing in the fig-tree beside the well. And, over by the pomegranate, a whole rose-bush had suddenly come out in bloom.

With the death of Federico, the Civil War became a personal matter for Juanito and his family. They were not blind to the murderous intrigues between the politicians, the party rivalries, the waste and muddle, nor to the machinations of foreign powers; but from now on their cause was inseparably bound up with the highly uncertain prospects of the Republic.

It took Theresa a long time to get used to the idea of Federico's being dead. She had thought of him as being safeguarded by his gaiety, rendered invulnerable by his laughter. His tragic death had been made to another man's measure. Federico had chosen it, however, when he had swum with all his might towards the sinking ship.

This second summer of war was overpowering. Juanito and his uncles worked frantically. Every sheaf of corn they bound, every cartful of vegetables they loaded, every crop of maize or rice they delivered, made them feel that they were fighting.

Bilbao fell, despite its fortified belt. Now Franco was taking over the mines and had control of the Galician coastline. The Brunete offensive had not succeeded in relieving the Asturian front. To gain a few inches of ground, the Republic had sacrificed so many troops that it had been compelled to form a special sapper corps to bury them. The men of the *huerta* were not afraid to face the truth: the North was lost.

The day the Valencia newspapers announced the fall of Gijon, the boys of Juanito's age-group were called up. On the farm, people avoided mentioning Belarmino Tomás's flight to France; instead, they voiced their views on Juanito's transformation into a soldier. He smiled, already intoxicated by this future in which grit and daring would be the qualities that counted, not patience and honest toil. He had forgotten Soledad.

On the morning on which he was due to leave, Theresa made up her mind to add a medal of the Virgin of the Forsaken to the scapular that he wore round his neck. Her hands trembled on the youth's throat. Beneath the transparent skin there flowed warm, jubilant blood, the blood that spurts from wounds, the blood that turns shirts into breastplates, the blood that adheres to lifeless uniforms. Theresa kept saying to herself, soundlessly and mechanically: 'Blood.'

A jingling sound announced the arrival of the cart. Juanito stood up and got someone to take his things out to the driver; they were packed in a sailor's kitbag that had belonged to Federico. He kissed his uncles on both cheeks, embraced his mother twice over, and then jumped nimbly aboard.

Theresa could not keep herself from proudly taking stock of the litheness and strength of his young body. To some invisible companion she claimed: 'That's my son, the finest-looking man in the whole *huerta*,' as though this claim might intimidate death. Juanito sat next to the driver, who was already taking up the reins. She managed to whisper: 'Juanito, if things go wrong the Madonna will protect you.'

To reassure her, he put his hand up to his neck. As they reached the crossroads, the vehicle gave a violent jolt and seemed about to overturn. Above the cracking of the whip came the sound of cursing and laughter.

Alone in her kitchen, Theresa knelt down on the mud floor, spread her arms in the shape of a cross and moaned: 'Blessed Virgin, you had a son of your own . . .'

II

THE CONSCRIPTS were enrolled in a requisitioned primary school near the Torres de Çuarte. On the blackboard there were some drawings and some childish lettering, as though lessons had been interrupted only a minute before. The formalities took a long time. There seemed to be some difficulty over finding the soldiers' particulars and dates of registration in the big black registers.

Juanito's initial excitement wilted under the influence of the playground. He could not take his mind off Soledad or her child by Pablo which would be a child of war. He felt no hatred, but his love, instead of holding out the prospect of great happiness, had turned into this withdrawn melancholy, a sickness that he would be ashamed to mention and that he had no hope of getting over.

Then he thought of the farm with a strange joy that was pure homesickness. He could have been striding about the kitchen and stirring the *paella* in the heavy cast-iron pan. He could have been planting out the last of the rice in the sodden drills . . . The *huerta* remained untouched. If he came back from this war, he would find it all waiting for him: his mother's voice, old Anselmo's lined face, the dazzling walls of the farmhouse at high noon and the scent of the new roses. Sun and shade would caress his body as they had in the past; water and wine would still have the same honest taste, for people change but things remain loyal.

Late in the afternoon, a gruff sergeant came along to call the roll and distribute some thin blankets. They were to leave that night.

'I don't know when you'll get there,' he thought fit to add.

Nationalist forces had made several attempts to cut communications between Barcelona and Valencia. The lorries would keep to the coastal road for as long as they could. Then, fearing that he might demoralize these raw recruits, he went on to say that enemy infiltrations in the area were confined to a pocket that would soon be disposed of . . .

Inside each lorry were two benches, running lengthwise. Juanito sat at the far end and dangled his legs. No sooner were they out of Valencia than his neighbour fell asleep with his head on Juanito's shoulder. A damp coldness began to penetrate their thin civilian suits. To unfold his blanket, Juanito would have had to wake his neighbour, whose head grew heavier with every jolt. Juanito was deriving a secret happiness from looking after someone more helpless than himself.

At the first break in the journey, the driver asked Juanito to keep him company up front. He was afraid of falling asleep at the wheel. When Juanito got in beside him, the driver handed him the wineskin. Juanito drank, for the sake of politeness, but the chill wine simply tasted of iron.

They reached Barcelona in the small hours. Broad, straight avenues fanned out before them, studded with street lamps. Who could possibly live behind those façades that reared up like hoardings on the edge of a building site? The Plaza de Cataluña, empty under this wan lighting, looked huge to them. Sleepy voices were raised as they drove under General Goded's windows. The failure of the pronunciamento already seemed as remote as the battles against Soult and Napoleon, but the bronze statuaries surrounding the square were scarred by bullets and had lost a few limbs.

The lorry was running more smoothly now. The wineskin was circulating. The light of a street lamp would suddenly fall on the tilted throat and gaping mouth of whoever happened to be drinking. All the bars were open, claimed Gugliemo, who had cast himself in the role of Tempter. Juanito thought of Alfonso as Gugliemo enumerated the merits of the night clubs along the Parallelo: never, he kept saying, had Barcelona seen so much singing and dancing and loving. The young peasants' eyes shone with innocent longing. Juanito shrugged. Now Gugliemo was lowering his voice to rhapsodize upon the vice-dens of the Barrio Chino. In this lawless district, love had the flavour of blood; liquor, drugs and vice were on offer all night long. There were sniggers in the darkness of the lorry. Gugliemo broke off, offended.

When the vehicle drove through the gateway of a barracks, shouts rang out and the future soldiers drew themselves up like actors about to go on stage. The Valencia-Barcelona run was growing trickier every day. With their next offensive, the Nationalists would reach the sea. The troops were hailing these reinforcements as though the Valencians had just carried out a perilous sortie through enemy lines.

That evening, Juanito and his companions approached the barrack gates rather hesitantly, but the sentry waved them on.

Despite the icy November wind that blew straight down the Parallelo, the crowd was conglomerating round the lottery stalls and coming to a standstill by the posters outside the cabarets. The war was intensifying the need for night life which every Spaniard feels. Freedom to stroll among the fierce neon signs was one of the highest pleasures that the government could accord its citizens—a little light, a little music, a little gaiety. Between offensives, the troops were able to titillate their nostrils and their palates.

They ambled along the wide boulevards, and then made their way into the Plaza Real through arcades lined with cafés. The customers, anchored to their tables, were calling out to passers-by. The smell of fried squid hung in the air. The soldiers followed the walls of the town hall, till they plunged into a maze of medieval streets as narrow as those in Valencia. A courtyard took shape in the moonlight. A solitary column was set in one of its corners, like a sentry. This weird place was like the crater of an extinct volcano. There must have been slaughter, up here on these ramparts, after an interminable siege. A tower with massive arches was surveying, through its dark-invested slits, a pillage several centuries old. The Valencians felt bewildered. Juanito peered through an iron grating. What could these vaults be used for today? Plunderers and defenders, arms and treasures, had long since turned to dust. They retraced their steps. They admired these walls and turrets and ramparts, a suit of stone armour that had withstood cannon fire. Gugliemo spoke of the vaults hollowed out of the rock which had in olden times housed horses, cattle and crops, enabling the defenders to survive even the lengthiest siege. These barns and stables receding into the darkness, these wells and reservoirs . . . it all fired the boys' imagination. The cathedral rose like a keep still standing amid demolished castle walls. Clinging to its sides, so many strange molluscs secreted over the centuries, were chapels, cloisters and chapter rooms. This holy township formed a veritable labyrinth. The soldiers slowly made their way round the outside of this other citadel.

The police were keeping close watch on the cathedral, for a fire would rapidly spread to the town hall, where the government was sitting. The wrought-iron screens had been torn down from in front of the side-chapels, the rich altars broken up and the saints evacuated higgledy-piggledy, in carts, like refugees. No harm had come to the tombs that paved this silent and shadowy grotto. Standing inviolate in the heart of the city, like the tower from which the Counts of Barcelona had watched the comings and goings of their vessels, the cathedral was a witness to the looting and rioting.

Next day they were taken to the Montjuich fortress for training. Juanito, who was used to mending farming implements, soon learned how to strip a machine-gun, sight a target and read an ordnance survey map. The instructor got him to demonstrate these things to the others. And Juanito had, in turn, to explain to Fernando, a shoemaker from Lerida who could only handle an awl, and to Ansaldo, whose practical experience had hitherto been confined to mixing mortar for a Saragossa builder, how to assemble and load a machine-gun.

These outdoor days in the biting cold on the slopes below the fortress brought back memories of working in the fields and playing games at school. Abruptly uprooted from their natural surroundings, these men still had their youth as a bond between them, and their gaiety to enrich them. When they returned to barracks at the end of the day, they would race to the taps and jostle each other to get at the thinly trickling water, so that they could wash and have a close shave. Then they would stroll in groups along the Parallelo, or the Ramblas, or in the Plaza de Cataluña. They would dart prodigious compliments at a girl, quite at random. She would accept these crude gallantries, or reject them with fluttering eyelashes. Juanito would slip away. If he remained faithful to Soledad, she would come back to him one day. His companions would disappear into some nightspot where the dancers came and sat at the customers' tables. The police had better things to do than keep a check on these all too hospitable establishments. Juanito would listen disdainfully to the others' accounts of their exploits when they got back to the barrack-room.

He preferred to walk by himself along the spacious avenues which, now that the crowds had gone and the stalls had been cleared away, afforded a prospect of infinity between the bare trees. Each of the dimmed street lamps housed a puny flame. A few more steps, and Juanito would reach another; again there flickered, level with the lowest branches of a tree, this fragile star, this pulsating and almost human brightness that quivered through the thick glass and brought companionship to his loneliness.

Fires had left charred gaps among the elegant façades on the other side of the Plaza de Cataluña. In the fog, the Sagrada Familia, the church with the ceramic walls, looked like an underwater madrepore. Its unfinished doorways opened like caverns bristling with stalactites, its towers were built on the lines of fantastically ramifying coral reefs. This weird construction was now just an engulfed cathedral, a rock coated with shells and bedecked with seaweed. In Juanito's eyes, this aquatic palace, which seemed to have emerged from some dusty pantomime backdrop, would turn into Valencia Cathedral, where the gold and silver saints keep watch in their niches, among the smoke from the incense and candles. Under the gaze of the Angels and the Blessed Ones, the Water Tribunal was passing its unchallengeable sentences. The same sunshine, the same rain had alike produced the cracks on the sculptured features and the lines on the faces of the judges sitting enthroned on the imitation leather chairs. A litigant was clenching his teeth to keep himself from answering back. He was stealing away, with laughter and gibes ringing in his ears . . . In the midst of the wary buyers on the dried-up bed of the Turia, the horses were prancing . . . The flower-beds in the Botanical Gardens were glowing through the railings; in the evening breeze, the roses and pinks and geraniums were reduced to scent.

Juanito would quicken his stride to escape from the images dancing on the wet asphalt. Other visions would appear in the puddles or on the shiny pavement. The nimble bodies of young men and girls were moving in time with each other in a jota, were swaying to achieve greater momentum. These attuned expressions, threaded hands and garlanded bare arms were going through every movement of the dance, all with an obvious joy at being alive. Juanito would hurry on. A fevered longing would pursue him relentlessly. At the foot of every street lamp, in the ring of speckled light on the tar, the girls' laughter would go fluttering on. He would murmur: 'Solita!' This diminutive was the only declaration of love that he would have dared voice. The iron trees, each overhung by a star, were turning into a real forest; a lake shimmered between their trunks. In it, fish were darting through the reeds. The eels looked like snakes in Juanito's pot. The moor-hens were flapping their wings at the water's edge. Juanito would practically run to work off his homesickness, to prove to himself that it really was all a dream. By this time, darkness would have blotted out the rows of buildings. The fog would be blurring the shapes of things; the frigid posturing of the monuments, with their bronze heroes and marble horses rooted to the city squares, would turn into the lively bustle of masts and sails in El Grao harbour. The throb of the sea showed, above the surface, in the gentle rocking of the barges leaving El Grao, bound for the Balearics or Oran. The fruit was spilling over into the water. The fishermen's nets were drawing in oranges eaten up with salt. Close by were the deep grottoes in which Juanito and Federico had played together. Their arches looked out on to water that was almost black . . .

Winter was casting its pallor over the Albufera lake . . . The sky was reflecting the earth. A young woman was handing a peasant boy a packet of cigarettes. But Sybil, like Federico, had been swept away in this whirl of absurd hatred, blind justice and limitless cruelty. War, like an outbreak of leprosy, was destroying even the memory of happy days. People were changing for the worse, things were degenerating. This fratricidal struggle was a crime, an original sin willed by man and corrupting the very elements. Earth, rivers, seasons, were all gone; all that remained was this cataclysm of steel, this maelstrom of fire . . . Would Juanito ever again be able to trim the climbing vine in the garden, or shake the olive trees to bring down the crop, or sort oranges, or plant seeds in the warm mud? To stave off despair, Juanito would run hell for leather and get back to barracks gasping for breath.

12

DEEP IN THE ARMOURED HUB OF THE BARRACKS, the canteen was filled—just like the inns back in Valencia—with a bittersweet smell of *anis* and white wine, and with sudden loud bursts of talk and laughter that quickly turned into quarrelling. Yet the men kept off politics. The gamblers would lose themselves in endless games of cards. The others would sit quietly comparing their provinces and villages. Every Spaniard derived the same feeling of pride from the poverty or richness of the soil of his birthplace. An Aragonese would claim: 'Where I come from, things have a job to grow; but in Saragossa we bake the best bread in the whole of Spain.' Fernando the shoemaker would hold his head high, as though he shared the baker's skill, and the two men would exchange looks of glowing friendship.

Juanito would be tempted to answer the Aragonese: 'In the *huerta*, things grow just like in the garden of Eden. Vegetables, rice, oranges . . . they all ripen so quickly that we barely have time to gather them. The women of Valencia are as dazzling as huge basketfuls of fruit, but their skin is daintier than flower petals. If the whole of Spain were like the *huerta*, there would be neither poor nor rich—just happy human beings.'

Every member of a group would speak in turn, and the others would listen attentively, then weigh his words. Courteousness does not prevent a Spaniard from passing judgment. But these men, with their thin faces and flashing eyes, would describe, as though it were a mistress, a desolate plateau in Estremadura or a burnt-up field in Castile. They would account for their feeble crops, their poor harvests, by those ingenious arguments which parents sometimes concoct in an effort to praise their stunted offspring.

'We get so much sunshine where I come from,' the Andalusian would say, 'that even the mightiest rivers dry up. But when a fig-tree or an olive-tree bears fruit, you won't find a more succulent fig or a pulpier olive anywhere on earth.'

When they were all content that they had done justice to their various provinces, the soldiers would sometimes swap memories and enthusiasms, bandying names. These names would spurt forth like flames from a cigarette lighter passing from hand to hand—the names of the matadors and dancers, of the singers and actresses, whose praises they happened to be singing. Those who lived in Barcelona or Madrid would display their superiority.

Juanito, for his part, would recall the feast-day processions in Valencia and the hours that he had spent in the cinema: life on the grand scale in New York slums and London palaces; the lengthy outbursts, the distraught behaviour of rich men finding out that nobody loves them . . . As a boy, he had felt perturbed by those fierce passions. Today, his experience went beyond all that noise and bustle, all that weeping and lamenting and shooting.

A few days before Christmas, at about the time when the fighting at Teruel was intensifying, a soldier came into the canteen. There was movement at the tables as people made room for him. Without replying to their invitations, he sat down next to Juanito.

Stubble gave a grimy look to his bony face; his sombre eyes exchanged a swift conniving signal with the white walls, the bar, the rows of bottles, the scattered glasses. His furtive glance was making certain of accomplices or allies in preparation for some mysterious battle, and of a refuge in case of rout. As they came to rest on Juanito, a fond gleam appeared in his restless pupils.

'I've been looking for you,' the stranger said. He smiled. A silence came over the surrounding tables. Cards hung poised in the players' hands.

'Don't you remember me?' the man went on with a note of satisfaction in his voice, as though he had been counting on the uneasiness that was beginning to assail Juanito. 'I'm Agustin. I used to teach in a school near Saragossa . . . It was I who booked you in, the night your detachment arrived . . .'

The main gate was creaking open. Sounds of a rather comical scramble came from the guardhouse, barked orders mingling with the curses of men rudely awakened. The hubbub ensuing from this false alarm had died down at once when a man had appeared from out of the shadows. In the first light of day it was impossible to make out his insignia . . . Juanito recognized the smile that seemed to be deriding itself, the crisp voice that had restored order in a matter of moments.

'You were sitting next to the driver,' Agustin said. 'He could hardly keep his eyes open. You saved the lives of the whole detachment by spinning yarns to him . . .' Agustin seemed to be enjoying Juanito's confusion.

He was reliving that bitterly cold morning when a peasant from Valencia had jumped nimbly down from the leading lorry in a convoy. His eyes were like those lagoons in which salt water and spring water combine. Agustin had shouted: '*Salud!*' and in the guardhouse he had handed him a mugful of steaming coffee. Juanito had drunk it slowly, and then thanked him in the lilting voice of the *huerta*. And in that dawn which was laden with all the sins of the day ahead, Agustin had begun to love again . . .

All day long he had fought down this giddiness, this feeling of being uprooted, but in his room that night Agustin had sat staring at faded photographs. Was it the same smile on two different mouths? But how could the intangible truth about a human being, the irrecusable admission of a soul be lodged in the curl of a lip? On these yellowing snapshots, Luis's face was growing blurred. Was the portrait losing its outlines simultaneously with the model, just as the spirit is extinguished with the body? This likeness was growing faint in Agustin's memory, even as Luis's body was slowly amalgamating with the soil of Belchite. But a boy from the *huerta* was restoring to Agustin the light that had transfigured the face of a miner from the Asturias. . . . Both came from such a long way off; both were of the same breed, and their desultory talk and far-away expressions held the same gift and the same refusal . . .

Joy at a resurrection was combined with remorse at a hidden betrayal. Agustin had lived for several weeks sustained by this singular stroke of fortune. He had subjected Juanito to a rigid scrutiny. As political commissar, entrusted with the task of keeping up the troops' morale, it was easy for him to engage in the most tortuous investigations. As though grappling with a foreign language, he had made out, word by word, Juanito's opinions and friendships and pursuits. Through spying on him, he was—all unbeknown to the boy—getting closer to him. In what other form of hunt would he derive the same joy from catching up with his quarry? From his instructors, Agustin learned that Juanito knew how to give orders to these unfledged soldiers, just as he knew how to handle the motley collection of weapons being turned out by the factories still in the hands of the Republican government, together with the rifles and machine-guns coming from France or Mexico.

Juanito had a lively disposition, but rather than sit about talking he preferred to go on long walks through Barcelona. Sometimes he would stay by himself in the barrack-room or the canteen. How could one track down the innermost thoughts, the desires, the daydreams, the longings of this withdrawn peasant? Stealing into Juanito's barrack-room would have aroused suspicion. Agustin was less afraid of the perspicacity of others than of his own weakness. Any semblance of partnership, any attempt at innocent camaraderie, holds out a promise of happiness all too intense for the recluse. Would he be able to hide it from the others? Would he have the courage to reject this chance of bliss? Was he not going to lose Juanito, just as he had lost Luis? Was it to get away from him that Luis had packed his kit one morning in May? He had only a few hours left to live; he seemed as intoxicated by his reclaimed freedom as a man who had broken out of gaol.

'Are you so glad to be leaving me?'

For answer, Luis had merely shrugged. He kept his eyelids lowered and his lips together, with that expression of pure cruelty forever worn by young Davids and Judiths, youths and girls as anxious to kill as if shedding blood afforded them a thrill more compelling than carnal pleasure. Never had Luis looked so beautiful as in that moment of breaking free, without a word of explanation. As Agustin looked back on the scene, Luis became re-endowed with the radiance that his portraits had lost. Now he saw, in memory, the earnest face, the long fluttering lashes obscuring the boy's expression as they took their leave of one another. Luis was stooping to fasten his pack, and his muscles were rippling. In his arms, the pack seemed to bear a resemblance to the monster head that David turns in his hands with the arrogance of a victor and the underhand spitefulness of a child. When the last piece of webbing had been buckled in place, Luis had straightened up with an air of contentment.

'There,' he had said, as though leaving for the front presented no further difficulties. Sitting on the next bed, Agustin admired for the last time the firm, clean-cut head above the fine neck, the dancing body, and girlishly slender waist that nature had conferred on a miner. Luis imagined that he was going off to defend the Asturias, even though he would be fighting within a few miles of Madrid. He pictured himself as being in a mining gallery blocked by a fall: he wanted to cut his way through and save his comrades . . .

The capture of Belchite had been just a flash in the pan. The offensive had failed: Gijon had fallen. On a roadside, far from the bleak mountains and the pale and wrathful sea, Luis slept under a bank with his mouth full of earth and blood. 'I am not to blame!' murmured Agustin.

Because he had not witnessed Luis's death, the tall headstrong boy was still alive for Agustin. He would visualize him crouched over his rifle or poring over a newspaper. He was whittling away at a piece of wood with his knife and whistling a hackneyed tune. Luis was smiling. Was he smiling at himself, as youngsters everywhere do, or at the bullet that was to go clean through his heart? The man next to him in the trench had told Agustin how Luis had fallen, with no vomiting or heavy bleeding: a clean death . . . The man had unbuckled Luis's belt, such a handsome belt, with raised eyelets, a belt fit for a general. Agustin had wept: death had returned his present. He was sorry that the lad had not been buried in his ornamental belt.

Agustin had been unable to shield his friend from his own nature. Of all his failures, this was the only one for which he could not forgive himself. Thereafter, he had felt nothing but contempt for his useless authority, his absurd contrivings. He had begun to hate himself, until that dingy November dawn when his heart had softly started beating again.

Juanito looked more knowing today. Army life soon gave peasants the poise and glibness of townsfolk. Perhaps Luis and Juanito shared the same strongly delineated mouth, those lips with their compressed and rather disdainful corners, and the exacting expression of young men who imagine that they are standing face to face with destiny! Was that the only point of resemblance between Luis and Juanito—the impression that they both gave of looking the Sphinx straight in the eye? Agustin gave up comparing the two, and dismissed all thought of Luis as a bad omen. Juanito's glass was empty. Agustin stood him a brandy. He began to talk about Andalusia, pretending to believe that Juanito was from Seville or Granada.

Juanito smilingly corrected him, in a slow and rather sing-song voice: his village was in the Valencian *huerta*, by the banks of the Albufera lake. The hand that he had rested on the sticky table had a broad palm and long fingers. It possessed the beauty of a tool perfectly suited to its task. It was good at tilling the earth and judging fruit by its feel, at lopping off branches and patting an animal's flank. Agustin restrained his fierce desire to take hold of this hand that work had not misshapen, to imprison these fingers that must have effected so many indissoluble bonds with objects and creatures. He raised his glass as though taking an oath.

He told himself with cold resolution: 'He is not yet twenty . . . he mustn't die.' But even as he sat deciding another man's fate, Agustin heard himself talking about the Levante. Twenty years earlier he had travelled from Murcia to Valencia through this lush region where life seemed too easy. With its boisterous men and gay women, its fertile plains, its towns sweet-smelling as gardens by the sea, its hot, humid climate and hazy sky, it had soon proved too much for him. He had cut short his journey. Yielding to a curious feeling of impatience, he had returned to his first post, back in that Aragon village where nobody was expecting him but where he did not have to repel, like an intrusive caress, this voluptuous sweetness in everything and everybody, this languid embrace of the days and nights. To justify his aversion, he would say to himself: 'The Levante isn't Spain: it's Naples, it's Carthage, it's the Mediterranean—the seething cauldron, for centuries past, of every foul cult, of all the sacrificing to idols and surrendering to the gods of the flesh. Spain is wrought from tension and purity: a hamlet in Castile and a ruined town in Aragon are expressions of the same striving and the same starkness, whereas these towns are gorged with their lushness, as though with blood that is too rich for them.'

Subsequently he had felt no urge to revisit these stretches of country that open out like flowers, or these towns that ripen in a few weeks of spring weather like over-sweet grapes.

Agustin was turning over these names that lay dormant and untarnished in his memory. He was using them guardedly, in the manner of an explorer employing a few words of a foreign language as feelers in the presence of strange tribesmen: is it to be peace or war between them, friendship or hostility? Juanito was won over. His face was lighting up in a smile . . . One by one, he was responding to these names which Agustin handled so circumspectly, as though they were weapons. He was repeating them. He was fondling these syllables that evoked the countryside round Valencia, these oasis-names handed down from the Moors, these magic words conjuring up enclosed gardens cooled by spring water: Ruzafa, Alboraya . . . He was feeling his way through these dewy sounds as though he were parting leaves. Just as he might have sunk his teeth into fruit that had burst its peel, he was biting into these names gorged with shade and juice. He was turning them into a glorious litany: Liria, Denia, Carcagente, Sueca, Alcira—were these simply the villages in the Levante that Agustin had spent a few days roaming among? Juanito's incantation was conjuring up vast shimmering expanses, a single orchard in which firm, serried, deep green orange-trees displayed row upon row of fabulous fruit. The palms rose, soared like shrill voices above a choir, towering over the mulberries and lemons and olives. Against the blue of the sky, the palms were quivering and glittering like firebirds. Beneath them lay the spuming foliage, an endless entanglement of branches, a swell of greenery. This sunswept display of wealth was contained in a single word: *huerta*. But on the other side of the Valencian plain lay another Paradise, another Garden of Eden, another orchard in which plants and trees and fruits and flowers mingled, all tossed by the same breeze, all nourished by the same sap, all full of the same heady vitality. Just as the sky is reflected in a mirror, so the Valencian *huerta* was reflected beyond the horizon in the

Murcia plain and the palm groves of Elche. Juanito was taking in at a glance this fertile, inexhaustible stretch of country, as though he were calculating the yield of his own small plot. Then, to trap Juanito into giving himself away, Agustin started praising the famous novelist who had portrayed the peasants of the *huerta* in a fierce and melodramatic light. Juanito smiled.

'We are not like that,' he said. 'Vengefulness and superstition are all right for Andalusians. Where I come from, the earth is too rich for there to be any of that. We are too fond of laughing and singing . . . And if we *do* fight, it's just for fun . . .'

His shyness had vanished. He had the volubility and the unforced laughter of a race whose members are always vying with one another for eloquence. Agustin listened, fascinated. He would not have wanted Juanito different in any way. Already kindled between them by their faltering words to one another was a tall bright flame feeding on whatever came its way: old memories, forgotten names . . . Agustin could not keep from stretching hands towards this chance blaze. He was no longer afraid of the excessively fierce impulse urging him towards another human being. 'Shall I suffer through Juanito, one of these days, just as I suffered through Luis?' But the wrench endured yesterday does not steel us for the agony awaiting us tomorrow. Agustin rose rather abruptly.

'If you need anything, you'll find me in the company office.'

He gave a patronizing wave of the hand, as though in self-derision. Talk picked up again. On the stained and sticky table stood the glass that Agustin had drained at a gulp. Gazing at it, Juanito recalled the November morning when he had felt that he was beginning a new life . . . But all we ever do is use up our lives, like those old clothes that we simply cannot wear out. Juanito was glad that Agustin had known the *huerta* before the harmony that had always prevailed there, between nature and man, and man and God, had been destroyed by the war.

Back in his office, Agustin opened a file and pushed away the cluttered ashtray. With a curious mixture of joy and sadness, he found himself feeling remote from events. The future of Spain, victory for the Republic, the triumph of freedom, now seemed mere talking points for the journalists and politicians. Had Luis flung himself into the butchery at Belchite to help his brothers in distress when they had been on the point of giving way? Had he wished, thereby, to break off a relationship that was becoming odious to him? The conjectures of the living were as irrelevant as the dead boy's motives. No amount of trumps will benefit the player who lets his cards spill on to the table. How could it matter, now, what or for whom his last thought had been? Why try to force words from his silent lips? A different man was being born again in Agustin. Lines from Lorca were stirring in his memory like memories of an earlier life. He murmured:

Canción de estrella viva
Sobre un perpetuo día . . .

A cluster of beams slanted into his cell: day and night were marrying. And glimpses of days gone by, of virgin mornings, dazzling noons and nights colder than crystal rose in his blood, summoning other lines:

La luz juega el ajedrez
Alto de la celosía . . .

Who better than Lorca to convey the pulsations of light in a shadowy room? Agustin pushed aside a report on the operations at Teruel and their effect on the army's morale.

Tucked away beneath a tottery pile of folders was a little book with a grubby binding. The tobacco-stained pages opened of their own accord in Agustin's hands. He saw himself as a young teacher at a school near Saragossa, thrusting this book into his pocket at the end of the day. Lorca was his companion on his long walks through the bare fields, the red clay hills and the ash-coloured rocks.

Sitting astride a felled tree, or the parapet of a bridge, he would stare down at the water racing over the pebbly bed. A hail from one of his pupils would not break in upon his grave musings, upon that sadness in which twenty-year-olds bury themselves when they think they are renouncing themselves and the world. His thankless sweating and toiling in a building after the style of a peasant's hovel, or of a poor village presbytery, would have been a heavy burden to Agustin, had he not felt the presence, like the Tempter near Christ in the Wilderness, of this poet who paraded the splendours of the world in a Genesis-like brightness.

The Aragon villages in which he had taught—Darroca, Alquezar, Albarracin—were in memory indistinguishable. Like splendid tramps wrapped up in their overcoats, they draped themselves in their ruined ramparts. Daring minor kings had made capitals or lairs of these look-out towers or eagles'-nests. Their palaces, distinguished merely by a huge battered doorway and an uneffaced escutcheon, were embedded somewhere between the schoolhouse, the inn and the village hall. Agustin had lived in the one, interchangeable cell-like room next to the unvarying whitewashed barn of a classroom. When he got out of bed at night and strolled to his desk, he would see, always, the same glittering sky above the slumbering countryside. He would return to his reading. The walls would reflect the merciless electric light. Agustin would no longer be certain whether he was asleep or awake. He would feel as though he were on a mountain-top, withstanding every ordeal, braving every danger, fighting off every kind of foe. These nights given over to reading constituted, in memory, a single spell of insomnia, a single timeless gallop. Agustin's mind and heart were going out to meet this Don Quixote who had not even jousted with windmills, or men, but only with ideas and words. He was absorbed, then, by the tremor of a flowering almond branch in the spring breeze, or the frothing of a torrent intoxicated by its own strength, or the smile of a lift-boy, in a hotel, apologizing for prompting pity.

For Agustin would get away from his surroundings at times. He did not care for looking round churches and museums and palaces; he liked to spend hours wandering through an unknown town, catching a stealthy glimpse of other people's lives. One evening in Gerona, he was strolling past the arcaded houses down by the river. A young craftsman was stooping over his workbench. Daylight and the shimmer of water were mingling with the golden glow of an oil lamp. And the face of this watchmaker, so absorbed in his task, was as eerily suffused as if he were engaged in some mystic rite. Agustin watched him unobserved. He imagined the lapping of the water enveloping his rapt industry with a caress and a prayer. Agustin felt entirely free of worry as he stood outside that window. All over Spain, workers and peasants were enjoying this indefinable sensation of being at peace with themselves; for life is sweet to those who have neither the time to dream nor the strength to yearn.

Perhaps even at this moment, in some village in Castile or Aragon, there was a teacher just like Agustin. He would have liked to step into this recluse's cell and promise him that, in some inexplicable way, the tables would one day be turned . . .

He had not yet broken the circle of his loneliness, the circle of his private hell. Emerging from his escapist flights of fancy, Agustin would find himself still surrounded by his classroom, with his pupils' exercise-books piled on his desk, together with that other book in which he wrote at fever pitch in an attempt to exorcise his demons. And then he would reopen his copy of Lorca. Suddenly he was no longer deprived of every happiness, no longer cheated of every taste of bliss. An act of grace was rising in him and intoxicating him. To be alive was an immeasurable stroke of fortune, an inexhaustible source of riches. He was falling in with the pronouncement of a sage: 'To be alive is ecstasy!' This was true even for Agustin, when a Poet's voice filled the night silence of the village, kindling a joyous blaze in the chilly schoolhouse. To convey the resplendency of daylight, or the enveloping spell of darkness, or the hunger of human minds and bodies, Lorca employed familiar words, everyday sensations and the songs that have lulled every child to sleep; in this, he was like those painters who compose their still-lifes with ordinary fruit, a hunk of bread, a half-peeled water melon bulging with aqueous blood, a cabbage with granular leaves lying beside the bedewed water-cooler, and a pile of lemons in a wicker basket. In the small, low-ceilinged rooms that gave on to the larger room where Agustin taught, there were, in place of holy pictures, some reproductions of the frescoes in the Sistine Chapel, an engraving of an Avila monastery, and El Greco's portrait of a nobleman with his hand on his chest. A friend who was an art student claimed that there was a likeness between Agustin and this *hidalgo*, whose other hand is resting on the pommel of his sword and who seems to be attesting his honour before God. Agustin would laugh at this assertion. He would lean forward and look at himself in the small circular mirror hanging from the espagnolette. What, with his pinched face and hangdog expression, could he possibly have in common with this aristocrat, who was so like his strong and flexible sword and whose eyes looked so confident of cowing Supreme Justice? He would say rather bitterly: 'But, Roberto! Everything about this man proclaims the haughty pride that made others bend to his will! Everything about *me* proclaims abjectness!'

Roberto would snap back: 'The only similarities that are worth grasping are similarities of expression: there are times when a cat puts one in mind of a beast of the jungle . . .'

Agustin would yield the point.

'After all,' he would say, 'I have no ancestors . . . Why not choose them at will from El Greco's portraits, or Rembrandt's, or Tintoretto's? When I'm looking through your art books, I can draw up my family tree soon enough: an Old Testament prophet, an Amsterdam rabbi, a doge and a corsair and—from now on, I claim him as mine—the man with his hand on his chest.'

Amid monstrous profanities, Roberto would insist that these undeniable genealogical affinities would emerge clearly from the portrait that he was going to paint of Agustin.

The book was still open in Agustin's hands; the lines were dancing on the page; his early years were flying at his throat, like watchdogs attacking a man who, on a quiet walk, steps unthinkingly through a garden gate. Perhaps remembering was the only way of being happy.

Juanito's face had revived dried-up springs within him. A strange thaw was occurring somewhere deep in his memory, and his soul rejoiced that it had found a fresh opportunity for suffering, a new excuse for waiting and trembling. Agustin was sitting in the raw wind that blew through the mountain passes.

A woman was going by with her copper-hooped wooden pail, and from it came the smell of churning milk. In an orchard, a cherry tree surrounded by walnuts and blackthorns was like a young girl who is hesitant to join in the dance. In this harsh landscape, the smallest touch of greenery or a flowering branch had to serve as a proclamation of spring. The men spoke but little, yet their words were warm and friendly. Agustin loved their dusky faces, their mistrustful eyes, so quick to light up, their rebel hearts. When he got back from his walks through these arid fields, there was something cosy about the sputtering of a log fire. There would be a letter waiting for him on his desk, from Roberto or a friend in Madrid. Agustin would greedily devour these pages, with their contradictory news, their half-confessions, their tartness and gaiety; for such letters are like the play of young animals, in which bites and caresses alternate.

I wasn't so very unhappy, thought Agustin, turning the pages as though his life were inscribed in this book. He felt as though he were surveying the tortuous path that he had followed, the intricate series of moves made by accident or from a sense of expediency. I was a little pained by my loneliness in the midst of those simple people. I still did not know what name to apply to a loneliness which I could only aggravate by seeking to break free of it . . . He carefully smoothed down the dog-eared page on which was printed a poem that he had read so often: I tried to escape by going into politics; poetry was better at appeasing my impatience to live, my frenzied need to love and be loved. He felt a secret pity for his own blunder. The bond of brotherhood that one professes to feel with thousands of human beings is no substitute for a single personal link. What had been his real wish when he had left that village for Barcelona and the political life? To lie in the shadows beside a fellow creature to whom he could admit everything. Yes, Agustin thought: a partner—someone who can neither forgive nor condemn, but who merely consents. He was frightened by his own lucidity. He lowered his head over the poem and read the titie in an undertone: 'San Gabriel'. He started to intone the opening lines:

Un bello niño de junco,
anchos hombros, fino talle,
piel de nocturna manzana,
boca triste y ojos grandes . . .

Suddenly he broke off, as though Juanito were snatching the book from his hands.

13

A SUPPLY OF NEW CLOTHING was delivered to the barracks, but there could be no question of fitting out all the troops. Juanito was given a uniform, whereas most of the recruits completed their training in the threadbare jackets and frayed trousers that had been issued to them on arrival. Before Juanito had time to get over his surprise at being singled out in this way, his name appeared on the promotion list. One morning, between manœuvres in the grounds of the Montjuich fortress, Agustin strode up to the new sergeant and casually offered his congratulations.

Casualties were daily arriving from Teruel, by plane and ambulance. The hospitals were detaining only those who had to undergo operations. Each barracks received its quota of minor wounded, who told of days and nights during which the only victory lay in the silent resistance of bodies to the torturing cold. These shivering men, gripping the barrels of their rifles with numb fingers, were performing the feats of a new Romancero.

Reports of the Nationalist capitulation in early January caused a wave of enthusiasm in Barcelona. For the first time, Franco was on the retreat and his generals were surrendering. The war was going to be over soon, and all that Juanito would have experienced would be the muddy training ground and Agustin's pep talks. Twice he volunteered for service at the front, to no avail. When he tried yet again, the officer who dealt with troops' requests explained that sergeants were needed for licking new platoons into shape. The zeal that dictated his action might be interpreted as eagerness to win further stripes.

After arms drill, that day, Juanito knocked on Agustin's door. The room was full of fumes from a small makeshift stove whose outlet jutted out of the window. A blue paper lampshade distributed a soothing light. Juanito made room for himself to sit by shifting some tins of food over against the wall. He glanced briefly at some photographs of political leaders which had been cut out of newspapers and pinned up round the room. Agustin broke into a laugh.

'No dancing girls, I'm afraid, no matadors . . . you're disappointed.' Then, pointing to a face in which a pair of keen eyes shone out between bushy eyebrows and heavy lips, he asked: 'Recognize him?'

In squares all over Spain, in the shade of the town hall, actors responding to this man's voice had performed the plays of Calderon and Lope de Vega among improvised scenery, on a dais loaned by the school, or on trestles hauled from some sacristy where they had lain among the processional floats and figures. The performances were timed to coincide with the feast day of the town's patron saint, or the annual agricultural show, or the local elections. Juanito had laughed and gasped and cheered with the best of them while Lorca and his troupe gravely bestirred themselves on the crudely finished boards. Sometimes the curtain refused to rise or fall between acts. Inordinate ambitions, heroic surges of joy, pathetic outbursts of sorrow, would cast shadows over the hard face of the peasants. Just as soon as they had cleaned off their make-up, the students would join their audience at table. They had the appetites of a wolf-pack and the spirit of crusaders; they had set their minds on giving a people back its inheritance. They were going to pluck great works of art from the museums and libraries, and turn the Spaniards of the present day into the contemporaries of Cervantes.

All these riches must be put back in circulation, Agustin would say, his taste for the theatrical joining forces with his political convictions. He had no wish to put life into a nation with no history, a race with nothing to attest to its greatness. Agustin sat picturing the little red or white towns of Estremadura and Aragon, hewn out of chalk or moulded from clay; but at the same time, for he was used to functioning on two levels, he was encouraging Juanito to describe the failure of his pleas to be sent to the front.

Why does he reawaken the past so strongly? wondered Agustin. Why do I feel this wave of enthusiasm, of resurgent fervour?

The very sight of the young Valencian's face—with his eyes, at once bold and bewildered, and the earnest set of his mouth—was enough to breathe life into any earlier phase, even though that phase might be doubly dead for Agustin. He found himself being carried right back to the schoolhouse near Saragossa, to the *barraca* at . . .

Juanito had finished. What is really dead within us, and what is capable of coming to life at any moment, wondered Agustin, in a sudden whirl of happiness. Even our betrayals are flimsily based. To whatever we have profoundly desired, profoundly loved, we remain faithful, in spite of other people, in spite of ourselves.

Agustin congratulated Juanito on his conscientiousness, his determination to fight. He spoke to him as though Juanito were the young Republican soldier for whom all his lectures were designed, as though he were a live dummy—the equivalent, for propaganda purposes, of the wood and wire lay figures that painters use in order to study the movements of the human body.

Juanito listened in embarrassment, much as he would have listened to Padre Enrique praying for him alone. The moment had not yet come, Agustin was insisting, for the Republic to throw all its strength into the balance . . . The way must be paved. The ablest and most determined men in Spain must gird themselves for that moment. Agustin was bidding Juanito to this second mobilization, which would be, simply, the overwhelming concentration of the finest and pluckiest volunteers. And to convince the boy, Agustin was recapturing the fervour with which, as a young schoolmaster, he had lauded the men of '89. The French Revolution had triumphed through the efforts of barefoot soldiers, of officers who had turned their backs on their own class in order to train recruits, of chemists, of scholars . . .

'There can be no victory for freedom, Juanito, without collaboration between the forces of enlightenment and the untapped resources of the common people . . .' Agustin's gaze rested on Lorca as though in search of advice, but the young, plump-faced, sensuous-lipped Andalusian would not reply.

'Lorca has been dead a year now, man! He thought it was possible to trust an enemy. For a poet and a monk, one cell is the same as another. Lorca chose a cell in Granada gaol. It was a poet's trick. He wanted to make friends with rifle-fire. Early one morning they propped him up against a wall . . . The silencing of his voice is as great a blow to us as the loss of a whole squadron of planes. When Franco is crushed, life will be tame without his gipsy *coplas*. With a guitar tune, or the whir of a cicada, or the shade of a thorn bush, he set the hearts of free men beating in a way no amount of speeches could. His poems were his "Marseillaise". He knew the flavour of every spring . . .'

Juanito kept his eyes lowered as he listened. With a new note in his voice, Agustin resumed violently: 'Yes, the Revolution needs Poets and strategists, sergeants and engineers! We must all conserve our energies for the moment of truth. I'm heartily glad your applications were turned down. For once, I bless our army's slowness and inefficiency . . .'

Agustin broke off, ostensibly to search for a lighter under the sea of papers. He found it, lit his cigarette as though his mind were still on his words, and then suddenly looked up. This time Juanito smiled. I've won, Agustin said to himself; but he knew he must turn this moment of harmony to good account.

'Do you imagine I enjoy my own job . . .? Oh yes, I know what they say in the barracks—that is what I'm here for—but who else is to track down the spies who are as active behind the lines as they are at the front, as rife in the depots as on the H.Q. staff?' He paused, to give his words time to sink in. 'And yet, when the decisive moment comes and we must throw everything we have into the battle, it will be thanks to an obscure political commissar like me that countless lives will not be sacrificed in vain, and that the balance will be tilted in our favour.'

Awareness of his own strength, pride in the essential and arduous role that he had been called upon to play, and a secret thrill of pleasure at dropping his mask in front of Juanito were giving Agustin a new face: the anaemic intellectual, whose poorly fitting uniform seemed like fancy dress, was turning into a haughty Saint-Just, as convinced of his omnipotence as he was of the truth of his convictions.

His words poured out in a disdainful hiss: he was vouching to an unseen Committee of Public Safety that treason and sabotage would never undermine the long patient struggle of the Republic.

On the desk, the cluttered ashtrays acted as paperweights for the food and ammunition supply chits. The folders were bursting at the seams with memoranda, reports, demands, protests. These documents, whose pointless classifications—'urgent', 'secret', 'confidential'—merely prompted a shrug of the shoulders from Agustin, bore witness to his vigilance. He had no hope of ever bringing this chaos, this squandering of energy, completely under control. Agustin pushed the mountain of papers aside. These entreaties, these threats, these denunciations, these appeals for help, these misleading statistics, dinned through his days like the roar of high tide. Now the vain tumult was dying down. Juanito's silence was smothering these conflicting voices, each one of which grew overemphatic in its eagerness to make its weight felt and swelled to huge proportions in an attempt to sound unique. This cacophony of doubts and hopes, these forecasts cancelling one another out, these claims already belied by events by the time they reached Agustin: these were war. But what did it matter that messages were tapped on their way from source, that figures got to headquarters too late? All was not in vain, since this Valencian was weighing every word that fell from Agustin's bitter lips.

We are all looking for someone to bear witness to our worth, thought Agustin, as he went on with the speech he was making for Juanito's benefit. Friendship, love, literature, politics: what's in a name, so long as a fellow-creature believes in us with all his heart?

'A bureaucrat?' He laughed shortly. 'Well, why not? If that bureaucrat has a better grasp of the situation than a good many ministers.'

Again he gave the proud, slighted grunt of mirth that served as laughter.

'Oh yes, I know more than a good many members of the War Cabinet. I've a clearer picture of the front than most generals. I'm more familiar with the feelings of our troops than any politician.'

He despised all the powers-that-be, but promised to let Juanito know when the time was ripe. How could Juanito argue? He knew, from having heard it more than once in the canteen, that Agustin was capable of explaining the vastest operations and of depicting the imminent Russian intervention and the subsequent torpedoing of the Italian and German cruisers in Nationalist-held ports. Agustin was making excuses for the shilly-shallying of the fainthearted British, and for the cautiousness of the French, who demanded evidence of fascist intervention before throwing off the pretence of neutrality. Agustin's views on strategy were prophecies. Juanito thanked him with a great surge of gratitude. They were sealing a pact among the faded registers, the unanswered petitions, the wine-containers stacked in one of the corners, the office stamps on the moist red and mauve ink-pads. They got up. Agustin opened the door on to the dark corridor. The blue lamplight picked out his mocking smile which gave Juanito a feeling of uneasiness.

The Valencian's footsteps clattered away down the iron staircase. Agustin finished what remained of a bottle of brandy. He was pleased with himself. Juanito imagined it would be easy for him to become a combatant. Agustin would save him, even if he did not want to be saved. Nothing can come between us, he thought. This ability to exercise remote control over another man's life was enough for Agustin. He was dismissing all thought of a grotesque pursuit, of dangerous advances. He would not try to get anything more out of Juanito than this trusting handshake, this shy smile. These were sufficient. He said quietly, as though Juanito were still there: 'You, at least, will live, Juanito.' This would be his way of getting even with Luis, with the war, with the whole human breed, in whose presence he would always be an outsider. Because an accident of mind and body made acknowledgeable desires alien to him, Agustin had developed a sinister taste for power and secrecy. Drink, and the emotion resulting from this soliloquy, in which he sought to rob death of its prey, were making him feverish. He forced open the window, which was stuck, and leaned out over the silent barracks square. It was a mild night. Agustin went back to his desk. A photograph of Luis was tucked away under his revolver. He had been unable to puzzle out the secrets of this star-like face, the face of a flower anxious to yield all its scent before nightfall. What foreboding gave this manly face its calm assurance, or the mouth its twist of childish arrogance? The boy's lips were lovelier for their failure to pronounce the words expected of them. His sealed face was still enclosed in the blurred ring of light with which the flicker of candles surrounds the carved features of the saints. Agustin's hand was shaking slightly. He was filled with a mounting temptation to destroy the photograph. 'I've had too much to drink,' he said to himself, pushing it to the back of the drawer.

14

JUANITO RECEIVED NEWS from the village. Padre Enrique had fled to Valencia. The churches were still closed. Looting of sacristies had been followed by sacrilegious masqueradings in the streets. The *huerta* continued to keep Republican Spain fed. Tremendous pride could be read between the lines of Theresa's letters. The bitter fighting at Teruel dragged on and on, but

Domingo wrote that the Republicans now held the town and that neither snow nor artillery fire would dislodge them. Theresa bade her son do nothing that might pain the Virgin. This gave Juanito plenty to think about. Two conflicting parties were rending Spain asunder. It seemed impossible for either of them to triumph. Each, furthermore, was cruelly divided against itself. Agustin was only too glad to recount the quarrels coming to light among the rebel forces, the bickerings between the Royalists and the Carlists and Antonio Primo de Rivera's Falangists and the power-hungry generals. The Italians and Germans were getting bogged down in these family quarrels, claimed Agustin; but the soldiers retorted sceptically: 'What about us? '

They all remembered the bloody purging of the anarchists, and later of the Trotskyists; the kidnapping of Nin; the campaign against Largo Caballero. The Republic, too, had its domestic squabbles, its habit of making an example of men who were idolized till the day they had resignation or silence or suicide forced upon them. Agustin shrugged; hadn't the Revolution of '89 been troubled by its Girondins and Montagnards, its warring cliques, its sectarian cross-currents, its fanatics bent on mutual self-destruction? Neither Robespierre nor Barras, neither the out-and-out Jacobins nor the time-servers had been able to check the triumph of liberty. Through opposing temperaments there flowed the same determination, the same unalloyed energy. How could these growing pains be compared with the palace intrigues centred round Franco?

La Pasionaria was in Paris . . . Her cries were going to awaken public opinion, take the wind out of the sails of the politicians, rouse the whole nation . . . Once France took up the cudgels for the Spanish Republic, the whole complexion of the war would change . . . Together with his visionary style, Agustin was recovering his seer-like conviction. French arsenals, if he was to be believed, were already producing for the Republicans. Squadrons of planes were shining above the Pyrenees. Tanks were barely unloaded at Barcelona before they were rumbling across the plateaus of Aragon and Castile. The Republic was counter-attacking furiously, all along the line.

Agustin was hailing the triumph of the righteous in apocalyptic terms, but in the superstitious hearts of the peasants and shopkeepers, La Pasionaria assumed the features of the Virgin. Instead of pointing to her son's wounds in an attitude of resignation, she was daring to defend him; in Paris, she was inveighing against the restrictive practices of the arms manufacturers and the cowardice of the statesmen . . .

Agustin harked back to the days of the Reconquest in an attempt to revive the age-old hatred of the Moor: the infidels would be hurled back into Africa together with the Nationalist generals. The Civil War was no longer merely the latest episode in the history of Spain. In her stand against the invader, modern Spain was coming into her own again.

From his front-row seat, Juanito was growing familiar with Agustin's strange dialectics, his colloquial yet splendid eloquence, his abrupt transitions, his readiness to employ every means of stirring the unsophisticated emotions of his listeners, and—when he thought his words had done their work—with the nervous tic that ran through his face like a twitch of pain and pleasure. Juanito remained unconvinced: a woman's rantings were no match for the Italian bombers and German U-boats.

Then, searching out his listeners' weak spot, Agustin dwelt on the scenes of murder and looting that had occurred in Madrid and Barcelona after the failure of the pronunciamento. The revenge of the underdog was openly exposed. In his crude imagery, the workers were a wild beast whom it was dangerous to rouse. The Spanish Republic, threatened by the plotting of the priests and generals, had witnessed the equivalent of the September massacre: in these bloody bacchanalia, the people had purged themselves of fear and humiliation. The summary executions should be seen as a purifying ritual, as the only offering acceptable to the gods of the past. The very men who had sought to plunge Spain back into the days of the Inquisition had been the first victims of the autos-da-fé. Amid the carnage resulting from the conspiracies of a few self-seekers, how could anyone be unduly moved by the sacrifice of an innocent victim, or the rape of a woman, or the burning of a church?

Agustin scanned his audience's faces for signs of agreement. Juanito looked away. The people of Valencia are humanitarian and superstitious liberals, ignorant of the iron laws of history. Agustin despised these timid Republicans, just as Saint-Just must have despised the garrulous lawyers of the Gironde. To enflame the young men's imagination, Agustin described the bonfires that had greeted the capture of the Montana barracks. The ancient palaces of Madrid, which had concealed their opulence behind bare façades emblazoned with eagles and plumed helmets, were ablaze. Their costly panelling, their silk-hung walls, their fine plate and glassware, their lavishly bejewelled patron saints, their bronzes, their paintings, their furniture inlaid with ivory and pearl—these were all fuel to the flames. The poor stood and watched it burn, the loot amassed over the centuries by a handful of families. Agustin was jumping for joy. He was dancing round the flames consuming the Liria Palace as though it were a hayrick. The great works of art that belonged to the Spanish people had been put in safekeeping. What right, cried Agustin, had the Duke of Alba to keep Christopher Columbus's logbook in his personal archives? He was trying to awaken in these property-minded peasants the feeling that they had won something back. He failed to convince them that a fabulous inheritance had been restored to them. Yielding to some unfathomable instinct, he roused his audience to that pitch of frenzy which in the old days had been called forth by bullfighting and the worship of gory statues. He conjured up pictures of those women caught unawares in the false security of their homes; instead of prompting pity, their heaving bosoms and rent clothes and tear-stained faces and straggling hair gave rise to anger and desire, desire barely distinguishable from anger, an anger like a raging desire. Perhaps, Agustin said sardonically, the number of victims had been exaggerated. His hatred for women was finding an outlet. He lingered over their passionate surrenders, their feigned sacrifices, their cries of terror that ended in coos of pleasure. Malicious smiles appeared on the men's stubbly faces. Agustin recalled the case of the Duchess of Villahermosa. She had defied the workers and insulted the troops. A bullet had struck her in the temple. A militiaman had raped her, and then her quivering body had been dragged through the streets. An elderly duenna had met with the same fate. The Republicans had no cause to blush: these excesses were the public expiation of prolonged insolence. There had been nothing to stop the young woman from answering the militia in unabusive terms. Agustin made much of these caresses in which the delights of profanation and revenge were darkly mingled. This corpse, displayed for everyone to see in all the disarray of murder, was inviting the passionate embrace of a whole city. The man who had raped this half-dead woman had been merely consummating the desire of the people. It was Madrid itself that possessed and trampled this creature hitherto reserved for the enjoyment of a caste . . .

Juanito had turned pale. The newspapers had merely reported the unavailing protests of foreign diplomats, and the government's reply. Agustin's words were tearing away the sheet that hides the obscene nakedness of a corpse. How was it possible to visualize this defiled body, marked less by bullets than by men's hands? The audience was wandering off. Agustin strode up to Juanito.

'What's troubling you, my sensitive friend?'

He was amused by Juanito's reaction, though unable to guess its ramifications.

'Nothing,' said Juanito, 'but what you have just been saying has nothing whatever to do with the war. It isn't for the Republic to encourage rape.'

He spoke harshly, with a kind of resentment.

Agustin smiled. The pure in heart do not know that pain is ecstasy, and ecstasy pain.

'Don't be alarmed, lad. You look like a boy who has just gone with a woman for the first time . . . What the situation called for was a good-looking youngster like you. The lady would soon have given up wanting to be a martyr. Englishwomen take to Spaniards the way the snow takes to the sun.'

A tremendous buzzing filled Juanito's ears, drowning Agustin's breezy comments. Flights of wild duck were flapping their wings in the crisp morning air, amid the echoing cries of a shooting party. A fresh-faced young woman was smiling at a boy. Her smile was too stunning an endearment for a ten-year-old, a stifling wave of perfumes that dispelled all other sensations, all other memories. She was still directing this smile at him, but he was no longer a child. He had become a murderer.

'What's the matter with you?' cried Agustin.

Juanito was toppling into his arms. Agustin braced himself against the wall to withstand the weight of the boy's sturdy body. He managed to propel him to the nearest bench. Soldiers were shouting to one another through the open window of the canteen. The post orderly appeared on the other side of the barrack square, and the men all crowded round him.

Sagging against the wall with his eyes shut, Juanito looked as though he were asleep. Agustin unfastened the collar of the coarse khaki shirt. A slender chain, with a medal attached to it, hung round the Valencian's neck. Beside the rusted metal, the skin looked as delicate as a child's. Agustin leaned still closer: was it Juanito's breathing that made the boy's chest rise and fall beneath the faint covering of down, or was it his own? On the rosy skin he sought the thin, bite-shaped wounds that the arrows are depicted as leaving on the body of St Sebastian. Round his neck, the metal chain marked the spot where the axe would fall.

Agustin was carried away by the mental pictures that he had conjured up in connection with Sybil. But this time the victim was Juanito: it was his head that was being struck off by the executioner. It retained that abundant halo of sandy hair clotted with blood. Juanito's head, like the Baptist's, was rolling on a golden charger with its tough and frisky mane. The man was grasping it by the longest locks and brandishing it like a trophy . . .

Juanito opened his eyes. Agustin was peering at him like a murderer watching his victim's last convulsions before finishing him off, and all the while trembling with impatience and remorse . . .

15

IN A CAMPAIGN which, for the Republicans, had consisted of one setback after another, Teruel stood out as a brief victory. They had barely had time to celebrate this episode as a decisive success before Franco recaptured the town.

A member of Juanito's detachment who came from Figueras recalled that in the old days his town had changed hands so quickly that it had belonged to Spain in time of peace and to France in time of war. Toledo and Teruel would be useful propaganda for the two sides, in much the same manner.

'This is a war of false victories and false alliances,' pronounced Agustin. 'Britain is not prepared to act without France, France will not commit herself without Russia, and Russia claims that she cannot intervene, for by doing so she would be playing into the hands of Germany and Italy. In plainer words, our friends are letting us choke to death while they keep an eye on our enemies. It would be a rich joke if it weren't at our expense. Everyone is out for the lion's share in our gratitude. The Non-Intervention Agreement is a pact between onlookers who, from the safety of the riverbank, decide not to go to the aid of a drowning man!'

In private conversation with Juanito, he no longer bothered to disguise what he was thinking. But in his pep-talks to the troops, he went on recalling the defensive nature of the Franco-Russian Pact, which prevented Paris and Moscow from acting, and pretended to believe in the support of the free nations.

In the course of the latest clashes at Teruel, Domingo disappeared. Juanito went from hospital to hospital, searching for his brother among the wounded brought back to Barcelona as and when ambulances were available. He wandered about in the stale and treacherous smell of ether. Through those unvarying wards, among all that pain, amidst all those sweaty faces pressed against their pillows. From every ward he would emerge at once disappointed and reassured. Then panic would take hold of him again. Was Domingo going to vanish without trace, was he going to join the host of the missing, like Federico, leaving not even a plain wooden crucifix behind him, or a penknife, or an identity disc? Juanito's quest was like a nightmare in which you finally forget what you are looking for. Perhaps war had no other purpose than to prepare the living for a death without farewells, for a kind of elimination.

But he did discover a casualty from the same company as Domingo. One of his legs had just been amputated. He had lost a good deal of blood. He responded to Juanito's questions with the barest wave of the hand, like those seers who take in the whole of the future, as though it were a landscape, but cannot pick out an isolated feature: a man's life or the end of the war held little significance for Ramon now. All was over for him.

Juanito called to see him again. Ramon recognized him.

'When you came looking for your brother, I was too tired to talk . . . They took some prisoners . . . There comes a time when you are ready to surrender, just as you would be ready to kill . . .'

Ramon's gesture of doubt or renunciation was echoed in the words that flowed haltingly from his lips. He was beyond courage and fear. Juanito had brought him some cigarettes. Ramon took them, even though he was not allowed to smoke. His lungs were still riddled with shrapnel; the doctors had given up trying to get it out. Ramon asked that his family be told. His father was a fisherman at Lloret, a village along the Costa Brava, pure white beside the blue of the sea which was as rich as a vatful of paint.

Juanito knew little of the sea, except for the stretch of coast near Valencia. Ramon recovered a hint of life to describe the sand-coated streets. In the evenings the womenfolk go home with a tunny fish slung over their shoulders, newly caught and still twitching. The surf breaks over the blood-red stone jetty. Two by two, the fishing boats head out to sea in the warm breeze.

Ramon was in the pilot boat. His father, aboard the companion boat, was directing powerful electric lamps sternwards. Blinded by the sudden brilliance of the beams, the fish were responding to this source of light, as though to a warmer current, and swarming into the net. Ramon smiled at their stupidity. Now all that they had to do was haul this scaly, shuddering mass back to harbour. There, the fish were laid out on great stone slabs, to be counted and weighed.

'In the *huerta*,' said Juanito, 'the sportsmen use the same trick when they go out shooting. In wintertime they light torches on the lake, and the wild duck come swooping down . . .'

But Ramon did not hear. He was handling, ecstatically, those slippery fish, those coral gills, those mother-of-pearl fins which were still flapping, as though the rhythm of the swell were continuing to inhabit them.

Juanito sat wondering whether the shining, hypnotizing words that the opposing sides bandied about—freedom, order, tradition, brotherhood—did not resemble these false signals, these promises of warmth and light, which men use the more easily to kill animals.

Gangrene developed in the other leg. There was no hope for Ramon. He was moved into a small private room: in hospital, being alone is the privilege of the dying. Juanito had to wander from ward to ward before he found him groaning faintly to himself, his eyes shut.

The operation had been performed too late, declared the nurse sitting at his bedside. It should have been carried out at the front. She did not lower her voice. Such precautions were superfluous. Was there anyone in Barcelona who ought to be informed? she asked in the same impersonal tone. For her, Ramon's death was a formality already concluded. Within a few weeks, people would come looking for his grave just as Juanito had come looking for his bed.

Ramon opened his eyes and smiled broadly at Juanito.

'You're here for the catch,' he said. 'We're none too early.'

He pricked up his ears, as though to make out the distant chug-chug of boats' engines in the warm, evening air.

'Never mind,' he said, 'there are bound to be a few fish left for us.' He broke into a laugh. 'The main thing is to be back in time for the *sardana.*' He began to whistle a tune with a strange rhythm. The nurse grew alarmed. These boys retained a terrifying degree of energy, a disconcerting outlook, to the very end. They were incapable of dying the way a lamp burns out: by degrees ... Ramon was addressing her now. He was inviting her to join the ring that was already weaving in and out beside the sea. Perhaps he was confusing her with another girl. He broke off his whistling to reassure her: 'It's so easy—just you see if it isn't. All you have to do is count: any Catalan will tell you that.' The ring kept opening to admit further dancers, who plunged boldly into the spirit of the thing. He turned to Juanito. 'Do you know the *sardana*? We were dancing it before Christ was born.' A tourist had told him that the *sardana* dated back to the beginnings of time. Ramon was naïvely proud of the fact. It was a proof of Catalonia's antiquity. And yet it was a living dance, which men and women of all ages and conditions danced along the coast. All you had to do was step into the moving circle that swelled and split into other concentric circles, and each ring danced to its own rhythm and impulse.

'It's a democratic dance,' Ramon continued, 'the one truly democratic dance.' This, too, had been explained to him by men who had come to Lloret to collect tunes, and to record folk-lore.

A dance fit for free men. The dancers, linking hands, would leap high in the air, with their faces tilted skywards and their chests arched. And they would all greet the sun with a laugh.

Ramon arched his body similarly on the pillow. He imagined that he was in the thick of the *sardana*, surrounded by those radiant faces and that garland of bare arms, and all about him the dance was giving birth to other rings, other corollas, was turning into that living rose, while the *cobla* blared forth like the voice of Judgment, sounding at once joyous and solemn.

Ramon was participating in this dionysiac round, in this dance of the living and the dead. He gave a sudden violent start and cried out in pain. 'For heaven's sake, hold him!' said the nurse, with something like irritation. Juanito sat down on the edge of the bed and slid his arm under Ramon's waist. The clammy shirt was stuck to the sheet. Juanito was holding merely a human trunk.

'I must have caught my clothes on a nail,' said Ramon. ' It's nothing to worry about. Stand close to me: it will make it easier for us to tack.' He imagined that he was on the boat again. The nurse shook her head.

Ramon drew a deep breath, to savour the moist offshore wind. The frenzied echo of the *sardana* was dying away in the distance.

'I never realized,' he said, 'that you knew the *sardana* in Valencia. You have the *jota*, which can't compare with it.' Near the surface, bulging eyes were lighting up and sending clusters of beams through the dark waters. Ramon was no longer struggling.

The nurse sprang to her feet and stared down at the cropped head sagging on to the pillow. Ramon was blinking slightly, as though caught in the blaze of a fishing lamp. His lips parted. A glittering net was closing on this prey in the enveloping darkness.

'You might help me,' the nurse said. Her voice still had the same note of hostility. Perhaps she was sick of seeing these soldiers die, disjointedly shedding their boyish memories, their childlike longings. She rubbed a wet flannel over Ramon's face and drew the sheet high over his chest. She adjusted the folds carefully, to hide the stump.

'Were you at Teruel?' she asked Juanito, and without waiting for his answer added: 'Do close his eyes.'

Overcoming his revulsion, Juanito lightly touched this human flesh which, though still warm, already belonged to death. The lids closed unresistingly under his fingers. Juanito drew slightly away from the bed. The sheet hung in noble folds, like the draperies with which sculptors surround recumbent figures, so as to give them greater dignity in death. For all eternity, Ramon was adrift in a sea full of strange jellyfish with phosphorescent eyes. Perhaps, despite the drone of the engine in the stern of the boat, he was able to make out the exuberant cries of the *sardana*, softened by distance, ringing out on the shore.

'He looks happy,' observed Juanito. The nurse seemed annoyed and upset.

'Happy?' she said. 'Happy . . .? There isn't even a crucifix to join his hands on. We could ransack the hospital and still not find one.'

Awkwardly, Juanito took off the chain that he wore round his neck. On the slim medal, the nurse recognized the Virgin of the Forsaken.

'Are you from Valencia?'

They gazed at one another in surprise, delight almost.

The nurse folded Ramon's hands in at attitude of prayer, then threaded the metal chain between his fingers as though it were a rosary.

16

A RENEWED WAVE OF TERROR was sweeping through Barcelona. Even members of the government trembled at the thought of early morning arrests followed by summary executions. How was anyone to tell one political police force from another? Men of the highest position chose to sleep in hiding-places on the outskirts of Barcelona. The anarchists, crushed soon after the start of the uprising, were reappearing; their hand was strengthened by all the setbacks and disappointments on the Republican side, and they were now proposing to liquidate not only the rebels, but the lukewarm, not only the Nationalists, but those who dared to place limitations on freedom. Their harangues and proclamations were rousing the worst instincts of the mob, inciting them to murder and suicide. It was not simply a matter of quelling the the enemy's resistance and doing away with a few traitors, but of breaking, once and for all, with law and order and with God. This 'freedom' invoked by the agitators was fermenting like wine overlong in the vat.

Units leaving for the front would encounter processions aping religious cortèges, and march-pasts akin to riots. Sometimes troops and demonstrators would merge in a single whirl of intoxication. Courage and the thirst for revenge, sacrilege and destructiveness, would fuse in an indistinguishable frenzy, giving rise to senseless acts. The statues of harmless politicians would be toppled from their pedestals. Shops that had stood empty for months would have their shutters battered down by the impatient mob. Foiled, the plunderers would set fire to the premises before they left.

Every day brought further destruction to the shabby houses down by the harbour, no less than to the tall blocks of flats lining the avenues round the Plaza de Cataluña. These terrifying and unaccountable conflagrations filled in the idle periods, the inevitable entr'actes, providing a diversion between the shots that suddenly rang out in a quiet street and the air raids, the smoke from which was driven through the town by the sea breeze.

Juanito refused to believe that these disturbances were whipped up by supporters of Franco. It was to alarm foreign journalists, claimed Agustin, that the priests were destroying their own churches after carefully storing away their relics and treasures. Before long they would be parading their pious trophies, quite unharmed, on lavishly reconstructed altars . . . Had not the Grail been hidden from view in Valencia on the very first day? The Madonna had followed, with all her jewels and finery . . .

'What peasant,' Juanito protested hotly, 'would set fire to his own farmhouse? What priest would dare burn the House of God with his own hands?'

Agustin flared up at this challenge.

'The House of God . . .? Do you still believe in all that twaddle? Do you believe in the Church, working hand in glove with Franco? In the bishops, who have proclaimed him heir to the Catholic kings?'

'God isn't Franco's property. He belongs to every Spaniard.'

'That is why every Spaniard is so poor,' declared Agustin.

'A word is no substitute for iron and coal, for bread and machinery.'

God belongs to every Spaniard . . . Is that what Luis believed as he lay in the Belchite earth? Agustin took a grip on himself.

'You are all like that in Valencia: rich soil nourishes superstition even better than flint. It is Spain that belongs to every Spaniard, Juanito: that's a lot of land and sky for a fellow to have on his hands.'

Suddenly he broke off and whispered in Juanito's ear: 'Juanito, I love you as strength loves weakness, as reason loves illusion, and in my way I love the gullible peasants of your *huerta* and the poor townsfolk who adorn their Madonnas with diamonds and lace. On feast days, their crowns and robes set even beggars' eyes ablaze. Your superstition wraps these idols in a mantle of fire . . . It is from you that they draw the blood that flows from their wounds . . . It is your tears, human tears, that stream down their waxen faces. Yes, Juanito, this miracle is wrought day after day throughout the length and breadth of Spain, and the thought doesn't even occur to those, like yourself, who work it . . .'

The Nationalist offensive was building up in the area north of the Ebro. The Germans were pouring in, with brand-new weapons and equipment. Some of the Republican newspapers were still claiming that this would be the last spring of the war, but communications between Barcelona and Valencia were imperilled daily.

Soledad had followed her cousin to Madrid; the baby was due early in the summer. When he heard the news Juanito averted his head, as though from an ugly wound. In the same letter his mother wrote that his brother Domingo was reported to have been seen, after the fall of Teruel, in a camp where prisoners were sorted. Theresa thanked the Virgin for sparing her son.

One morning, Juanito was sent for in the middle of arms drill. He handed his men over to another sergeant and raced down the goatsherds' tracks towards the barracks. The training ground was below the Montjuich fortress, in the narrow valley between the cemetery and the park. Explosive thuds came from the chalk-pits which, in the early days of the war, had re-echoed to the rat-tat-tat of firing squads. In the distance, beyond the thin woods and bare hills, Barcelona was rousing herself in the grey morning and quivering like an anvil being pounded by a blacksmith. A patch of sunlight on a roof was making the tiles gleam like fishes' scales . . . . Juanito stopped to get his breath back. From the blue produced by the first smoke of the factories, and by the exhalation of the schools and houses, there emerged an abstracted pediment, a dome as light as an arch, a spire that Juanito was unable to identify.

He hailed an army lorry and the driver agreed to take him to the barracks. Along the Ramblas, the flower-sellers were arranging their wares while the last of the night dew evaporated under the trees. It was a June morning with its deceitful flavour of eternity.

'I just wanted to see you!' said Agustin, with a shake of the head. He apologized for disrupting Juanito's arms drill and for needlessly putting him to so much trouble . . . Then apologies gave way to sarcasm: 'I suppose the Republican troops are carrying all before them on the hills of Barcelona? On the Saragossa front, it's a very different story . . . Well, what do you expect, man? Armies aren't made of heroes, or nations of great men. The uncommitted swim with the tide: in Burgos they are pro-Franco; in Madrid they think they are pro-government.'

As a rule, Agustin took a militant view of events. He would extol desperate stands and hopeless sacrifices. 'Every great gesture that has brought advancement to the human race seemed an act of madness at first,' he would often tell Juanito. 'The crucifixion of your God, for example.'

Was he trying to convince himself that there was neither choice nor freedom in this war?

'How many enlistments are the result of a journey? The Republicans who were on holiday in the Balearics have disguised themselves as Knights of Christ. The conservatives in Madrid will play at being heroes of the barricades till the end of the war!

Mere chance has split the enemy forces into two camps. History is a series of tedious repetitions: the *marranos*—whether you call them Republicans or Nationalists—changed sides yesterday, just as they are doing today, to escape the auto-da-fé. Who can blame them? If, tomorrow, a lost battle enables them to change back again, they cease to be traitors by becoming deserters. But I haven't even put my bed away.' Agustin was referring to the horsehair mattress which he kept rolled up during the day. Beside it, on the ground, was the big black ebonite receiver which was his link with headquarters. Juanito started to untangle the telephone cord. Agustin's talkativeness was merely a cloak for the few brief words that he was reluctant to utter, or perhaps even for silence.

Juanito observed coldly: 'You are letting your tongue run away with you, Agustin! If I understand you aright, all the participants are recruited by force: they regain their freedom by cheating. And yet you have told me over and over again that this isn't a war of mercenaries, but—in your own words—a holy war in which every soldier is defending his body and saving his soul . . .'

'Yes,' Agustin admitted, 'the only justifiable war in our history. It isn't a question of putting a pretender on the throne, or turning to foreign powers for help, or preserving the vestiges of an empire. This is *our* War of Succession: it will be settled between men of the same blood . . .'

He drew his hand across his face, as though he were very tired.

'You are right, Juanito. It is I who am weakening. Perhaps a political commissar has his moments of irresolution, just as great generals do.' He made an effort to laugh. Juanito went on looking serious. There was a silence. 'All human truth is eclipsed at times. You mustn't condemn those who give way to tiredness or fear . . .'

Agustin rolled up the horsehair mattress and the blanket in a single operation and shut them in the cupboard. His movements were the deferment of other movements, his words the postponement of an ultimate explanation. Juanito started towards the door. Agustin stopped him.

'You want to go away and sleep, like the favourite disciple in the Garden of Gethsemane. Yes, you want to leave me to grope with these insoluble problems all alone? Today, Spain is a family of feuding brothers . . . And yet it is wonderful to see two brothers fighting for the same cause . . . In Malaga, José Antonio was in the same prison as his brother. He was to be executed first. He was in terror lest his brother should step on his blood: the same gallery was used for exercise and executions. This obsession with defiled blood . . .! It makes one think of Lorca . . .'

Agustin's strange soliloquy was guiding Juanito like a hand through a darkened room. In an attempt to break free, he said: 'Surely you didn't send for me just to sing José Antonio's praises?'

For the first time, he was staring angrily at Agustin. Agustin averted his eyes from this accusing face. He filed one of the documents lying on his desk, as though his thoughts were far away; then he swung round.

'Your brother is alive.'

'Domingo?' murmured Juanito.

Agustin had won back the advantage.

'Stupendous progress!' he said. 'Taken prisoner in January, joined the shock troops in February, decorated by Franco in March for entering Alcañiz with the Italians . . . You've nothing to say?'

Juanito was staring down at the floor. Could he feel particularly glad that his brother was alive? Agustin's sardonic tone had set his innermost thoughts racing. He could see even farther into his mind and heart than his companion.

'Don't be too quick to judge him . . . Your brother will emerge as a coward or as a man with his head screwed on, depending on how the war turns out. The Republicans will be generous if they win: it's one of their principles. Domingo has backed both sides and been successful, but his main success lies in the fact that he is alive.'

Juanito broke in imploringly: 'Agustin, I thought the moment had come . . .'

Agustin's face hardened. Domingo's defection was not going to induce him to provide the Minotaur with another victim.

'Yes, Juanito, the moment has come for every Spaniard to do his duty. I've explained more than once that in '89 the Revolution triumphed thanks to the officers of the *ancien régime* and to a few twenty-year-old generals. As yet, you are neither.'

He had regained control over himself and over others; he was setting forth his well-furbished arguments and unchallengeable precedents. Juanito had no choice but to obey this clipped, angry voice.

'Today,' continued Agustin, 'peace and war are being determined by every soldier. But the outcome is as much in the hands of you instructors as of the general staff. The Republic certainly isn't going to triumph through the efforts of fanatical peasants and righteous lawyers. They behave as though they were living in the time of the guerrillas who fought against Bonaparte. And every morning Negrín banks more and more heavily on the outbreak of a world war. He imagines that the Apocalypse will save us, and that the Four Horsemen will halt the Tercio . . .'

The ringing of the telephone cut short his derisive laugh. As he lifted the receiver, he motioned Juanito to stay. His hands were clenched tightly on the instrument. At regular intervals he would nod and say: 'Yes.' The call must have been coming from a long way off. Agustin was repeating what the man at the other end was saying, clearly enunciating each word. The information that had come in during the night was being confirmed by an absolutely reliable source. Agustin's informant was emphatic: emergency positions must be taken up at once . . . Agustin slowly replaced the receiver and walked over to where Juanito was standing.

'This time the moment, as you put it, has really come . . .' He spoke with difficulty, between his teeth. 'The moment has come too soon, lad.' He paused for a few seconds, then resumed: 'Franco's detachments reached the sea last evening. Barcelona is cut off, both from Valencia and from Madrid. There isn't a Republican zone any longer—simply a number of towns and cities that will hold out for a longer or shorter period . . . The units that have ventured too far must at once fall back to close the breach . . .'

Juanito was silent. This splitting of the front was still going on inside him. He was those beleaguered cities, those straggling units which, under the impression that they were joining up with the main body of the Republican Army, were about to fall into the yawning trap that was opening between Barcelona and Valencia. Closing breaches, dealing with infiltrations: he had heard these euphemisms before. Into his mind came the N.C.O. in the playground of that school in Valencia.

Agustin spread out an ordnance survey map. The railways and the roads and the contour lines of the hills made it hard to follow at first glance, but the names of remote villages were familiar to Juanito. Agustin swept his hand across the whole area from Belchite and Alcañiz to the mouth of the Ebro. 'They're everywhere,' he said. Like a doctor, he seemed to be assessing the spread of the disease in a tissue, the consuming action of a group of cells called tuberculosis or cancer. It was a ruined lung, a leg that had to be cut off because of gangrene. Juanito dismissed the memory of Ramon from his mind and pored over the brand-new map, from which the names shone out, in ink that had barely had time to dry, amid the greens and blues. The Ebro wound through the placid hills, all the way down to the Golfo de San Yorge. In just the same manner were the Nationalists flowing through the peaceful villages, many of them surmounted by a ruined castle, and the renowned vineyards. Already Agustin was asking the switchboard for a number. He was checking that all available transport was being used to stabilize the front as swiftly as possible.

'Stabilize the front . . .' Juanito repeated the words to himself. Men had already been sacrificed, swept away by this current like miners by a flood. These troops had been taken prisoner before they had set eyes on the enemy.

'It's monotonous, being right all the time,' said Agustin. He had been predicting this thrust to the sea ever since Franco had recaptured Teruel. Yet he was deriving a new lease of energy from this disaster.

Juanito made as if to go, but again he held him back.

'You've stopped thinking about your brother . . . You see:

one man's waverings are of little account in comparison with a break-through like this!'

He pointed to the full bottle of brandy on his desk.

'Open it, boy! When you are shooting dice, you mustn't give in because of a single bad throw . . . Let's drink to the counter-offensive!'

17

A SUDDEN SPELL OF SPRING WEATHER was bringing a new softness to Barcelona. The flower-sellers' stalls turned the Ramblas into lanes of pinks and roses. The aphrodisiac scent of narcissi and jasmine masked all the less pleasant smells, and in the warm evenings it stagnated like an invitation to happiness. Despite all that threatened them, people were allowing themselves to be carried away. All their faces shone with the same impatience to have a last fling. Some strolled about the town from sunset till dawn. Darkness was preceded by a long pale twilight, during which the sky above the harbour turned the faintest shade of pink. This twilight existed for the sole purpose of enabling one-night lovers to meet, of allowing their eyes to accord and their fevered hands to grope for one another. To every couple, each night presented itself as the last. Daytime hopes and anxieties faded at the approach of darkness. Till tomorrow, despite the air-raid warnings, despite the plumes of fire that suddenly showed above the roadstead, they inhabited another time. In this world, kisses and caresses alone retained any meaning. Juanito, too, was surrendering to the promise disseminated upon so many lips. The city was coming apart in his arms, like a disintegrating sheaf of flowers whose scent was, in itself, an embrace . . .

A single night could contain the last happiness of a man under sentence of death, a single night held all eternity. The lovers did not seek to extend their one-evening encounters. Before ending up in a battle that was lost even before it started, Juanito was discovering an ally in his own body. He was deriving an ever-fresh joy from this contest in which his youthfulness triumphed.

Other soldiers, in the dives of the Barrio Chino, were replacing the tourists of earlier years; gambling and drink were a means of escape, reinforced by the throaty voice of a male singer or by the antics of a dancing girl miming the love-grapple and the ecstatic swoon. Juanito was demanding from these proffered bodies the lightning upheaval of gratification. How could he possibly turn down a single promise of happiness? In this war, everything about which struck him as corrupt—since nations and parties alike were cheating—the only thing that did not deceive was the frenzy that took hold of a human frame in which he was allowed to find enjoyment. Amazed, Juanito recalled the imprecations that Padre Enrique had poured out against the pleasures of the flesh. These women who hugged him to them were, in their way, bringing him absolution. They asked nothing of him but kisses in the dark, imprecise words, caresses. War was freeing souls from fear, bodies from hypocrisy. Every woman that Juanito held clasped in his arms imagined that in grappling with him she was grappling with death.

One evening in April, he thought he recognized a girl making her way uncertainly down the Rambla de los Estudiantes. It was Soledad. He called after her, feeling a lump come into his throat. She turned round: for a moment they just stood there, speechless, paralysed with joy. Then the silence that was choking them shattered into a thousand and one questions. They had been playing hide-and-seek behind the obstacles of war. Soledad laughed awkwardly, and her laugh brought them together again.

Shoulder to shoulder, they walked as far as the Paseo de Gracia. The crowd was bearing them along. They were shyly questioning each other: in charming confusion they were groping their way between reproaches and regrets. Groups of people would come between them or edge them into the roadway. They would call out breathlessly, as though they were about to lose one another again. To practically every word, to reassure herself that he was really there, she added: 'Juanito!' and he, feeling his head in a whirl, said to himself: I wasn't through with loving her: one's never through with loving.

They passed a women's demonstration. The women were demanding that every available man be sent to the front. They were proudly chanting their slogan, but the soldiers—both those who were back from the trenches and those who were soon to undergo the baptism of fire—responded with crude gibes. And the crowd were ridiculing these citizenesses.

Juanito and Soledad gave the scene the most fleeting of smiles; the amazons were vainly attempting to regroup in the midst of all the cat-calls. The two young people made their way across the Plaza de Cataluña. Shots rang out under the trees in the centre of the square. A woman's screams caused panic on the pavements. Juanito and Soledad went on walking at the same pace. This burst of gunfire made no more impression on them than the squibs which the children used to let off under people's feet.

The great avenues opened out like bowers to hide the lovers beneath their green canopy. The throng was less dense. They let their feet guide them. In front of them rose an aquatic bush sprouting seaweed and bristling with shells. The two highest boughs were burgeoning in the moonlight, as though they in turn were about to put forth branches. It was the unfinished church of the Sagrada Familia. Soledad stared in amazement at this rock built by a man and eroded by the sky's currents. She had once gone into this grotto. Needles of crystal tinkled on the ceilings. The thin walls vibrated in the wind, giving rise to a kind of dizziness.

'It isn't a church,' said Soledad, 'but something wonderful and useless.'

Juanito, for his part, compared it to a reef covered with moss and aquatic plants. Adhering to it were sponges, flowers, jellyfish. Coral branches were its vegetation. The porches were merely a bristling of stalactites. The sky showed through the hollowed-out façades. There was nothing so rich and fragile in Valencia. They started talking about the old cathedral, where men dispensed justice beneath the eyes of the saints. It had been turned into a magazine; the Virgin's basilica was empty.

'You haven't changed, Juanito!' Soledad kept saying, though there was no telling whether this was meant in praise or condemnation. The abetting darkness enveloped them. A clock struck midnight, as though to restore them to the measurable realms of time. But, sensing that it was being importunate, it muffled its strokes. Gateways were deep in shadow, their darkness welcoming the couples marauding after pleasure. The wind was shaking the trees so gently that the branches, as they caressed one another, exchanged avowals and haltingly whispered secrets. Between Juanito and Soledad, words turned to kisses. At intervals, Soledad spoke openly of her affair with Pablo. The whole thing had ended as swiftly as it had begun. The child had come before its time. Pablo, after dazzling Madrid with his sartorial splendour, had been called to the front. He had not married Soledad, for the child had not lived and Pablo did not love Soledad . . . Soledad did not condemn him for his frankness, nor for walking out on her. She had become too indifferent to him. The memory of another love, linked with her childhood and with the labours and seasons of the *huerta*, made her cry as she lived all alone in Madrid. She was destitute. How could she describe the poverty, the hardship of her existence there? A friend of Pablo's, a workman in a Barcelona factory, had found her a job. Arriving a few weeks after Juanito in this city, where everything proclaimed the burden of war, Soledad had got used to the clothing factory where she cut and sewed service tunics, and to the rather shabby room that she rented from an old woman. She had put off till later her chances of being happy. Spring had come. Despite her tiredness, Soledad had been unable to resist the urge to go for a walk . . . Juanito's voice calling to her in the Rambla had almost frightened her . . . She broke off . . . The night was not a night like other nights, but another world, beyond time and space, in which lovers ended up meeting as they did in dreams. Soledad's glances enveloped Juanito with a desperate admiration, an almost imploring tenderness. To end the night in his arms was the only way of effacing memories, regrets and feelings of remorse.

. . . By becoming his mistress, Soledad had the impression of becoming his fiancée again.

As they caressed one another, they started talking about the village, and Federico's death in Almeria, and Domingo of whose fate Juanito pretended to be in ignorance. What could Valencia possibly be like without fiestas, or the *huerta* without dances?

Juanito returned to the barracks at first light. In the passageway, Agustin's door was ajar. He always slept with one eye open, being more afraid of an uprising behind the lines than of the news from the front. The defection of a single unit or a surprise attack on a barracks was enough, he would say, to alter the course of a revolution or a war. He called Juanito in. He had already rolled up his horsehair mattress. The days began very early for him and never finished. He was in a good mood:

'You see what early risers we priests are, Juanito! The only thing that keeps the church going is men like us who drag ourselves out of bed at dawn to say Mass. Without this act of discipline and courage, the Spanish Church would have collapsed long ago beneath the weight of its vices and cupidity. But come in, come in . . . I can't say you look like a choirboy . . . Your uniform reeks like a barber's shop . . . Your friend must be a manicurist . . . Don't be offended at my indiscretion . . ' In the blue lamplight, Agustin's face was gay and relaxed: perhaps he enjoyed being at his lookout post so early, while the rest of the barracks was still sluggishly rousing itself. A door was banging at the far end of a corridor. From the kitchens rose the smoke of a log fire. But Agustin was merely savouring, like an act of revenge, the joy of snatching Juanito away from the easy-going spring, from this complaisant city, from his flirtations, from the whole sentimental and rather nauseating state of happiness that was ensnaring the Valencian.

'Sit down.'

Augustin shut the door carefully. He switched off the lamp, which was no longer needed, and flung open the dirty casement window. The grey light invaded the room. It was going to be a fine day. Agustin lowered his voice with a certain affectation.

'I wasn't waiting just to welcome you back like the Prodigal

Son. No, I have something better in store for you today: we're going home, Juanito—back to *your* home . . .'

Juanito sat up with a start. Soledad was restored to him, but Valencia was claiming him again. Never would both be his. City and woman were at once connected and in conflict. No sooner was one of them within reach than the other sought to lay hold of him.

'We'll go to Valencia first,' continued Agustin. 'The Army of the Levante must be ready to march the moment Barcelona launches the offensive . . . Today, the front is everywhere: the threat to the Republic is as great in Barcelona as in Valencia or Madrid. Perhaps your city will be the gateway to victory! While we are smashing Franco's positions along the Ebro, Valencia will rise as one man. They will be caught in a pincer movement, do you see?'

'Yes,' said Juanito, 'they will be trapped.'

All that he wanted was to share this ecstasy. Agustin collected himself.

'We shall only stay in Valencia for a few days . . . While I'm dealing with things, you will be able to go off and see your farm and your fiancée . . .' He made this return to Valencia sound like an outing. With Juanito he would escape from these barracks, to which the ghost of Luis still clung. He squeezed the boy's arm. 'What do you say, man? I've been better than my word.'

Juanito was silent. To see Valencia again, and the *huerta* in the June sunlight, was to return to the Garden of Eden before the Fall; but it meant losing Soledad a second time. Desire and regret tugged at him with equal force, throwing him into a whirl. Agustin was revelling in his strength and astuteness. He was sure of his argument: if the rebels resumed their offensive, the Republic would regroup its forces at a point farther south. Were Barcelona to be permanently cut off from Valencia and Madrid, there was a danger of its becoming a death-trap for the Republican government.

'Too many fanatics have been blown to bits setting fire to Franco's tanks . . . We've always had too many desperadoes. It is in Valencia that the Republic will win the final hand, but we shall play our last trumps with a cool head. There will be no more anarchists, no more fights between Trotskyists and Stalinists, no more waiting for miracles from abroad . . . Spain is going to work her own miracle . . . Men like you and me are going to bring it about!'

Scorn and doubt had gone from Agustin's voice. His eloquence was irresistible because he was the first to be won over by it. The Republic was going to save itself. But Agustin was going to save Juanito, whether the boy liked it or not. It was because Luis had left Agustin that Luis was dead. Agustin was constantly talking in the name of reason and condemning Juanito's vestiges of primitive mentality. But he shared the ill-grounded faith of all human beings in love. Juanito was invulnerable. Neither chance nor fate, neither man nor God, would dare to lay a finger on Agustin's guiltless happiness. Other soldiers might die. Juanito alone was immortal. Agustin had decreed it. If the offensive failed, they would find another country, another name, another occupation. They would go on walking straight ahead, hand in hand. To other men, this was friendship. To Agustin, it would be love. He let go of Juanito's arm and smiled.

'Are you happy? We two are going to save Spain.'

Agustin had it all mapped out. His supervisory duties with the units at the front enabled him to transfer from division to division as often as he liked . . . He would be able to fool Juanito to the very end; he would leave him with the illusion that he was free to fight and get himself killed. He was talking quietly, yet his words rang with the arrogance that reminded Juanito of his speeches after the first Republican victory at Teruel.

'The heroes are building bridges and roads. The armies go by overhead. At night they hear the rumble of tanks shaking the girders. We shall be like that, Juanito—working in the dark while the others advance.'

'When do we start?' asked Juanito.

'In a few days' time! Keep it to yourself till then.'

They said good-bye in the corridor. Juanito was still tense and earnest, but Agustin was so happy that he could not help joking: 'You put me in mind of Tobias—you know: the boy in the Bible who sets off to recover a debt on the other side of the world . . . He finds a companion who shares every danger with him: the stranger is an angel disguised as a man and looks like Tobias's big brother. He teaches him how to catch sea-monsters, and how to extract medicine from the livers of fish, and how to exorcise a woman possessed by the devil. He brings him safely home . . . then he vanishes. I should love to perform that service for you. You've a good hour's sleep ahead of you yet. Good night, Juanito.'

As he undressed, Juanito caught the musky odour that Agustin had noticed. When the time had come for them to take their leave of each other, Soledad had hugged him to her with the same maternal and impure frenzy as Mercedes. They assumed, in the act of love, the same expression of drowning women sinking to the bottom of the sea with their rescuer.

All round him, the men were breathing in time with one another; it was as though only one person lay asleep in the barrack hut. In Juanito's brain, scenes from the past were jumbled up with glimpses of the future. He was already in Valencia, since Soledad was in his arms; but it was Mercedes who had acquired Soledad's face. She was admitting her imposture and Juanito was leaving her. He was walking beneath the arches of a bridge with Agustin. The Turia was all but dry, but Agustin was explaining that the outcome of the war depended on the bridge . . . Juanito had a hankering to bathe in the fine thread of water trickling over the pebbles. He wanted to cleanse himself of Mercedes's over-scented caresses, of her clammy hands. When Juanito stooped over the narrow stream, his own reflection was replaced by Agustin's. His face wore the same loving and anguished look as on the day when Juanito had fainted. It was as though he were aching to disclose his secret at long last, but the distant sounds of an army on the march came to Juanito's rescue.

18

THE ADVANCE on Castellon de la Plana came as a further thunderbolt. More exposed than Barcelona or Madrid, Valencia was becoming the main objective of the Nationalist units that had established their positions within a few miles of the coast. Contrary to Agustin's anticipations, the rebels were bent on determining the issue in the south and, by attacking the Republic's final stronghold, were draining the loyalists' last resources. How was Valencia to bear the brunt of the war unaided? How could Barcelona and Madrid—the former encircled, the latter bled dry—help the Levante, which till now had kept them going?

In Barcelona, this imminent disaster provided ammunition for the demonstrations against the 'pro-armistice' group. Juanito gave no thought to anything but to defending his soil, his city. He was the descendant of the craftsmen and burgesses of Valencia, whose insurrection had shaken the power of the throne more dramatically than had the revolt of the Castilian dignitaries. Agustin was fond of recalling the reckless stand of these associations of silversmiths and carpenters, of weavers and bricklayers. He would bring Juanito's ancestors back to life for the boy: 'Like you, they were sombre and bellicose beneath their calm and smiling exteriors: true Valencians.'

The monarchist historians dismissed their insurrection as a 'peasants' uprising', but in these bloody convulsions the people of Valencia had woken up to their strength and dignity before any of the other cities.

'Now that Valencia is threatened, you are the most ardent patriot in Spain.'

Juanito shrugged and said: 'If a single shot is fired at the gates of Valencia, I shall desert—and that's all there is to it.'

Agustin gave in at once.

'You won't need to do anything silly, since we'll soon be on our way . . . I too feel a longing for barricades and for guerrilla fighting . . .' He pushed away the half-empty brandy bottle that lingered among the ink-pads on his desk. 'Oh! I nearly forgot . . . Your brother is in charge of road transport in the Oviedo area . . . There is no danger of your running into each other . . .'

After three long years of war, Negrin was still obstinately banking on an outbreak of international hostilities as a solution to every problem. Barcelona, with only turnips and lentils to sustain it, was accusing the army of monopolizing food supplies. Rich and poor protested with equal heat, for nobody escaped the consequences of the shortage. The government was saving up its supplies of grain and tinned foods, of sugar and oil, with the intention of making them last till the democracies entered the fray. It was serenely awaiting this final reckoning between the the nations. Seeing things in this light, and sensing that world history was about to combine with the history of Spain, how could it possibly pay much attention to the discontent prompted by inadequate distributions of rice? Barcelona had suffered from not experiencing the baptism of fire, as Madrid had, from not uttering the '*No pasaran*' that still hovered on the lips of the capital's inhabitants, like the name of a victory.

Every evening, Juanito would meet Soledad in the secluded walks of the Montjuich Park, up by the fortress. They would wander through the thickets, the glades, the sunken paths that imitated nature as the stucco façades of the Pueblo Espagnol reproduced the squares of Castile or the narrow streets of the Levante. The park was no longer tended; clusters of mastics and tufts of broom grew all over the place.

Lying beneath a pine, Juanito and Soledad would forget the city which, in the fading light, spied on them with its millions of eyes. The dusk would thicken beneath the branches. They were more alone in this derelict garden than in the middle of the *huerta*. Juanito would try to catch the babbling of the warm water in the canals. Soledad sensed that Juanito was slipping through her fingers. She would say: 'You are going to leave me, too.' War consisted of farewells and betrayals. Peace would settle nothing.

Soledad's impatient kisses and caresses and bites betrayed an experience acquired in other encounters. Soledad kept quiet about the lovers who had succeeded Pablo, but her laughter in the act of love bore witness to them. At the factory, the foreman would criticize her work, but at the end of the day he would insist, in a fatherly fashion, on seeing her home. Soledad was afraid that he might follow her. Every evening she would slip into the park, losing her breath by taking so many short cuts, and wending her way through thickets and up and down steps as though she were taking part in some intricate children's game. She would meet Juanito near the Spanish village and fling herself upon him, snuggling against him so that he could cradle her. To enmesh him, she would talk on and on about their Sundays back at the village and about the fiestas in Valencia. And, trembling at the thought that she might disappoint him by chattering so much, she would rouse him. He would take her and despise her a little for giving herself like a prostitute on this hard earth bed strewn with pine-needles. Yet after the first embraces they experienced the peacefulness of carefree moments that resembled the night of their first meeting. They made their way slowly down towards the town. Before taking their leave of each other, they lingered in an empty café, where they staved off hunger with the insipid, rubbery flesh of octopus.

'We are not so badly off,' Soledad sighed. She was thinking of the walk back to Badalona, of the next day's work at the factory, of the improbable time when there would be no war.

She said, offhandedly, so that she should not appear to be laying claims on the future: 'When all this is over, Juanito, you will go back to Valencia, and there will be no reason for me to stay on here.'

Juanito did not answer. He longed to be rid of this girl who looked so tousled from their hasty caresses.

Soledad continued with something approaching despair: 'You are so handsome, Juanito, you are so handsome.' Her words were merely an unavailing prayer which reminded Juanito of Mercedes's greedy hands straying over his body and Señora Martinez's moist glances . . .

When Juanito got back to the barracks in the middle of the night, Agustin was still up. He hailed him as he went by. Tired of calculating the repercussions of each new defeat, he was glad to speak openly: 'The front is like an old darned jacket. Repair it at one point and the material gives at another.'

The lines in the face that he turned towards this beholder had been scooped out by satiety and disgust. As he himself said: 'My face has at least ten years' start on me.'

He examined Juanito in the manner of a painter studying his model, or of a traveller gazing at an unusual species of man in an unknown region.

'You know, Spain isn't just the old grannies bawling their wares in the Ramblas, or the shopkeepers torn from behind their counters, or the bourgeois who have hidden away their best silver plate to serve dinner on it to Franco's staff. If the Republic goes down, Spain will live on in men like you, who know how to till and reap, men who eat slowly in the farmhouses of the *huerta*, sitting round the table . . . The meals they eat, day in, day out, are more like the Last Supper than the farce enacted in the churches on Sundays. Men who speak with your assurance—the assurance of shy people who are in the right—and who laugh unreservedly, as the serious know how to laugh. Thanks to men like you, there will always be, if not freedom, at least friendship between Spaniards.'

He would return to the present to run a critical and contented eye over Juanito, as though he were his son.

'You are sturdy . . . Your arms are bursting out of your sleeves . . . You have a full, strong, manly face, but a dimple like a little boy's. And you have the chin of a true Valencian. Your eyes are full of life . . . When you spoke to me in the canteen, they were the colour of a pool under the trees. You were still out of your element then . . . Now somebody has taken the place of the *huerta* for you . . .'

Juanito would remain on his guard. His meetings with

Soledad, and the turning of their engagement into an affair, were too sordid to be discussed. A man such as Agustin had no need of pleasure or emotion or romance. He had books and ideas. Juanito would change the subject.

'I'd like to go back to Valencia.'

'Valencia shall be yours, and today Valencia is the front line! The workers of Madrid defended freedom within a hundred yards of their houses. They used their furniture to strengthen the barricades. They fired from their windows, from behind their mattresses . . . Look at this!'

The headline of the evening paper, rather smudged by the wet newsprint, ran: 'Valencia will be another Madrid.' The Nationalists were nearing Castellon de la Plana, only a few miles down the coast from Valencia.

Juanito took the newspaper from him. The article added nothing to this statement.

'There,' said Agustin, 'now are you happy? This time you are going to fight . . . A fraction of an inch, this way or that, in the trajectory of a bullet and . . .'

'When do we leave?'

Agustin shrugged at this display of childishness.

'We're not going to walk slap into a rebel outpost. The front is all over the place at the moment.'

His voice was hoarse. He reached for the brandy bottle. It was empty. He made another attempt at clowning.

'You see: it's time we pulled out . . . We can't hold out here any longer, the cellars are empty. Negrin is saving up the *anis* and the brandy too, so that Franco can celebrate his arrival in Barcelona. There will be enough for every Moor and every Knight of Christ to get drunk on . . .'

19

A WARM WIND scattered the scents of June through the city, crushing them like flowers in a clammy hand. On the hills overlooking Barcelona, Juanito drank in the sweet smell of grapes hung to dry on screens. He was spacing out his meetings with Soledad. What was the point of prolonging this simulacrum of love, this imperfect substitution of one woman for another? The *huerta* was all that he longed for. Soledad talked about the village in an attempt to carry him back, through the evocation of this familiar scene, to the first gropings of their hearts.

Juanito preferred to dream aloud to Agustin: 'In February, the orange trees blossom at home . . . Nobody knows why one row of trees, or a particular orchard, makes up its mind before the rest. When the peasants come in from the fields at night, they forget everything. They fling themselves down on a bank, they put aside their tools and their baskets, as though they needed to be empty-handed to enjoy the smell to the full. They stay on the roadside, not saying a word. Night falls. Their wives are waiting for them. They don't feel hunger or thirst any more . . . The scent coats their chests like snow or castor sugar . . . You wouldn't believe, Agustin, how happy you feel because the orange trees in a field have suddenly come out in blossom.'

Agustin was silent. He would have liked to sprawl against the hedge, drugged by this scent, beside strapping youngsters, and to share their aimless ecstasy . . .

'Tell me more, Juanito.'

'What do you want me to tell you? In the *huerta*, the year isn't long enough for sowing and reaping; when the cold weather comes, there is duck-shooting on the frozen lake . . .' A pale blue sky stretched over the plain like a second lake. Juanito saw a woman huddled up in her furs, smelt the scent on her hand, took the packet of cigarettes . . .

'What about the floods?' asked Agustin, to foster this confiding mood in which a man of few words was finally intoxicated by his own flow of speech. 'Are they an invention of the newspapers to get the poor Aragonese and the poor Castilians to shed tears over the rich peasants of the *huerta*?'

'No,' Juanito laughingly protested, 'there are real floods, they're as terrifying as they are unexpected. People have to live in their lofts. They go from farmhouse to farmhouse by boat. Furniture floats about, boxes drift all over the place. The water continues to rise . . . Each village collects its patron saint, takes him out for a row and treats him to a procession, complete with prayers and music. But if the level continues to rise, everyone —parish priest included—begins to blaspheme and to threaten the saint . . . Suddenly it's over. All that is left is the sodden earth strewn with branches, and the banks are carpeted with reeds, and in the middle of a field, where the water has left them, are tables with missing legs, and the backs of chairs, and cupboard doors. The mess is soon cleared up; out of superstition, nobody mentions the flood again . . . The women whitewash the houses so as not to see any longer where the water rose to, and the village saint gets a little present after all . . .'

Agustin pulled a face. With these superstitious peasants, shortage and abundance, disasters and rich vine-harvests, all redounded to the greater glory of the saints and the profit of the parish priests. God, like a broker dabbling in every human undertaking, always took his cut.

'Do you pray, Juanito?'

The suspicious voice brought a blush to Juanito's cheeks.

'Why not? I've every right to pray.'

There was a silence. With these Valencians, Agustin said to himself, credulity came under the heading of human rights. How was this hurdle to be got over? To Juanito, freedom of thought was freedom to prostrate himself before idols, to cover them with jewels and sumptuous cloths. Agustin tried a slightly different tack: 'I know that you are a tool in the hands of the monks, but who do you pray to—St James or St Teresa? How do you know which is which? They change their names and faces just like actors. The Virgin in Barcelona is paler than wax, and she is Our Lady of Mercy. In Saragossa, she is the colour of gingerbread, a real darky for Franco's Moroccans, and she is Our Lady of the Pillar.'

Juanito smiled disdainfully.

'In Valencia, the Virgin has had only one name and one face for hundreds of years: we call her Our Lady of the Forsaken . . .'

There was a tremor of respectful familiarity in Juanito's voice.

'Anyone would think you were talking about a woman,' observed Agustin. 'My word, yes—it's as though she were a very beautiful cousin, a bit older than you, who will never treat you as anything but a kid, and as though she were also your mother and your sister and your fiancée.'

But Juanito did not weaken in the face of this mockery.

'You don't know how right you are . . . To every Valencian she is all you say. Day and night, rich and poor flock in to see her; they cast themselves down before her. The congregation changes all the time, but everyone, immersed in his tête-à-tête with the Madonna, imagins that he is there one his own. . . You cannot imagine it: the mother whose child is at death's door turns to her as she would to a neighbour, and the woman who has lost her lover talks to her as she would to a friend . . . The man who has been betrayed, the thief about to be arrested, the great industrialist facing ruin, all who are afraid, or hungry, or in need of love, lay their burden at her feet and rise more slowly than they knelt, as though their prayers had already been answered.'

Agustin tried to fight back.

'Superstition is a prop for the weak,' he said. 'It appeals to petit-bourgeois æsthetes; but any hang-over from the past enslaves the people and hampers their march towards the future . . .'

Juanito was not listening. He was in the circular chapel of the Virgin of the Forsaken. The Madonna, in her cloak of gold, embroidered with flowers that had rigid stems and blazing calyces, was stooping towards him. For each of her sons was entitled to her attention, each demanded her help, and nobody would have dreamed of questioning the compassion that shone out from her sad face. Her silence was more consoling than any amount of words, and her discerning gaze healed wounds even as she perceived them.

Controlling his irritation, Agustin racked his brain for arguments, as though to get Juanito out of the clutches of an old mistress: 'Your idol owes her power to the worship of woman, not to faith! The world's most sensual peoples wallow in this incestuous feeling for the Madonna!'

Juanito shrugged; for centuries this frail creature had been sharing human happiness and distress, just as she had shared the life of Christ. She had believed, as all mothers do, in the signs that attend a birth. She had forced the first miracle out of Christ, as she had wrung from him his last words on Calvary. She was God's pledge to man, just as she was man's guarantee to God.

And to Juanito this timeless creature was as young as himself. She had all the experience of the human race, but she embodied in a single face all the powers that bring reassurance and enlightenment to sinners. She was strength and pity, wisdom and beauty. Through her was accomplished the mysterious promise of immortality made to the city of Valencia at the very dawn of time. Those who went down on their knees before the Virgin of the Forsaken were venerating its presiding spirit. And in that oratory, Valencia was stooping, in the guise of Mary, towards the poor and infirm, as though these were her most favoured children.

Agustin said with a groan: 'It would take twenty centuries and twenty civil wars to rid you of your illusion!'

He hated this silent and motionless rival who emerged unscathed from his attacks. Juanito invested this doll, tricked out in brocade and covered with imitation jewellery, with the mystery that surrounds all women. In her he confided what he would never entrust to a friend. And his fervour surrounded this idol's altar no less than did the copper hearts and the glow of the candles . . .

'Valencia has nothing to fear,' Agustin continued. 'You will simply parade the statue the way you do for the floods . . . Our marching orders are ready . . .'

In the bluish light, Agustin produced two sheets of crackly yellow paper. Juanito made out their names and a few words in which the terse military style was slightly softened by the less clipped phrases of the intelligence service: '. . . will report to Valencia garrison . . . to establish communications . . . after carrying out this mission will return to the theatre of operations, to take up the posts previously assigned to them . . .' The details of execution were left to the initiative of the parties concerned, to chance or to fate: no time-limit was stipulated.

'When do we leave?' asked Juanito.

Agustin turned away. Why did the Valencian reproduce, at times, the exact tone of Luis's voice, the demanding look in his eyes? Juanito was issuing the same summons, like those imperious interrogations that roar out in the middle of a symphony. The harmonies drown them in a concerted tumult: another instrument repeats the same unanswerable question on a higher note . . . Moths were fluttering round the bright electric bulb. In the distance, Barcelona was now just an outpost benumbed with fatigue. Everything was taking on a heartrending, valedictory gentleness.

'Tomorrow!' said Agustin, lowering his voice. He imagined that he was still dictating Juanito's future. He was merely obeying. He was handing him back to his city. In the end, he would hand him back to the war.

'How?' inquired Juanito. The face that he turned towards Agustin wore the same trustful expression.

'By sea,' said Agustin. 'We are cut off from Valencia, and I am not keen to fall into Franco's hands!'

Juanito was thinking about the voyage. He was Oedipus provoking the sphinx, a youth anxious to run off to his war, impatient to kill or be killed. Once again Luis's face asserted itself, obliterating Juanito's very expression. Had Luis preserved, even at Belchite, that grave beauty, that resolute air of a knight on the eve of battle? Had pain fashioned a different face for him when his head burrowed into the earth on that bank? But from his death Agustin would remain forever excluded.

'Well, Juanito? Are you shedding tears for the barracks and the parade ground, for the Ramblas and the Barrio Chino?'

Agustin spoke mockingly, but he knew that Juanito would leave Barcelona with the indifference of the very young to whom towns are merely a transitory setting and human beings mere substitutes for the actors who will one day figure in their lives. In their eyes, the moments of farce are part of the rehearsal . . . The prompter's voice drowns the text . . . These spectators are waiting detachedly for the curtain to go up on the tragedy of their lives. But in the real drama of a person's existence, extras too have their parts to play, and the destiny of every one of us is made up of accidents. One day, Juanito would discover that our passions, our heartbreaks and our moments of ecstasy are coincidences allied to faces that are gone before they have lived up to or fallen short of their promise. One day, he would rediscover in his memory, like an unintelligible and incontrovertible oracle, this night, and the moths with the outsize shadows dancing in the ash-like beams of the lamp, and Agustin's pale hands resting on a litter of paper, and the phosphorescent glow of a slumbering city.

Agustin wore a pained look.

'One town gives way to another,' he said. 'Everything changes, except ourselves . . . One day we shall look back on Barcelona with regret.'

He was thinking of what the Gospel said: 'From him that hath not shall be taken away even that which he hath.'

'Don't be sad, Agustin,' said Juanito, 'we're leaving together.'

At this, Agustin turned away from the sight of the boy's face, too beautiful in the lamplight. In a strangled voice he said: 'Lad, you don't always have to give to the poor and the infirm . . .'

But his heart raced with a gratitude deeper and more mysterious than love.

Next day Agustin roamed through the barracks, going into one room after another. The soldiers stared after him. What was he after? Juanito was checking Agustin's kit as well as his own.

'Are you sure you've got all your shirts?' he asked, but already Agustin was gone again. He was wandering through deserted messes, empty halls. In the canteen he slowly rubbed his hand along a wooden table-top, as though to absorb an impression. At the end of a corridor, stooping in front of the dirty window, he found once more a radiant face . . . Luis loved looking at himself in mirrors. Agustin had caught him examining his reflection in this pane, on which dust and spiders' webs formed a kind of foil. In this glass, Luis already had the look of a dead man.

Agustin's hand closed frenziedly on the window-fastening. Was it really over this pool that Luis, with the narcissism of the very young man, had fawned upon his own image? Agustin's gibes had brought the blood to his cheeks. His early morning face went carnation-red . . . Even though he was furious, he could not help laughing at his own vanity, and disguised his temper by saying in a provocative tone: 'Why? Aren't I entitled to look at myself in a mirror? Do I need written permission?'

Was there no other reality than that face beyond space and time, than those words which were as pointless as the taunts exchanged by a pair of young soldiers?

The window opened on to a backyard, full of refuse and wild grass. Agustin automatically rubbed the dirty pane, as though it were obscuring some mysterious landscape. Through this veil of dust he could not see the waste-ground into which a cook-boy was tipping a saucepanful of water.

With something very like violence, he was trying to come to terms, once and for all, with the questions that were stifling him, with the dead boy, with himself. Did this moment contain the whole justification for his existence? That smiling, sulky face had quivered in this makeshift mirror. Was this fleeting chance —the fragile image of an ephemeral being—the most secret and durable phase in his life? Agustin's love, like a stray beam from a long sunset, still brought a blaze to his sombre, outsider's heart . . .

'What is the real me?' Agustin kept saying to himself. In the old days, when he had been reading a classical tragedy, a single phrase had been enough to electrify him. Had he simply been hamming or indulging in hysterics? Amid the clash of swords and armour, a line of dialogue had compelled him to break off his reading and stride up and down his room to expend the superhuman energy, the resolution, the daring, the pride that had accumulated in him. As though unmasking his face to his partisans, as though revealing his soul to a mob, Agustin had shouted, on the verge of tears: 'Me! Me!' He had discovered, beyond the confines of frontiers, the sublime brotherhood that reigns between great men and reconciles the victors and vanquished of yesterday's fighting.

On the murky window, Agustin thought he could make out impressions of rain; he scanned these huge tears absorbed by the dust. And Coriolanus's proud declaration still reverberated in his mind: 'I'll stand as if a man were author of himself and knew no other kin.'

Yet these demi-gods were still vulnerable: Cæsar was submissive to his wife's dreams and Coriolanus yielded to his mother's tears . . . Agustin, who had imagined that he was endowed with the spirit of a conqueror and the heart of a hero, was scanning the glass, so hazy with memories, for the reflection of a perished human form, for the ghost of a ghost.

20

JUANITO SLEPT ON HIS BED FULLY CLOTHED, like a refugee on a railway platform, twitching at the slightest sound. But their departure had been put back twenty-four hours. A German warship was on the prowl off the coast of Barcelona.

Juanito had made his farewells, and his kitbag and blanket

were stacked in readiness under Agustin's desk. In the afternoon he walked down the Parellelo to the Montjuich Park. He was longing to break with this town. The final kisses that he exchanged with Soledad would free him from a past that was too recent to affect him. In Barcelona he had found neither war nor love, but their counterfeits.

The June afternoon was stifling. Juanito sought the shade of the deepest thickets. As he went along, he dipped his hands in the fountain basins dotted about the paths. In a pine grove some children lay asleep, snuggling close to an old woman. Juanito could not help thinking of bodies thrown about by an explosion. Soledad would not arrive before sunset. Juanito longed to have done with the words, the inevitable gestures, the promises in which the lingering fire of an affair burns itself out. In the distance, the city was dozing under the implacable afternoon sky. The pine branches filtered the light somewhat. Juanito fell asleep. The lorry that had carried him off from the *huerta* was taking him back by a strange, roundabout route. Juanito could hardly recognize the devastated villages. He was amazed that the fighting zones of which there had been so much talk—Teruel, Brunete, Belchite—were within a few miles of the Albufera lake. Bombers were roaring over the rice fields and orange plantations. Juanito just had time to throw himself down behind a flimsy dike; the water was flowing peacefully past, almost touching his face. An exploding bomb was covering him with earth. A man was stooping over Juanito as he lay wounded.

He opened his eyes. One of the children was sprinkling him with gravel, delighted at having escaped the vigilant eye of his grandmother and felled this giant. The buckle of the giant's belt fascinated him. He dropped the remaining gravel so that he could touch the buckle, and promptly tripped. Juanito caught him under the armpits and, lifting him up in the air, asked: 'What's your name?'

The child swayed in his arms without the slightest hint of fear and thought the question over.

'Jorge,' he said. It was a recent discovery, and he was none too sure of it.

He was as lovely and as sticky as a bunch of autumn grapes. Suddenly there was a stream of imprecations. The old woman calmed down when she saw Jorge sitting beside Juanito, but as she dusted her skirt she showered kisses and reproaches upon the truant's head. A proper gipsy, she kept saying: he would duck under the stalls when she went to the market, climb all over the orange carts and hide from her from morning till night. He had made a pact with the devil to torment his grandmother. The old woman explained to Juanito that her son-in-law was fighting on the Ebro. She repeated this name several times, as though she were talking about a foreign country or some fantastic and familiar place, like Hell. Wasn't Juanito off to the Ebro too? He did not know; the old woman shook her head: in wartime you must expect the worst. Her daughter had been wounded in an air raid, and the youngsters had not recognized their mother under her bandages. The family was on its way back from the hospital . . .

Having nothing better to do, Juanito listened politely to the old woman's chatter. Perhaps those who are soon to die fasten on to such everyday words, which give a new and more reassuring sound to the pronouncement of the oracle. The Ebro was no longer the river whose course Juanito had traced on an ordnance map one evening: it was the last-minute Ally, the terrifying Archangel who in olden times had come to the aid of the knights crushed by the Moors.

A gang of youths came rushing down the steps. Without so much as a glance at Juanito, they got ready for a bullfight. Those who were playing the parts of the matador and picadors pulled off their shirts to show that they were more exposed. The others, sitting on the steps, formed a simmering arena from which gibes and advice were constantly darted. The youngest boy present spread a wine-coloured cape over a wooden sword. Armed with his *muleta*, he went down on his knees in front of an imaginary bull. But a latecomer unwrapped a strip of cloth and produced a pair of horns. The boy who was substituting for the four-legged animal was puffing and blowing and scratching the earth with his hoof to gather strength for a charge. He was mimicking the bull so well that he seemed to have its muzzle and its look of obstinacy and dull fury. The arena rang with applause. Already another boy was snatching the red cape from the first.

Juanito smiled at the efforts of these boys, all so anxious to surpass themselves and triumph in the eyes of the crowd. The war would be over before they could show their paces in the arena. It would leave them with the memory of a night of uproar: marching columns and blazing buildings, looting and demonstrations. They would look back with regret on the days when the adults, absorbed in this bloody game, had let them train every day, in the hope of eclipsing Dominguez and Belmonte.

The oldest member of the gang came over and sat down next to Juanito.

'Esteban is terrific,' he said. 'Some of his passes are sensational.'

In the dusty 'ring', Esteban was gyrating nobly, as though the whole of Seville were following his movements, his provocations, his summonses to the bull. His adversary was out of breath from galloping on all fours. The spectators were stamping their feet. Esteban managed to position himself perpendicularly to the horns. He touched the bull lightly on the frontal arch with his wooden sword. The bull slumped to the ground, to the accompaniment of shrieks of joy from the arena. The boy who had been playing the part of the bull handed the horns to someone else and sat down, looking displeased with himself.

'We haven't had any real bullfights since the war,' Juanito's neighbour continued. 'All the cattle-ranches are in their hands . . . In Seville, for a big bullfight, they drew the map of Spain on the sand in the ring, with coloured chalks. It was so well done that from the seats you could recognize every province, every town. In the last fight, the matador thrust the sword in right between the eyes—a brilliant *faena*, like the stroke Esteban brought off just now. Before it collapsed the bull swerved slightly and rushed forward: the matador was gored right in the middle of his body. . . . His blood came spurting out to join the bull's. They both had to be dragged off at the same time: the man, whose guts were spilling out, and the animal, which was shedding its blood through its nostrils. The map was all smudged. It was a bad omen for the Nationalists at the beginning of the war.'

'There's no telling who the bad omen was for,' said Juanito. He broke off, amazed at his pessimism. To retrieve himself he added: 'I'm off to the front tomorrow: omens don't concern me any more.'

'Of course not,' the boy said, looking rather nettled. 'They're old wives' tales.'

His friends were shouting to him. He ran back to them.

In the evening, Juanito stood staring down the path that Soledad would take to join him. Was she ill? Inwardly, Juanito was hoping that she would not come. He had said good-bye to Barcelona in the shape of the people strolling through the park, of that old woman, of those boys. Soledad's kisses and caresses, her promises and plans for the future, would be merely a repetition. Night had fallen. It cost Juanito an effort to walk slowly out of the Montjuich Park, with the apparent reluctance of a man cheated of a final rendezvous.

In the warm darkness, the water lapped gently against the jetty. Through the clouds, the moon shed a wary light on this section of the harbour, which had been pounded by bombs and shells and in which all that survived was a few blind stretches of wall, an undamaged window-frame, a gateway opening on to a gutted corridor. On a balcony poised in mid-air, some rags conjured up images of washing hung up to dry and of the world of birdcages, rickety cradles and evergreens which the poor contrive to maintain behind balustrades decorated with an Elche palm.

A soldier was talking regretfully of the open-air cafés whose wooden terraces still jutted out over the sea. There had been dancing to the strains of a barrel organ, and afterwards people had eaten huge helpings of fish and prawns. And shop assistants and hard-up office workers had blown their savings once a month and lived like lords. He gave Juanito an account of this lavish living within smell of the sea.

Juanito shook his head.

'In Valencia we had fiestas, battles of flowers . . .'

But the Catalan was not to be outdone: 'In Barcelona, before the war, you could sing and dance and drink at any hour of the day or night!'

On one of the café terraces, shadowy figures were on the move, human shapes crawling about and dragging strange burdens after them: some old women were ripping planks of wood from the ruins, to heat their homes.

A number of lamps were placed at the foot of the awnings protecting the cargo. Agustin tiptoed over in the darkness. He laid his hand on Juanito's shoulder.

'Listen,' he said, 'don't expect a cruiser or a luxury liner . . .'

A shadowy bulk was now blocking the view.

'You see,' said Agustin, 'that old barge, disguised as a warship? It carries supplies between Valencia and Barcelona. On the return journey its holds are full of wounded, and men on leave and people on special service, such as us.'

They were soon embarked. Agustin wanted to go down into the hold, but when they got there they were confronted by the tart smell of fruit and vegetables, mingled with the stench of grease. They preferred to sleep on deck. With their packs and kitbags, they settled down at the foot of a mast.

'We have protection,' said Agustin. The vessel boasted a pair of guns—one fore, the other aft—that would not have scared even smugglers away. Juanito felt sleepy. They stacked coils of ropes under their heads.

'Everything is fine,' Juanito said with conviction. 'What are you thinking about, Agustin?'

'I'm thinking,' said Agustin, 'that we have a fifty-fifty chance of getting caught.'

'In wartime those are good odds,' observed Juanito.

'You're right,' admitted Agustin. He reproached himself for the bitter twist that he gave to his slightest remarks. 'Everything is fine, and tomorrow you will wake up in Valencia.'

The big black clouds covering the sky parted with the silent ease of theatre curtains. The full moon appeared. The stars seemed to be signalling messages to each other, like beacons.

The wind had dropped. The engines were gently pulsating in the heart of the ship. Juanito was artlessly happy at making this trip on the open sea. Previously he had made only a single crossing to Cadiz, aboard a felucca laden with oranges. He gave himself over to his happiness which derived from a feeling of detachment and perhaps from the simple intoxication of being alive.

'We shall be at El Grao before sunrise,' Juanito continued.

Already he was relishing this first sight of Valencia in the early hours, as of a woman caught leaping out of bed.

The boat was gliding over a luminous plain. Her stem barely clove the water, beneath which the reflection of the sky trembled like burnished sand. She was hugging the coastline. It was impossible to tell, now, whether the faint points of light on the horizon were lamps or stars. A flock of birds took wing. They circled the rigging, then vanished.

'This is wonderful!' said Juanito.

It was as pointless to think of the day that would follow this vigil as of the day that had preceded it. The night drifted on, leaving no wake upon time . . .

Other soldiers lay asleep, with their heads propped against the rail. Like sentries giving way to fatigue, they seemed, defenceless, to be exposed to attack from an unseen enemy. Their packs were down on the deck beside their rifles. They had unfastened their cartridge belts. The moonlight was turning these dusty soldiers into silver-clad knights. Handsomely built as those heroes who are barely distinguishable from one another in legends, they looked as though they were sharing the same dreams, smiling at the same love affairs, heading for the same battle. The light fell on their sturdy necks, their firm chins, their muscular arms folded beneath their heads.

'There lie the latest reinforcements for the courageous city of Valencia,' thought Agustin. The inadequacy of the resources brought into play by the Republic made him sad. This egoism on the part of those responsible betrayed the death-wish, for Valencia was now Franco's principal objective. Yet Barcelona was jealously holding on to its men and its war materials.

But this peaceful night, with the sound of Juanito's regular breathing, soothed Agustin. It was cleansing him of his grievances and doubts. It was putting an end to the indictment constituted by his every thought. It was essential for him to abandon himself to this great peacefulness that was forming within him. Again he tried to give precise expression to it: I have acted wisely, he thought. He was no longer thinking of his political convictions, but of a creature of flesh and blood. I have made no demands on him: the very fact of his existence gives me more than any amount of caresses and declarations, more than all those lies whereby the mind makes use of the body to render its betrayal more complete . . . I need you to live, Juanito, let me watch you live!

'Are you asleep, Juanito?'

'No!' said Juanito. 'It would be a pity to sleep away a lovely night like this.'

'Didn't you have a fiancée in Valencia?' asked Agustin.

Juanito hesitated.

'I thought I had,' he said. 'I was little more than a child. Then the war came . . . We both changed. I don't think of her any more . . .'

He was stating the inevitable and the irreparable.

'All the girls in the *huerta* are yours for the asking,' Agustin said, to close the subject.

Juanito broke into a laugh.

'Now you'll be able to see just how beautiful our girls are in Valencia,' he said.

These last words finally set Agustin's mind at rest. Nobody was going to contend with him for Juanito, except the war. Once more, words took shape uncertainly in this inexpressible peacefulness, bursting like air bubbles on the surface of the water: I have no regrets . . . I have acted wisely . . . He felt rewarded in advance by this feeling of confidence for everything that he was giving up. The act of love was just a simulation. Agustin was achieving at the outset the state of repose which lovers experience but rarely after their grapplings, achieving that freedom in which the partners' minds seem to hover above their sated bodies.

Agustin took Juanito's hand between his two. The Valencian was asleep. He seemed to be swimming on the shiny deck, ascending and descending the currents of his dream. Beyond the dark rail rose wave after wave, each effacing its predecessor.

It must be midnight . . . I still have a whole night in which to be happy, Agustin said to himself. Suddenly he was overcome by a tremendous feeling of unease. Being happy, happiness: he had never used these outmoded expressions except to scoff at them. Happiness, he was fond of proclaiming, was the Declaration of Human Rights for fools. And now this happiness was suddenly being inflicted upon him. Not the frenzied complicity of the act of love, but the feeling that his existence was finally attuned to another existence, that his heart was beating to the same rhythm as another heart in another breast.

'I have conquered my loneliness . . . I am not alone any longer . . . Because I have experienced this moment of communion, I shall never be alone again.'

A sudden commotion in the stern of the ship broke in upon his thoughts. The gunner was claiming that he had spotted a submarine periscope in the distance. Agustin saw the captain and crew hurrying aft. Majorca was not far away. Agustin pictured the trawler going down with her cargo of sleeping soldiers, like those vessels laden with slabs of ancient marble and pillars and amphoras which divers discover off the coasts of Greek islands. But he knew that the ship would reach El Grao in the early morning. These angels disguised as troops would be yawning and stretching on the deck at sunrise.

The alarm had died down. Everything was still again. He spread a blanket over himself. Other pure, starlit nights came back to him. He groped for the names of those villages in Castile and Aragon where, after enacting, by the light of the lamps in the arcaded main square, the roles of those shady characters which were inevitably assigned to him, he had wandered—shunning the inn where the audience would address him as though he were still the pimp or the traitor or the parasite in the play—along a ruined fortified wall, losing his footing on refuse and scaring the starved-looking cats away. He would pluck a length of honeysuckle from a wall and take a long whiff at its voluptuous and virginal scent. The stars shone down with a kind of rivalry upon this village, still enclosed in its shell-like ramparts, like the dwellings of early man. Agustin would feel sorry for himself. He would walk along like Robinson Crusoe, unbearably alone on his island, looking for a footprint in the sand . . .

He would tell himself bitterly: 'After every victory and every defeat, one is back on one's own again.' The performance had been, as it was every night, a hectic struggle. He had enjoyed, in the midst of their exertions, the intoxication of taking risks and sharing in delight . . . With the closing line, the illusion of being a member of a community would vanish. Art would fail to create those bonds between human minds which religion and the act of love are incapable of establishing. There is no exertion, no sensuality, which lasts; every embrace must come to an end. After this attempt, Agustin would once again begin to lose faith in the idea of spreading the word in country districts by means of plays: what brotherly feelings could possibly endure between these unskilfully made-up apostles who nightly, on unstable boards, imagined that they were breaking bread with other suffering and humiliated human beings?

Who, at this moment, was so much as aware of his absence from the massive arcades, where the audience was now taking its revenge on the actors, interrupting and shattering them with catcalls? There would be a crunch of footsteps on the gravel path. Some apprentice, some shop assistant, was making his way home through the side streets. He would recognize the actor. A clammy hand would guide Agustin to a shed: a few faltering words, a few gestures were enough to make them accomplices.

'Will you come back?' the youth would say in the darkness.

Perhaps he was good-looking. Agustin would answer: 'Why yes, of course.' He would say so, not so much to deceive this chance acquaintance as to lie to himself. He was lying for a single human being just as, a few hours earlier, he had lied for the crowd. He was trying to prove to himself that the hell of his loneliness had its moments of remission . . . But the pleasure of those nights was a charitable gift from chance, the result of an imbroglio like those plays in which masters disguise themselves as valets, and lovers as indifferent bystanders—whereupon two people hiding from each other under assumed names end up by admitting everything to each other from behind their masks . . .

The moonlight poured down on to the boat. Agustin no longer had to pretend in order to prolong a furtive happiness enjoyed in the leathery smell of a shed, nor an intoxication which retained the scent of new-mown hay. Nothing can threaten a joy founded upon renunciation. Agustin lay silently intoning an act of grace: 'You are alive . . . I have acted wisely . . . And nobody, not even you, will share my secret.' These assertions rose within him, giving place to one another like the soundless waves on the still sea, dying away in a mysterious surf-like tenderness.

'Juanito, my son, my brother, my friend . . .'

All that we ever possess of another human being is his supreme absence: sleep. Just as the ship was submissive to the watery depths that bore it aloft, so Agustin was abandoning himself, open-eyed, to the motionless drift of happiness.

The shouts of the crew awakened the sleeping troops. A darker line on the horizon proclaimed El Grao harbour. The grey water was shivering in a perpetual breeze. Daybreak was lighting a distant glow in the sky. Agustin seized Juanito's arm.

'Wake up, man, here is your city.'

Juanito woke up. The lively waves were reflected in his astonished eyes. In the sky, another headland was advancing above a swirl of clouds. And on the sea, dawn was reflected, with its breaches of light and blazing barricades, in a vast roseate and snowy confusion. But already it was possible to make out the pine trees on the shore, waving in the morning breeze.

Juanito broke into a laugh.

'Even while I was asleep,' he said, 'I could feel myself drawing closer to Valencia second by second.'

He went over and propped himself against the rail. With his whole body, he could feel the bend of the coves that were now in sight. He was steeped in this water, where the old trees clinging to the bank with their thick dark roots were like paddlers afraid of losing their footing.

He spotted a neighbour standing on the quayside. The man promptly offered them a lift to the village. Agustin and Juanito squeezed into the seat beside him.

Juanito sounded his neighbour for news of the *huerta*: the war was taking its place among the calamities that afflicted the area at lengthy intervals, like flooding and foot-and-mouth disease. Agustin was re-experiencing his rather contemptuous aversion for these peasants, so bound up in their trees, their crops, their vine-harvests. But every year the villages of the plain sent their best musicians to Valencia. After bending all day over their furrows, these peasants, at night, would tussle with difficult scores. This competition gave rise to a good deal of rivalry: the announcement of the results would end in scuffles, and victors and vanquished would return to the applause of their villages with swollen faces, bruised hands and open cuts, as though they had just stepped out of a boxing ring.

Juanito was sorry that the competition had not been held this year. Jaime would have taken the guitar prize. Agustin gave the impression that he was scanning the rice fields and the canals.

'If only you could see this competition, Agustin, you would realize that we Valencians are as crazy as can be.'

'Have you seen anything of Soledad?' the man asked casually. 'I hear she is going to marry her cousin.'

'No,' said Juanito, 'it's all off. She is working in Barcelona in a clothing factory.'

'You are home,' said the man. 'I'd rather not stay, on account of the horse.'

Juanito hurried his companion through the little garden and up to the *barraca*. The door was ajar.

'Come in,' said Juanito. The straw-bottomed chairs were drawn up to the table. Black against the harsh white walls, the roasting tins and gridirons, designed like jewels and chased like guns, formed—with their flowing lines, their plant-like arabesques, their superb tendrils, their incisive scalloping—a lacework as precise and intricate as the shadow cast by a flowering bush.

But the water jugs and the bulging jars for containing oil, turned with love and patience by the village potter, spoke the same language of discreet opulence and pride.

Juanito strove to conceal his pleasure. 'You see, Agustin, it's just an ordinary *barraca*!' He broke off. 'Here comes my mother.'

Theresa flung her arms round her son and covered him with kisses, without deigning to notice that he had a companion with him. Her hands wandered over his shoulders, neck and arms, to assure themselves of his reality.

Theresa then bestowed a smile on Agustin. Her face, beneath its early wrinkles, retained a grave beauty. Juanito had inherited her slender nose and her proud and secretive mouth.

As though to justify the ardour of her welcome, she said: 'Of my three sons, Juanito is the only one who is left to me.'

She insisted on Juanito's bringing in their neighbour and bade the three men sit round the table.

'I've been expecting Juanito,' she said, covering the cloth with crisp white bread and some seed-cakes. She took her time over filling their cups. Her every movement was endowed with extraordinary dignity and inbred simplicity, with the courtesy of a race to whom a warm welcome and hospitality are primary duties.

While they were drinking, she opened the shutters a few inches. The light brought a gleam to the red tile flooring. On the window ledge, pinks and sweet basil were opening in their pots. Juanito could rest assured that the war had not brought dirtiness or untidiness to the *barraca*.

Theresa came back and sat down next to her son, but it was into Agustin's eyes that she stared.

'Is the war ever going to end?'

Juanito's uncles had been conscripted for clerical jobs on account of their age. Alonso had been allowed to remain on the farm because he was incapable of doing any kind of work. Theresa was not complaining. Children, women and old men were cultivating the *huerta*, and the *huerta* was continuing to keep Spain nourished. There was a tremor of pride in her calm voice.

How Juanito takes after her, Agustin was thinking: beneath their restraint, they have the same fierce and imperious nature. For this peasant woman, the 'point of honour' which St Teresa accused herself of carrying over into mystical life was to keep Spain nourished.

Juanito took up his mother's remarks with ice-cold conviction: 'As long as the *huerta* is free, the Republic will have bread and the strength to fight.'

Their neighbour, concerned at the Nationalist thrust towards Castellon de la Plana, was dubious.

'Valencia is in danger of being encircled before long,' he said.

Nettled at this, Theresa swung round to face him.

'If Valencia is threatened, Valencia will defend herself. The communists and anarchists ruined everything in Barcelona and Madrid. The Republicans in Valencia will have to get rid of them.'

Their neighbour stood up.

'Valencia will hold out, just as Madrid has held out,' he said.

Theresa walked out to the cart with the men. She smiled warmly at Agustin: 'Treat this house as your own.' And, slipping her arm round Juanito's waist as though he were her fiancé, she said, thrusting her face close to his: 'Respect the churches and the priests, Juanito. Sacrileges offend God and bring tears to the Virgin's eyes. If we lose the war, it will be on account of a handful of murderers and incendiaries.'

She kissed Juanito three times and arranged, with their neighbour, a swift way of exchanging letters and news.

The three men drove for a time without speaking.

Agustin was turning over Theresa's last words in his mind. She speaks of freedom, he thought, just as the knights of Calatrava spoke of Christ. Even though they are Republicans, these Valencians use mystical language. They see everything in terms of expiation and punishment. They at once demand and implore a miracle from heaven. He sighed.

'Your mother is right,' he said.

Juanito was silently rejoicing that his mother should have spoken with such ardour. He recognized every jolt in the road, and his eyes lingered caressingly on the long lines of orange trees with their swirling leaves, the white outhouses, the battlemented ramparts, the keep-like gateways that would protect his city from the Moors.

21

LIKE A BODY AWAKENING cell by cell as a swifter blood flows through its arteries, every house and every street in Valencia was filled with a secret buzzing. Since the start of the uprising, the Republic had been forced to withstand one blow of fortune after another. It had met the surprise of the pronunciamento, the staggering gains of the rebels and the unexpected capitulations of its own troops with a faith which had simply been strengthened by adversity. It had not despaired in the face of indifference from abroad. But as the Nationalist threat to Sagunto intensified, word went round which made even the gloomiest faces light up with impatience and gaiety. It was no longer a question of waiting, or of having faith, but of acting. The Republican army was going to hit back. The idea of crossing the Ebro, hacking through obstacles, crashing through every barrier and flying in the face of the elements in order to annihilate the enemy was of a recklessness, a do-or-die determination, a cheerful bravado, which went to the heads of all Valencians. The wounded were holding themselves erect, as blithe as volunteers for the first skirmish. The offensive, by its boldness, enchanted the daydreamers as well as the strategists. It excited the zealots and the sceptics. In this final battle, it was not the communications between Valencia and Barcelona and Madrid that were at stake. It was the fate of Spain, it was her past and her future. The hidden wildness that lies dormant beneath the even temper of the Valencian people broke loose at the very mention of the Ebro.

As Agustin put it: 'In your part of the country, Juanito, every able-bodied man is running a fever . . .'

But Juanito was deriving a new conviction from contact with his native soil.

'On the contrary, the people of Valencia are the first to have realized that the Russians are keeping the war going the way a donkey-driver perpetuates his donkey's sore . . . From now on, the Spanish will count on nobody but themselves . . . If we hadn't gone on waiting, all this time, for Russian tanks and Mexican rifles and British planes, we would have put an end to it by now. The Valencians will defend themselves with the rifles made in Sagunto, and with the shells that the women have learnt to turn out!'

'Don't flare up at the slightest objection,' sighed Agustin. 'In this town, bravery turns to poison. Queue up for tobacco and you'll hear talk that would make Don Quixote's hair stand on end . . . The people of Sagunto hurled themselves into the flames, so as not to fall into the clutches of the Carthaginians. Now the Republicans are haring towards the Ebro . . . For an army to swim across a river isn't a military manœuvre: it's an exploit straight out of Homer, an episode from some mediaeval epic. The idea of a handful of men seizing control of a town or subjugating a fortress by a feat of daring belongs to the world of literature, not of strategy . . . Don't look cold and put-out, Juanito. I am glad to see a miracle being wrought before our eyes: it is maturing in every mind. Before expressing itself in song, the epic is silently taking shape in men's hearts . . . A heroic aspiration is taking hold of an entire people . . . I am not viewing this mood as a sceptic or as an inquisitive bystander, but as a sociologist who may be witnessing the foundation of a place of pilgrimage, the establishment of a religion, complete with its prophets and its miracles . . .'

'You no longer believe in miracles. Because it seems to you to be happening too late, you are denying this miracle, you even want to scoff at it!'

'I'm trying to see it in perspective, Juanito . . . Do you know that some of the churches are reopening on the quiet? Statues are reappearing in chapels. The atheists and iconoclasts are trying to get Heaven on their side . . . When the Republican army was on the retreat, Christians were asking themselves uneasily whether God was on Franco's side . . . Now the same army, split into three small groups, is about to counterattack. Immediately, believers and free-thinkers alike count on the support of the angels . . . A gale of holy fanaticism is blowing through Valencia. . . . Left-wingers and right-wingers are equally desperate to be in on the act. This mixture of faith and despair is carrying us right back to the days of the Crusades. Now I understand the Reconquest. It wasn't the work of the Grand Orders of Chivalry, but of the craftsmen, the shopkeepers, the peasants, gripped by the same inspired lunacy.'

Juanito rejected all comparisons with the past.

'Speech-making was all very well in Barcelona,' he said. 'Here, we don't need lectures or propaganda. It's quite simple: the city is rising as one man to resist invasion and the threat of being trampled underfoot. Valencians may be hot-blooded, but they are also clear-headed . . .'

'And they even have marvellous rifles,' joked Agustin. 'The only trouble is, there are just about enough to arm one crack company! In Barcelona, our arsenals were bursting with them, but they dated back to the times of Maria Christina.'

Juanito was not to be discouraged: 'The government is just waiting for the offensive, then it will distribute the latest models. . . . As soon as we reach the Ebro you will believe in the miracle.'

Agustin pretended to be terrified.

'You make it sound like a country outing. The Ebro? I can't even swim! I'll sink like a stone. At least the water is warm in July. I shall be laid out like a hero before you even have time to notice what has happened . . . Later, you will pray to the Madonna of the Forsaken for a blasphemer.'

'I'll teach you to swim . . . In July, at Mora del Ebro and Gandesa, the Ebro doesn't cover the whole river-bed. It's just a pool: you just paddle about among the tall reeds.'

Agustin gave in.

'You're trying to impress yourself,' he said. 'You're a true

Valencian. Before the war, the men of the *huerta* were always determined to have the most striking saint in the carnival, the handsomest float in the procession. Even the musical contests ended in a pitched battle. What you really need is those mediaeval jousts, when each side picked its boldest knight to be its champion. In Valencia, the Civil War is like an historical romance, but it may be for that very reason that Valencia will be the Republic's liegeman, that Valencia will triumph over this swarm of Italians and Germans and rebel generals, like the knight valiant who unseats all his enemies in the end or—if you prefer it, Juanito—like the little shepherd-boy David slaying the giant Goliath. Don't think I'm laughing at your town: it has the arrogance that heroes are made of . . .'

He was pretending to share Juanito's illusion, just as they would together have drained a bottle of cheap brandy. Inwardly, he was addressing him in that other language which he had learned while acting Lorca on those summer evenings when only the cicadas persist in their song on the arid plateaus of Castile and Aragon.

What does it matter whether the offensive succeeds or fails, Juanito? You will live, wearing the brave and puzzled expression of young victors on their pedestals. One day I shall leave you without saying good-bye . . . Political commissars vanish from the scene in the same way as they have lived. They receive their due in the summary justice which they have dispensed, in a quick death, in an anonymous grave.

I shall have no difficulty in finding my way back to the *huerta*. I shall arrive at your farmhouse, just as we did that morning, unannounced. My steps will leave no imprint on the damp floor. I shall stand by the window, not daring to inhale the smell of the pinks, which is the smell of blood, of sunshine, of desire.

The daylight will filter through the shutters like birdsong: nothing will be capable of destroying this hymn to joy. The eternity for which I thirst is the shadow of the countryside washing the walls of your *barraca* at dawn, like blue water; but during your hot midday sleep I shall be that Jacob's ladder at your window which the sun picks out in bars of fire . . .

When you come in from the fields you will linger in the house to enjoy the touch of cool water on your warm skin. I shall be in the garden, by the fig tree . . . Then the warm evening springs like a dog on to people's knees as they sit chatting. Their everyday words take on a mysterious tone. During silences the shade accumulates at the corners of their mouths, like drops of milk on babies' lips. Half-solved riddles glimmer in their eyes. Scents prowl the countryside . . . By now, life is merely a wonderful intimation, a confidence too sweet to be voiced . . . Forgotten names, unconstrued words, inexplicable gestures, vanished faces, haunt the living. And you will suddenly say: 'Agustin!' But no one will know who you are calling or who, in the twilight, answers you.

'What are you thinking?' asked Juanito.

'I was wondering how we're going to keep the guns and equipment dry. If the troops swim across the Ebro in the middle of the night . . .'

The Nationalists controlled the bridges over the Ebro, and to them this river, with its powerful underwater currents, seemed an invincible barrier. But a single Republican division reaching the other bank would wreak incalculable havoc among their positions, for the enemy forces threatening Madrid and Barcelona presented a huge and vulnerable flank.

A well-staged offensive would destroy, link by link, the enemy's network of aerodromes, roads and training centres. Agustin sat picturing the shattered supply lines, the chaos-ridden headquarters, the ever-mounting paralysis among their divisions.

'Don't you see, Juanito? All a person's blood can be lost through a single wound. Instead of keeping up a hand-to-hand battle with Franco, the thing to do is produce this haemorrhage or, if you prefer it, this clot of blood which impairs the working of the whole bodily system . . . Once we have done that, the rebels' Italian and German friends will prove less generous . . . When prices slump, investors grow wary . . . Rome will recall her pilots and Berlin her instructors. The idea of non-intervention will find support on both sides. The Portuguese will be troubled by an uneasy conscience! Britain will spare a thought for our people, instead of worrying about our mines . . . France will send us something better than manifestoes proclaiming her sympathy. Yes, Juanito, a single victory for our army and the Russians will take the plunge and provide us with something more useful than spies and interrogators . . .'

He gave a nervous laugh, for the great upsurge of hope inspired by the final twitchings of life in the Republic was at last taking hold of him.

Juanito did not have time to show him round his city. With its closed churches and shuttered premises, Valencia was no longer a fervent and sensual town, enraptured with enjoyment and colour and noise, but a grim, austere centre straining in a heroic effort to equip an army. The *huerta* was amassing its crops, emptying its silos and its tanks. And Valencia was frenziedly preparing to sustain the final offensive.

The very people who at the beginning had protested against the massive requisitions made at gun-point were the first to deliver their vegetables and corn and rice. The roads were crowded with vehicles converging on Valencia and creating a bottle-neck at its gates, like some fabulous tributary procession. And these carts groaning beneath their load, these wagons into which living animals had been piled higgledy-piggledy, these old hairy goatskins whose full-bodied wine would be emptied into the service vats, these sheaves of corn, were like preparations for the triumphal banquet which would bring years of horror to a close.

Proud and sullen, Valencia was proclaiming her role as nourisher. In the winding streets round the cathedral, the crowd would make way for the patient cortège. As the jolting line of creaking carts, of tumble-down forage wagons, of short-winded old lorries went by, Valencia would salute the corn and fruit and livestock, all the riches of a fertile soil. Instead of regaling the Virgin with heaps of flowers and meadows of pinks and roses, Valencia was offering up to the Republic this living gold plucked by her menfolk from the mud of the rice-fields and moulded by their hands . . .

The Huerta

22

EVERY EVENING, Juanito rode out to the farm. The road to the *huerta* ran along the coast. And as he pedalled along on his bicycle he inhaled a heady gust of brine, resin and tar. He proceeded more slowly on the banks of earth dividing the flooded fields. Yellow flags lined the path. The rice-fields emitted a smell of warm, fertile mud, the sticky heat of a drowsy body. In the distance, frogs were striking up. The sun was going down. Juanito savoured, in anticipation, the water from the well, whose coolness, with its secret hint of aniseed, held the flavour of the blue shade of summer days. And his mother, rejuvenated by her years, graver and gayer than before, stood smiling at him in the doorway.

In vain did Juanito try to entice Agustin to the *barraca*.

'Come and spend a night at our place!' he would say. 'Night after night my mother is on at me to ask you. You sleep easier in a *barraca* than in an H.Q. office. Even your dreams take on a different colour.'

Agustin would make a show of temper: 'I've no superstitious love for any house. Rich or poor, all houses are of equal worth, like the tents which camel-drivers set up under the stars every night . . . How can people grow attached to walls, to stone, treating them as though they were human beings? You call that legal and sentimental fetishism "pride of ownership". But happiness is only to be derived from possessing men and women who are unaware of their beauty or objects which are perfect and cannot deteriorate. I can just about understand the craze for collecting rough-hewn stones, uncut diamonds, crude gems. You can play with those cold, glittering objects, like a child with a shell that lies forgotten in his pocket . . . But a house! It is the most corrupt form of ownership, the most irksome form of slavery! Rather a hermit's cave! Your *barracas* are so absurdly spick and span that they put me in mind of those babies, covered with lace and ribbons, being wheeled in their prams through the public gardens of Madrid. There is something carnal about your attachment to walls made of reeds and mud: as you would say, it's a sin!'

This doctrinaire tirade amused Juanito.

'There is nothing sinful about preferring to sleep under your own solid roof, rather than in a tent or a cave. And ours is the best *barraca* in the village!'

Agustin laughed at his own exaggerations: 'I know . . . Your trees bear the sweetest fruit, your ramblers put forth the richest-scented roses, and even your well somehow contains purer water . . . These absurd and irrational possessives—*my* soil, *my* spring—don't irritate me coming from you, because you are ready to share everything, shade as well as sunshine . . .'

'Well then,' Juanito insisted, 'are you coming tonight?'

'Some other night . . . I have to finish my report for tomorrow's meeting.'

Juanito eyed him suspiciously, as though seeking other motives for his refusal.

'Have you got something against us?'

'Us' was Juanito's *barraca* and his mother, the village and the men of the *huerta*, the creatures and plants thriving on a bountiful soil.

'How can you think such a thing? I should be so happy to come . . . But I have only a few days, a few hours in which to assess the strength of the Levante . . . Our whole future depends on this chancy estimate, this risky inventory, this patchwork of guesses . . . I'm not unduly troubled with qualms, but I'm like a magnetic needle run wild and incapable of pointing true north. Every time I come across a new piece of information, I'm afraid the total may change . . . Somebody has worked out that if the factories at Sagunto were reorganized they could produce three times as much . . . In which case, Valencia would be able to equip its army . . . Like a dunce, every time I add the figures together I get a different answer . . . Then I try to track down the error . . .'

Agustin's confiding in him allayed Juanito's sullen pride.

'You'll find it,' he said, 'and tomorrow you will come with me. Just you see if you don't.'

Hospitality was the prime duty and prime virtue for a man of the *huerta*. It was also an opportunity to show off to a stranger the splendour of his existence. Theresa, like her son, would rise to the occasion. Agustin would have to taste every Valencian dish, sample every local wine; the neighbours would join in this banquet, from which only the parish priest would be missing. Soon after dark, voices and guitars would ring out under the night sky, drowning the croakings from the rushes at the edge of the lake.

'Promise?'

A lingering distrust darkened Juanito's eyes and brought a pout to his sulky, small-boy's lips.

'I promise!' Agustin answered, propping his elbows on the sill of the ground-floor window.

'*Salud!*' Down in the courtyard, Juanito was getting on to his bike, and was already pedalling along beneath the bowl of the sky. Agustin was left all alone till the following day in this stifling office overlooking the courtyard of the Archbishop's Palace, where Military Intelligence had set up its headquarters. If Juanito had changed his mind and turned back, Agustin would have given in. He knew that his victory was precarious, but admissions would leap into his mind, as irrepressible and jerky and contradictory as the words of a drunk in the confessional. Juanito's remarks would come back to him: 'Have you got something against us?' Oh yes, Juanito: everything. Against the boys who were at school with you, against Francisco, who came home on leave yesterday, against your absent friends, whom you will spend all night talking about, against the old people in the village, calmly remembering the way you looked and moved and laughed as a child. And I loathe your mother because you are like her and because you love her—isn't that sufficient reason? On account of her, I shall remain in your eyes a man from the outside world, a guest who is given the best bedroom for a night, a stranger. But still more do I detest the fields that you till, the trees that you prune, the roses that you graft, and even the fruit and flowers in which you glory like an untutored poet revelling in the lines that he has just composed.

Oh, Juanito! In Barcelona, I didn't bother my head about your mistresses. Those momentary accomplices were nothing in comparison with this *huerta* which laps you day and night in caresses and solicitations and countless moments of sensuality which are all the more terrible for being innocent. To that soil you are truly wedded. I can see you now, out on the road . . . you are racing along, with your head low over the handlebars; just for fun, you are describing wide, pointless curves, like the swirling flight of swallows. You are haring back to your orchard, your house, your child's bed next to the fruit loft. You are keeping a rendezvous. You will never weary of that embrace, of that kiss—the first kiss you received.

In Barcelona, I used to prick up my ears for your return. All that I felt for the girl whose scent lingered in your hair was a faint distaste; but here I am truly ousted. With all my heart and all the strength in my body, Juanito, I hate the houses of the *huerta*, with their gleaming red floor-tiles, and their spotless windows, and their blinding white walls, and—in the window-boxes, like alms for the relief of passers-by—their full-blown flowers. Ah! Rather than a *barraca*, it's the deck of a ship that I should like for a home—that deck on which you lay among all the other sleeping troops. When a cloud hid the stars I could still see your head tilted back under the sky . . . The dog-weary centurions lie asleep like that, surrounded by their useless lances, their scattered shields. And none of them even notices that Christ's tomb is empty. Oh, Juanito! That is the finest moment of the Resurrection. God Himself has disappeared, and His guards are talking in their sleep . . .

At this very moment, your mother is throwing herself into your arms and showering you with kisses. She takes you with her arm round your waist to show you, before nightfall, the withered rose tree which has started to blossom again. You told me about it yesterday. She sees a lucky omen in this shrub putting forth shoots again so that it shall not be pulled up; and the neighbours wave to your mother over the hedge. They whisper: 'Theresa is happy, she has her son with her,' and they refuse to go into the house. What are the pair of you talking about? The need to repair the well, the curtains of trees protecting the delicate seedlings from the wind, the last stages of the fruit harvest? Despite the first wrinkles, the first grey hairs, despite Federico's death and Domingo's silence, your mother is roaring with laughter. War, poverty, old age, are gone, because you are there. And you also are unwittingly forgetting everything, denying everything . . . Juanito, I hate your gardens and your houses!

And yet one evening, to replace one form of suffering with another, I shall go out there with you. In your garden I shall savour, astonished, the false respite, the fleeting euphoria which sedatives grant to the gravely ill. Your mother will say: 'At last! I've been expecting you every evening.' These phrases which are not even lies, these old, worn, ritual expressions of politeness will bring the tears to my eyes. Your mother will add: 'You will have Juanito's room. It's a very simple little room, but from the window you can see the lake on the skyline. Juanito will sleep in his brothers' room. In the loft next to Juanito's room we have hung some fruit to dry: it's a pleasant smell and won't interfere with your sleep.'

Lying on your bed, Juanito, I shall dream your adolescent dreams. It will be a short-cut to those incredible years when I did not know that you were alive. I shall keep my eyes wide open as I drift motionlessly along . . . Till dawn breaks, every star in the sky, every frog in the rice-fields, every animal cry from the farms, every creak of the floorboards in your house will belong to me. . . . You will sleep. My own sleeplessness will be the stuff of your dreams. The blood in your veins, the water in the canals, the sap in the trees, the juice in the fruit, everything that nourishes the *huerta* will flow from my soul, as from a mysterious wound.

I need this illusion and I am afraid of this temptation: to

mingle forever with your life, to become, through the magical agency of a single night, a member of your race, to share with you the memories, the echoes, the laughter, the flavour, the sad and gay remarks of good days and bad, to relive, by spending this isolated night under your roof, the nights of your childhood and youth . . .

When Juanito appeared in his office at the beginning of the day's work, Agustin would find a heightened radiance in his face, just as he would have discerned in it the signs of a night of debauchery. The Valencian produced some fruit from his pocket. Out of his jacket he whisked a huge ruffled pink which seemed to be made up of several pinks.

'There!'

In his voice there was the satisfied note of the prospector who has found the nugget that he was looking for, of the sportsman laying out the contents of his game-bag. He had returned to the *huerta* only to bring back this evidence.

Agustino pretended incredulity: he had never seen such a massive orange or a pink notched like an ornate lace frill. Juanito burst the resilient skin of the fruit with his nail.

'Look!'

Beads of blood appeared on the orange peel. The pomegranate that Juanito was wrenching open with his strong hands was a dank cavern full of rubies. Agustin inclined his head over the pink: all the nights and days of the *huerta* blazed forth in a single whiff of scent. Juanito tried, unsuccessfully, to choke back the proud cry that rose to his lips: 'You see: there is nowhere else on earth like the *huerta*, and even in the *huerta* nothing grows as it does in our garden.'

Agustin slowly put the orange down on his desk: in his sudden exhilaration it seemed to him that Juanito was this dazzling fruit, this flower with its giant calyx, the artless and glorious offering of the Valencian plain beneath the morning sky.

'My mother chose it for you,' Juanito added.

As he unruffled the pink, Agustin inhaled the whirl of scents. Hiding his intoxication, he turned the pomegranate this way and that, eyeing its leathery skin, its lips parted to reveal a gaping jaw. He said to himself, over and over again, with a sudden bound of pain and happiness: They talked about me . . .

It irritated Agustin to see Juanito as subject to the spell of the *huerta* as he would have been to a woman's.

'We have only a few days left. Accurate or not, my report is nearly finished and we'll soon be on our way . . . Don't pull that face! Haven't you had enough of the fatted calf?'

He was quickly touched at the sight of Juanito's abashed expression. He ascribed his ill-humour to overwork, to the wide variety of functions that he had to assume.

'There are moments when I'm no longer sure whether I'm a political commissar or a strategist or Commander-in-Chief or Minister of Supply. Everything is my concern, and there is not a detail on which the success of the manœuvre does not depend. When I get back, I have to vouch for Valencia's morale, for its military potential. If Valencia can equip an army and begin to join up with us as soon as we have crossed the Ebro, victory is ours. Otherwise it will be suicide. What the people back in Barcelona require of me isn't an investigation or a balance-sheet listing the pros and cons, but a total answer, a yes or no. And I have only to utter the word "offensive" for the man across the table to stare at me star-struck, like a lover promised the woman of his desire. Everyone in Valencia is tipsy without having touched the bottle, ready to cry and laugh over imaginary disasters and successes. But how am I to assess the contribution that the Levante will make at the decisive moment?'

Juanito's face darkened.

'You have no grounds for doubt! The fact that people here show more enthusiasm than those in Aragon or Castile doesn't make them less reliable or less courageous or less strong.'

'Don't take offence,' said Agustin. 'But put yourself in my position. I need you, not just to type out an urgent report but, by discussion, to clarify these jostling views, these blurred impressions, these statements which, for all their sincerity, contradict one another or get mixed up. I know as much as it is possible to know. I have sounded everybody who represents something: a party, a movement, an experiment. I shall get a better overall picture of the situation when we fly over Valencia. In the plane which is to take us to the Ebro, I shall draw my final conclusion. Why torment ourselves? Another few days and the offensive will be unleashed: then we shall see clearly enough whether the enthusiasm lasts, whether it was sensible to rely on Valencia . . .'

They drove through the outskirts of the city: huge empty goods-sheds were reminders of the days when fruit and vegetables had to wait for a buyer. In long, regular lines, the orange trees unfurled the Garden of the Hesperides as far as the eye could see. Juanito stared out of the window at this landscape, these trees, these fields. All of it was his, down to the heaps of compost and manure which at times gave off an intolerable stench.

'This is your first flight,' said Agustin, 'but we have been allotted a machine good enough for a cabinet minister . . .'

The factory-buildings of the Manises district came into view. At the aerodrome, formalities were quickly over. A huge, glittering, metal bird was poised on the red runway. Juanito stood marvelling at it. The pilot informed them that he intended to fly at a very high altitude to discourage fighter planes. They climbed into the cabin. A man attached safety-belts to Juanito's legs and arms. Thus bound, he turned to Agustin and gave him a smile. The machine began to move along the runway. A rumbling invaded the cabin. Agustin sat surveying his companion out of the corner of his eye. Was he concealing his apprehension? But a wonderful feeling of freedom was taking hold of Juanito and intoxicating him. The plane was climbing straight into the sun, which was reflected on its dazzling wings . . . And to Juanito it seemed that he was the first human being to go cleaving through space in this lightning manner.

A few air-pockets restored Juanito to the human condition. The sky and the floor of the plane were giving way beneath him. The scenery toppled over on to its side. The markings on the map gave no indication of the positions held by the Nationalists. These laminated hills were studded with the same white villages, the same churches; ruined castles afforded the protection of their rust-clogged drawbridges, their innocuous towers, their dismantled ramparts, to the cheerful and prosperous market-towns of the Levante. And there was no hint of the canker of war which held the whole of Spain in its grip.

When the plane flew over Tarragona, Juanito picked out the harbour, the compact city walls, the arches of the aqueduct, and the arena, where pools of shadow lay in the gangways between the rows of seats. The town looked like a beehive ripped open by a brutal hand. From the deep cells, the June sunlight flowed like thick honey. Beneath the splinters and the shrapnel, beneath the gaping rafters, beneath the rubble, lay the town's indestructible foundations, those huge blocks of gold-coloured stone, worn at the corners as the feet of bronze statues are worn by human lips.

The past was emerging through the recent ruins. Another Spain was preserved intact in the soil, with its temples and its treasures. The Civil War was merely a protracted episode. The breaking of this single thread was not enough to destroy the tenacious web in which a people inextricably mingles falsehood and clearsightedness, truth and error, courage and weakness, just as an individual shapes his destiny with what he has inherited and what he has rejected, with his virtues and vices, his chance of salvation and his urge to self-destruction.

The plane climbed to evade Nationalist fighters. Huge tracts of wooded country lay spread out like a sea of a darker green. In the grottoes, Republican troops were in hiding. With the collusion of the peasants, snipers lurked behind the barkless cork-trees, waiting for the Nationalist front to cave in. In their hunger they occasionally set an ambush, as though still living in the age of the stage-coach, but these bandits had only one aim: to reconquer the mouths of the Ebro . . .

The river meandered through dense and undulating vines. Innocent villages were dotted about on its banks. Only the demolished arches of the bridges served as a reminder that this long pale blue trail divided warring brothers.

Down in the plain, some buildings clustered round a chapel

with an undamaged spire. The aircraft circled the monastery. In the midst of the old slate roofs, like a silk handkerchief spread on the ground by a passer-by, appeared a sand-coloured rectangle. The machine came to rest on it with infallible precision. While Agustin was making his report, Juanito wandered through the stark, imposing cloisters. There were no battle-scars to be seen, but in the chapel, instead of kneeling monks, Juanito caught a glimpse of officers in their shirt-sleeves poring over huge maps spread out on wooden trestles or pinned to the walls.

This was the H.Q. in charge of operations on the Ebro.

23

ON MOONLESS NIGHTS, a strange scene was enacted on the banks of the river. Lorry loads of troops were brought up from their encampments after dark, standing as closely packed as cattle on their way to market. The overloaded vehicles were jolted about as they drove along the tracks to which the warmth of the day still clung, together with the scents of early summer. Protests would ring out, then somebody would break into song. The war was turning into a game of hide-and-seek which had all the gaiety of boys playing truant from school.

These night exercises were like hectic preparations for a party, interspersed with outbursts of temper that turned into roars of laughter. The offensive on the Ebro was a conspiracy between youth and courage. There would never be pluck and high spirits enough in this fine trick which the Republic was about to play on the solemn Nationalist generals. And there was unanimity in the absurd confidence with which these gamblers were laying down their last card.

Juanito could not help exulting. The Valencians were not the only ones to believe in victory with all their heart. Agustin left his command post to go with them on night training. Juanito twitted him.

'Just look at you, ensconced in your prior's cell! It took those monks three hundred years to get your quarters ready for you.'

'Everything is up to standard,' Agustin acknowledged, 'though I *did* have to bring my own service maps and my own brandy and Lorca's poems . . .'

A violent quarrel flared up at the back of the lorry. A soldier was claiming that he was being pushed by his comrades. Agustin restored order quickly and curtly: 'Haven't you got something better to fight about?'

The dispute died down.

'It's a great weakness of the Spanish,' Agustin growled, 'this urge to exchange blows and curses.'

Juanito did not answer. He was savouring every moment of this journey through the sleeping countryside. The silence was delicious, it was a living silence containing endless flutterings in the trees, endless scufflings in the undergrowth. Suddenly the toads struck up their tune. There was always one which waited for the choir to cease before it started to croak, like a soloist waiting for his entry. Juanito would say aloud, to himself, to Agustin: 'I love the darkness, I love the countryside, I love the summer . . .'

So as to take up less room, Agustin would slip his arm round his companion's shoulders. When the lorry lurched, the back of Juanito's neck glided along his arm. Agustin stopped weighing up the chances of a successful offensive. As on the boat which had brought them to Valencia, he gave way to happiness, letting it carry him where it would. He pretended to make a joke of Juanito's words: 'I love the darkness, I love the summer . . .' The driver handed him the flask, in its felt covering. Agustin declined it, but Juanito tilted the raw warm wine into his mouth from a great height, as though it held the very flavour of the night.

A sudden jerk of brakes brought the vehicle to a halt close to the bank. There was a screeching sound as the driver let down the back of the lorry. Faces remained hidden in the gloom, and nobody could detect the gleam of inexplicable happiness in Agustin's eyes.

When the training period began, the strongest swimmers, selected as instructors and disposed at intervals along the bank, were barely distinguishable from the bushes. The stooping shrub signalling to Juanito was Javier or Gaspar.

The men hurriedly took off their clothes. Standing knee-deep in water, the instructors urged on the laggards: 'At this rate, Franco will be in Valencia before you get to the other bank!'

Juanito transformed himself into a ferryman, a half-naked St Christopher poised on muscular legs. The water rippled over his skin, quivering round his knees. He advanced till it was up to his neck to show a beginner how to keep going without getting out of breath. In the tranquil darkness, these patient exertions reminded him of working in the fields. He loved ploughing his way through the Ebro step by step, teaching others to master this obstacle, stroke by stroke. Even the most nervous troops felt safe with him. In the midst of these frenzied preparations, he enjoyed the peacefulness, the caresses of the air and water on his naked skin. These superbly built peasants and muscular bricklayers and round-shouldered office workers were his brothers—even the 'churros', the ones who did not come from the Levante. They all believed in freedom, just as they all pinned their hopes on a victory wrested forcibly from men and from God. This victory would restore a desire for unity to those who wanted to break away from Spain—the Catalans and the Basques and the Navarrese. Less obviously, it would be a triumph for Valencia, for its artisans, who long ago had stood up to the nobles just as they had to the king.

Some of Agustin's remarks came back to Juanito as he conscientiously carried out his duties as swimming instructor. Valencia had been the first free territory in Spain. It would likewise be the last free territory, and from it a second Reconquest would be launched.

'But you can see you aren't going to drown!'

The soldier regained his footing. Juanito returned to his dreaming. The moonless night was its accomplice. The water glistened faintly. Probably it was after midnight. If Juanito was tired, he did not feel it.

These naked troops were shouldering the task of the hidalgos with their massive armour and costly swords, were taking up the mission of the Knights of Santiago and Calatrava. The Ebro was cleansing them of their smell of hide and sweat. These factory hands and peasants and shopkeepers were sharing the experience of Don Quixote on the eve of battle.

In the end, Fernando was the only one left who still cried for help; his comrades poked fun at him, but Juanito reassured him: 'You're getting on all right, don't listen to them! You're nearly there . . .'

Fernando staggered proudly over the pebbles and slumped on to the bank. It was agony for him to be the company duffer. To join the fight, he had left his job in the grocery near the market, where he had unctuously served the most fashionable clientèle in Valencia. A distant relationship bound him to Juanito. While he was recovering his breath, Fernando would admire Juanito without envy, as though by mere personal effort he could turn himself into this strapping youth.

The troops who had completed their training were practising crossing the Ebro in groups. The water stifled its murmurs on the reeds growing by the bank: a faint lapping was the only evidence of the swimmers crossing the river in rhythm.

PART TWO

The Crossing of the Ebro

Thou hast affected the fine strains of honour,
To imitate the graces of the gods;
To tear with thunder the wide cheeks o' the air . . .

SHAKESPEARE: *Coriolanus*

24

ON 15TH JULY, Juanito opened the top-secret order from headquarters. His hands were trembling slightly as he unfolded this sheet of paper which contained the date of the offensive. Agustin came down several times to examine the equipment piled up by the riverside: the barrels and ladders and stout oak planks that would enable a makeshift bridge to be slung across the river as soon as a party of volunteers had reached the other bank.

Juanito broke into a laugh: 'There isn't a single barrel, empty or full, left in Tortosa.'

'So I see, but get it all hidden away among the reeds. The offensive has been put back twenty-four hours. Is that disappointment on your face?'

Agustin was eyeing the Valencian suspiciously. Juanito mastered his feelings.

'Why should it be? We're ready. A day one way or the other makes no difference.'

'Good,' said Agustin. 'I didn't mean to hurt you . . . But an offensive is an enormously complicated mechanism which can be thrown out of gear by the slightest thing.'

They sat down under a tree, some little distance from the others. Agustin opened his brief-case and took out a map stained with printer's ink. The colours and lettering were slightly smudged, because greasy hands had tried to feel the rise and fall of the natural features on this flat surface. Agustin saw a pair of hands running over the battlefield, as benumbed and sensitive, as clumsy and discerning as a blind man's. They seemed to be reading these representations of hills and roads and waterways with the intention of thoroughly embracing them; they were caressing the river that had to be crossed. They were spelling out these slopes and ridges to increase their sense of towering over them. They were sliding more gently over these swellings of earth which would cover men's bodies. For reassurance, Agustin said to himself: I'm drinking too much, I'm not getting enough sleep . . . my head's swimming. These premonitions merely externalized his fear. He had experienced the same signs, the same obsessions during the battle of Belchite. Everything had forewarned him of Luis's death . . . Agustin pulled himself together. The hands straying over the map were his own hands. They were obeying him by folding up the crumpled sheets of paper. A few yards away, Juanito's men were shifting the materials for the pontoon bridge, setting them down among the leafy stems of the tall reeds. There were long steel girders glinting in the sun, so heavy that it took eight men to carry them. Every time they set one down under the reeds they would give a triumphant cry, as if a matador had just felled his bull, in the ring, with a magisterial thrust.

Agustin raised his voice. His hand smoothed out the ruffled map.

'Listen carefully, man. We are here, right at the south of the Ebro, not far from Tortosa. You are attempting to cross the Ebro with your men. Right at the north of the river, near Mequinenza, other men are doing the same, and doing it at the same time. Franco is just as nervous as we are at this moment; he is expecting the offensive, but he doesn't know whereabouts on the Ebro it will be launched. He dare not weaken his front in the Levante, nor his front in the area of Madrid. He is going to have to turn the whole distribution of his forces upside down.'

Agustin broke off. Juanito's face was glowing. For him, this staggering manœuvre was already in progress. Franco was hastily recalling his troops in an attempt to close the two breaches. By crossing the Ebro near the mouth of the river, the Republicans were re-establishing communications between Barcelona and Valencia.

'When I came to Barcelona, the road along the coast was still free . . .'

Juanito was not in the least disturbed that he should be the humble instrument which would enable the Republic to breathe again.

Agustin watched the blood rush into the boy's radiant face. He thought: Nothing is lost while there are twenty-year-old Spaniards beside themselves with joy at the prospect of victory. He felt the need to encourage and share this exhilaration.

'At the same time, the units which cross the Ebro at Mequinenza will cut the road to Fayon, and every Nationalist division in Aragon will be tied down.' He paused to weigh the full effect of his words. 'And when the two operations at the extreme ends of the front have been successfully carried through, when Franco's thoughts are wholly occupied with the need to smash these two dangerous bridgeheads, the main body of the Republican army is going to surge forward in the centre, in the Gandesa loop.'

'Show me, show me.'

Agustin's thin hand indicated the bend of the Ebro, thrusting deep into the territory held by the Republicans.

'Look! At this point, the Ebro forms a salient right in the middle of our lines. How could Franco, attacked from the north and south, possibly maintain more than a thin protective screen round Gandesa? This is where we shall throw in the 3rd and 35th Divisions, followed by the International Brigades—the 13th and the 11th and the 15th . . .'

'And what will be the effect of that? ' Juanito begged of him breathlessly. 'Quick! Tell me!'

'This is the point where we shall make our break-through and demolish the first hinge in the Nationalist line. After our double diversion, Franco won't even be able to bring up reinforcements . . .'

'I understand; but who will support our attack in the south?'

'The French of the Commune de Paris Battalion—men who are used to fighting both in the snow of the Sierra and in the midst of blazing pine forests. To them, crossing the Ebro will be a joy-ride.'

'I know,' said Juanito. 'They were at University City and at the Battle of Aragon and at Las Navas and at La Cuesta de la Reina.'

Agustin instinctively lowered his voice, even though the men were now some way off.

'When night comes, you will cross the river in three groups. You and your men will cross at Campredo. I mean: you will try to cross.'

A terrible apprehension was taking hold of him: an animal fear was invading every fibre of his being, like a poison beginning to take effect. The very scenery surrounding him was decomposing before his eyes. This was no longer a summer morning on the bank of a river, amid the bustle of preparations which were so like a game of hide-and-seek. The tall leafy reeds were quivering in an ominous wind. The ripples on the surface of the water were trying to efface something. The planks that the soldiers let fall were hammering out an order, an enigmatic warning. Was this just a morning like so many other mornings, or was it one of those moments which topple over into another time with all the sensations and passing thoughts that they contain, all the words and silences? Ought Agustin to mistrust these fleeting seconds which were assuming a false mask of eternity? Would he one day see this morning of leave-taking the way you see a ship lying undamaged at the bottom of the sea? Already he was sinking, drowning aboard that ship . . .

'What's the matter? Don't you have confidence in my men?'

'Of course I have,' Agustin protested. 'It's myself I'm worried about. As the years go by, I no longer have any confidence whatever in myself.'

'Why, you're mad!' said Juanito. He supposed that Agustin had doubts about their victory.

Agustin gazed with a mixture of despair and joy at his companion's ruddy face and bronzed shoulders and quivering body, stripped to the waist. The heat was causing fine beads of sweat to stand out on Juanito's temples and making his sandy locks cling to his forehead. He was beautiful. His lips were parted and he was smiling. He was Juanito Sanchez, a peasant from the Levante, chosen from among all other men to be the first to cross the Ebro.

Through him, Agustin was surveying those fearless youths —St George and Hercules, David and Perseus—who are all depicted as spurning the monster's convulsed head with their foot. When he was young, Agustin had delighted in these heroes straining towards their achievement, tougher than the weapons that they brandished, and in their smiles of disdain—for, to them, any adversary was merely the simulacrum of an enemy. For the last time, Agustin compared Juanito with Luis, searching for a ray of hope in their dissimilarity. Luis had set off for Belchite with an affected swaggering ease designed to impress the other men in his barrack room. Juanito was armour-clad with enthusiasm . . .

An absurd prayer trembled on Agustin's lips: 'God, you took Luis from me, but leave me Juanito. Luis was my accomplice: you punished me through him. He lies buried in the soil of Belchite, beneath the ashes and brimstone that have rained down on Sodom since time began.'

But Agustin did not believe in a God whom you could turn to. The need to pray was merely a relic of primitive mentality.

'I'm not mad,' he burst out. 'I weigh causes and effects. Perhaps there are times when you have to be a bit mad to succeed . . . Oh, Juanito! Today I wish that, like you, I had been born in Valencia.'

The small craft were ready to sail, hidden in the creeks. Like the bare and shivering men lined up on the bank at regular intervals, the countryside was holding its breath in the darkness. The Ebro was lapping gently over the pebbles, like a child at play. The signal was no more than a whisper passed from lip to lip.

Juanito was the first to step into the water. It felt warm. So that they should be freer of movement, the dozen volunteers wore no clothing except for a belt from which a couple of grenades were strung. At the mouth of the river, the current was strong. Juanito made a few easy strokes, then he had to struggle against this sly force which was trying to carry him back to the bank. This contest between a young naked body and the river was like an embrace, one that Juanito was obliged to thwart. In midstream, some tree-stumps were causing the water to eddy. Juanito advanced cautiously. He used his agility to break free of these obstacles which clung to his legs, wrapped themselves round his belly and chest and enfolded him closely. From head to foot, he felt wonderfully alive to this watery caress which at once threatened and protected him. He was not afraid. To the strategists, the offensive was a gamble. To Juanito it was a wager between himself and his luck. It was not to the enemy lurking behind the trees on the other bank, but to himself that he was flinging down this challenge, and in his own eyes that he was taking it up. In a single trial of strength he was running the risks that in other lives are spread over years. For the first and perhaps the last time, Juanito was measuring swords with his destiny. He was artlessly happy at being naked and alone for this initiation, more secret than that of love, more complete than that of death. He had always been fascinated by cards, not so much by the stake itself as by the thought of losing everything or winning everything in a single moment. Every silent stroke he made was a victory for mind and body. No night of love would ever match this night spent alone. He wondered whether the others were experiencing this same delight which, far from stemming from peaceful submission, sprang from an amazing concentration of all his faculties. Never would his muscles respond more perfectly, never would his senses achieve a higher pitch of alertness. In the middle of the river he had the impression that he could hear the rustle of every leaf on the bank, the murmur of every reed brushed by the current. To avoid cramp, he adopted a regular rhythm. The thrust of the river grew fiercer on his hardened thighs and arms. Maintaining the even measure of his strokes, he pricked up his ears. Had his companions followed him, or had the current already carried them downstream? I shan't even know what to call out to them, he thought. Most of them were French, and in the afternoon they had vainly tried to swap impressions with a mixture of mime and a handful of Spanish words. But on their lips those words were unintelligible, and the miming had only added to the confusion. It had all ended in roars of laughter. The French had offered round harsh-tasting cigarettes, the Spanish a red wine from the Priorato district, which is never quite free of dregs. Back there on the bank, despite the mood of expectancy, all the volunteers had been gay; they had all sat picturing this midnight crossing of the Ebro being written up by dumbfounded journalists and glowered over, in Franco's headquarters, by officers whose eyes were puffy with sleep and rage.

The strength of the Ebro declined rapidly in midstream. Juanito began to swim at speed again.

It's just like being in a swimming pool. The bank isn't far away. He felt for the bottom with his toes, but did not encounter it. The darkness obscured everything from which he might have taken his bearings. Yet, to judge from the tiredness that had accumulated in his forearms, he had been swimming for a long time. He tested the depth again, and his foot touched some large pebbles. He stood up. It had been as simple as that. He had crossed the Ebro, but behind the reeds rifles might already be trained upon him and his companions. Death did not alarm him. It was merely a rendezvous with a stranger. Out of a sense of caution he advanced slightly stooped, but when he felt a mixture of sand and grass under his feet he straightened up. Close behind him he heard bare feet splashing about in shallow water.

'Juanito! We've made it!'

Despite the darkness of the shelter of a clump of trees chosen as a rallying point several days before, Juanito could visualize Esteban, with his bright eyes, bearded chin and bantering smile.

He repeated with the same proud modesty: 'Yes, we've made it.' Other figures approached. Naked and still dripping from this strange baptism, the Frenchmen were smiling. This smile of victory was the password between these men who had escaped death.

'What about the others?' whispered Juanito.

Esteban did not answer. A faint, regular sound carried to them. The first boat, towing the cable that would connect the pontoons, had just touched the bank. Juanito and his companions sprang forward. They had rehearsed the job so often that as they twined the cord round the stoutest of the tree-trunks they felt as though they were still only practising. The planks followed on other boats. Juanito and his companions did not have time to rejoice or wonder how the offensive would turn out. The black boats moved back and forth across the dully shining river. Juanito was down on his knees, helping the first of the pontoon builders to secure further cables. He stood up. In the gloom, an invisible craftsman was nimbly gliding the boats to and fro, like dark shuttles on a loom, at ever-increasing speed. The men were jumping down on to the beach and disappearing into the thickets. The supporting waves had to advance very quickly to widen the bridgehead. The element of surprise had to be exploited before sunrise. No resistance was being encountered. This is too good to last, thought Juanito. Darkness was on the side of the Republicans; it was their accomplice. The silence of the early moments of the landing was giving way to an endless cracking of twigs and branches. The troops were advancing through the undergrowth. The whole battalion had crossed the Ebro, but had the operation been successful farther up or down the river? Into Juanito's head came scraps of Agustin's explanations, recalled in the older man's tones: 'The crossings in the north and south are a single manœuvre. With this pincer movement we shall demolish all Franco's defences. Then the whole army will be able to pour through in the centre.'

A mysterious tremor began to run through the earth. Esteban threw himself flat on the ground. He was capable of interpreting all the sounds of war. He could tell the calibre of a shell from the way it burst and recognize a low-flying aircraft by the roar of its engine. He said: 'It's Franco's tanks. They're at the canal.' The French volunteers were crowding round Esteban and Juanito. They knew enough about the operation to realize what was happening. In their advance, the Republicans had to cross a canal that ran almost parallel to the Ebro. It was there that battle was already being joined. Day was breaking. Juanito turned towards the river. Building was proceeding apace: the piers were about to be linked up. It was Juanito's task to defend the troops erecting the flimsy pontoon bridge which would enable the guns and the heavy equipment and the lorryloads of men and ammunition to surge forward. The pontoneers were working with clenched teeth, without seeing what was going on around them; their every movement was calculated to make the least possible noise, to expend the least possible energy. They are working like insects, thought Juanito. The object of their toil would have collapsed, had these men looked up. Despite the cool of dawn, sweat was streaming down the carpenters' bodies. They were silently handing round a water-bottle and taking long swigs at the clear liquid. As they hurriedly nailed the uprights into position, they listened for the staccato chatter of the machine-guns which were preventing the Republicans from crossing the canal. In this race against time, everything counted: the insertion of a bolt, the fitting of a metal component. Floating rafts would bear the weight of the girders which teams of eight men had difficulty in shifting and which they dropped in the appropriate position with a slightly hoarse groan.

As the sun dispersed the shades of night with its sudden piercing shafts, savage flashes raced across the sky. Juanito and his companions were breathless with impatience. A few hundred yards away, behind a curtain of trees, a furious battle was raging in which they were not allowed to participate. Their mission was to defend the bridge. Up on the scaffolding a tall thin officer was waving his arms about. He was using his hands to test the strength of every part. His pathetic and comic gestures seemed to accelerate the work of construction, then slow it down. Standing alone in the midst of the kneeling pontoneers, clambering up and down the girders, he was weaving about like an orchestral conductor. And for his rostrum he had the frail and slender bridge which already connected the two banks. With the derisive spirit of all Valencians, Juanito could not help laughing at him, even while admiring him.

On the other side of the bridge, reinforcements were waiting —lorries, fresh units, brand-new guns. As soon as the plank-work on the bridge could stand the weight, a second river, above the Ebro, would convey the living might of the Republican army. The dull thud of mortars, the crisp chatter of machine-gun fire, were getting nearer. Esteban eyed Juanito uneasily. On the canal, the troops of the 14th International Brigade were counter-attacking. Shells were exploding all over the place. Between reports, Esteban was following the rumble of the tanks advancing on their caterpillars. Huge rents were appearing in the sky, some of them whitish, others streaked with red flashes. The framework of the bridge was already bestriding the river, while the Italian planes were machine-gunning the bank, almost shaving the ground. How could the bridge possibly survive daylight air-raids? Like a tightrope-walker, the officer was performing a perilous feat of balance above the Ebro. On either side of the river, the pontoneers were working with feverish haste within the flimsy shelter of the piers. The coming and going of the boats continued rapidly in the water, where the first reflections of the clear sky were now appearing. Machine-gunned, the troops were toppling into the river and the survivors swimming to the nearest bank. It was a midsummer morning, without a breath of wind or a cloud in the sky: the first of the mornings that Juanito was to live through on the other bank. A boat brought over the kit left behind by the volunteers: Juanito and his companions put aboard some wounded who had been dumped on the bank; then they got dressed. The men were once more encumbered by their sticky shirts and shiny trousers and tough leather boots; it seemed a particular hardship to have to put them on again after these hours in which their bodies had been wrapped only in night's warm caress. They left the belongings and equipment of the other volunteers stacked in a pile.

'They must be hiding stark naked under the trees.'

Juanito did not have time to smile at the thought of these heroes in search of their clothes. The Nationalist artillery had found its range. Shells were raining down within a few yards of Juanito and the pontoneers, showering them with earth and torn-off branches.

'German guns,' said Esteban.

The officer who had been prancing about in the middle of the bridge see-sawed above the river and disappeared with a splash. Juanito wanted to hurry to his rescue. Esteban held him back. The Italian planes had spotted the bridge; the mortars and heavy guns concentrated near the canal were scouring the bank. Some of the projectiles were making direct hits on the metal girders, which groaned under their impact.

The coming and going of boats was suspended. One of them went down. As he fell into the water, a man screamed at the top of his voice. I know that voice, thought Juanito. On makeshift rafts, other soldiers were rowing furiously to get out of the machine-guns' line of fire. Juanito turned to Esteban: 'We must dig a trench.'

Within minutes their pickaxes had burst the pebbly crust of the soil. Water was oozing into the sandy earth. They were below the level of the river. With the earth that they had dug out they built a parapet which would enable them to stand upright without danger of being hit by bullets. Reassured by this paltry cover, they looked out over the top. Another officer was striding about on the bridge. Less gawky than his predecessor, he seemed to rely on crisp orders rather than mime. But suddenly the sky was ablaze, all the way from one bank of the river to the other. Juanito's companions flung themselves into the barely completed trench, blinded and deafened. Juanito was the first to glance out. The bridge had vanished. All that was left was some twisted girders jutting out of the water. The Ebro was sweeping away, pell-mell, both the rafts—whose connecting cable had broken—and the bodies of the pontoneers. From the ruins of the pier on the bank, Juanito and Esteban dragged out a number of wounded. A boat came for them, then a man arrived with orders for Juanito and his team to join up with the International Brigades fighting near the canal.

Of this day spent on a few square feet of soil swept by machine-gun fire, Juanito was to retain, not memories so much as sensations that slowly but surely invaded his consciousness: the taste of earth and blood in his mouth, a torturing thirst combined with a mental picture of the cold clear water of the river sweeping along a few hundred yards away.

With Esteban, he had crept into one of the trenches dug

during the night by the first arrivals. From these precarious shelters successive counter-attacks had been launched, as a result of which the approaches to the canal were strewn with bodies. Next to Juanito, a gunner was intently at work on his machine-gun. The weapon was clogged with reddish earth, but the man was patiently taking it to bits and putting it together again, carefully laying the components on the earth ledge inside the trench. He toiled with wrinkled brow but without a hint of panic, like a craftsman faced with the prospect of a long series of peaceful hours at his bench. Esteban and Juanito exchanged pitying glances. Anyone would have taken him for a clockmaker performing an intricate repair. Within a few yards of the trench, the bodies of the gunners killed in the course of the last attack lay sprawled full-length. The man explained that he had had a hell of a job saving his gun. He was so busy getting it back into working order that it did not occur to him that it was of no further use. There would be no more counter-attacks. Juanito's instructions were clear. Now that the pontoon bridge had been destroyed, there was no question of crossing the canal; far from it—sheltered by the narrow waterway, they were to hold out for a few hours so as to immobilize the enemy positions. A delaying action. Juanito recalled what Agustin had said. The crossing of the Ebro in the north and south was a diversionary move.

The bodies lay fermenting in the sun. Juanito seemed to catch a whiff of putrefaction. There was no hope of reinforcement. It was impossible even to evacuate the wounded, and an emergency dressing station had been set up on the riverbank, near the spot where Juanito and his companions had landed. A medical orderly came to the trench to collect a casualty. He told Juanito that the enemy across the canal were the Ifni Rifle Regiment. They were a much-feared unit. The diversion had been a success. Through the haze of stupor resulting from the heat and his tiredness, through the agony of his thirst, through the fear that expressed itself in a tightening of the bowels whenever a shell landed near the trench—or on it, so it seemed—Juanito clutched at this word: diversion. Esteban was staring at him in silence. The earth was heaving as though it were about to cave in on them. If I have to die, why should it be today, here and with Esteban? Juanito wondered. He needed to live. When he had been crawling his way to the trench, he had been fully aware of his whole body, from the roots of his hair to the soles of his feet. Every cell, every muscle of that body had contracted to escape annihilation. A diversion. Perhaps the offensive, bogged down at Campredo by concentrated artillery and by the fire of the Ifni Rifle Regiment, was progressing with infallible sureness in other directions? This thought, which at other times would have gone to Juanito's head, left him cold at that moment. A diversion . . . The man with the machine-gun was examining his weapon. He was unaware of being a mere unit in the total of forces already sacrificed. A diversion: that meant the loss of a great many troops, a great many machine-guns. In an H.Q. office, a specialist had worked it out mathematically. Other officers had discussed the efficacy of such a manœuvre. They had even assessed, to the nearest figure, the cost of its success; they had weighed its strategic value, its effect on public opinion. This operation, put into effect to ensure the stability of the rest of the line, had seemed necessary in the interests of bolstering the morale of those who were not taking part in this diversion . . .

What am I doing here? Juanito kept asking himself, with a mixture of anger, despair and shame. True, I'm a Republican, but of what possible use can my death be to the Republic? And on the other side of the canal there may well be a man born in Caceres or Burgos performing the self-same movements as me and asking himself the self-same questions. If a bullet has his name written on it, what does that prove—that he was less lucky than me?

The shells were raining down at briefer and briefer intervals. Esteban whispered: 'If they cross the canal now, we've had it.' He must have been even more afraid than Juanito. When a shell whistled over the trench, he no longer even drew his body tightly together in an instinctive attempt to offer death a smaller target. His breathing was getting louder. He was panting slightly, standing as close as he could to Juanito. What can I do for him?

wondered Juanito. He laid his head on Esteban's shoulder, as though he were tired. Esteban did not stir. He seemed comforted. His breathing became more even. He had fallen asleep from exhaustion.

We're like a litter of kittens huddling together in their mother's basket, thought Juanito.

The rate of fire was falling off again. The soldiers remained curled up in sleep, mingling in this warmth which was preserving them from death. 'This thirst is too much for me,' Juanito said, as though to himself. The gunner broke off from his labours, with a reproachful expression, to hand him his water-bottle. Juanito eased himself from Esteban's grip to close his lips on the cold metal rim. The liquid had a rusty flavour in his mouth. 'It's wine!' he said. Now his parched palate recognized the heavy juice that swells the grapes of the Priorato district. This was not a mouthful of coolness but an infusion of life. This wine was strength, courage, passion and coolness all rolled into one.

'I've never drunk such a wine,' said Juanito, handing the flask back to his neighbour. The man shrugged. He was checking the feed of his machine-gun.

Juanito could feel this fierce, harsh caress spreading through his whole blood-stream. He had not had anything to eat since the previous day, and a slightly drunken feeling came over him. It was as though he had consumed a whole year's grape harvest, countless other mellow and fruity wines, redolent of other summers, other autumns. The heat was less severe now. At lengthy intervals the Republican artillery would open up, but the shells had only one aim: to discourage a possible attack by the 'Moros'. Esteban was staring straight ahead of him. He waved aside the flask when Juanito handed it to him. The man with the machine-gun had abandoned his weapon. He looked terribly at a loss for something to do. Perhaps he was sensing that the offensive had failed. He would have liked to drag his fellow-gunners back into the trench, but they lay a considerable distance away. Esteban shrugged. 'What's the point of doing that?' he asked. 'They've been dead since this morning . . .'

The man explained that the Moros mutilated corpses in the

most hideous manner. He wanted to bury his mates to prevent their bodies from being defiled. Esteban and Juanito conferred with their eyes.

'Stop thinking about them,' said Juanito. 'As soon as it's dark our orders are to get back to the other side of the Ebro any way we can . . .'

The three of them waited in silence for the dusk to thicken. Esteban was the first to leave the trench. Juanito followed. They picked their way slowly. The Republican artillery was firing off a few rounds, as though nothing special were happening, to prevent the Nationalists from crossing the canal and to keep up a pretence of resistance. It took the best part of an hour to cover the few hundred yards that lay between the battlefield and the bank of the river. They crawled along, with nothing to protect them, occasionally making a detour to avoid a body. Juanito would reach out and give this sleeping comrade a gentle shake. Once, a wounded man groaned. Juanito flattened himself beside this body which still had some warmth in it and pressed his mouth to the stranger's ear: 'Make an effort, man, follow us!' Perhaps there would be a boat that they could load the wounded on to, but the man gestured briefly and fell flat on his face again. Esteban, growing alarmed, was calling Juanito's name in a whisper. The man with the machine-gun had vanished as soon as they left the trench. He must have gone back to bury his mates.

'He's nuts!' said Esteban, by way of farewell.

They crawled on, and never had Juanito's will to live been more active or more intensely felt. On the edge of the bank they spotted the pile of weapons and equipment which still marked the spot where they had landed. Without a word, they tore off their clothes. They were as naked as when they had emerged from the Ebro the day before. Other ghostly figures loomed out of the reeds: they were unsteady on their feet, as though they had forgotten the upright walk of living human beings. This procession of naked men reminded Juanito of those grimy canvases in churches which show Christ being baptized while other men, in the background, are hurriedly pulling off their garments. These phantoms slipping about on the bank formed a strange cortège.

Juanito glanced up at the sky. Luckily, the moon was hidden behind thick clouds. The night was so hot that tunics, belts and cartridge-pouches would have weighed the men down like suits of armour.

On the right, the outlines of the ruined bridge emerged ominously. Esteban and Juanito clung to the girders to conserve their strength. Strips of khaki material still adhered to the framework. The two men let go their hold of this dangerous support. They swam cautiously, like a pair of divers picking their way round a mysterious wreck. As he exerted his muscles, Juanito took stock of what he supposed was a failure. But every touch of vegetation on his legs, every piece of driftwood which his hands knocked out of the way, together with the resistant pressure of the water on his trunk, filled him with the stunning sensation of surviving a disaster.

On the other bank they splashed about among the reeds and the slippery pebbles again. Behind them, a number of other survivors materialized, spluttering, whispering, even daring to laugh. Juanito and Esteban, exhausted from their exertions, came upon the dressing station behind a curtain of trees. They asked for some blankets, for they were shivering with cold.

The medical orderly handed them a cup of steaming hot coffee. He had laid some unneeded stretchers on the ground, to serve as beds. These naked men, coming to life one by one and emerging shyly from the shadows, did not seem to surprise him. While they drank, he casually informed them that the offensive was proceeding according to plan. At Mequinenza, as at Campredo, the units concentrated on the flank had succeeded in crossing the river and gaining a footing on the other bank. In the centre, the Nationalist front had caved in. There was no telling how far the Republican troops had got. Perhaps they had already exceeded all their objectives. There was something fabulous, something altogether immeasurable, about this success. It wasn't just carefully selected units of the Republican army that were pouring through this breach towards Gandesa. It was the hope that had suddenly been restored to Juanito and his companion. They stood gazing at one another with dazzled expressions on their faces. Esteban kept saying, as though it were himself whom he was trying to convince: 'You see, Juanito . . . You see . . .' Juanito could find no words to describe this victory which had at first confronted them in the guise of defeat. He simply repeated some of the names and figures that were the testimony of this miracle. More than five thousand prisoners had been taken in the course of this lightning advance. Flix, Asco, Fatarella, Mora del Ebro, Gandesa: the Republican units had invested or captured these villages. In Barcelona and Valencia and Madrid, these syllables were on everybody's lips and were being intoned as though they were an act of grace.

New arrivals were wresting themselves from the shadows, with water streaming down their naked bodies. Like dead men still trailing their winding sheets, they were drying themselves with bits of rag. The survivors of the Commune de Paris Battalion promptly gave up counting one another and started firing a host of questions at the orderly.

'Put some clothes on!' he answered, pointing to a pile of old uniforms and torn shirts, a rag-and-bone-man's delight from which they all had to outfit themselves as best they could. He appeared to be repeating an official communiqué but, despite the tired look on his face, his words invested him with a fantastic air of adventure. The exploits of the Romancero paled before these deeds. The main body had crossed the Ebro at Asco. Now the Republican army was fanning out towards Fatarella in the north and Mora del Ebro in the south. In the centre, the vanguard had reached Gandesa, more than twenty miles from the starting-point.

These words, which the orderly repeated without embellishment of any kind, seemed to hold a magic power. Like spectres obeying a sorcerer's summons, other soldiers appeared. Despite the coming of night, despite the crossing of the river, they still had in their ears the hellish roar of artillery and mortars, and in their mouths the taste of earth, and in their nostrils the smell of death and excrement and urine. Exhausted from the tension to which they had been subjected, they groped about as though they were learning to walk again. Many of them did not even attempt to dress. When they were handed the mug of hot coffee, they burnt their fingers trying to drink from it and passed it on to a neighbour. When they had crossed the river the night before, the majority of them had experienced, not fear, but a kind of obscure apprehension. That crossing had been an initiation, a mysterious rite which had promised to bring about a metamorphosis within them. On the far bank they had found only the ordinary horror of the battlefield, the counter-attacks in which their battalion had lost most of its men, the bitter satisfaction of keeping several enemy battalions at bay. As they listened to the medical orderly, they were finding out, with the same sense of dazzlement, the same gratitude as Juanito, that together with the whole Republican army they had crossed the mysterious frontier which divides defeat from victory. In their weariness and their superstitious joy, they were staring—as though he were an apparition, as though he too were part of the miracle—at this medical student in his dirty overall who was reciting, without excitement or weariness, the same familiar story interspersed with unheeded words of advice.

'You could lie down if you wanted to. No? Some of the stretchers are as soft as mattresses. Try them!'

But all these half-clad men were clustering round him like those who, on the banks of the Jordan, sought baptism at the hands of John the Baptist. An acetylene lamp perched on a medicine chest gave a savage light to the orderly's face, and to his hands when he refilled the saucepan to brew some more coffee on the spirit-stove.

The ghosts who ventured into this bright light reacquired the substance of living creatures. Juanito found himself wondering what was dream and what reality. Would he wake up in the midst of victory in a few hours' time? Wasn't this man—with his subdued voice and his ready laughter when an over-eager soldier burnt himself on the tin mug—going to vanish like a sorcerer, together with his spell? Yet, in the event, all estimates and prophecies had been exceeded: sixty thousand men had crossed the Ebro in a single night.

The Crossing of the Ebro

25

WAKING EARLY NEXT MORNING, after a few hours of confused dreams, Juanito and his companions hurried off to join the 11th Spanish Division. The dawn clouds were dispersing and giving place to a radiant July sky. Everything seemed to augur wonderfully well.

They made their way briskly up the left bank of the Ebro. There was nothing to encumber their progress. A few of the men still had rifles or some grenades. The majority looked like scantily-dressed tramps. They came to Benisamet: the area was in the hands of the Republicans. Small isolated detachments were occupying the villages from which two battalions of Moroccans had been driven out. The main body of the division had proceeded on its way to Mora del Ebro, where it was to relieve the International Brigade. At every halt they made, fantastic news would burst like a bomb in the midst of the band of young soldiers. They proudly totted up their booty: the thousands of prisoners, the whole batteries of artillery, the ammunition depots and the bridge-building materials which would now enable the Republican army to cross the Ebro at an incredible rate.

Esteban, who normally had little to say for himself, was now talking and laughing as though he were drunk.

'Juanito,' he asked, 'do you suppose we'll ever catch up with our unit?'

Juanito said nothing; by remaining silent, he was better able to enjoy this reversal of fortunes.

At Mora del Ebro, they crossed the river with the first armour and the light artillery. In the cool light of this summer morning, the men were amazed to find the same hawthorn bushes and gorse, the same olive trees rustling at the slightest breeze, as on the other bank. The white and red farmhouses were surrounded by vines and almond trees. They passed through the first villages. Supporting walls held the cultivated land in check, but the gardens had been left to run wild for months past. Hidden away in the fleecy foliage of the olive trees was the shiny black fruit that the peasants had not had time to pick. In the fields, the big square reservoirs from which the water was piped were empty and cracked from the heat. Juanito, who was used to seeing water race briskly along the irrigation canals, stared disdainfully at these tubs standing apparently forgotten in the middle of the fields.

The soldiers passed through some vineyards. Beneath the bronze-green leaves, the wasps had left a few dead clusters which the men shared out among themselves as though they had unearthed a treasure. On the horizon, a faint line of hazy blue hills lay steaming under the scorching sun. A voice inquired after Fernando. Another replied that he was in Franco's headquarters by now, and Juanito roared with laughter. Other detachments were joining up with them. The whole offensive was running smoothly and with perfect synchronization.

A hand fell on Juanito's shoulder: it was Agustin. They strode on, as amazed at seeing one another again as if they were meeting in another world.

'I thought you were at the bottom of the Ebro,' said Juanito, to hide his pleasure. He had never before felt such warmth of friendship for Agustin.

'Providence picked the wrong man. I crossed the Ebro in a barge, with boots and belts all round me, like a warehouseman. As I stepped ingloriously ashore, your cousin's body was being laid out, blue all over and puffed up like a balloon . . .'

'Fernando!' gasped Juanito.

In the distance there was a rumble of artillery. Nationalist units were grimly defending the villages spread in a protective arc round Gandesa, but the offensive was progressing with machine-like regularity. The unexpectedness of the attack was paralysing all Franco's communications within the Ebro loop. In vain did he recall his air squadrons from the Levante to destroy the bridges. From north and east and west, the Republicans were converging: it was the roads and communication centres round Gandesa that they were after, not a particular wood or a particular farmhouse. In the north, too, they were endeavouring to cut the road to Fayon, so as to prevent Franco from summoning his crack units to the rescue. Already he had flung two army corps into the battle: the Banderas of the Tercio and the Tabors of the Regulares. In an attempt to withstand the speed with which the taste of victory had invested the Republican onslaught, Franco's troops were clinging like grim death to the mountainous sierras of Fatarella and Pecha and La Picosa.

Despite the glare, Juanito was staring up at the ash-grey peaks and reddish cliffs which the Republicans were skirting. The Nationalists must be hiding out in those lofty redoubts, like guerrillas. Occasionally, making use of a favourable position, they would engage in a rearguard skirmish. But they would very quickly break off the encounter in the face of this irresistible tide which swept wave by wave over the isolated farms, the rudely awakened villages.

Agustin, whose mission was to set up a forward command post, was partaking to the full of the exhilaration prompted by this lightning offensive.

'Just think of the war correspondents in Madrid and Burgos . . . They're rubbing their eyes as they read last night's communiqués. They are turning on their radios to grieve over our misfortunes. They are ready to go back to sleep on hearing confirmation of a fresh disaster . . . But, instead of talking about a few hundred yards gained or lost, a voice is telling them that chessboard, table and opponent have all been sent flying! Where is the front? Nobody knows, not even we who are determining it . . .'

Agustin was beside himself with joy. Marching straight into the sun like this was going to his head like neat spirits.

'Juanito, I'm drunk without having touched a drop of brandy all night long. Just imagine the non-intervention extortionists, the shady dealers in human cattle, struck all of a heap by this daring feat, quaking in their boots at the thought of having backed the loser. I can see them now, like the heirs in a play: they imagine that the moment has come for them to share out the spoils, when hey presto! the old uncle recovers!'

A platoon joined them. Juanito recognized Fernando's comrades. Their boat had capsized in midstream the day before. One of them had heard a scream. Had it been Fernando? On that apocalyptic night, one mother had been deprived of her son forever . . . The men lowered their voices: who would have thought that Fernando, with his shiny face and skinny body and the way he moved, typical of a man who had always been cooped up in a shop, would be one of the first to die in the offensive, one of those victims whom time would transform into a hero?

'I'm making for Gandesa,' said Agustin. 'It's the best position for an H.Q., right in the centre of the loop.'

Juanito stared unseeingly ahead.

'Thinking about Fernando?'

Juanito was pondering. Never had he felt so closely wedded to another man's destiny. Why couldn't people even mention Fernando's name without contempt or pity? Had he lived, they would all have gone on laughing at his amiability, at his simple remarks, at his mind, which was as awkward and constrained as his body. Yet he had lived through that unprecedented moment: he had shared the final bid of the Spanish Republic. While the water had whistled in his ears, the convulsion of a whole people had raced in his blood. For the first time in his life Fernando had been a doer, and not just a watcher. He had stopped submitting to men and events. He who had never chosen anything—neither his work nor his pleasure—had chosen this moment of pride and wild passion, in which he had bartered his meagre share of happiness for the mythical destiny of a conqueror.

But among the fighting men there existed that communion of the living and the dead of which the Church speaks. Like a lesser saint in a disused side-chapel, Fernando too would work miracles for his companions.

'Don't laugh at him, Agustin. He gave his life so that the offensive might succeed.'

The Virgin of the Forsaken must have been napping

at the time, thought Agustin. But he kept the joke to himself.

'Why not? The gods have always loved human sacrifices.'

A half-demolished steeple proclaimed the village where Juanito and his men were to make camp.

A demolished balcony barred the way into the village hall. Goats had strayed through the gaping doorway of the church and were chewing the grass that was already springing up among the debris. The undamaged well marked the centre of the village. Juanito jangled the chain. Water slopped out of the bucket as it swayed against the side. Esteban held the bucket still while Juanito drank. Images were reflected in the glistening water: the white houses with their wooden pillars forming a gallery round the square, and that large fragment of July sky like a length of dazzling silk in the hands of a dealer. What is more beautiful than a July morning? thought Juanito as he wiped his mouth. What is more peaceful than a village square on a day of victory? A small boy shooed the goats out of the church, and then, surrounded by his herd, came over to question the soldiers.

'How far have the Republicans got?'

Soon a whole circle had formed round them: shy women anxious for news, old men with shining eyes. A tall dark girl strolled diffidently towards them. The ring of onlookers made way for her: it was Encarnacion, the mayor's daughter-in-law. Her husband and his father had been taken as hostages. Encarnacion listened with indifference as her own story was whispered by one of the old women. She had attacked the Nationalist soldiers tooth and nail when they had called to arrest her husband. If only all women were to defend their sons and brothers and husbands like that, said the old woman, there would be no war. Wars break out when womenfolk allow their menfolk to kill one another. Encarnacion remained grave and withdrawn. How could she possibly recognize herself in this heroine?

'Her father-in-law was the best-looking man in the village,' the old woman persisted. 'In the old days, he lived in Madrid.' Encarnacion bore out this statement with a flutter of her eyelashes. It was all quite true. In her youth she had spent a few weeks holidaying in these parts. She had got engaged here. When Enrico was taken ill, the doctors had insisted on their leaving Madrid. And the house in the Avenida de la Castellana had seemed dreary to Pablo. He had come down and joined the young couple in this country house where he had always spent the summer. Pablo was nearly fifty. He had completely fallen in love with this village, of which he was mayor. He would crack jokes about his mission of enlightenment. The school and the co-operative, the library, the scientific breeding-farm, the model dairy: these became his toys. 'I've been reading too much Tolstoy,' he used to say. But this philanthropy was the by-product of a fiercer and more hidden inclination, of an uncontrollable whim that ruled him body and soul.

Encarnacion questioned herself, as she had questioned herself day after day in the silent and empty house. Had not Enrico guessed everything? What a lot an invalid can conceal behind his detachment. His constant tiredness allowed him to evade questioning, and when he smiled he seemed to be apologizing for his doggedness in staying alive.

Encarnacion was scrutinizing the young officer. He was good-looking, this boy, and there was an innocent boldness about him. He was gazing at Encarnacion as though she were the prize for victory.

The old woman was still enumerating the blessings that Pablo had heaped on the district: the maternity home, the new cinema, the fruit-tree nurseries. Encarnacion checked a smile: these ambitious and extravagant acts of benevolence had enabled Pablo to resist temptation. The old woman turned to Encarnacion. Nobody would dare to question the mayor's generosity, and even in Madrid people talked about this model village in the Priorato district.

'Yes,' said Encarnacion, 'some praised him, others attacked him, but here everyone loved him.' She broke off abruptly, as though even the most commonplace words might give her away. Wasn't everything that Pablo had done simply an alibi to mislead himself and others?

It was as though the old woman were delivering an address over his deathbed. Pablo had all the shining merits, all the virtues perceived in retrospect, that go to make up an epitaph: he was handsome and generous, as wise as a man of mature years and as plucky as a youth. Swinging round to face Juanito, who seemed to be in charge of the detachment, Encarnacion interrupted this funeral oration.

'In our house,' she said, 'there is room for up to twenty men.'

She was no longer thinking of her husband or of her father-in-law. On this peaceful and radiant morning, in the course of which men would go to their death, she felt a child again. In this unknown face, Juanito was rediscovering the *huerta* under the midsummer sky, the ice-cold water in the garden well, the soil already hot from the sun . . .

Agustin was talking to him: Good-bye. And keep your men away from the local wines till victory is won!'

The onlookers fastened their eyes on to this puny figure in the crumpled uniform and suddenly spotted the captain's insignia on his sleeve. A note of triumph blazed through the derision in his voice:

'Spain salutes the sons of the Cid!'

His mock-heroic tone could not fool his simple-hearted audience. In these presumptuous words, the Republic was celebrating its revenge. The soldiers, rather pale from their sleepless night, straightened their backs as though for inspection.

Juanito closed his eyes for a moment. The exhaustion he felt was due to this game of hide-and-seek with destiny. A great cry of rapture went up, delivered with all the strength in their lungs, and through these hoarse voices the besieged cities of Madrid and Barcelona and Valencia were already acclaiming their liberators.

26

IN A HARBOUR, it takes only a sudden silence in the middle of the day, only the poising of the hammer over the anvil, for the sea's heavy breathing to emerge and for its low-pitched song to drown the noise of human industry and enjoyment. Similarly, on this first day of the offensive, Juanito would cock his ear at moments. 'What's on your mind?' his companions asked. They supposed that he was worrying about a surprise attack, the rat-tat-tat of bullets on a street-corner in the deserted village, or the grenade that would explode when they paused for rest and when weariness abolished all thought of danger. Juanito was listening in the depths of his soul, in the innermost fibres of his body, to the blurred and endless rumble of victory. It seemed to him that other voices were taking up this act of grace, carrying it on and on to the ends of the earth . . . Whenever a tumbledown farm-house was rid of the last of its Nationalist defenders, Spain was shaking with impatience. Soon, thought Juanito, there will be no war. The only solution was to win. There would be no hangings, as there had been in the days of the French. The holy statues and the priests would return to the churches. Juanito would go back to the *huerta*. He pictured the sodden fields in the middle of spring. The horses were drawing the plough. Their hooves were sinking deep into the furrows. Perched up on the plough, the driver looked as though he was gliding over a lake of gold or silver, depending on what time of day it was. There was nothing on earth more beautiful than this tilling of the fertile soil, than this magnificent mud, which made it seem that God had yet to separate the elements, to distinguish between sunlight and shade. The peasant was cutting into the clay to add seed to the water.

The detachment would chance upon a derelict vineyard,

or a hamlet reduced to a few sections of wall which the war had rent capriciously, like an earthquake, sparing a tottering porch or an old tower with an all but human stoop, only to pulverize a proud, brand-new village hall or a stately house adorned with gleaming *azulejos*.[1] Juanito's mind was carried back to the night they had embarked at Barcelonnetta, he saw those balconies hanging in mid-air, those stage props. But it was essential to infiltrate quickly through the arid chains of hills that constituted Franco's defences. The young soldiers were advancing as though this was harvest-time: they were moving hurriedly, as though to gather one last cartful before nightfall. Juanito pointed out a spur of reddish clay on their right, over towards Alcanitz—Franco's headquarters . . . Even the least bold of them thought longingly of a surprise attack. Juanito strove to calm their impatience. But the wild-eyed fanatics and the timid were at one in their serene confidence that this victory would put an end to the party rivalries in Barcelona and Madrid. Juanito sighed. Who would ever rid the Republic of the divisions between anarchists and communists, of the struggles between syndicalists and liberals?

Hoots of joy broke in upon Juanito's reflections: a patrol had discovered a shedful of arms and ammunition. Juanito pushed open the creaking door which in the old days had closed on the rusty old ploughs, the primitive scythes, the reaping-machines with their enormous cutters. He drew up sharp. The sight took his breath away: neatly aligned on the shelves were stacks of cartridge belts and boxes crammed with bullets. In the corners stood dense clusters of rifles. Grenades were heaped in pyramids at even intervals. Juanito eyed this windfall like a fisherman or a member of a shoot examining his haul. It would be dangerous to move the grenades, he thought, and they had best keep the machine-gun under cover for the time being. He handed out the rifles made in Germany, the first-aid packs originally intended for Abyssinia. All this booty roused childish longings in these destitute warriors. It occurred to Juanito that what could not be used immediately must be hidden away. Ammunition must be expended sparingly, like lives.

[1]Sevillian tiles, Moorish in style, famous for reflecting the play of light.

But, exhilarated by their first success, these victors greedily absorbed the news bulletin which they picked up on a skeleton radio. As soon as the instrument began to belch forth predictions, uncorroborated figures and proclamations, they gathered round in a circle. Felix, who had worked in an electrical shop in Barcelona, persuaded the god to speak and then interpreted the oracle. Juanito loved him because he shared his unshakable faith in victory.

The voice broke off. Felix expressed the opinion that Franco could not last much longer. His bright eyes found the same assurance written on Juanito's face. The men round about them filled out these fragmentary communiqués with their own wild hopes; they mingled solid news and invention, already shaping the legend that would later surround the offensive. The loudspeaker claimed that Russia was on the point of intervening in the war. A vast fleet was about to come steaming down the Mediterranean. This armada would soon be at Cadiz and Barcelona, at Valencia and Almeria. How were the men to distinguish between the unsettled dust of actual achievement and this gold-dust which was suddenly glittering before their eyes? The success of the offensive would galvanize the Republic's wavering friends into action . . .

Juanito dared not disillusion them. Figures and calculations went by the board; everyone round about him believed only in prophecies and miracles.

Visitors were few and far between. Two planes had to land because they were out of fuel. It was evening. The crew shared the lentils and stale bread which were Juanito's usual fare, but wine flowed plentifully. Even in the smallest farmhouse, there were bottles thick with dust and spiders' webs hidden away in the deep cellars. When they were opened, the contents would first give off a smell like the dank exhalation of a tomb; then came a superb vintage aroma, the suggestion of vats fermenting in the sun, which went to the soldiers' heads at the very first mouthful. The airmen talked and talked, they fell about with laughter while the wine deposited a reddish sediment in their tin mugs. Voices were raised in criticism of the generals' stupidity, the ministers' incompetence. And yet the offensive had been a success.

One of the crew, encouraged by roars of laughter, was aping the panic and confusion of the Nationalist units, making gibberish of the denials broadcast from enemy radio stations. He mimicked the bewildered sentries, the precipitous rush from the fighting line and from the officers' messes. His concern was now for the ammunition, now for the tins of food. He had all the comic verve which turns a story-teller into an actor. He was the whole Nationalist army being rudely awakened from its sleep.

The captain broke in upon this pantomime with his calm voice.

'The surprise element has soon gone out of the attack,' he said.

It was as though he were talking to himself. A sergeant added to the picture: 'Franco's planes are back in the sky; we had some of them on our tail today.'

These words were lost in the thunderous applause. Juanito and Felix exchanged glances. Their faith was too fervent not to be vulnerable. The troops were dispersing for the night. They were to share with the air crew the greyish blankets which constituted the whole of their bedding. Felix and Juanito lingered beside the captain. They went on sitting at the schoolmaster's desk as though to finish a game of cards. The candlelight fell only on an empty glass, a ring of tobacco smoke, the captain's hand playing with a bunch of keys.

'They are the keys to my house,' he said, as though bringing himself to answer a question. 'I had filled it with everything that I loved: mementoes of my travels—I'm a journalist, everything interests me—shells, tribal masks, photographs of remote islands on which I imagined that I was the only human being ever to set foot, and also . . .' He paused. 'Also a woman whom I had brought back from those parts. A single high-explosive, and all that was left was a jar from Italica, a present from a friend . . . The house was still under fire. I made a dash when the light faded; I opened the gate, as though a house still stood behind it. . . . In an alcove by the front door I could just make out the amphora, standing on its head. I ran my hand over it in the dark: it wasn't even grazed. I stood there crying for a long time—though exactly why, I couldn't have said. Whenever I handle this bunch of keys, I get the feeling that they are still going to open rooms and cupboards for me, that all I have to do is put my hand to a door, that someone will be there waiting for me.'

Juanito said, with some embarrassment: 'The keys will be useful again some time . . .'

The man shrugged.

'No more houses for me,' he said, 'but in Spain there will always be laws and reforms, press campaigns, meetings, strikes, demonstrations and possibly other outbreaks of arson and war. For the words of men are explosive, and politics breed war . . .'

He lowered his voice slightly, as though he were afraid of his own thoughts: 'Whatever the party, its programme isn't simply made up of phrases, slogans, empty words. The stakes are human blood. War is the day of reckoning, the day on which we all have to pay.'

Agustin's words were often tinged with strange doubts. But for the first time Juanito was seeing the history of Spain with different eyes. Pronunciamentos and coups d'état, monarchist restorations and democratic insurrections, followed one another as fight follows fight in the bullring. Perhaps the Republic was nothing more than this interval between kills, lasting as long as it takes to drag the dead bull from the arena and release another from the pen, dazzled and furious, scraping the sand with its hoof.

The captain was silent now. He ran his eye over these sleeping men who already looked like corpses on the battlefield. They were breathing almost in rhythm. Some of them had improvised a bed out of a door torn from its hinges and laid on top of some empty packing cases. No doubt there were other makeshift dormitories, only a few miles away. Other youths were playing this children's game with the ferocity of adults. And these sleeping figures were divided only by dried-up rivers, scarred fields and shattered houses.

Felix in turn went off to bed. They were alone. A temptation was growing in the captain and dispelling all sense of caution: the temptation to pluck a man from the infernal ring, to give this grave and stubborn Valencian as a hostage to life instead of to death . . .

'I thought,' Juanito persisted, 'that in this war men were facing bullets instead of goading an animal . . . Are we the animal which can't make out why it is being forced to advance, to attack, to defend itself?'

'Let's just say "why it is being forced to die" . . .'

They paused. The silence was rent by a salvo of shells. The Nationalists were aiming blind from the other side of the mountain range.

'They've got ammunition to waste,' Juanito said bitterly. He saw the captain to the school teacher's lodgings where he was to spend the night. There was a half-consumed candle on the table. Juanito thought of Agustin who was always talking about the long nights that he had spent reading. A straw mattress had been laid on the bedstead. It gave a crunch as the captain flopped on to it. He looked very old and very tired. He laid his bunch of keys down beside the candle.

'Good night,' said Juanito, deep in thought.

'Good night.' The captain sat up on the mattress. 'Listen, boy, don't forget my name. I'd like to help you one day. You're right: this war is a bullfight, but there have been bullfights in which bulls have smashed through the barriers and gored the spectators. You never know: there are many forms of courage, you see, and acknowledging that we have made a mistake is one of them. You are brave . . .'

'I'm not brave,' protested Juanito, 'but in the *huerta* the soil belongs to us. The bread we eat tastes of freedom. I'm not fighting for a régime. I'm defending what is mine.'

The man sprang off the bed. He flung his arms round Juanito, as he would have flung them round a drowning man in an attempt to bring him up to the surface.

'If you are defending what is yours, don't just defend your field and your soil—defend your youth, save your life. You have got to understand that nothing is worth such a sacrifice. Nobody has the right to dispose of your life, not even God.'

He broke off. He had neither the words nor the strength to wrest the boy from this bloody game of dice. His arms dropped to his sides. He slumped back on to the bed; again there was a crunch of straw.

'Blow the candle out, will you?' the captain said softly.

'There,' said Juanito, 'it's done.'

He groped his way back to the school assembly room where, huddled up in his blankets, Felix was clenching his fists in his sleep. When the airman had been talking so frenziedly, Juanito had not known what to say in reply. Now such a terrible anguish took hold of him that he called out: 'Felix! Felix!'

'What are you shouting for?' asked Felix, as he woke.

'Nothing,' said Juanito, 'it was only a nightmare.'

Juanito told Agustin about the two planes which had forced-landed. But his companion seemed suspicious.

'Why didn't they signal the break-down to their base?' he asked. 'If they took off at dawn, they must have had enough fuel to get back. But what were they doing in this sector anyway? They were flying in the opposite direction from their normal route.'

Agustin had known the captain in the days when he wrote for a progressive newspaper in Barcelona.

'Day after day he propounded, instead of any solution, the most noble ideas. He roused enthusiasm. He fostered a mood of passionate fervour, of lofty aspiration . . . He was a revolutionary who wouldn't dirty his hands. To him, the blood and grime of the battlefield were impurities that might upset his calculations. To him, the liberation of the people was a laboratory experiment carried out in antiseptic surroundings with rubber gloves and, it could be, even a mask like those the best surgeons wear. But in a war, truth persists in the guise of chance and incoherence. The squandering of lives and the destruction of treasures are expressions of necessity.'

Juanito did not dare to mention the ruined house, the ironical talisman, the bunch of keys. Weakly, he protested: 'He must have changed. He saw everything from a standpoint that was almost *too* human . . .'

The captain's words came back to him, and that disillusioned tone of voice. He had given the impression that he had weighed everything up. The force of what he said came from that hint of weariness. He seemed to be talking to himself, as though Felix or Juanito were of no more account to him than the sleeping figures curled up under their blankets. He had expressed their hidden doubts. The men struggled in their dreams, imploring some mysterious judge for a stay of execution. They were looking for reasons for their courage or their cowardice. To exist had seemed to them the worst of nightmares. The sleeping men were striving through their dreams to establish an alibi for living and for dying.

'What did he have to say for himself?' growled Agustin, mistrustfully.

Juanito was evasive: '. . . He said that politics breed war, that every party programme is staked on human blood, that words turn to dust in the end.'

'A fine closing paragraph for an article, and one that can be used time and again.'

Juanito could find no words to express his anguish when the journalist had made his half-voiced confession. Had war no other object than to rob millions of men of their only chance of existing?

Beside the empty beer-bottle on the desk, the candle-flame had flickered like the tongues of fire on the brows of the apostles . . . In the schoolmaster's bedroom, through their faltering words, a friendship, a pact, had been sealed between the older and the younger man: 'Defend your youth, save your life!'

To Felix, Juanito had made no further mention of the captain, as though he had been to some extent his accomplice.

Ten days after the crossing of the Ebro, the Nationalist army launched a counter-attack with powerful artillery support. It followed the same pattern as the Republican offensive: pressure in the north and south was followed by a wide breach in the centre, the thrust being made towards Venta de Composines.

Juanito stared gloomily at the bluish line of the mountains, which imitated the ramparts of a mediaeval citadel. For them, the offensive would not extend beyond that horizon. Several times they were ordered to move camp. As a result, they exchanged a derelict village hall for a schoolhouse. They were merely circling, within a radius of a few miles, the village where Juanito had re-encountered Agustin one July morning. Then the air had tasted of victory, the sunlight had been as exhilarating as a fanfare.

'I cover more ground on my way to and from work in Barcelona,' Carlos said.

His comrades laughed bitterly. Carlos would exploit his success. His thirst for popularity could make only an idol or a martyr of him. In Barcelona he was enough to reduce the post office where he worked to fits of laughter. Now he was having to draw the long bow to defend his star role. Like an ageing actor seeking to explain the public's betrayal, he attributed the soldiers' indifference to the jealousy that Catalans inspire—or so he claimed—throughout the rest of Spain. To shock the Andalusians and the Valencians, he boasted of heinous and quite imaginary crimes.

'You've raped all the nuns, set fire to all the churches and plundered all the sacristies,' said Juanito ironically.

The epic had become just a news item. The crossing of the Ebro was reduced to the level of advances and communiqués. For every scouting mission there was a surplus of volunteers. Instead of handpicking the men he required, Juanito drew their names by lot. Every one of them wanted to have a hand in reviving the offensive.

When H.Q. ordered a reconnaissance of the approaches to Alcañiz, where the Nationalists had their headquarters, Felix was all eagerness.

'Alcañiz? I'd love to get a good look at Franco . . . I mean, it's ridiculous fighting a war all on account of some geezer you've never set eyes on.'

At once, looking angry, Carlos broke in: 'If you choose

Felix, you've got to send me too! I'm just as keen to get a good look at that gang.'

Juanito turned to Felix. He was reluctant to enter his name on this priority list for death. Since the captain's visit, Felix and Juanito had lost their belief in victory, and yet they refused to accept defeat.

'It's all right by me, but you're the only one who can get anything out of the radio. If they take you prisoner, we won't get any news till the end of the war.'

Juanito's little joke rang false. Carlos turned to his comrades.

'Aren't you capable of twiddling a knob?' he asked.

They set out before nightfall. Over the ruined farmhouse, over the neglected vines, over the flinty road, hung the diffuse glory of late afternoons in August. Carlos got up from the wooden seat where he had been sitting with Felix, to go, he said, and say good-bye to the local girls.

The other soldiers wandered off. Juanito went over to Felix.

'Remember those two planes?' he asked abruptly. 'They landed at Burgos next day. It was all arranged . . .'

Felix pulled a face. Was he showing his contempt for the deserters? Was he reflecting that his mission would just be one more sacrifice in this accumulation of absurd, heroic and inconsistent acts that make up a war?

'If I deserted, Juanito, it wouldn't be to go and fight for the other side, as the captain has done, but to get back to a world in which there was no war, no bloodshed, no hate . . . What's the use of just changing uniforms and sides?'

'Yes,' said Juanito, 'what's the use?'

Two days went by. Juanito was alone in the village hall, reading a dispatch.

'Lieutenant!'

The voice made him jump. It was a peasant whose face and body were a mass of scars. He lived close to the farm, which he had been unwilling to leave, despite the shelling. His arms hung straight at this sides, clutching a pair of rifles.

'I haven't had time to clean them,' he said.

He laid them down on the desk. Juanito recoiled. They were

the brand-new rifles that he had issued the week before, the splendid German rifles that Carlos and Felix had taken with them on their mission.

'And the bodies?' asked Juanito.

The man cleared his throat.

'There wasn't much left of them. Arms, legs. I buried what there was.'

I've seen other men die, thought Juanito. Why should the death of Carlos and Felix be different from other deaths? But he got a grip on himself.

'Thanks for bringing the guns in,' he said. 'You'll have a drink with us, won't you?'

He left the rifles on the desk. The lamp bathed them in a flickering light that flowed along the barrels. They were covered with a strange rustiness, a sort of mouldiness. The night enveloped Juanito in its warmth, a perfect August night, a concert of stars in the deep bowl of the sky, a concert of smells mounting from this sterile earth devastated by warring humans.

The troops sat talking in the doorway. Juanito thrust the man forward. His hands shook as he poured him a drink, but nobody noticed. When he announced the deaths of Carlos and Felix, there was a silence. The old man sat calmly drinking his wine. It was time for the news bulletin; the troops hovered round the wireless-set with a lost look on their faces, not daring to switch it on.

Juanito walked back to the office in the village hall. The rifles were still there on the desk beside the papers. Juanito held the barrels up to the flickering lamplight. They were spattered with particles of human brain. There were strips of hairy skin on the trigger. Nobody could see Juanito turning the rifles over and over in despair. Finally he laid them down on the desk and started to cry.

27

AN OLD LORRY arrived fitfully with their rations, pulling up with a squeal of brakes and a clatter of tins. The soldiers would greet with cries of equal derision the bully beef, the half-rotten vegetables, the bacon well past its prime and the canful of rancid oil—the hallowed foodstuff of Spain. The catering officer, taking no notice of the gibes, would measure out the provisions as though he were afraid of committing a flagrant injustice.

'I suppose you've brought us a few lentils?' an Andalusian would jeer.

'We've a large enough supply of lentils to last us several wars!' the catering officer replied, straight-faced. He shared Dr Negrín's conviction. The Republic would hold out, thanks to this heaven-sent vegetable. If the troops kept on at him, the man pointed at the overgrown fields and vineyards, at the empty cattle-sheds.

'There's nothing in standing orders to prevent you from adding to your rations!'

This suggestion gave rise to a storm of indignation. It was a long time since they had taken, either peacefully or by force, the meagre stocks hidden away in the neighbouring farmhouses. To bolster the men's morale, Juanito made plans for an expedition.

'I'm bound to find a ham that somebody in the village has overlooked, and a sackful of rice, and a loaf made from flour instead of sawdust.' But it was essential to avoid any suggestion that they were requisitioning these things. 'I shall take Vicente with me,' added Juanito. This was a shrewd, wiry fellow from Cadiz. He shamelessly quoted the proverb according to which the dogs in Cadiz are unmannerly, the children uneducated and the girls unchaste.

'We'll have to go carefully with the people hereabouts,' he

said. 'They're stingy because they're rich. We'll start by asking them for a glass of water . . . Once we're sitting down to table, we'll ask for a drop of wine to wash the taste away.'

As he talked, he kept adjusting his stool. Top people, he would say—bishops and ministers—always had their own personal seats. It wasn't a question of comfort, but of dignity. Because he believed in nothing, Vicente was a respecter of ceremonial. He would claim humorously that his native city was the only one in Spain that was populated with sensible people.

'In Seville, during Holy Week, the women of Triana clamour for the Virgin and swoon with ecstasy when an old stuffed dummy is heaved out of the sacristy. In Valencia they laugh and cry all the year round, without rhyme or reason. They go straight from processions to battles of flowers, from quarrels to firework displays.'

Juanito did not take offence.

'It doesn't stop us from working,' he said.

Esteban the Aragonese backed him up: 'Where I come from, we do our best dancing after we have picked the olives or brought in the harvest.'

Juanito decided to take this reliable shepherd along; from him, there was no fear of either bragging or looting. Before they set off, Vicente solemnly bequeathed his stool to the Republican army but dared anybody to use it while he was away.

Juanito was counting on reaching the village before nightfall and returning with the food next morning. The three men strode out at a good pace. Between the hills above the fleeciness of the vines, the steeple was coming into view. Suddenly a roar filled the sky. They flung themselves down, full-length, at the edge of the road. A squadron of planes flew overhead. Esteban counted them. They seemed to waver and dance in the twilit sky like hornets. But they were converging above the village, circling persistently round the steeple, hunting for signs of an airfield or a command post hidden under the trees. The explosions reverberated in the evening silence. From close at hand came a panic-stricken trotting, sounding like a cloudburst of hail. It was some goats. The fence of their enclosure had been blown down, and they were racing dementedly through the vineyard, colliding with the plants. A few of them came over and sniffed these human bodies lying in shallow ditches which they more than filled.

'Here come our rations,' said Vicente, not moving a muscle.

The goats mistrustfully skirted the sham corpses and set off in the direction of the village. The explosive thuds diminished. Through the russet leaves that still clung to the vine-stalks, Juanito kept track of the wider and wider rings described by the aircraft. Vicente was the first to sit up. He was enchanted at this unsuccessful attack.

'Franco's looking after us . . .'

Esteban was silent. All this time, he had been merged with the granulous soil. Its every shudder had spread through his primitive body and soul. He crossed himself.

'We were lucky,' said Juanito. He was thinking of Carlos and Felix. They must have heard that mosquito-like buzzing when the plane was swooping down on them.

They went on their way. Night had fallen. The village was abuzz with cheerful excitement, as though a procession were due to pass through. What had drawn Franco's pilots so persistently to the empty schoolhouse, the abandoned post office, the church with the gaping roof? A bomb had fallen close to the arcades in the square and smashed the bottles in the front part of the café. The syrupy smell of the *anis*, the sweet, heavy bouquet of the wine, completed the villagers' intoxication. In the market-place, Juanito propped himself against the edge of the fountain. The house next to the village hall was undamaged; even its projecting, wrought-iron balcony was intact. The door opened. Juanito recognized the young woman who had walked across the square on the first morning of the offensive. He stared at her, quite motionless. That white face, beneath the sleek hair with its centre parting, was reviving the radiance of that victorious dawn, the virginal blue of the sky in the shimmering water from the well. And the stranger was coming towards him as though, that other morning, they had arranged this meeting.

'Hullo, lieutenant, what a lovely day you chose for your visit!'

The voice flowed into him, slow and familiar. He glanced quickly about him. Vicente and Esteban had taken advantage of the general high spirits to insinuate themselves into friendly households. There was a faint galloping sound: the goats were roaming about, intoxicated by their freedom. For them too, this abortive air-raid was a distraction. Shaking their heads, they seemed to be commenting on its absurdity.

'Were you afraid?' asked Juanito.

The words slipped from him like clothes when two bodies are about to fuse.

Encarnacion repeated the last two syllables with a note of amusement.

'Afraid? Why should I have been afraid?'

On the smooth rim of the fountain, their hands had already joined. She threw back her head. Her teeth flashed in the fading light. Those lips parted in a smile were summoning Juanito, but he was startled by the fierceness of his own desire.

Encarnacion was thinking aloud: 'I was afraid when the Nationalists left the village and took their hostages with them. My father-in-law was a man of strength. One had a sense of security when he was about . . . Then one morning other men came. I wasn't afraid any more.'

There was no mistaking the stress on the words: '*Other men came.*'

'I remember that morning, too.'

In the distance, a guitar began to pulsate. The truce between them was like a mysterious prelude.

'Are you thirsty?'

Encarnacion's hand was drawing him towards the silent house. After she had lit the candle standing on a chest in the hall, he allowed himself to be led farther on, into the white-walled room which was kept for guests. He had to pretend to drink without impatience the wine which looked black in the porrón set in front of him. But he waved aside the bowl of fruit.

'Aren't you hungry?'

He did not answer. How could he say to this woman: 'It is your body for which I hunger and thirst'? Down on the table, their hands had united. They stood up. Encarnacion took the lamp with the milky globe from the centre of the table. They walked across the large hall. Encarnacion threw open a door. The bedroom overlooked a darkened garden. Through the half-open shutters stole the heady smell of honeysuckle and the pale phosphorescence of the night sky. Juanito did not wish Encarnacion to close the outer shutters. But for the sake of modesty he blew out the lamp before taking her into his arms.

Early next morning Juanito woke alone in this unfamiliar room which was still full of the scents from the garden. He dressed hastily. He found Encarnacion bustling about in the main room. He took her in his arms, amazed that the ecstasy of that summer night could be over. Confidences had given way to caresses. They had imagined, as they woke or succumbed to sleep, that they were proceeding directly from one embrace to the next. Juanito had got up at times to rest his brow on that star-washed sky, as though on a window-pane. The trees had been astir with startled scamperings, winged escapes, long whispers in the dark. Encarnacion had called out laughing: 'Where are you, Juanito?'

He had walked back to the bed and buried his head in her shoulder again; his lips had gently closed on that breast which tasted of jasmine leaves. He had interrupted his kisses to ask whether she had experienced keener pleasure with any other man. She had protested.

'I've only had one man—my husband. He loved me too much, and I didn't love him. Nobody knows what has become of him. Who is there for you to be jealous of?'

To reassure him, she had given him a sporadic account of the drabbest episode in her life: her marriage. Juanito had never felt so much curiosity towards another human being. He needed to master the course of this woman's life so that he might possess her more fully. Encarnacion had lain talking to herself. Juanito had fallen asleep amid the shadows and the faint breeze laden with garden smells . . .

That smouldering, dream-woven sleeplessness had existed

outside time . . . How can you wake from such a night? Now everything was ready on the table, as it always had been in the *barraca* before he went out into the fields. Juanito ate and drank slowly, a stranger to himself. Encarnacion sat staring at him. Their farewells were speedy.

Encarnacion carefully loaded up his knapsack. When he rose from the table, she said: 'Juanito, wait just a moment.'

He heard her rush into the bedroom. Already she was back. She was pressing herself against him to unbutton the neck of his shirt. She had picked a long sprig of honeysuckle. The pale flowers clung to his chain and medal. Beneath the coarse khaki flannelette, he would carry away this necklace of caresses, these warm and ruffled petals.

'That's to stop you forgetting me too soon!' she said with a sad smile.

28

THE TRIO REASSEMBLED IN THE MARKET-PLACE, stooping under the weight of strangely misshapen bundles.

'You look as though you've got a dismembered body in your haversack,' Esteban said to Vicente as they started back along the road leading away from the village.

Juanito scarcely heard. He had not yet recovered from the intoxication of the night in that bedroom which, opening on to the shadowy garden, was like a grotto full of voices, tremors, mysterious harmonizings, intermittent caresses. Was it only a woman's body that he had clasped? Hadn't it been the night, enfolding him with its myriad arms, brushing his skin with its myriad breaths . . .? All he had to do was quicken his stride and incline his body slightly over the sunstrewn roadway: the scent of the honeysuckle would stream from the neck of his shirt, mingled with the smell of his warm, moist body. Had his companions, too, experienced this sating of body and soul, this wonderful complicity? He had not the courage to ask them.

A derisive hooting greeted them at the camp. Their answer was simply to tip out on to the kitchen flagstones the tins of biscuits, the sacks of rice and flour, the sausages as brown and compact as the gnarled roots of a tree. And the war seemed won on account of a day of plenty.

'You ought to have been a priest,' said Agustin. 'They hang round you like the devout waiting to confess . . .?'

He was irritated by this ring of silent devotion round Juanito, by the trusting expressions on the people's faces. Day after day he had to fabricate wildly improbable missions that would allow him to spend a few moments gazing into the Valencian's round, full face, into those eyes whose tranquil surface reminded him of pools on which dead leaves lay rotting.

Juanito shrugged.

'They only come for news of the offensive. You can't imagine what it's like . . . No papers, no letters, a wireless set that suddenly dries up in the middle of a bulletin.'

Yet, tenaciously clinging to this narrow strip of land which gave them control of the Tarragona-Alcañiz road, they had just dug another trench. When the day came for them to abandon this position, all would be lost. Yes, it seemed to Juanito that if this one mesh were to give, the whole net would be ripped wide open.

Agustin was becoming more outspoken: 'Positioning, artillery, air support—they all count, and we take them into consideration. But they are not enough . . . You must have seen a man performing the most incredible antics on the strength of a good drink. That was the whole secret of the offensive . . . We were drunk with anger and despair and rage at ourselves and everyone else. Franco could have doubled his defences: we should still have got through. But you can't swim across a new river every night. The Ebro wasn't a manœuvre, it was an exploit. It was the strategy of suicide.'

Juanito shook his head. He had not wakened from that heroic dream which he had wrought naked and open-eyed.

'Don't say that, Agustin. There has never been a night to compare with it. It wasn't the night of suicide, but the night of victory.'

Agustin pretended to be above such boyish nostalgia.

'Yes, Juanito, it was the sublime night on which the Spain of the Cid united with the Spain of Don Quixote—but what manner of day could have followed such a night?'

Juanito stood listening to Agustin. The Republic's moment of glory was now linked to that chain of bloody reverses and disappointments of which a war is made up. Enthusiasm was no substitute for ammunition, a just cause no replacement for tanks and planes. The captain had drawn the appropriate inference—and deserted. Agustin, for his part, accused Spain and the foreign powers.

'You are always looking for people to blame!' observed Juanito.

'No, there are too many of them . . . Yes, Juanito, the crossing of the Ebro was the Cid's last feat of valour, or Don Quixote's last battle in Barcelona, when he suddenly realizes that he is just an old fool.'

'He rides home to the village to make his will.'

Juanito knew his Cervantes, just like every other Spaniard, but it was a joy for Agustin to hear him quoting from *Don Quixote*.

'I have no village, and no will to make.' There was nothing for Agustin to fall back on—no roots, no family, no other side to his nature for him to come to terms with. Juanito had his love of the soil, his appetite for life. Agustin returned to his inventory: 'The only thing I have staked in this war is myself. I've nothing to lose, nothing to recoup. If I go down, all the other players are extinguished with me . . .'

But with his peasant's obstinacy, Juanito denied that the troops were exhausted. He was determined that his labours and his courage should bear fruit. Like a harvest forcibly wrested from the soil, victory was something that God owed him.

'Why aren't our garrisons in Madrid and Valencia on the move?' asked Juanito.

Agustin gave an exasperated shrug.

'Another offensive would drain the last of our resources. It would expose Madrid and leave the way to the *huerta* wide open.'

An air-raid warning interrupted their talk. They raced to the dug-out, which was dug flush with the foundations of the building. A score of men were piling in, helter-skelter. Juanito and Agustin slumped down on to these bodies, which looked like corpses heaped in a ditch after facing a firing squad. Nobody spoke, but breathing grew heavier as the drone of the aircraft seemed to draw nearer. Juanito thought of the sustained humming of the strings of a guitar. He felt a jolt in the air, as though somebody had breathed down the back of his neck. Esteban let out a faint groan. He was not wounded, but Vicente, in a convulsion of fear, was hitting him in the face. Abuse mingled with the laughter. Again the droning started towards them. It was a mosquito-like hum, of the kind that will shatter the silence of a room. Juanito thought confusedly of Encarnacion and of the abetting darkness in which he had clutched her to him with all his might, yielding to an intensity of desire which he would now never experience again. Then he reproached himself for his impiety: 'Blessed Madonna, have pity on Juanito! Our Lady of the Forsaken, pray for us!'

The bomb had fallen a hundred yards away. The planes were moving off. The soldiers picked themselves up, looking shaken, covered with earth. They were shaking themselves like children emerging from a haystack.

'I thought we'd had it that time,' Juanito said calmly.

'So did I,' admitted Agustin. To himself he added: I wouldn't have seen the end of the war; I'd have bowed out with Juanito. But a feeling of superstitious remorse took hold of him. What right have I to choose a companion in death? he thought. War is not a pretext for a suicide pact.

He eyed Juanito with the prescience which love finally achieves when, by dint of renunciation, it becomes only lucidity.

'You're changing, Juanito!'

For a split second he seemed to catch a glimpse of a sturdy young peasant jumping down from a lorry, a round-faced boy with an air of boldness and faith, a Valencian who was as yet nameless to him . . . Agustin felt very rich. He owned so many different mental pictures of Juanito to mark out those months of waiting, hoping and enduring.

There was no other reality than this meeting on a road: two strangers exchanging cordial words, faint smiles, a quick handshake. I've changed too, Agustin was thinking. I'm like Robinson Crusoe, forgetting the fact of being shipwrecked and on an island at the discovery of another human being's existence.

'I'm not changing,' said Juanito. 'You know very well that we men of the *huerta* never change. The only way we change is by dying.'

'Be quiet . . .!' Agustin felt another admission about to escape him. '*You* won't die.'

Juanito took a short-cut through the fields practically every evening, hurrying as far as the garden gate. As he raced along, he inhaled the scent of the withered roses. He rapped his hand feverishly on the closed shutters. The window opened and he vaulted over the sill.

'I knew you would come tonight!' Encarnacion was sure of it.

Her mouth glowed. All the summer scents that had deserted the powdery flower-beds rose from her proffered body. The bunches of pinks, the clusters of roses, which are flung at the Virgin's feet in Valencia seemed to be there on her silky throat for Juanito to rumple and knead.

All day long, behind the closed shutters, she had no other diversion than to review the sum of chance occurrences, of accidents, subterfuges and expedients that constitute any life. The ardent caresses of her lover delivered her from these futile considerations. In the evenings, his soft taps on the shutters plucked Encarnacion from that inner theatre where the actors and supernumeraries who play their parts in the drama of a human life filed past on the stage. For a long while she had been living with Pablo's ghost; now Juanito's exorcized all other phantoms from her loneliness.

Behind the closed outer shutters, throughout those glaring August afternoons, Encarnacion talked to an absent Juanito as she talked to him at night when he lay asleep beside her. She answered the questions that she had evaded when the Valencian's gaze had been harrying her, when his kisses and caresses had been seeking to extort other confessions from her. When she was alone, she dared to think back and to explain her actions to herself: By getting engaged to Enrico, I was marrying Pablo by proxy. Everything conspired to make the substitution easy. Pablo loved going about with high-spirited gangs, he loved to laugh, to go to late-night concerts. Enrico might easily have been his younger brother: he was shy, he was dreamy, he had no go in him. Enrico's mother died very young, bringing her son into the world. 'She was just like Enrico,' Pablo used to say. 'She let life slip through her fingers. I can never remember her really taking to a play, or a friend, or a dress-design, or a length of material. That's how Enrico is: devoid of appetites. He has no roots in this world.' But when Juanito was beside her, Encarnacion—instead of describing Enrico, with his premature wisdom and sad gentleness—conjured up another companion.

'My father-in-law was a friend to me. It was he who steered me into his son's arms. He wanted to engineer Enrico's happiness. That sounds a bit crazy to me today . . . Engineer someone else's happiness? Why, we barely manage to live our own lives . . .!'

Juanito was eager to understand everything, to know all there was to know about Encarnacion.

'Why did you marry Enrico?'

Encarnacion's body weighed on his arm like a compact sheaf of corn.

'My mother and I suffered from the dreadful poverty of people who have known better days. I had the vague feeling that there was some lapse, some fault to make good. Marriages and funerals enabled my mother to keep a few desirable connections alive by pouring out congratulations and paying constant visits of condolence. One day, with a kindness that seemed like a blunder, one of her cousins invited me to spend the summer down here with her daughter . . . I met Enrico . . . Within weeks we were engaged. It is easy to write on a blank page, Juanito, but after a few years one has to strain to make out the original words beneath the erasures . . .'

She looked back on that period in her life with a strange nostalgia.

When his fits of breathlessness confined him to his room, Enrico would insist on his father's accompanying his fiancée on any outings that they might have planned. Encarnacion's engagement left her with the delightful memory of a long tête-à-tête with Pablo. The horses' hooves rang out on the flinty roads. As they roamed the wooded hills, the couple progressed from general discussion to confidences. Encarnacion's unhappy girlhood found an echo in Pablo's disappointed life.

One morning Pablo expressed a wish to show her Poblet Abbey. They wandered among the ruins and the fragmentary pillars scattered about the cloisters. The singing of the birds did not succeed in drowning the rippling laugh of a fountain. Pablo picked his way across the chaos of flagstones. He came to the fountain, surrounded by slender columns and delicate ogives. The water was spurting out and scattering in the wind. When Encarnacion wanted to drink from the spring, Pablo cupped his hands for her.

Encarnacion paused in her ramblings. What was discreditable about that? Could she not tell Juanito of that innocent game between a young girl and a man of ripe years, of how wonderfully stirred she had felt? She would tell him: 'At Poblet, only a short distance from here, spring-water rises in the heart of a ruined monastery. One summer's day, I drank some from the hands of a man who might have been my father. He has never been my lover . . . And yet, in that ice-cool water, I must have been drinking a love-potion.'

That day, Pablo had been frightened of the words that he was on the point of uttering, the actions that he was on the point of taking. He had sought Encarnacion's hand for his son, to establish something irrevocable between them.

Juanito discovered a man's portrait half-hidden behind some books. The face was deeply scored, but a handsome row of teeth was exposed in a derisive smile. This mixture of experience and youthfulness gave his features a fetching quality.

'Who is this?' asked Juanito.

She took the portrait from his hands.

'My father-in-law, a week before he was arrested.'

Juanito felt that his question had awakened a painful memory. He did not understand why Encarnacion was crushing her lips against his, as though to dispel an intruder.

29

WHEN HE OPENED HIS EYES first thing in the morning Juanito would imagine, with impatient joy, that he was about to trim the garden trees before going out into the fields. Benumbed impulses would awaken in his arms, too. But the walls of the *barraca*, beneath their blinding coat of limewash, as taut as dress material starched for some special occasion, had vanished. Juanito stared about him in vain for the shutters, parted to reveal the pots of sweet basil, a bed of pinks and, over by the well, the fig-tree with its plump leaves and its strange branches, contorted like a man who has just plunged his head into the water and is now shaking himself purely for the pleasure of sprinkling the drops of coolness over his skin. Juanito allotted the day's duties and sent somebody into the village to try to get some vegetables.

'Don't spend all day at the inn,' he enjoined the volunteer, for the inn still had its vine-trellis and a wooden seat, its insecure tables and an attentive circle of old men and small boys.

The day dragged by, hot and barren, quite unalleviated except by some item of news which a passer-by might shout in their direction, and by the orders delivered by a dispatch-rider streaming with sweat. In the evenings, a light breeze from the sea lent a hint of brine to the smell of the vineyards. From the plants, still covered with grapes, rose a musty aroma. A warm breath was exhaled from the overheated soil. The setting sun, like a weary vineyard hand, seemed to slow down in his task of treading the grapes heaped in a glowing vat. Juanito filled his lungs with the intoxicating smell.

A man from Alicante said, as though to himself: 'Where I come from, we take the grapes to the press run by the co-operative. The bees go with us, on the carts; when we toss the bunches out, the bees are still clinging to them, their wings all sticky from the juice. While the grapes are being weighed, we go off and drink some of last year's wine. By the time we get back, other carts have arrived, other basketfuls, and the bees are a bit drunk—just like us men.' He mopped his brow as though he had just that moment unloaded the baskets. Juanito dreamt of other evenings, during other wine-harvests, buzzing with bees and laughter.

This was the time of day when the card-players laid aside their hands, when even the most irascible stopped arguing. Everyone would dream aloud. A corporal who came from Burgos heaved a sigh . . . At sunset, the city pavements were watered, to settle the dust. Girls were walking by. They seemed to disdain the compliments that were launched at them, but as the daylight faded every town in Spain turned into a strange court of love. Beneath the arcades, still full of the afternoon shade, everyone was restored to the world of misty carafes and glasses, of words likewise full of coolness, of nimble jests. Life was a lounging lit by a woman's brisk walk and fleeting smile, was an idleness punctuated by the singing of the swallows and the shouts of the news-vendors. Juanito closed his eyes to savour this perfect moment to the full. The smell of the soil conjured up pictures of the *huerta* rousing itself at sunset like a woman demanding further caresses after the act. To safeguard this peacefulness, it was only to himself that he said: Hang it, they've forgotten us! No orders, no rations, no newspapers . . . He would have liked to talk to Agustin about a future existence, as though about a blank day that could not be filled. Nobody knew how this war would end, but there would be fruit-picking and wine-harvests again, dancing and processions. Year after year, the elections and music contests in Valencia would end in pitched battles and reconciliations. Women would come into Juanito's life, more aloof than Sybil, more considerate than Soledad, more reserved than Encarnacion. Would he one day re-experience that fluid and rather dreary time when you are not yet in love and can barely remember being in love?

From the road which, farther down the hill, followed the line of the Ebro came the roar of a motor-cycle. The troops hurriedly gathered round Agustin and fired questions at him. But Agustin drew Juanito aside. The offensive had failed. Only Juanito still believed in that wild-goose chase. When he found him kneeling over his machine-gun in a farmyard, Agustin was gripped by a feeling of hallucination. Luis, stooping over his pack, had fastened the straps with the same childish absorption. Was Juanito going to run away from him now? Beads of sweat stood out on Agustin's forehead. But Juanito smiled serenely at him. Life was possible. The air became breatheable again because Juanito was saying, in the lilting tones of Valencia: 'I thought you must be up at the front, testing your trigger-finger with the International Brigades.'

'You know as well as I do that they have been disbanded. Do leave that thing alone.'

Juanito carefully loaded the machine-gun, frowning as though he were checking the water-level in the ditch at irrigation time. Was there another Juanito, on Franco's side, checking the working of his machine-gun with the same expression of concentration, the same adept hands? A superstitious feeling stole into Agustin's mind. He felt like shouting: 'Juanito, don't kill—then you won't be killed yourself.' But he dared not voice his anguish.

'What are you staring at me like that for?'

'You make me laugh. You're handling that gun as though you were operating a reaping-machine.'

'Tools are made to go rusty in some hands and to function in others . . .'

Juanito answered without looking up. And his words were sententious and gay, in the style of the people of the *huerta*, who turn all life's misadventures into proverbs. In a flash, Juanito was up on his feet again. The brickwork of the well had given way and would have to be rebuilt: such a perfectly sited well, he insisted; the water was wonderful . . .

He talked about it with the greed and tenderness that the Spanish feel for water.

'Won't you have some?'

'Brandy is more in my line,' Agustin answered with a grin. 'Even before the war I couldn't stand water.'

'That's just your bad luck!'

Juanito lowered the bucket on its creaking chain. When it came up again, sparkling in the sunlight, he plunged his face in and absorbed, through every pore, this water which held the flavour of shade. Then he snorted ecstatically, showering Agustin with drips.

'Come and see the roof: we've repaired most of it.'

With laths of skilfully plaited reeds and palms, the troops had filled in the gaping tear. Now they were applying thick mortar and laying undamaged tiles, proud to be restoring this ruin to the dignity of a habitable dwelling. Working within a few yards of Agustin, they pricked up their ears for compliments—though naturally they pretended to be watching the darting, swirling flight of the swallows in the sky above them, where shades of green were now appearing. This domesticity exasperated Agustin.

'To think that we are branded anarchists and vandals! You people are waging war with trowels in your hands. With warriors like you, a farmhouse is soon turned into a manor. If the offensive is resumed, you are bound to have to turn your backs on this palace! If it fails, you will have prepared a fine billet for Franco's Moroccans.'

'By your next visit,' Juanito laughed, 'it will be a *barraca* just like my family's! Where I come from, we say that tumbledown houses bring bad luck on the whole neighbourhood. Gaping roofs and broken windows attract evil spirits.'

'What is more important is that you shouldn't attract enemy aircraft in your craze for reconstruction.'

Agustin strode away, glowering at himself and at the others. 'Congratulate your team of builders!'

When the moment came for him to take leave of Juanito, his rancour melted.

'Everyone is on edge at H.Q. We're trying to find a way to get the offensive on the move again.'

Juanito nodded approvingly.

'Agustin, I keep thinking of the first few days, of that army pouring over the bridges the moment they were erected! Now the war is like water stagnating and turning the land into a quagmire instead of racing through the fields . . .'

'And how is the discipline?' Agustin asked. 'How is the morale?'

Despondency was stealing insidiously into the minds and hearts of the inactive troops. Juanito tried to make excuses for them.

'You know how it is. If they had tobacco and newspapers and letters, I'd be strict with them. But just think of the lives they lead. They spend day after day flat on their bellies, trying to find a bit of shade, and at night they have to do sentry-go or march off to relieve an outpost for twenty-four hours . . .'

He vented his feelings against Barcelona, which demanded victories but neglected to keep the men supplied.

'Come and take a look at the rations I got yesterday!'

Juanito plunged the blade of his knife into one of the tins, which were covered with curious protuberances. With a hiss, a whitish foam came shooting out of the lips of the wound.

'I can't issue putrid food.'

The tin landed with a clatter in the middle of the vines. He stared after it, deep in thought.

Agustin thought he had got thin and weatherbeaten, and that there was a certain wildness about him. His expression was no longer that of a child who is put out over something. The sun was bleaching his hair and eyebrows.

While they stood debating how large an amount of meat was necessary to a soldier in the field, strange words danced in Agustin's brain, composing a hymn to the harvesters, standing erect and as golden as their sheaves of corn in the midst of the fields. He stared at these soldiers, with their bare and sunburnt chests. Juanito remained a creature of another breed. And yet his muscular arms had sowed, had steered the team so that the plough should produce a straight furrow.

He is only a peasant from the *huerta*. What made me choose him from among millions of others? But how could I have failed to love him?

Juanito's voice angrily broke in upon his reflections: 'You are not even listening to what I am saying. Like all staff-officers, you imagine that wine is all the troops need; they need meat and rice as well. Look at them: they're dressed in rags, they're filthy. The fact that they have only one shirt makes it more imperative that they should have soap to wash it with. One of them is a tailor from Gerona, and he sews better than any woman. Bring us some thread . . . And next time don't forget the ink: I'd like to write a letter home.'

'Don't entrust your letter to any pilots: it might find its way to Burgos.'

'You leave fortune-telling to the gipsies!'

Juanito shook his head, as though to dispel an obstinate fly. He changed the subject: 'Do try and come over one night. There is a fellow from Caceres who has found a battered old guitar in one of the peasants' houses. It's only got one string, but when he mutes it he could get tears out of a stone.'

30

HAVE I THE RIGHT TO BE HAPPY? Encarnacion kept saying to herself. In Juanito's arms she was finding a new zest, a zest tinged with old dilemmas, with questions that had been worn threadbare. All the haphazard and circuitous events that shape a life, all the bruising endeavours and irksome failures, were acquiring a meaning. Colour was being restored to even the most commonplace memories. Till now, her whole existence had been merely a prolonged, agonized shedding of the cocoon; the uncertainty of that long wait had been the prelude to the ungovernable joy, the revelation which now blazed in her mind and body.

The blank days, the drab and stagnant years, had paved the way for a miraculous blossoming. Happiness, unhappiness, love, loneliness: these words no longer seemed to her the false and pathetic highlights which third-rate painters abuse in an attempt to give a magical relief to commonplace objects, to lend a hint of mystery to flat compositions. She thought back to the early days of her marriage, in Madrid; to Enrico's misanthropic outbursts masking the spread of the disease; to the kind attentions of the father-in-law who had been too young to be a fitting companion for a married woman with time on her hands. The doctors had advised them to move to the Riviera or the Basque coast. 'If I need a milder climate,' Enrico had said, 'why not Santa Creus?' Down here, he had previously experienced a taste of happiness which would be sufficient for his survival.

Encarnacion had come back to these vineyards, these white country houses, these ruined abbeys which were already mingled with the story of her life . . .

On the night of their return, Encarnacion had a dream: on a huge blackboard, a man's hand was rubbing out crude chalk-marks, illegible characters. In place of these doodlings it was tracing a perfect face, a name . . . Encarnacion knew this fine, virile hand, without being able to put a name to it.

After the first embraces, Juanito slept till dawn. When he lay dreaming beside her, Encarnacion was better able to remember that concurrence of chance and predestination, of loneliness and illusion, which we call our love. With a companion beside her, and with her eyes closed in the dark, she floated along more easily aboard that motionless bark. Abandoning herself to the current of the past, she was borne past the drifting islands, past the reefs, along the uncertain shores of memory. To recapture the present, she switched on the bedside lamp. Juanito was sleeping with his arm folded over his face, like a harvester trying to shelter from the August sunlight. The lamp burnt out. Absurd thoughts came flooding into Encarnacion's brain: I lacked the courage to choose between Pablo and Enrico; that was why I lost them both. Life is nothing but this option which is imposed upon us at every moment. By clasping Juanito to me, I have at last brought myself to make a choice. Who could possibly blame me? Neither Pablo nor Enrico. Whatever happens from now on, I have had my share. Nobody can deprive us of what has truly belonged to us.

By contrast, she returned to the days when she had suffered most from this indecision, this ambiguity. Everything—events, people, objects—had seemed to conspire to add to her malaise. While Enrico slowly recovered, it was as though Encarnacion, thanks to his illness, were renewing an engagement temporarily broken off by the contracting of a misguided marriage. Enrico insisted that he was capable of being his own doctor and nurse. He adhered strictly to the timetable and diet that he had given himself. Pablo plunged, with all the wild enthusiasm of a student, both into the running of the farm and the affairs of the community. He was the first to laugh at the sight of himself disguised as a village politician and gentleman farmer . . .

Juanito opened his eyes. His dreams seemed to be rooted deeper and deeper in Encarnacion's innermost thoughts.

'Did you ever go back to Poblet with your father-in-law?'

'Yes.' Encarnacion's voice feigned indifference. 'The same fountain was playing in the midst of the same ruins.'

Again she saw Pablo, standing among those comic-opera ruins. His expression was no longer that of a lover who dared not declare himself. This time he did not talk about the Kings of Aragon or about Gothic architecture, but his plan to open a maternity home in the village and the new plum-tree plantations.

Encarnacion had the feeling that she understood what, haltingly and in whispers, the fountain was saying. The water was talking like a woman who has too much to say, and who mingles laughter with sobbing and breaks off because she has confessed, yet feels regretful that she has not entirely bared her soul . . .

'Pablo, you make me think of Dr Faust, who is determined to do good to people whether they like it or not.'

He had puckered his face, childishly and disarmingly.

'But before embarking on his high endeavours, Faust loses his wrinkles and recovers his black hair,' he had said. 'He seduces Margarita before devoting himself to humanity.'

Encarnacion had smiled.

'Oh, come now, Pablo, don't be coy! A man must still be very young to want to change everything like you do, to deliver bodies, to win souls.'

'No, no, Encarnacion, this is simply the echo of the turbulent enthusiasms of one's youth. When I read *War and Peace* in those days, all my heart used to go out to Levin, the kind landowner —sentimental, utopian and, I think, rather inclined to freemasonry. On the threshold of old age, men are like women: when they can no longer hope to inspire love, they seek to prompt gratitude. They "compensate", as I believe your psychoanalysts put it . . .'

'Why don't you say something, Encarnacion?'

'Juanito darling, I want you to get some sleep, that's all. I have all day for sleeping.'

'So have I,' Juanito said. 'You know quite well we've stopped advancing. There is nothing for us to do except wait for orders that never come . . .' He tore himself away from this too stagnant present. 'It strikes me, Encarnacion, that you are a bit in love with Pablo. But one of these days we shall go to Poblet together. You will drink some of that ice-cool water from my hands. My mother knows about magic. She says that there is only one thing that can break a spell—another spell.'

Encarnacion was barely conscious of his words. In her mind, she was sitting in the drawing-room. Enrico was already rising from his chair in compliance, as he put it, with his monastic routine. Pablo was sighing: 'I've just been listening to *Tristan* on the radio. Wagner believed that he was renewing the art of music. In fact, all he did was invent, so that he might tell of his love, a language that was at once more chaste and more passionate than the poets'. A masterpiece is never anything more than a confession, the account of a mysterious choice.'

Encarnacion listened, with lowered eyelids. Novels, symphonies, canvases, were compounded of these impenetrable confidences. But she was disdainful of the amazing subterfuges, the extraordinary roundabout ways whereby some human beings give voice to a passion.

'Why do men always want to bare their souls, Pablo? There must surely be *some* masterpieces that have disappeared without trace, *some* passions that have ripened without a word of admission . . .' She marvelled at her own sense of security in saying these words. Destiny was a chance to be taken, and her own chance was named Pablo . . .

Juanito ran his hand along her arm, searching for her shoulder. 'What are you thinking?'

Gripped by an indefinable feeling of remorse, she asked herself whether she was betraying Pablo with Juanito, or Juanito with Pablo.

'Juanito,' she said, 'I was thinking that love ought to have no beginning . . . Those who are destined for us, we ought to know and love for all eternity.'

'But that is true of us,' Juanito protested. 'I have always known you. Where I come from, there is a Madonna so beautiful that all the women are jealous of her. She has hair like yours:

black, and sleek, and parted in the middle. Her eyes give the impression of knowing everything, her nostrils are transparent, and her lips are trembling as though she had just betrayed a secret.'

'Hush!' Encarnacion cried. 'You're a pagan, a Moor like all Valencians.'

But behind that downward-tilted head there sparkled a shield of precious stones. In the darkness, Juanito could see that living sun gently revolving on its spokes.

'That morning when you came over to the well, I thought the Virgin was manifesting herself in our hour of victory, the way she slips into the crowd on feast-days in Valencia . . .'

'Juanito, you are mad.'

To silence him, she crushed her lips against his. She returned to her confessions.

'To Pablo, in those days, I was at once a pupil and an equal. To share the same ideas is to be the same age . . . Are you asleep, Juanito?'

There was no answer.

The same age . . . Encarnacion continued her ramblings in silence. Like a pair of students carried away by the same dreams, Pablo and Encarnacion would sit over the fireside late into the night. It was a hard winter. The flames would shoot up from the grate like trees, fed not so much by the old moss-grown logs as by the wild notions, the reckless projects which they flung thick and fast into the hearth, their faces glowing from the blaze, their pupils dilated by this incandescent landscape. They could not tear themselves away from these moments of wonderful openness with one another. The slumbering household stood guard over their tête-à-tête. They did not even look at one another. With their faces turned towards the fire, they were like soothsayers spreading their hands and staring into the future.

31

A VILLAGE IN THE PRIORATO DISTRICT became the Future City. The same forward-looking spirit was making two hearts beat to the same rhythm. The same sea-breeze filled their lungs. Were Pablo and Encarnacion to be the only ones excluded from this happiness which they were building for others with such cold intensity?

The moment a talent showed signs of emerging, the moment a child in the village or in one of the neighbouring farmhouses displayed any ability to draw, or an interest in mechanical things, Pablo felt responsible for this spark which had found its way into a human mind. Out of the entire New Testament, the only parable that Pablo cared to quote was the one about the servant entrusted with the increase of his master's wealth. Out of this peasant boy in whom a scientific aptitude was coming to light, Pablo would make an inventor or a technician. This small child who spent all day sketching would one day give expression to the new face of Spain. The experiment frequently revealed the mediocrity of the 'subject' and the graspingness of those about him. Such mishaps brought Pablo and Encarnacion even closer together than the successes.

Pablo refused to be discouraged.

'Our percentage of disappointments is quite normal,' he said.

This generous creed isolated Pablo from other members of his class. But criticism, like praise, merely impelled him to widen the scope of his experiments. Election to parliament enabled him to apply his ideas on a larger scale. Just when Pablo was emerging as a politician, the disease tightened its grip on Enrico. Pablo's work in his first session as deputy was interrupted by medical examinations, X-rays and visits to specialists. For a few weeks, a change of treatment gave Enrico the outward semblance of health. Deceived by this remission, Enrico admitted that he had imagined the end was near after the first alarm. 'I wanted to come down here to Santa Creus because I hadn't the courage to die in Menton or Davos.'

Encarnacion felt as though she were still in the car which had driven her down to Santa Creus, a few miles at a time. Past the window drifted the rocky plateaus, the banks of red clay. In the deserted villages the shutters were closed, for the inhabitants—living equally in fear of light and wind, sunshine and darkness barricaded themselves against the elements, against poverty and famine . . . We are just the same, thought Encarnacion, we shut our eyes, we stop our ears, we lie with words and silences.

Enrico's powers of dissimulation became apparent to her for the first time. For months, believing that there was no hope for him, he had made no demands on Encarnacion, apart from getting her to read him novels in which women forswear love and, soon afterwards, die from the sacrifice.

'I didn't want to subject you to a heartrending deathbed scene until I had to.'

Enrico apologized for upsetting all the doctors' pronouncements. The driver swerved to avoid the quagmires. After this, just as one is suspicious of a partner who sees things too clearly, Encarnacion was always to dread Enrico's lucidity and that kindness which was akin to the rather contemptuous compassion of God towards his creatures.

'I thought I knew the date. Any time-limit arouses fear and impatience. Whenever Pablo made plans in front of me, at lunchtime, I would say to myself: The day the modern dairy-farm, or the schoolhouse or the maternity home is completed, I shall be gone. And when you talked of redecorating the house, I was in agony . . .'

More quietly, almost ashamed, he continued: 'That was weakness, for if death is total oblivion I shall not take a memory of your appearance with me, nor that of the house. And if ghosts return to roam the places where they have lived, a change of wallpaper or a rearrangement of furniture will hardly baffle them!'

He took her hand. Encarnacion shut her eyes. In the dining-room the midday sun traced a ladder of light on the shutters. Pablo was talking, laughing, growing intoxicated with his own voice. His son was silent, his lips slightly parted in a faint smile, as though he for his part were growing intoxicated with his silence and reserve.

'Today, I'm just like everyone else: I don't know the date of my execution. I am pardoned, or perhaps I'm simply on parole . . . To be alive is to know that you will still be breathing to-morrow.'

The new treatment had given him back his old gaiety and animation, but within a few days he was in the grip of a queer feeling of exhaustion.

'It's as though I were swimming in water that presses in on me like lead . . . I can't make headway . . . I've done some silly things since we came down here . . . I've lost the habit of being healthy . . .'

The relapse was attended by violent spittings of blood. They occurred at night. In the mornings, his face was ashen and there was an unhealthy gleam in his eyes: he looked like a man exhausted from a long journey.

Pablo was packing his bags for Paris. Encarnacion and Enrico kept the bad news from him: how could they deprive him of a happiness that he had been putting off for so long?

From his student years in Paris, Pablo retained for the city the inexplicable predilection that ties us to certain human beings. To catch the plane to France from Barcelona was to take a quick and easy flight back to his youth.

To get free of their souls human beings have little but prayer, drink and debauchery. To Pablo, Paris was all three: an orison to an unknown God, a confrontation with himself, an evasion. He wrote long, adolescent letters to Enrico—the letters of a man in love, thought Encarnacion; for, to write them, Pablo seemed to wrench himself from the caresses of Paris as from a woman's bed.

Encarnacion discovered the torture chamber which each of us carries inside him, and within which even the most innocent expressions of happiness, on the part of another, serve as racks and whips. In this innermost ring of hell, unlit except by longing, victim and torturer are one.

One evening they heard the jingle of a harness and the sound of horses' hooves on the gravel drive. Encarnacion set down the vase in which she had been pretending to arrange some flowers. The purple dahlias spun round on the table, turning into wheels of fire, wheels of joy, wheels of pain, grinding up her life. Pablo was back. When he stooped to kiss her, Encarnacion caught the familiar whiff of lavender. As he smiled at her, he stood swaying slightly, just as he always did; but his eyes were boring into her with boyish avidity. Both he and she were quivering with the same bridled surge of emotion. Encarnacion could feel sobs and laughter clutching at her throat. She wanted to dance and shout and weep, but Enrico was secretly observing her.

She said bravely: 'Tired of Paris already?'

'Not in the least tired of Paris, just worried about the wine-harvest.'

He was humorously readopting his role of landowner.

But Encarnacion was feasting her eyes on his sturdy frame. Phrases whirled dementedly in her brain: I love, I am loved. She gazed into his face, a face at once too virile and too tender, a youthful face despite its wrinkles. She kept saying to herself: He will never go away again. Enrico had vanished. They were standing there, face to face, more naked than lovers in the frenzy of the act. Pablo read her thoughts. He said, in a slightly strangled voice: 'I'm too old to travel.'

'Too old?' Encarnacion's gaze caressed the hollow cheeks, the fine lips. Pablo was hers. Encarnacion bowed to her fate: they would never experience the sating caresses, the shamefaced moments of remorse, the sensual memories, the impure longings that link two lovers. They would grow old side by side, and never would Encarnacion entwine Pablo's fingers with her own. They would stifle this leaping joy which was making them both tremble at this moment. They would conceal this great unspoken happiness beneath everyday tasks and concerns, but their love would be as beautiful as those beggars, almost naked beneath their rags, who come knocking at doors in late summer. And no one would ever guess how Pablo and Encarnacion had loved each other.

'What is it, Juanito?'

Her companion sighed, turned on to his other side and mumbled something. He plucked Encarnacion from her long reverie by changing dreams himself. Why, lying beside this burning young body, should she recapture Pablo's most trivial remarks, the note of impatience that sometimes came into his voice, his expression when he was interrupted in his reading, his childlike laughter over a tiny success, and his fits of temper, which would subside at the slightest word of reproach? None of this was painful to Encarnacion any longer. Even the thought of Pablo's being a prisoner was not a source of anguish to her. For the offensive would soon be on the move again. Pablo would be released. Between the shutters, the sky was turning pale. Juanito only just had time to get back to camp before sunrise. To awaken him, Encarnacion set her lips to his mouth and gave him the last kiss of the night, the first kiss of the day.

32

THE NATIONALIST ARMY was pitching violently into both extremities of the Republican front. To effect its breakthrough in the centre, it was concentrating its artillery and main strength in the regions of the Sierras. It was employing against the enemy the same manœuvre that had enabled the Republicans to cross the Ebro in July.

Juanito and his companions were clinging desperately to the rugged slopes of the Sierra Caballs. The rare items of news that reached them were as darkly foreboding as the sudden storms of late summer.

Europe was being divided into two camps, over the question of a Polish port. Would a world war earn Spain, *in extremis*, the help of allies who had hitherto held back? Agustin threw himself, body and soul, into an enlightened internationalism. The Danzig problem, he said, was compelling the League of Nations to fulfil its role as arbiter. But how were the issues in Spain to be laid before the great powers again? How was Pontius Pilate finally to be coerced into passing judgment?

Agustin knew how: the Spanish Republic would, on its own initiative, call for the withdrawal of volunteers. And this move would testify to its irreproachable conscience.

'Don't you see, Juanito? It is more compelling than the non-violence of the mystics and more effective than the strategy of the militarists. Instead of defending a mountain peak or a hillside, only to lose it to the Nationalists the following day, we shall be regaining, outright, a position of overwhelming moral superiority. World opinion: that is the real tribunal and the real sanction. The League will impose a solution to the Danzig problem upon the disputing parties. Then it will intervene in Spain.'

'In Valencia, the Water Tribunal settles disputes in the same way. Each man is his own lawyer; if the condemned party protests, his fine is doubled and he steals sheepishly away amid roars of laughter . . .'

This commonsensical approach irritated Agustin.

'You're a proper Valencian. You see everything in terms of harvests, of distributions of water!'

'When a man is attacked, he calls his friends to his assistance and everybody fights until there isn't an ounce of breath left in them. What do we want to send the volunteers home for? The only reason they came was to defend us!'

The Republic's fate was being determined abroad, claimed Agustin.

Juanito laughed at this: 'When Franco's guns start firing —this morning, for instance—our fate will be determined here.'

The war was lost but, like relics of an earlier life, sensations allied to the intoxication of victory persisted in Juanito. The warm

July darkness, the cool river-water still clung to his naked skin. He was still tottering about on the bankside pebbles, among the reeds. On that baptismal night, Juanito had felt as though he were crossing every frontier at one fell swoop . . . A few weeks had gone by. The miracle had turned out to be a lie. Juanito was capable of contending with human beings and with the elements. He was incapable of standing up to figures, interpreting statistics or struggling with abstractions. It was enough for him to glance upwards: the sky above the withered vines was still a sky of victory. Of what possible use was this stratagem, designed to impress world opinion and the League of Nations?

'There is no proof that we are beaten! And nobody has the right to take away our volunteers . . . If the International Brigades are disbanded, the world will suppose that we are defeated. They will all abandon us. We shall lose our airmen and technicians, but Franco won't: he will still have his specialists, his artillery, his armour . . . Franco will put paid to us without any help from outside.'

Agustin felt his conviction wavering: was this peasant arguing more convincingly than the politicians? To Juanito, every volunteer was the representative of a whole people. How dare governments break this alliance sealed between men of goodwill? These desperadoes, coming from every nation, had given themselves to Spain. This contract, in which death was merely a clause, could not be broken. A kind of despair came over Juanito.

'God, at least, is straight!' he shouted. 'He can't let us down!'

Agustin eyed him uneasily. He would never love him more than in this moment, when he was ascribing men's cowardice to the indifference of God.

'It is because God is straight that he is not intervening. He would slip us a few aces, but men are cowards, who will allow a stranger to be murdered before their eyes. To excuse themselves they say: "It's none of our business. He isn't from these parts." '

Some distance away from them, two soldiers were pretending to quarrel. The gallery was applauding their streams of invective, their challenges. They don't suspect a thing, thought Juanito.

Defeat is like death. You don't know anything, you are unwilling to believe what you hear. Suddenly you find out, and all is changed. He thought back to a spring morning in the *huerta*. The branches and the broad leaves of the fig-tree lay strewn on the ground. Francisco, struggling to get his breath back, was trying to find words to describe the shelling of Almeria. Federico's drowned body was being swept unresistingly along by the currents of the sea. The sunlight was glinting on the water racing through the canals, on and on as far as the eye could see.

'It's Vicente and Esteban,' said Juanito.

'I have to be at H.Q. at five.'

'*A las cinco de la tarde*,' Juanito repeated. It was the first line of the dirge that Lorca had flung over Ignacio Sanchez, like the cape still covered with the sand from the ring and stained with a mingling of blood, beast's and man's. Agustin intoned it frequently. Lorca was dead. Where was the poet who would weave such a sumptuous winding sheet to enwrap, not the quivering body of a matador, but the Spanish Republic?

'*A las cinco de la tarde . . .*'

The nervous voice was mingling the familiar words with the tranquil September sky, with the coppery vines, with the dusk which was gathering in total disregard of the beauty of the world, with the laughter of men who would go on living and hoping and fighting even when all was over for them.

Juanito stood listening with lowered lids, as though he were attending a religious ceremony. What was the point of discussing the arrangements for the withdrawal, of envisaging, in detail, the phases of a liquidation? They made their way back to the camp in silence.

33

BENEATH A RUST-COLOURED SKY, September was drawing to a close, with a humid smell and a breeze that carried a hint of corruption. In the clouds, too, as though across other vineyards oxidized by sulphur, men seemed to be awaiting the signal for the wine-harvest. The soil was regretfully allowing its riches to rot: nobody wanted to gather them any more. It was a breast heavy with milk, to which no child's lips clung, a breast tormented by its useless sap.

At lengthy intervals, Franco's artillery would open up. Vicente remarked that air-raids, and Nationalist attempts to break through their positions at dawn or dusk, had taken the place of the Angelus and the ringing of bells before Mass.

'We haven't surrendered a foot of ground in two months,' Juanito insisted. Am I lying to encourage the men or to fool myself? he wondered. The relieving of the International Brigades, scheduled for 21st September, had nearly ended in catastrophe. Agustin had put in a sudden appearance at dawn that day, looking pale with worry.

'Stand by, man! Your orders will arrive some time during the morning. The Nationalists have just smashed our line in the Sierra. We have to repair the situation, and quick, before the relief turns into a rout . . . What are you smiling about?'

'Nothing! It would be even more wonderful if Spanish troops were to re-establish the line. Don't worry: we are sure to find a way of stopping Franco!'

On his motor-bicycle, the political commissar listened with an expression of exasperated pity.

'You can say that again—it would be even more wonderful! Just the same, you'd better hurry up and alert your men!'

He sat staring at Juanito with desperate fondness, as though one or other of them were about to die.

'And then, Juanito, we shall talk the matter over tonight. I'd like to spend the evening calling you all the names under the sun. I'll explain how nothing is capable of rousing Don Quixote from his madness, or a Valencian from his illusion!'

Agustin had headed straight along the line of the mountains, along a rough, winding road from which his machine seemed, at every turn, on the point of crashing down into a precipice. Already the camp was the scene of feverish activity. Within an hour of Agustin's passing visit, in the full glare of the sun, the men were lending one another a hand with their kit, outside the ruined house that served as a command post. Juanito subjected each soldier to a thorough inspection. He shared out the rations. What was the good of hoarding what little food was left? The men were discussing the news. Franco had played his cards well. He had waited to launch the final assault until the relieving of the Brigades disorganized the front. The Sierra Caballs, despite all the shells that had been raining down on the outposts for the past fortnight, was still in Republican hands.

Time stood still. There was nothing in the whole wide world but this tender and too beautiful September sky and that distant rumbling. The whole of Franco's artillery must be firing. Never had Juanito felt such impatience burn within him. The hours were slipping slowly past. Everything had been said. The men sat silently on the roadside. Once again Juanito calculated the Republican forces in the Sierra. There were the 13th and 14th International Brigades—crack units—to deal with the Nationalist thrust. But the men's minds were troubled more by moral issues than by statistics relating to men and guns. Was a unit under any obligation to go on fighting after the time stipulated for its relief? The Brigades had carried out their contract up to 21st September. Were they in honour bound not to bequeath a jeopardized front to the Spanish units? These foreigners, retorted Esteban, had the same ties with Spain as if they had been born in Salamanca or Malaga. The argument grew more involved.

Was it enough to be a Republican to feel and act like a true Spaniard?

Juanito broke into a laugh: 'Soon we shall see how true Spaniards *do* feel and act! '

The midday sun was burning their skins. The soldiers had put down their rifles, their bursting haversacks, their cartridge belts; in this intense light, the paraphernalia of war seemed pointless and cumbersome. This day of waiting would never end . . . The stout blades of pocket-knives sank warily into the hard crust, the resilient flesh of the bread. They ate slowly, out of habit and possibly to stop themselves from thinking about the orders which did not come. Juanito laid his head on his pack and promptly fell asleep. He woke, with a start, an hour later. The wind brought only a faint rumble. The afternoon was slipping past, just as the morning had. If the order came now, thought Juanito, we should not have time to counter-attack.

Dusk was gathering when Agustin reappeared, looking grey with fatigue. He asked for a drink, and while he was slowly emptying the wine-jug, the men formed a circle round him in silence. Then he began to relate the day's happenings, as though reciting a well-learnt lesson. His words fell with the weight of things already accomplished. Events over and done with were being inscribed in a book. In the midst of the shuddering survivors of Campredo, restored to life on the bank of the Ebro, the medical orderly in the same impersonal voice had listed the villages already conquered, the successes of the offensive . . . Perhaps, thought Juanito, victory and defeat are final only when a man has given them this indelible quality by sharing them with other men.

Like the crossing of the Ebro, the last stand of the Brigades up in the Sierra Caballs was on a par with other incredible deeds in the remotest past. One night, these improbable feats of arms would set other adolescents dreaming.

Yet every one of these soldiers was listening as though spellbound to Agustin's dispassionate tones. The glaring, empty September day, spent on a roadside waiting for orders, was turning into a series of terrifying episodes. In the midst of the surprise blows, how were attackers to be distinguished from defenders, victors from vanquished? The Nationalist thrust had been supported by a torrent of steel and flames. The Republicans' command post had come under fire. Agustin made a wry face; he recalled crawling over to a brother-officer to pass on instructions to him. The cracked walls had shaken every time a gun fired. The ceiling had seemed about to cave in on them. The floor had been about to swallow them up. Then the bombardment had stopped. Taking advantage of the lull, Agustin had taken a glance out of the command post's only window, now completely shattered. The Nationalist flag, with its spread-eagle, was already fluttering on the ridge. Haggard-faced troops were scurrying into hollows in the ground, in search of shelter. More guns were firing, more shells were producing other craters, which the men had no time to take advantage of . . . All was lost . . .

In an impartial voice, as though he had omitted one of the factors of the situation, Agustin added: 'There were some really fine officers in charge of the battalion . . . The Brigade Commander had the orders for their relief in his pocket. He was sole master of his decision.'

Cigarettes were stubbed out. Darkness was blurring the men's faces, though their eyes still shone faintly. Juanito could see the terrified soldiers bounding across the fresh shell-holes. The earth walls were caving in on them. These shelters were burying them alive . . .

'Well, Agustin . . .?'

Unhurriedly, as though giving evidence at a trial, Agustin continued: 'Captain Rol was too badly wounded to take any further part . . . Major Sangnier and Commissar Tanguy launched the counter-attack.'

Juanito felt a change come over his entire body: the sense of anguish that had been making his skin crawl was giving way to a kind of drunkenness, to a palpitation so violent that his heart seemed about to burst. The same surge of courage was coursing through all the other men's bodies. The same touch of madness was silently turning all their minds.

Agustin was recapturing the voice of earlier days, those low vibrant tones that had so stirred Juanito in Barcelona. Telling the peasants about the revolution of '89, or the Commune, or Fermin Galan's uprising, on a barracks square of the slopes of Tibidabo hill, the political commissar had achieved the sudden flagging, the half-repressed sobbing, the momentary swooning of saeta singers. Like them, he had appeared to succumb at the paroxysm of his inspiration, at the supreme moment in which prayer and invective, the sigh of enjoyment and the cry of pain, are one.

Now Agustin was abandoning himself to this secret effusion to conjure up the manner in which the relief had been effected at the height of the disaster. His audience felt like urging him on, as though he were a matador performing a difficult pass, as he extolled the heroism of the French, their presence of mind, their grim determination to re-establish the damaged front. Without these coolheaded foreigners, all the achievements of the Spanish divisions and of the Brigades would have been in vain.

When he reached the end of his account, Agustin experienced that trembling of the glottis, that sharp intake of breath, that impassioned suffocation that are perceptible only to the initiates of the flamenco. And they all applauded him, as though he were a singer who had just hit a note in which his voice was beyond compare, or an actor who had achieved an intonation which carried all before it.

Those who had expressed doubt as to whether the Brigades would stand firm on the day they were relieved were now proclaiming their admiration.

'*Más valientes que nosotros!*'

Agustin asked for a cigarette. In the light from the match, he was seen to nod his head. Am I just a poet, he wondered, a man so made as to reveal to all others the beauty of a gesture, to hold up the torch to a sacrifice?

He refused to share some tinned food with the soldiers, but agreed to spend the night in their camp.

'They already have all the information at H.Q.,' he said.

'If I leave here first thing in the morning, I shall still have to wait a good hour while the General Staff recovers from its fear . . .'

Juanito and his comrades made up a bed for him in the ruined hovel. They worked in the dark, roaring with laughter as they swept away the empty bottles and pieces of broken stone. For a mattress, they spread several blankets on the mud floor. Out of courtesy, those who usually slept alongside Juanito under this gaping ceiling elected to spend the night in the open. One of them found a candle at the bottom of his haversack and gravely lit it in an attempt to lend more importance to this makeshift hospitality.

The September night was warm and humid, with a mass of stars which the wind seemed to extinguish in a single gust, but which then shone out again, dilated, in a purer sky. Juanito spread his blanket next to Agustin's. The attachment that the political commissar felt for him did not surprise him. Juanito was tender and violent: it was natural that everyone else should be like him. As soon as they were stretched out in the darkness, Agustin started yawning.

'Shall I tell you something?' said Juanito. 'Captain Rol reminds me of Fermin Galan and Garcia Hernandez . . .'

'There is nothing in common between a soldier doing his job to the very end and those two martyrs, or unlucky conspirators.'

Juanito was not to be discouraged: 'Yet in Barcelona you used to say . . .'

'Their action was a double suicide; tonight, their sublime behaviour strikes me as being madder than all the exploits of the age of chivalry . . . But you are right. In Barcelona, those two friends, each trying to save the other, seemed to me finer than the heroes of antiquity, nobler than the great leaders of the National Convention.'

Juanito went on dreaming in the dark, with his eyes wide open. He kept saying, like a child clamouring for a fairy-tale: 'Go on, Agustin! Tell me, tell me . . .'

'Fermin Galan and Garcia Hernandez were two young

officers—two friends, Juanito—who believed in the Republic with all their hearts . . .'

'Two friends,' repeated Juanito, 'who believed in the Republic with all their hearts . . . Agustin, isn't that what *we* are?'

'Yes,' said Agustin, 'but in those days there was no Republic. It happened in Jaca . . . Everything seemed easy at first. Fermin Galan was marching at the head of the troops; the crowd was following him . . . A Civil Guard sergeant tried to halt them in the Plaza de Portales. Somebody shot him. Galan was indignant: this murder had sullied an insurrection without barricades. As they marched out of the town, he hurled his revolver into a ditch . . . And they all went to meet the foe unarmed.'

The fatigue of his daylong vigil was taking hold of Juanito. Agustin's unemotional voice was suggesting familiar scenes to him, drawn from his own life. The story of the uprising was being enriched by incidents tapped from his dreams; the arid plateaus of Aragon were turning into the green Valencian plain, dotted about with white *barracas* and orchards in blossom. The revolt, so swiftly quelled, hovered in his memory like an embroiled episode from an earlier life.

That night, a pair of prowling figures knocked at a farmhouse door. Covered with mud, exhausted from their long trek, they were asking for shelter. The peasant was not alarmed by these guests with their hunted expressions, or by their torn uniforms, on which their officers' insignia still shone. He invited them to sit down in front of the dying fire . . . Fermin Galan and Garcia Hernandez sat arguing in an undertone while the man went out to get some food from the pantry.

That's just how it would happen in the *huerta*, thought Juanito. If a stranger comes knocking at your door at night, you welcome him like an old friend . . . Awakened by these two deserters just as he was about to doze off, Juanito was hurriedly tossing a few sticks on to the fire. Then he was offering them food and drink. But all that the pair wanted was a roof over their heads, a bit of warmth. Juanito was able to catch a few words:

'The responsibility is entirely mine, Garcia. Think of your family . . . Slip across the frontier!'

Garcia Hernandez was refusing, and Juanito was discreetly lowering his eyes.

'I am not going to leave you.'

The defeated pair were embracing, with tears in their eyes. Juanito was looking on so wholeheartedly that he was now identifying himself with one of the comrades. He was turning into Hernandez, the one who was refusing to make a dash for it. Galan has assumed Agustin's thin face, his feverish gaze, his eloquent mouth. The incredible metamorphosis was readily achieved. The two friends were recognizing one another; they had discarded their identities, as though these had been a mere disguise. Now each was reading his own courage in his companion's exposed face.

Agustin's voice jolted Juanito out of his dream truer than reality.

'The mayor would not hand them over to the authorities. Galan himself was compelled to make a telephone call to Huesca, to get somebody to come and arrest them. They had to wait three hours for the arrival of these soldiers who were to drive them away handcuffed, like a couple of burglars caught red-handed. Meanwhile, what little they said to one another was full of confidence and gaiety. The certainty that they were going to end their lives together drove all other thoughts from their minds. The mayor kept begging them to make a run for it. History is full of these comic and heartrending incidents. The village mayor, a man of decent feelings, stood wringing his hands. In his anguish, he ventured to tell them that the Republic would need officers like them. They had no right to sacrifice themselves. Galan replied courteously that one day the Republic would have an army worthy of it. They were merely two scouts who had strayed on to the road to the future.'

Juanito was slipping into another world, in which human beings could at any moment choose to be reincarnated; they did not have just one life, just one chance of making good; they were free to move backwards and forwards within their span of time, whenever they liked. Galan and Hernandez were yielding to the mayor's entreaties. They had assumed different names and appearances to shake off their enemies . . . They had changed their destinies.

'At the trial, in Huesca, the accused did not even defend themselves. Instead of denouncing his accomplices, Galan wanted to expound his ideas. The general in charge of the hearing asked uneasily: "Will it take long?" "Too long," replied Galan. He preferred to hold his peace and light a cigarette. In this way, he made the court's task easier and saved those who had supported him . . . Do you understand, Juanito?'

Juanito did not answer; he was continuing Agustin's story in his own manner. Galan would not be executed, since today he was concealed behind Agustin's features, but in his dream Juanito was trying to fill in the gap, the blank, that existed between Galan's escape and Agustin's arrival on the scene. In a wild village in the high plateaus of Aragon, Galan had adopted the appearance of a young schoolmaster. Agustin was the proof of this reincarnation. In a faraway voice, thick with sleep, Juanito asked: 'Galan isn't dead, is he, Agustin?'

'What do you mean? There is no telling what idea is going to ripen next in the brain of a Valencian. Not dead? He declined to have a priest attend him, but he kissed the lieutenant in charge of the firing squad . . . I picture that young officer as being alien to the scene, with the rather distant compassion of the Centurion in El Greco's painting. He was there to fulfil a role that he had not chosen, to carry out a sentence for which he was not responsible. His men stood in line, the regulation distance away, and everything was done in a dignified way. In Huesca, Galan had bidden farewell to his companions. But on the way, the lorry got stuck. They had to finish the journey on foot. The lieutenant and the two condemned prisoners walked side by side. They stopped several times, to give one another a light or to hand round cigarettes. Probably Galan experienced a hidden wave of friendship for this grave young officer who was exactly as he himself might have been had he not answered another call. I don't know why it is, Juanito, that in this whole strange and admirable story I should always come back to this moment, to this mysterious bond of feeling between two men. To me it seems that Galan chose his killer. He was glad that it was this officer, and not another, who was in charge of the firing squad. Galan did not believe in God, but he had faith in a brotherhood of men. When he had exchanged that kiss of peace with the lieutenant, he shared out among the soldiers everything that he had in his pockets: seven pesetas, thirty centimos. It was his entire fortune, and the men took the copper coins with proper gravity, as a final token of friendship. Then Galan placed himself in front of the stake and shouted to them: "Aim well, comrades! Don't hang your heads!"

'It is this familiarity, this courtesy towards his killers, this suggestion of being on an equal footing with death, that make the hero. Yes, Juanito, that forgiving kiss to the lieutenant, those pesetas shared out among the soldiers, are finer than the sublime farewell speeches of the great.

'And just picture that young lieutenant dropping his arm and shouting "Fire!" . . . Yet, as though in its simplicity this were not great enough, people have described how this lieutenant was converted to Galan's ideas, and how at Teruel he fought savagely for the Republic . . . Why should it not be so? Juanito, I'm sure that every one of those soldiers must have piously preserved the pesetas belonging to the martyrs of Jaca . . . A conversion, a miracle, signs from heaven at every hand, relics of every kind—well, what else can you expect, Juanito? This is still Spain. Freedom, too, has its saints. What do you have to say about it—you who see the hand of God in everything?'

Juanito was asleep. Agustin went on in an undertone: 'Only the imaginary is real in this country, and that spiritual frenzy that grips the mob at the sight of spilt blood, whether it is Christ's or a bull's, a Christian martyr's or a heretic's . . .'

He imagined that he was back in that sinister dawn, when the front was giving way under the force of the enemy thrust . . . Juanito was voicing his dreams that the Spanish would save the situation . . . The command post was collapsing under the weight of the artillery fire. Captain Rol lay dying on the ground, on a makeshift stretcher. In that ash-covered, hugely blistered, lunar landscape, the guns were scooping out fresh craters. Men were fleeing through a petrified chaos, like damned souls trying to hurl themselves into a deeper abyss . . . A morning of Hell . . .

In the still night, Agustin could barely make out the sound of Juanito's breathing. He touched his bare arm to assure himself that he was asleep, that he was alive. A strange thanksgiving welled up in Agustin's heart. He repeated, several times: 'A morning of Hell, a night of Paradise, a morning of Hell . . .' then promptly fell asleep.

34

NEXT DAY, they returned to their first encampment, on the edge of the village. They were coming home. Their hands recognized the walls that they had braced, caressed the well whose lip they had repaired. Uneasiness showed in the faces of the women and the old men. Was the village going to be turned into a battlefield again? Terrible accounts of summary executions were circulating. Any suspect quickly became a hostage, and any hostage was transformed, one morning, into a corpse riddled with bullets.

Juanito's companions were proudly reckoning up the enemy's losses: in the course of the latest fighting, the 13th Moroccan Division had been destroyed with all its equipment. As he listened to them, Juanito reflected that, even though crack units were wiped out in each new offensive, the Civil War was not leading up to a decisive total: the lists of debits and credits increased with every defeat, with every victory.

That very evening, his heart beating rapidly, Juanito raced over to Encarnacion's house. She was waiting for him. At the end of September she had received a short note from Pablo. He made no mention of Enrico, but on this single sheet of paper, slipped under Encarnacion's door by an unknown hand, he claimed that he was well and that he still had hope. These two lines, so commonplace as to be almost anonymous, seemed endowed with unbelievable strength. Do I still love Pablo? wondered Encarnacion.

Yet she abandoned herself to Juanito's caresses without seeking to justify her behaviour. She gave herself over, body and soul, to the brittle happiness of his return, to his tenderness and burning desire. Life was giving her this belated joy so that one day she might suffer more intensely . . . Life . . . She would say this vague word over and over again. It was less theatrical than 'destiny', less presumptuous than 'providence'. Sad and consoling, it was sufficient to evoke a power with all too human a face: life. This wretched, abetting and lucid God looked deep into Encarnacion's soul, with her own eyes . . .

In these clear, warm-hued October days, the soldiers quarrelled a good deal, having nothing better to do.

'It's like waiting for a train at the wrong station,' Vicente would say.

Siestas and card-games occupied the less exacting. The guitar-player from Caceres had broken the last remaining string and put his foot through the instrument. The sudden appearance of an aircraft or the explosion of a mine would momentarily put new life into the more loquacious. The tailor from Gerona would make a sweeping gesture with his hand, as though clearing his work-bench.

'What with the British navy in the Atlantic and the French navy in the Mediterranean,' he said, 'Morocco will soon be taken care of.'

His companions shrugged. To make forecasts was to invite disappointment. Some mysterious force was implacably at work against them. One town after another was falling to Franco, one province after another going over to him. But the Republicans' dearly bought successes at Brunete and Teruel and on the Ebro were crumbling away in paltry advances.

On that first afternoon, Juanito and Agustin were strolling, up and down a shell-blasted thicket within a few yards of the farmhouse. The vine-arbour had started putting forth shoots again. The walls displayed scars that had been filled in with fresh plaster, like that paler skin which forms over wounds.

'We aren't advancing any more,' Juanito observed, 'we are in neutral gear. This offensive is like a jammed machine-gun. No matter who tries, it won't fire any more.'

'We've had our miracle,' said Agustin.

Juanito stared unseeingly at the billowing terrain behind which Franco's artillery lay hidden. The guns were not even firing any longer. The offensive had been brought well and truly to a standstill. And yet Juanito had lived through that apocalyptic night on which half-naked men had imagined that by crossing a river they were overthrowing every frontier, demolishing every obstacle, forcing the hand of fate.

'This morning I had news from home,' said Juanito. 'The factories in Sagunto are working day and night.'

'Sagunto . . .' repeated his companion.

The Republic was exhausted, the war was lost, but the blast-furnaces of Sagunto were glowing and linking up, across the centuries, with other braziers lit by men who had been on the point of capitulating. History was not a remorseless progression, but a symmetrical interplay of images readjusted to suit the whim of a mountebank. A very poor poet shapes history, thought Agustin. He is concerned solely with repeating certain syllables, with organizing these connections and echoes and reflections within the cycle of events. Perhaps it is only a play in which the actors change: the text is debased or enriched by their every mistake. Yesterday saw the absurd sacrifice of the inhabitants of Sagunto setting the town ablaze out of loyalty to Rome; today sees the no less absurd sacrifice of the people of Valencia, men and women alike, toiling in the factories without respite.

'I've never told you about my earliest memory of the war, have I? It was right at the start, in Aragon . . . Durruti's men arrested a little fifteen-year-old Falangist. His comrades had been mown down, all round him. He was shaking with fright. He was shouting that he had been forcibly conscripted. They searched him. He had a Falangist party-card in his pocket: that didn't prove anything. So the militiamen sent him to Durruti. Making no attempt to find out why he was fighting against us, Durruti offered him the chance of joining our ranks. The boy didn't say a word. Durruti loved sublime attitudes. He would spare this child, who would soon admit himself defeated by his high-mindedness . . . All these anarchist leaders revelled in tragic situations . . . The little Falangist asked for twenty-four hours in which to make up his mind. He was given them. When Durruti sent for him, the scene was all set for the magnanimous pardon; delivered in the grand manner. But the boy ruined the whole thing. After carefully thinking it over, he refused to change sides. . . . They shot him. A hero or a lunatic, depending on which way you look at it! Juanito, you are just like that fifteen-year-old fanatic. Having time to think doesn't sober you. On the contrary, the stay of execution—the offensive on the Ebro—merely strengthened you in your illusions. And when the evidence was staring you in the face? Only the weakminded give in when the facts give the lie to their dreams. True visionaries are not to be swayed. You are Don Quixote all over again. Like him, nothing can bring you to your senses—neither the jeers of your fellow-men nor the pitfulls of destiny. What can I say to you? One doesn't wake a sleepwalker!'

'Keep talking,' said Juanito, clenching his teeth. The comparison with that fifteen-year-old Falangist nettled him, yet he also found it gratifying. He was saying to himself: Had I been in his place, I should have done the same, and his heart was thudding furiously.

Agustin hesitated. How could he destroy this hope which had sustained their friendship? Would Juanito forgive him for these words of doubt? He continued discreetly: 'The fact that Franco's guns are silent, Juanito, means that he is preparing a massive build-up of artillery. Do you want figures? Franco is concentrating hundreds of guns along a front of less than a mile and a half, and the whole of his air force will be there to make the battering more intense. Don't you see? No army can stand up to that. For me, the Sierra Caballs is already in Franco's hands, and within a few hours—or a few days, if you like—the Sierra de la Picosa will have fallen to him, and the Sierra de Fatarella, and Mora del Ebro, and Ribarroya.'

'It isn't possible,' said Juanito. The blood had left his face. He was refusing to accept this defeat, was denying it with all his heart. The little Falangist must have worn the same stubborn expression when he rejected Durruti's offer.

'This is the ebb-tide . . . Now, the essential thing is for us to fall back without too great a loss. For our army, the failure of the offensive is a haemorrhage suffered by a man already gravely ill. How can the haemorrhage be arrested? That would be a second miracle, even more amazing than the first!'

'Than the first?' Juanito repeated these unbelievable words to convince himself that they had really been said. There never had been more, and never *would* be more, than one miracle: the crossing of the Ebro. A second miracle would cancel out the first. Recross the Ebro? How could anyone contemplate anything so monstrous?

Juanito began to shout: 'When in the name of heaven are Valencia and Madrid going to launch their attacks? We smashed our way through Franco's lines—let them do the same!'

'Franco would have no difficulty in repulsing attacks on another front.'

'But we have proved that Franco can be beaten!'

Furious resentment showed clearly on Juanito's face. Was it on his account that Agustin was smarting from the defeat as though the knowledge of it were something quite new to him? How could he bear the expression of bitterness and distaste in those innocent eyes? A pout of disappointment marred the line of his lips.

'Listen,' Agustin said abruptly, 'only a strong swimmer can save a drowning man . . . If Madrid tries to launch an offensive, all will be lost within a matter of days. We have got to hold out till a compromise settlement is imposed on us . . .'

'You used to say that there was no compromise between the coup d'état and freedom!'

'. . . A compromise, for true Republicans, is the only chance of one day continuing the fight, by other methods, in other places.'

'A fortnight ago you were talking about victory!'

'You are young! When a man gets to be forty, he tells himself that life is worth saving.'

'That's what the journalist said. You called him a traitor!'

Juanito bent down and scooped up a handful of red earth. It trickled through his fingers, warm and granulous. Time was running out in the same manner. Events were turning to dust. Lives were trickling vainly through the fingers of the war. There was no justice, here on earth or in heaven. Feeling quite helpless, Agustin was silent.

'I don't hold it against you,' Juanito said gently.

35

WHILE SHE WAS WAITING FOR JUANITO, Encarnacion would wander about the house. With her finger-tip she traced a name on the thin layer of dust covering the furniture. On the first floor, she lingered in Enrico's bedroom. He was a tidy invalid, and everything in his sanctum was neatly arranged. The bookshelves and albums of gramophone records were set within reach of the divan. There was a gap in the middle of the bound books. Enrico had tossed the book into his suitcase while Pablo was arguing with the soldiers who had called to arrest his son. Encarnacion re-enacted Enrico's movements. She ran her eye over the smooth leather backs, as if she were leaving a familiar room for ever.

'If I knew what was at the back of his mind at that very moment, I should know everything.'

Similarly, at the bedside of a dying man, we imagine that by puzzling out his final thought we are sharing his most intimate experience as a living man and catching a glimpse, through his eyes, of another world.

Enrico had been quite unstartled: he had been expecting this visit. Javier was a name and a face known for a long time past. Pablo had tried to turn this last offspring of a poor family into an engineer. 'It is only too easy,' he said, 'to acclimatize seedlings, to try out new manures. With a boy like Javier, you can't distinguish the plant from the surrounding soil. It is a more complex experiment, a dual endeavour. We have to uproot this boy from his background, graft him on to another background, take advantage of his natural curiosity to give him the rudiments of a scientific training.' The failure of this venture was more mortifying to Pablo than to Javier.

'There are limits to the metamorphoses that can be achieved,' Pablo acknowledged. 'To me, Javier seemed the most gifted, the most needy of the bunch . . . I should have liked to give him another chance.'

As a result of this attempt to educate him, Javier read the papers, discussed the news in the café, aired his views on the programmes of the political parties and gave his opinions on the future of Spain. After wavering, for a time, between the communists and the anarchists and the Falange, he plumped for José Antonio whose speeches made a stronger appeal to his imagination. Javier regarded Pablo as a dangerous traitor, because in the Cortes he had always voted with the Centre. The liberals, partisans of reform, were by their efforts prolonging the life of the Republic; in the eyes of the extreme right, as of the extreme left, they were the enemies who were aiming to cheat the nation out of the great and gory reckoning from which justice, law and order, and prosperity would emerge.

On that June morning, Javier had called on Pablo without either bounce or awkwardness. He had received orders which were not for him to weigh. He did not know what fate was in store for the hostages. Pablo's questions were blocked by the courteous replies of his former protégé. Encarnacion strode into the room. Javier saluted her, slightly intimidated. Pablo turned to his daughter-in-law. 'They are here to arrest Enrico,' he said. The same anguish was reflected in both their faces. How could Enrico possibly endure the days of suspense, the interrogations, the nights in Tarragona gaol?

'You know perfectly well,' said Pablo, 'that Enrico has never had anything to do with politics. If you must arrest somebody, I'm the one who is in charge of everything here.'

Javier nodded his head in agreement. Pablo was the mayor. His arrest would give rise to violent reactions. But taking his son as hostage constituted a sufficient guarantee.

Encarnacion began to speak, almost in spite of herself. By sacrificing Pablo, was she seeking to atone for her love?

'Enrico is ill. He hasn't stepped outside this house in ten years. Why arrest him? He is your hostage where he is.'

Javier seemed not to hear, but he averted his eyes from Encarnacion.

'Go and tell Enrico,' said Pablo. 'Leave us by ourselves.'

He had no further hope of persuading Javier. Perhaps, behind his expressionless, executioner's face, this humiliated man was enjoying a wonderful sense of turning the tables. He dug the earth just like any other peasant, but the little that he had learned enabled him to play this decisive role: he could release father or son, whichever he chose.

'Listen,' said Pablo, 'it is so easy for you. All you need is a name on a list. It's the same name.' He gave a smile, in an attempt to convey the suggestion that they were both in this together. 'Surely I'm a fair substitute? I'll make a better hostage for you than a boy who has been ill with tuberculosis for the past ten years. You'll no sooner get Enrico to gaol than you'll have to move him into the infirmary and let him go.'

'In that case, he won't be parted from you for long,' said Javier, with indifference in his voice.

They walked through the hall, and Javier opened the front door. Shouts rang out in the street. Enrico retraced his steps to kiss his wife.

'Encarnacion!' His deep voice was suddenly solemn, as though he were speaking to her for the last time.

'Encarnacion!' He repeated the name with the strange accent of a man who knows at last.

'What is it?' she asked.

He stooped and murmured in her ear: 'Remember . . . From this moment on, you are free . . .'

When Enrico stepped outside the door, there was a silence. The crowd had supposed that the troops had come to arrest Pablo. Instead, the villagers were confronted by a hunched-up figure, grey at the temples, old before his time and dazzled by the bright daylight. They had forgotten Enrico's blunted features. Their abuse burst forth again, mingled with curses. Jeers were flung at Javier, thick and fast, like a shower of stones.

'How much do you make for doing a job like this?'

'You're trying to put the grave-diggers out of business!'

He did not have time to meet these gibes with threats. Encarnacion had rushed forward into the middle of the detachment. She was clutching Enrico as though the soldiers were about to shoot him. A sergeant grabbed her arm and tried to pull her towards the house. Without letting go of Enrico, she scratched the man's face. Small boys were clinging to the soldiers, who were trying to free themselves. Javier turned to Pablo. He said with icy hatred: 'That's what I get for showing too much humanity. Call your daughter-in-law back over here or I'll fire into the crowd!'

He unslung his automatic rifle and motioned to the troops to make themselves scarce. Stunned by all this commotion, Enrico was lurching about, jostled by the soldiers and by the women who were trying to defend him. Screams of fear mingled with the abuse. Children threw themselves flat on the ground, a response that air-raids had developed in them. There were cries of entreaty: Javier was about to shoot.

Pablo stared at Javier, who was aiming at the man and woman standing with their arms round one another in the midst of this howling throng. A stone hurled by a small boy cut his cheek, but he paid no need to it. Clenching his teeth and tightening his finger on the trigger, Javier was about to spray the street with bullets . . .

Pablo rushed out into the middle of the group.

'Encarnacion, let them take him! They're going to shoot!'

He managed to wrench Encarnacion free of Enrico's arms and drag her back to the door. Javier signalled to his men to march off. A child picked up Enrico's suitcase and handed it to him. Enrico's face lit up in a smile. He shot a glance at Encarnacion whom Pablo was holding in the doorway. She looked as though she were about to faint.

'Encarnacion, it's only a matter of a few days, a few hours.'

She opened her eyes. Was he talking about Enrico?

'You think they are going to release him?'

'I don't know, but I got a message last night: tomorrow the Republicans launch their offensive.'

Her whole face lit up.

'Tomorrow!' she repeated.

They walked back to the drawing-room. In the same armchairs in which, only a few minutes before, they had sat waiting to attend to any needs that Enrico might have, they silently shared this piece of news.

'Tomorrow night,' Pablo added, 'they are going to cross the Ebro.'

And neither of them had the slightest doubt that the offensive would succeed.

36

THE OFFENSIVE WAS POSTPONED. Next day, Javier reappeared. He demanded to see Encarnacion, and she supposed that he brought news of Enrico: Javier merely handed her some wads of banknotes wrapped in newspaper.

'Enrico gave them to me,' said Javier. 'I accepted this money because prisoners are always searched, but I have brought it to you because it is yours!'

'I'll pass it on to my father-in-law.'

Her extreme indifference touched him on the raw. Did she take him for a servant?

'There's talk of a further list of hostages.'

'Since Enrico was arrested, we have been ready to join him at any time.'

Javier's eyes flashed briefly.

'The Republicans aren't here yet,' he said. 'The Ebro is deeper than people think.'

His desire to protract his visit was obvious. He could not take his eyes off Encarnacion's face. She moved a step closer to him.

'You wouldn't take Enrico's money, but suppose it was I who offered it to you?'

Javier smiled disdainfully.

'It isn't your money I want, it's you!'

She walked over to the study door and calmly opened it.

'Good-bye, Javier.'

'I'll see you again soon, señora.'

His brain could find no words for the whirl of hatred and remorse, love and desire, that held him in its grip. He shook his head, as though abandoning hope of finding expression for all the conflicting emotions that had been stirring within him for years. He was relishing this opportunity of existing in Encarnacion's eyes—his only pleasure, his only revenge. He looked her straight in the face.

'Tomorrow, señora, I shall be back for Pablo.'

The window overlooking the garden was wide open; the front door was not bolted. There was something intoxicating about this pretence of security. Pablo was relating his trip to Paris, the way one thumbs through an album—skipping certain pages. Encarnacion was not pained by his concealments. By now, Paris was simply a fête for the young at heart, a city aflower with dance-halls, ablaze with fun-fairs, as noisy and sweet as a hurdy-gurdy, with its deserted parks, its secluded museums, its dark façades trimmed with a frieze of birds.

'There are so many couples in Paris, and all lovers have the courage to be happy there.'

Behind the railings of the Luxembourg, a frailer, headier springtime was born under the dense foliage, beside a long mirror of water.

'It is a garden for those who are too happy or too unhappy, a garden for first kisses and final partings. When I returned to it, I was nearing that moment in life when any new discovery becomes simultaneously a leavetaking. Yet my heart raced like a boy's. A green-coloured shadow caressed the smooth cheeks and untroubled brows that were all about me . . . The strolling figures glided along the avenues of blossoming trees like prisoners in a transparent aquarium. Couples sat on the seats, with their arms round one another. A gust of wind was parting the branches; a cascade of sunlight was pouring down upon two twenty-year-old faces. All day long they had been students obsessed with diplomas and examinations, caught up in a constant race against time, but as they opened their fat, dog-eared books they smiled as though they had cleared those paper hoops which life places in their path, as a substitute for obstacles. Over this garden, as in churches where much praying is done, there hung a mood of immense acquiescence.

'I was just a man returning to the scene of his youth and sentimentalizing over his early years . . .' He broke off for a moment, in an attempt to take stock of all that useless knowledge, all that unnecessary toil, all that idling, all that fanciful ambition. Youth—that time of boundless happiness, of imaginary unhappiness, of longings that nothing can satisfy or disappoint—had lingered on for him beneath the tender and acid greenness of these leaves.

'I think of my youth in the same way as explorers who search for a mountain pass, or a country, or a river, or a city with such intensity that in the end they can visualize it. Across the road from the Law School, I found the hotel where I lived in the old days, with its tall slim façade, like a lighthouse. I felt like marching in and taking my key from the rack . . . I went on sitting by the Medici fountain till the drum-roll sounded. It isn't a fountain, it's an enchanted mirror. The lovers gather round it, just as birds swoop down on to a tree in the evening and stay there singing till nightfall. There is something funereal about those heavy garlands of leaves. They put me in mind of ancient sarcophagi; they surround a shrine in which a Juliet lies waiting for a kiss to restore her to life . . .'

In that magic grotto-like brightness, upon that mirror-backing worn by the reflections of so many couples, Pablo had on several evenings sought Encarnacion's face. But by pouring out this final tête-à-tête he was preserved from the giddiness of declarations. He started talking about his cousins. He laughed at the exasperated Parisianism to which so many foreigners are inclined. Nicole had backed up Pablo when he had suggested a flamenco restaurant, but this eagerness for 'local colour' had angered Teddy. He was so determined to frequent all the smart restaurants and be in the swim in every possible way that he no longer had any freedom or leisure, merely a despairing awareness of a programme that could never be kept to. A lithe and all too handsome youth had recited Andalusian *coplas*. To emphasize the rhymes he had flashed his gaudy rings and he had coerced the customers into gulping down their wine without putting their lips to the glass. A plump dancer had flung herself about in the midst of the tables. The waiters had interrupted their serving to hammer out the rhythm of the guitars on the dividing rail. Between steps, the girl had made every attempt to rouse Pablo. He had remained indifferent to her inducements. When he got up from the table, she walked over to him. 'You are turning me down because you love another woman,' she said. 'That is the only good reason for scorning a woman.' Pablo was disconcerted. Unable to find an answer, he blushed. Nicole noticed, and afterwards, in the car, she took pleasure in badgering him with questions.

Pablo was deriving a secret joy from relating this episode.

'And did you love somebody, Pablo?'

'Yes, Encarnacion! That was why I was so disturbed by a dancing-girl's remarks, and by Nicole's jokes.'

The night flowed by, a night beyond time, a night on which

souls could be bared, on which no confession was to be feared, since day would never come.

Encarnacion made as though to rise.

'If they are coming at dawn, you ought to get some rest.'

'They will come at dawn, Encarnacion, and I shan't have slept—but I shall have so many days and nights for sleeping.' He grinned broadly. 'Prison seems such a long sleep that I haven't given a thought to what I shall do when I wake up. Will there even be an awakening for me, for you, for us?'

She said very softly: 'You know perfectly well there will, Pablo. The Republicans may be crossing the Ebro at this very moment.'

'Let's leave the future aside, Encarnacion. For once, the present is enough for me. I have never known such a night . . . It is when we are truly living in the present that the past is restored to us, not in the form of memory, but as our deep roots, our living roots in time. Instead of trying to make out what our future will be, I am reliving our journeys together, those detours that we made on our way to Madrid or Tarragona. How could we possibly have confused our existence with these reforms, these proposals, these constantly changing plans, these memoranda? Our life, Encarnacion, was that village in Aragon, that hamlet in Estremadura, that college, that chapel from which we couldn't tear ourselves away and to which we promised ourselves to return one day . . .'

While he was talking about Paris, Encarnacion was all attention; but now that Pablo was uttering these names that were invested with their own past, images flooded into her brain, casting a warm, hallucinatory spell over her. In a ruined patio in Alcala de Henares, the midday sun was burning her bare arms and the back of her neck. The Tajo, green and white like an old bronze pulled out of the sea, held Toledo in its ring. On a pale April evening, leaning against the balustrade of the bridge, Pablo dreamed aloud: 'Other cities have a black Virgin, but Toledo is itself the swarthy face of that timeless creature, with its patina of incense and prayers.'

Somewhere south of Tarragona, in a fishermen's inn, a

flamenco singer on the point of swooning was throwing up his thin hands as though to defend himself from his ecstasy. On the Alhambra hill, behind jealous walls, the water still sang in the humble aqueduct that St John of the Cross had built with his own hands. One Granada morning, Encarnacion and Pablo wandered through that wild garden in which a recluse had composed the mystical songs that brushed him with a wing of fire in his cell.

But the whole of Spain was a spring, a cell and an orchard, a road signposted with treasures and strewn with miracles. In the abandoned palaces of Valladolid, washing floated among the sturdy arcades that bore the blunted profiles of the great warriors and poets and sages. In the heart of grim Castile, a city barely capable of being stirred by the snow of almond blossom, monasteries like fortresses were the sanctuaries of their love, as also, on the parched hills of Andalusia, were those castles dating from the Reconquest, brick-clad and marble-flagged like knights still wearing their silk raiment beneath their armour. On the rock at Peñiscola, the evening wind was scattering, like a flight of eagles, the imprecations of the last Pope of Avignon: they had inhaled the spray of the open sea on this shelf which no storm could cover.

But, in their memories, these pilgrims were confusing the voluptuous retreats where days and nights had seemed to obey a shepherd's flute: Orihuela, Elche, Murcia with its sealed-in gardens filled with the long cooing of doves.

In the spring, the scent of the lilies guided them through the cloisters which turn the monastery of Guadalupe into a City of God. Like a naked captive, a jet of water shivered in a turquoise fountain-basin, beneath a mudejar dome, amid sumptuous and faded mosaics.

'It is like a green and blue enamel buckle on the belt of an odalisk.'

The lines of St John of the Cross enveloped their rapture:

> *. . . dejando mi cuidado*
> *entre las azucenas olvidado.*

They abandoned themselves to this sensuous ecstasy. They lost themselves in this sparkling of gems, this singing of spring water, this harmonizing of scents.

'Encarnacion, a shout from a stranger in this Persian garden would be enough to pull a man right out of himself, to give him another life, another face, so exposed and beautiful that he would not dare to recognize it . . .'

Pablo's voice was becoming hoarse and breathless. Encarnacion pretended not to understand this thirsting look which was giving him a new youthfulness.

'Rather than mystical canticles, these surroundings call for those Sufistic poems which are the *coup de foudre* of a conversion. Shackles fall, wounds heal, eyes open . . .' He broke off, then resumed with sudden savagery: 'All is purified, all is forgiven, two lovers die, impaled by the arrow of a single line of poetry! Encarnacion, this enlightenment of sinners comes close to the transports of the Elect . . .'

Encarnacion made herself smile.

'To the monks,' she said, 'this garden is simply an innocent serenading of the Virgin by the angels. You, Pablo, are the only one who dreams of Bathsheba.'

But Encarnacion was succumbing beneath this burden of colours and scents and rhythms, beneath this weight of their words and silences . . . She was gazing at Pablo. The unbearable beauty of this moment was shining in her eyes, trembling on her lips . . . All was allurement . . . All was temptation . . .

Encarnacion averted her eyes.

'These cloisters are within the sacred precinct,' she said. 'Any poor woman who dares to set foot in here is liable to excommunication.'

'We shall be damned among the lilies and the roses,' countered Pablo, 'standing beside the Fountain of Life . . .'

Inside the church, he accorded only a casual glance to the Zurbarans and the choir screen and the Velascos' tomb. More than to accepted masterpieces, Pablo was drawn to beauty that was 'filched', like fruit into which they sank their teeth. Shining out in the gloom of the chapel was an altarpiece in which the Virgin seemed to be defending her Son from the adoration of the Three Kings: presents and crowns were spilling at her feet. She was sitting enthroned in the heart of a vortex, and her aloof face was the motionless hub of the wheel of fervour formed by those imploring arms, those outstretched hands. Down on her knees, Encarnacion was begging the Madonna, like a pauper: 'Take pity on me, who have nothing!' She was lying, for Pablo was behind her in the shadows.

To their lips sprang the name of a wild town defended by its gorges and crowned by the widely circling flights of birds of prey: this name was a bond between them, more private than a shared sin, more exquisite than a short-lived ecstasy. Encarnacion repeated, speaking very softly: 'Cuenca . . .'

37

BY MOONLIGHT, they had wandered amid a scene that was like a stage set. The streets rose steeply, vertiginous flights of steps and vaulted passageways linked tiny squares, in each of which stood a single tree or a calvary. A fountain was singing in the darkness. They had the impression of being on a parapet-walk: below them, they sensed a sheer rock-face, a brawling river, an abyss of warm darkness . . .

'In daylight, Cuenca is even more fantastic and startling than Ronda, even fiercer than Toledo,' said Pablo. 'It stands guard over a maze of precipices in which two rivers with almost identical names are alone successful in finding one another again.'

Next day, Pablo went down to the lower end of the town to take a look at the car. Encarnacion walked through the breakneck streets alone. She was holding Cuenca gathered in the palm of her hand like a bronze door-knocker, like a sword whose edge can never be blunted, as firm and compact as the doors of its palaces, which bristled with shell-shaped studs. The town gave the visitor a contradictory impression of security and instability. The centuries had proved incapable of shattering this metal armour, this stone shield. When Encarnacion leaned over the side of one of the narrow terraces that overhang the abyss, she discovered a pale river whose windings were garrotting the town on its rock. Cuenca, like a magnet, was drawing together the lines of this landscape of ashes and lava, but on to this grim, Genesis-like chaos there fell a blossoming light.

Pablo was waiting for her at the hotel. According to the man at the garage, they would be unable to leave before next day. Encarnacion concealed a sudden leap of joy behind her habitual calm.

'Let's go and take a look at the cathedral!'

The screens flung their airy foliage of copper and blackened iron nearly to the vaulted roof. In this indestructible vegetation, sirens, angels and monsters were at play.

With their medallions and string-courses, the monastery's austerely decorated arcades smacked of Rome as much as of the *siècle d'or*. Pablo loved this hint of robustness, this restrained might, this pent-up pride in the architecture of the Spanish Renaissance, qualities which come to the surface in the churches of Herera and in that unfinished palace in Granada, which is bursting with the sullen pride of a conqueror. He drew his hand over the noble, haughty columns, much as he would have patted a horse. They pushed open a worm-eaten door. Above them rose a triumphal and funereal cupola. The Mendozas had decided to erect this Pantheon to their line. Damp rot was eating into the walls where occasionally a bird strayed in flight. Beneath the huge vaulted roof, deepset niches were aligned on either side of the altar. This protocol, upheld beyond life, would allow the bones of the Mendozas to escape contact with other human remains.

Pablo and Encarnacion stared at one another. Triumphant in this place were Spain's sad grandeur, her feeling for precedence and, in this macabre pomp, her concern that aloofness—the privilege and supreme vanity of the great—should be preserved even among the dead.

They returned to the patio, with its rank weeds, its happy lizards, its mighty columns.

Pablo sighed.

'Why don't we spend the rest of our lives here, Encarnacion?'

Yet in the afternoon they visited other churches, and the small square near the seminary, where a minaret, as out of place as a giraffe in a garden, stood with an air of boredom among the seminarists playing their fierce game of football. Then they made their way down the worn steps, hewn out of the rock, that led to the Carmelite hermitage. They passed some gardens. The scents from the flowerbeds seemed to reach fever-pitch on this June afternoon. Now and then, a faint breeze would waft the smell of innumerable unseen roses towards them.

'The Carmelites who breathe this air all day long enjoy the best of both worlds,' observed Pablo.

Everything seemed easy that day: renouncing the world like these women, bending it to one's will like Pablo, walling up love within oneself, yet living a full life.

While they were having dinner at the inn, they heard on the radio that the right-wing deputy, Calvo Sotelo, had disappeared. Up on the wall, next to the calendar, were a portrait of Alfonso XIII and a picture of Our Lady of Murcia. Pablo sat staring at her small face, the face of a young nun, edged with goffered frill. In the kitchen, a woman was setting down the jar of oil with a sigh. Everything about them was invested with the scrupulous cleanliness of a convent parlour. The whitewashed walls with their patches of bluish shade, the red-tiled floor, the earthenware plates, all reflected the peace, nobility and humility of everyday life. The concord that existed between people, this harmony long nurtured between objects and the hands that have worn them down, was about to vanish. The calendar would serve no purpose from now on, the portrait of Alfonso XIII would become a provocation, and the slogans on the walls would change according to whichever side was occupying the area. The moment in which Pablo and Encarnacion had stepped inside this inn was receding into a past so distant that by now it was simply a mental conjecture, like those fabulous civilizations brought back to life by a clay tablet.

Pablo and Encarnacion, alone in the dining-room, sat talking in undertones of Calvo Sotelo. Bold to the point of rashness, confident of escaping from every trap, of returning from every exile, he had smiled disdainfully when La Pasionaria had shrieked in the Cortes that he would not die in bed. Without threats and enemies, he would have felt at a loss. He was like those great ships that need a mighty draught if they are to make headway: hate provided him with such a draught, quite as much as adulation did.

Encarnacion was silent. A man imagines that he can envisage death when boos and cheers are raining down on him during a speech in parliament. But how can he foresee the startled awakening, the leering faces of the executioners, the bullet in the back of the neck?

Pablo said: 'A hole-and-corner death like this was no way for him to end his life.'

The waitress, pricking up her ears, pictured the man at the height of his powers, a courageous figure with a ready tongue and a bright, clear laugh. She turned in alarm to the picture of the Madonna, who looked so like a young, placid and rather thickset nun. Beneath the coquettishly pleated wimple, her chubby face had not changed expression, nor had the eyes, which might be gazing upon Calvo Sotelo's corpse. The waitress crossed herself . . .

But now, forgetting the places at which they had stopped off in their travels through Spain, they returned to the days when Encarnacion had reopened the white house in the Paseo de la Castellana. She voiced her illusions: 'I was a bluestocking. Politicians seemed to me to be more childish and more dangerous than anyone else. I imagined that I was establishing harmony between these fanatics by getting them to meet in my house.'

'Yes,' said Pablo, 'I remember those evenings in Madrid when there was a truce between those hostile parties. Monarchists and Republicans exchanged views instead of abuse . . . Your beauty jolted those bigots out of their fanaticism. Just for a moment they were tired of being in the right.'

'A true party-man is never tired of being in the right.'

'They had used up all their threats and invective during the day. They looked like monsters under a spell.'

'It was only an entr'acte!'

Encarnacion smiled at Pablo's dreams of a centre party of liberals, a third party, but the waverings of the orthodox had prevented the Right from forming a government or associating itself with attempted reforms. After innumerable oscillations, the needle had returned to zero: reports had been followed by debates, press campaigns had overthrown governments almost before they were formed . . . As he evoked these rolls of the dice, each of which had cancelled out the one before, Pablo experienced a curious delight: his plans had fallen through, but to a phrase of Azaña's, or to a statement by the Primate of Toledo, there still clung glimpses of Encarnacion, modulations in her voice as she strove to convince a sceptic, and those glances of secret complicity that made up the past of their love.

Encarnacion, too, was deriving an inexpressible happiness from treating the same names as landmarks in their passion. The Asturian revolt, the attempted pronunciamento in Madrid, the efforts to obtain self-government on the part of Catalonia and the Basques: these convulsive fits now simply constituted a secret language between them. And this code had enabled them to endure the denial of the flesh, just as tonight it was allowing them to exchange these memories which were at once more fiery and more chaste than any caresses.

They no longer knew whether they were talking about the Republic, as of a river painfully shaping its course, or about this feeling which was invading their hearts through all their hopes and disappointments. It took more than a day, Pablo affirmed, for a nation to wake up to its potentialities. It took more than a few years for a man and woman to triumph over all obstacles and meet in a single night of fulfilment and refusal.

Politics was merely the wonderful disguise that had enabled two human beings to love one another.

'You made everybody believe,' Pablo went on, 'that Spain would awaken peacefully to freedom, that she would become a great power again without being torn in two, that in this new nation trust would prevail between all men . . .'

'I used to pass on that saying of Michelet's that you were always quoting: "A Republic is a great friendship . . ." '

The refutation of their hopes could not wound them. They had believed in this peaceful Republic. Other men had preferred a system of government based on political assassination, rioting and civil war. They felt as though they were still in their drawing-room in the Castellana: in their ardent, new-found faith, each would instinctively turn to the other in order to overcome a contradiction.

'My father-in-law will tell you . . . Am I not right, Pablo?'

These commonplace words carried across the years, more stunning than any declaration. Nobody would ever be able to deprive Pablo of them. Some people claimed that in the little town-house in the Castellana a plot had been hatched between men of all parties. A conspiracy had indeed been woven, but between two individuals. This pact would outlive all changes of government. But Pablo and Encarnacion would never give it its true name.

The night drifted by, barely disturbed by the barking of a dog. From time to time Pablo would walk over to the open window. There were so many stars in the sky that a jasmine seemed to be blooming there, with all its might. He refused to go and lie down even for an hour, but said yes to a cup of coffee. Encarnacion's hands played with the china, the silver spoon. That tinkling, those controlled movements, that smile, had accompanied so many other occasions on which they had sat conversing far into the night. The pungent aroma of the coffee was dispelling the scents from the night garden, the smell of the earth freshened by the dawn dew. Pablo was still talking.

Just as one bids farewell to one's travelling companions, he was taking his leave of these friends and adversaries whom he would never see again. Torn between their religious faith and their ideas, eager to build the future yet consumed by nostalgia for the past, most of them retained in political life the good manners instilled in them by their Jesuit teachers, their writer's coquetry, their orator's charm. Pablo was recalling these veterans of parliament with their good-natured irony, these champions of the people for whom every debate became a joust in which they drained their powers of persuasion and their good humour and their bad faith till the Cortes rang with applause like a bullring when the deathblow is delivered.

Encarnacion, too, had the impression of walking to the door with these guests who came from all over Spain, with their gruff or too gentle accents, their hankering for law and order, their thirst for revenge, their hard or pampered early years. With their memories, they had composed the tragedy that they were interpreting. It was from their personal, humiliated lives that they had derived this dénouement. But, like all true actors, they imagined that they were interpreting a text of their own invention. And each of them, weighed down by a hidden, unsettled score of grievances and claims, was adding his own chaos to this world of confusion and violence, from which a new nation was to be born.

'Do you remember, Encarnacion, the evening when José Antonio . . .'

Pablo left the sentence unfinished. Their remembrances were only half-expressed. José Antonio, too, had wished, when he spoke of the future, to efface the past. Discernible behind the bold young leader was his father, the dictator who had ended his days sadly in exile. José Antonio, like all the others, had been seeking to avenge a ghost. His courage and eloquence and popularity had been intended as reparation for the old man forsaken by all his followers and rejected by his sovereign.

'And the day when Calvo Sotelo laughed when he told about his altercation with La Pasionaria, and the threats and curses that poured from that woman's mouth!'

They recalled his radiant face, rendered even more handsome and vulnerable and provocative by his own words of defiance. How immortal he had felt himself to be, this man who had only a few weeks left to live!

But tonight Pablo and Encarnacion no longer asked themselves those tragic questions which a victory on the part of either side would be incapable of resolving: had the Civil War been inevitable? What exactly had sparked it off? They simply remembered the bronzed face and easy bearing of the leader of the Falange. Calvo Sotelo, the young Minister of Finance, brimming over with plans, was a handsome Galician with the precise movements of a technician. Encarnacion was haunted by the everyday words, the crude or polished gallantry of these lion-tamers after they had laid aside their whips. Were they the same men—speaking in parliament, in their editorial offices, in the cafés and clubs where they had yielded to the temptation of violence, carried away by their own slogans and their own bluster—as on those cool and airy spring evenings when the ground-floor windows had stood open on to the little garden in the Castellana?

A mild intoxication was taking hold of Encarnacion. Was it all only a nightmare? Their visitors had lingered on. As he walked down to the gate with them, Pablo was groping for a remark that, in a burst of laughter, would reconcile those who had imagined themselves to be implacable enemies. There was a crunch of footsteps from the gravel path. Pablo was about to come back into the house.

'It looks as though the President is completely in control again,' he said.

Encarnacion opened her eyes. Pablo had not noticed her momentary loss of consciousness. He was still taking the bearings of the situation: by expelling Cardinal Segura, the Democrats had behaved in the same manner as the Inquisitors burning heretics, and the Catholic kings hunting down the Jews and driving out the Moors . . .

Encarnacion said gently: 'Pablo, we have only a few hours left together. Let's forget politics.'

He smiled at himself.

'I'm incorrigible,' he said. He glanced about him, as though to assure himself that they were still alone. The sky was getting paler beyond the open window. Not a sigh, not a rustle came from the garden. The whole world was holding its breath so that Pablo and Encarnacion might finally dare confess their love for one another. He laid his two hands on Encarnacion's bare arms. She did not even quiver.

'Yes,' he went on, 'all that is dead for us. The only thing that I shall carry away with me, Encarnacion, are all the summers that we have spent here together since the day you walked into this room with a party of young men and girls, with Enrico.'

He did not intend that the name and face of his son should be excluded from this moment. He seemed to hear that long pastoral symphony of summer days when the wasps buzzed amid the smell of the squashed grapes. He would take away the memory—heat, scent, light—of a single summer, a single wine-harvest.

'That was the day my life began . . .' said Encarnacion. There was a silence: Pablo's expression was entreating her to desist and to go on.

He repeated, dazed by this admission: 'The day your life . . .'

'The day it ended,' she supplied.

Pablo stared at her incredulously. He could expect nothing more from her than this consent, this stone-like immobility and this touch of her bare arms against his palms.

This sleepless night had been a long excursion through space, an intricate voyage through time. The politicians' names had been like the names of towns which train-passengers spell out on the signboards of stations. Those professors who imagined that they were holding forth to their pupils, those statesmen who seemed to be haranguing a mutinous crew, those condottieri so like the bronze generals who sit on horseback in city squares and who may or may not have restored the monarchy or crushed a revolt—all these supernumeraries had vanished. The streets and houses where they had lived had suddenly toppled over into the void like stage-props. Only Encarnacion and Pablo still existed, face to face . . .

The world of other human beings had sunk like a stone in this breach between two days. Then Pablo began to talk feverishly of Paris. It was no longer a whiff of youth that he was inhaling beneath the tree-lined walks of the Luxembourg. He was no longer envious of the happiness of the lovers on the clear spring evenings. He was strolling all over the city with Encarnacion at his side. They were walking in step. They were making their way through the crowd, which was pushing them closer together. Pablo was taking Encarnacion's arm, like a fellow-student. Now he had his arm round her waist, like a fiancé.

Beyond the scenes that he was conjuring up, Encarnacion could discern other scenes, beyond the words that he was uttering she could make out other words. He was arranging countless assignations with her in this imaginary city, in this improbable future.

'Why do people always talk about Paris in the spring? Early June is even more limpid, even more intoxicating. The Seine looks as though it is racing towards some mysterious happiness. The water has a human tremor under the bridges, and the trees seem to be abetting it. Up on the embankments, the lovers walk with a quicker stride. These young men and women are consumed with a kind of impatience: it is as though they thought someone was going to rob them of their ecstasy. Without so much as glancing at one another, they glide along the riverside, between the roadway and the mass of second-hand bookstalls on the parapets, as though swept intoxicatingly along in the front seat of a charabanc. Suddenly they stop to look at a book; they thumb through it feverishly as though their fates were inscribed in it; they laugh at the tops of their voices; they buy it. Twenty years later, when one of them opens this book, without knowing why he has taken it from the shelf, he or she will be shot clean through the heart by a profile sculpted from gleaming marble, hair tousled by the wind, and the moist radiance of lips parted in a smile.'

He broke off abruptly. The image of the colonnades, of the pediments, of the marble goddesses sitting on the banks of a nacre-coloured, pearl-coloured river, was trembling in his heart. This silky water was taking on the colour of youth and longing. Pablo was breathing the summer twilight that was unwilling to die on the embankments. He was back among the restaurants hidden behind their box-trees, among the vermilion trails on the grey surface of the Seine, among the crowd who looked as though they were celebrating a victory or the arrival of a sovereign. But the only triumphal entry was this long sunset, the river with its gleams of slate and chiffon, puffed out like a bird's throat, and the men and women exhilarated by some unfathomable item of news, by the amazing promise of a June evening.

Encarnacion was yielding to this invitation to happiness, Paris was no longer a capital like other capitals, with their splendours and squalors. It was the city of Temptation. Encarnacion was walking along by the river at Pablo's side. They were striding through the seasons like a couple clasped tightly in one another's arms. And under every kind of sky, in every kind of light, Pablo was unfolding at her feet the imaginary and real city where they would dare to love one another . . .

'This nightmare must come to an end . . . It won't be in spring or early summer, it will be in October that we shall discover Paris. The trees are still russet and green along the main boulevards. This is my first Paris, the one I found waiting for me every year before the Law School reopened its doors. You cannot imagine the sweetness of this false spring. The children make huge bouquets of the plane-tree leaves, which are like hands made of red copper. The autumn breeze is enough to capsize all the boats in the big pool. I used to wander from Sainte-Geneviève hill to the Luxembourg gardens. I strolled among the thinning trees and yellowing lawns; there was nobody in the deserted walks. I would renew my acquaintance, as though with old friends, with the stone queens in their flowing cloaks who form a grave assembly on the terrace. I would spell out the names engraved on their pedestals as though they constituted a poem that was intelligible to me alone . . . Over and over again I would say: "Blanche of Castile, Eleonore of Aquitaine, Anne of Beaujeu . . ." These figures, sculpted so alike in their grey stone, each had a different smile for me. I was not yet in love . . . Never have I felt freer than during those delightful vacations . . . You will see for yourself . . . In Paris, the late October days are as warm as spring, but they leave on the lips that faint hint of nostalgia, that touch of longing that are beyond happiness . . .

Today I am better equipped to savour that late autumn, or late spring . . .'

Pablo was jumbling up seasons and years, all the different phases of his life. Was he speaking of the future or the past, of the few days that lay ahead of them, or of his youth, lost and preserved for ever? Entering into the spirit of the thing, Encarnacion was making no attempt to find her bearings in this labyrinth shaped from Pablo's memories and longings and repressed desires. With all her heart, she too wanted to confuse spring and autumn, Paris and Madrid, the beginning of love, that day when she had first set foot in this house, and the imminent separation, the moment when two human beings compelled to part imagine that they are offering one another all the past days of their love, the way one cups one's hands and offers a drink of water . . .

There was a crash of rifle-butts on the front door. They rose with smiles on their faces. This night of sleeplessness and anticipation, this seething and ice-cold night lingered between them like a life that had already been lived to its conclusion. Without embraces, or promises, or caresses, or kisses, they had celebrated their wedding. Nothing was interrupted by Javier's brusque intrusion, by all this shouting, by this absurd clatter of rifles. Instead of promising themselves, as all lovers do, an eternity of joy which a few hours of pleasure are sufficient to exhaust, Pablo and Encarnacion had met in this mythical and familiar city, which would henceforth be their secret country . . .

Encarnacion held her face slightly averted as she described these final moments.

'In the end,' she said, 'Pablo had no thought for anything but Paris. He spoke of it in the tone in which believers speak of the City of God.'

'Your father-in-law ought to have made a getaway,' protested Juanito. 'We crossed the Ebro the next day . . .'

Encarnacion shook her head.

'The house was surrounded. And Pablo would have been recognized wherever he went. Javier had forewarned him, the way they forewarn a condemned prisoner of his execution.'

'Was he afraid that Javier might have lied?'

A reflective look appeared on Encarnacion's lowered brow. Why had Pablo not attempted to escape? Was it laziness? Was it suspicion?

'He should have tried,' insisted Juanito.

'It's hard to explain. He wasn't the kind of prisoner who turns a guard's inattention or a momentarily unbolted door to his own account . . . He was unwilling either to admit his guilt or to force the hand of fate. There is no telling what motives one obeys at such times. Perhaps it was defiance . . .'

Encarnacion faltered, but already Juanito had seized upon her words: 'Yes, it was defiance. He didn't want to flee because he didn't want to be slaughtered in a ditch or shot down like a burglar outside his own house. It was courage that made him stay . . . The hardest thing for him to do was to wait for them to come and arrest him!'

Deep in thought, Encarnacion repeated: 'The hardest?'

She had the impression of being beside Pablo, with her eyes half-closed, following that river of life which mysteriously flows through a city. She smiled into empty space, at an invisible companion.

'The hardest?' she said again. 'We sat up all night. I felt as though I had a huge book open on my knees . . . There were so many pictures in it, everything that we had discovered, everything that we had loved, and even the countries that I had seen only through Pablo's eyes . . . As we thumbed through the pages, we would skip a chapter or go backwards instead of forwards. Just think of it, Juanito: this is what we did *that night*! A drowning man relives his whole life in a few seconds . . . In a few hours we relived all those years of hopes and disappointments . . . First thing next morning, they came and arrested Pablo . . . It was as though we were drugged, anaesthetized, from having remembered so much.'

The Crossing of the Ebro

38

THE ROAR OF THE MOTOR-BICYCLE became a signal for the men. As soon as its throbbing carried to them in the calm evening air, they would hurry forward. Agustin would hand out newspapers, tobacco, tins of food. Like a sportsman depositing his bulging game-bag, he would toss a haversackful of coffee into the doorway of the billet.

Juanito would leave go of the pump of the well, which he had been repairing. He would listen to the news with indifference: the camouflaging of truth in these official bulletins was of no interest to him. The men would wander off. Then the two companions would take a stroll between two rows of vines.

'Nothing could be more like a cemetery,' Agustin observed. 'All these neatly aligned crosses.'

Now that the future was sealed off, Juanito's every thought was for Valencia. Once or twice a week he would steal off to the village at night. But the happiness that he found there left him with a bad conscience. He could not talk to anybody about Encarnacion.

'Last night I dreamed that we pushed open the door of the *barraca*. The table was laid, but guess who was calmly sitting there waiting for us? Fernando! Is it a good sign when the dead visit us in our dreams?'

Agustin side-stepped the question.

'Dreams and omens aren't my forte.'

They walked on another few paces. Each of them was looking to the other for help. Never had their friendship been more alive or harder to express.

Juanito would say shyly: 'There isn't even a book here. Recite something, Agustin.'

In his fine, grave voice Agustin would intone the poems

which occasionally he had reread the previous night, before going to sleep. This was a kingdom that he could still share with Juanito. He would bring out the rhythm in Lorca's brief songs, as though a guitar were accompanying him. He appeared to invent, to lose the thread of a ballad, to amaze himself with a sudden discovery. He would mime this innermost quest with a movement of the hand, as though to lay hold of a haunting presence. On Juanito's spellbound face he gauged the effectiveness of this moving eloquence. Moulded by his voice and gesturing, the poem would acquire a more confiding tone, a more mysterious melody, than when it was set out on the page in even lines, under the harsh electric light. Juanito would clamour for more. Shedding a strange light, employing unexpected words, Lorca would carry him back to the familiar trees that he pruned every year, to the farm animals, to the shade and sunlight, to the creak of the bucket-chain. These everyday images merely served to evoke other realities, as close to him and as durable: blood and death, physical desire and spiritual hunger, the feeling of peace that Encarnacion's face gave him. Agustin was more drawn to other, rather enigmatic poems, the closing lines of 'Narcissus', for example:

Cuando se perdio en el agua
comprendí. Pero no explico.

He enlarged on the poem for his own benefit rather than Juanito's.

'Narcissus never understands. Like the water, he reflects. Like fruit, he ripens. If he understood, he would no longer be reflection nor fruit, no longer mere semblance and sensual delight. And Narcissus destroys himself before destroying another. In this, he is rather like Don Juan . . .'

But Juanito, smiling with pleasure, was repeating:

Sueño que no sueño
dentro del surtidor.

He relished the poems in which the Holy Week processions blazed forth. Seville would light up like a midnight sun; each *paso*, with its statues and candles, would describe its orbit like a heavenly body. From these nebulas of flowers, stars and incense emerged the tear-stained face of the Virgin or of Christ.

In Valencia, likewise borne aloft by human arms, the saints oscillated in the heart of a burning bush. Juanito's boyish heart raced as it did on feast-days, when Christ, covered with the green shadows of death, lay outstretched on his mother's knees.

Agustin said: 'Man! You haven't heard the girls of Triana yelling at Christ, that day, as though he were a lover coming home from a scrap with blood all over him. They tend his wounds and abuse him, they rail at him as though he were an infidel. They heap reproaches on him as though he were a seducer, the better to envelop him with words more burning-hot than hands, more fevered than mouths . . .'

He described Seville celebrating by torchlight its marriage to Christ. As Nuestra Señora del Desprecio or La Macarena went by, *saetas* rang out. These prayers buried themselves in the Madonna's breast like quivering arrows. In the heart of the winding streets, amid the sweet smell of squashed fruit and the puddles of *anis*, the girls from the cigar factories and the waitresses and the barmaids, clustering round this silent Saviour, as though round the bedside of a lover or a prodigal son, interspersed their cries of adoration with vituperative howls, cursing the cruelty of his executioners and their own sins. Like the Bacchantes, they tore their victim to pieces, like hired mourners they clawed their own faces. Like the Holy Women, they wrapped their Dearly Beloved in his shroud; they folded his body in a winding sheet of pure linen. They nourished this precious chrysalis with spices and balms. In the candlelight, their shrill cries seemed to wrest a final convulsion of pain and life from Christ as he crossed the Triana bridge to return, damp and dusty, to his chapel. Then the Sevillian dirge burst forth like a voluptuous bridal song. Lorca had caught the mood of this first Resurrection:

Cristo moreno
pasa
de lirio de Judea
a clavel de España . . .

Agustin was getting on his motor-bicycle.

'I'm late. Good luck!"

Juanito was jolted out of his dreams. He said with warm feeling: 'Good-bye, and thank you!'

But Agustin, above the roar of the engine, was ironically intoning the 'Lamento':

Cuando yo me muera,
enterradme con mi guitarra
bajo la arena . . .

One October evening, Agustin propped his motor-bicycle against the cracked wall of the schoolhouse to which the detachment had fallen back. Brushing past the children's desks, each a mass of carved initials, and a blackboard, which still had sums on it, he threw open the door.

Juanito sat surrounded by his men, dipping his iron spoon into the pea soup in his mess-tin. He ate with his eyes lowered, displaying the respect that men who work on the land have for food.

When Agustin stopped in front of him, Juanito looked up.

'Have some food!'

Agustin declined.

'I'll wait for you on the road.'

Juanito joined him outside the schoolhouse. Agustin decided to attack with brusque directness.

'This time we're done for, Juanito. In forty-eight hours, we shall be back across the Ebro.'

The sun was going down behind a hill, and the sky was rusting above the neglected vineyards. An emaciated dog sniffed at the two men and, detecting the smell of defeat on them, tore across the fields, which were littered with tins, shrapnel, broken bottle-ends and fragments of window panes.

'Back across the Ebro!' Juanito repeated the words incredulously. His throat was still full of those rasping names which he had recited at the start of the offensive as a litany and thanksgiving as an all-powerful incantation and an unrepealable magic formula which would cause other villages to fall into Republican hands: Ribarroya, Campesinos, Corbera. The Republic had arisen, like the man sick of the palsy who takes up his bed and walks. Everybody shook with amazement: how far would the cure go?

'Now,' said Agustin, 'nobody will know at what a cost, or by what means, Franco will have triumphed. If we are beaten, *we* shall be known as the rebels!'

'Who will dare judge us?' Anger was flaming in Juanito's cheeks and bringing a note of shrillness into his voice. 'Only the volunteers have the right to do that: they fought with us!'

'That is why France, Britain and Russia so hurriedly agreed to recall them. A single British pilot was an indictment of the whole Labour Party, a single Frenchman was the living evidence of Blum's betrayal. Europe would rather we butchered one another in private!'

'It's all right for Franco! He still has his technicians and his instructors and his war materials. He has nothing to fear. He is armed, against men fighting with their bare hands.'

As he spoke, Agustin stood relishing this surge of violence in Juanito, this determination to fly in the face of the facts, this refusal to kowtow to other men. He will never be beaten, he thought. An absurd feeling of pride welled up in him, as though he had invested Juanito with extraordinary powers that would allow him to escape the human condition, as though he had taught him to walk on water, to stride through flames, to be oblivious to pain, to cheat death. The heart of a Valencian was not to be daunted by the base scheming of the U.S.S.R., selling poor-quality equipment at an exorbitant price, or by Italy's and Germany's shady conspiracy with Franco, or by the permanent peace treaty that England had signed with Hitler at Munich.

They walked back to the schoolhouse. The night would be quiet. Franco would allow the Republican army to fall back unmolested. The soldiers were squatting on their haunches, playing cards by whatever light they could find. Candle-flames flickered just above the floor. In the midst of disaster, a strange sense of security prevailed. Life remained disturbingly normal.

'What's going to happen, then?' asked Juanito.

'Barcelona will hold out for another few weeks . . .'

It was as though Agustin were afraid of precipitating events by announcing them.

'And if Barcelona surrenders?'

'The government will take refuge in Valencia . . . Your dream will have been truly prophetic, Juanito!'

Juanito did not answer. The lime-trees in the playground had been gashed as though by a savage gardener. Somewhere a guitar was pulsating. A voice began to sing. It was a ballad that both men knew. Juanito thought of Encarnacion, with intense and instant pain. The singer was dwelling on certain words. Juanito's love would not have lasted much longer than this pause between two notes.

Two days later, the first waves of government forces fell back across the Ebro. To cover the withdrawal, Republican units had to cling to the hilltops that had been captured in the enthusiasm of the early days of the offensive. The foreign radio stations reported the shrinking of the Gandesa pocket . . . The Republicans were compelled to make grenade assaults on positions that were destined to be abandoned almost as soon as they were won back.

Juanito's and Encarnacion's farewells were brief. Already their first night together seemed very remote, an August night full of scents and breezes, warm and fiery. Encarnacion stared humbly at Juanito: 'I shall not see him again in this life, but thanks to him I have been loved just like any other woman.' He had broken the magic circle which had stood between her and human happiness.

'Juanito,' she said aloud, 'I was going to tell you today . . .' The carefully chosen words with which she had intended to break the news eluded her now. An expression of such fear and joy appeared on her face that Juanito gasped, speaking almost directly into her ear: 'Out with it, Encarnacion!'

She hesitated, as though they were being spied upon.

'I can't say it . . . Juanito, it would be too wonderful . . . I'll write to you.'

This happiness was coming either too early or too late for her.

In the market-place, by the fountain, the troops were lined up, ready to go. Juanito walked back to them. Standing impassive in her doorway, Encarnacion watched them march off.

39

THE RAMBLAS flowed down to the sea in a single river of leafiness. The flower-stalls had disappeared from the central avenue. The city was rousing itself uncertainly, like a man coming to in a strange bed after an operation. But this feeling of disquiet soon wore off in the presence of the dazzling sunshine and warmth of a November morning. Early strollers were abandoning themselves to this holiday climate. Barcelona was about to bid farewell to the International Brigades, and the optimists were expressing satisfaction at their withdrawal. The Republican army had no further need of instructors: it had evolved its own tactics and discipline.

Agustin crossed the Rambla de los Estudiantes, on his way to headquarters, where he was to pick up his final instructions. He shot a disdainful glance at the crowd spilling over the pavements and gathering in the windows.

They are expecting a pageant or a feast-day procession, he thought. Giving way to the enticement of the spectacle, he slipped into a café and installed himself right next to the window. He barely had time to put his lips to a glass of woody-flavoured brandy before a great wave of cheering broke out in the distance.

I should have brought Juanito along to show him Don Quixote intoxicated by defeat.

Agustin was guarding himself against his own feelings. Surely, he thought, I'm not going to be taken in by this farce! Who's going to march past, anyway? Not the bravest, the ones who arrived hidden among the coal in a tender, or in the holds of a ship, not those who hurried here without passports or contracts to form a first rampart in Madrid! They, as the poets say, sleep in the Spanish soil: the freedom that they came to defend tastes of the red dust that fills their mouths.

Somewhere near Belchite, under a bank of earth, lacking both coffin and cross, lay the body of a miner, and the icy wind of the high plateaus of Aragon was singing an endless dirge for Luis.

Luis . . .! This march-past was not a calling-up of spirits: there were too many dead to be raised.

He broke off his thought abruptly. The onlookers were blocking his view. Agustin pushed forward to the doorway of the café. A continuous roar was mounting from the Ramblas. In the centre of the avenue, above the heads of the crowd, he could make out a tidal flow of forage caps, berets, battered helmets and other, stranger headgear.

There must be thousands of them, Agustin said to himself.

They were having to force their way through the outstretched hands. People were clutching at their sleeves, as though to hold them back. Men and women were thrusting children towards them. Occasionally a soldier would good-humouredly hoist a small boy on to his shoulder. Cheers would ring out, a bellow of adoration go up. Soon Agustin found himself being pushed out on to the pavement by other customers till he was practically in the front row of the crowd. Men from the northern countries were going by: Swedes, Canadians, British, Americans. The spectators could not make out their badges or distinguish among all these equally ruddy faces and equally bleached heads of hair. The eyebrows of many of the troops showed almost white against their tanned skins. With their ragged uniforms, and their gaping shirts which afforded a glimpse of sunburnt chests, they held the crowd spellbound. These foreigners were emerging from another continent, another planet, a legendary mist, a fabulous North, full of islands and monsters. They marched along embarrassed by this frenzy of enthusiasm, by these shouts that they did not understand; the flowers that were being flung full in their faces at point-blank range were smothering them like confetti at a carnival. And their faint smiles were addressed to the city, to the November sky, to this Republic whose call they had answered, to this Spain which was tearing itself away from them with tears and wails, like a quivering mistress.

Their ill-assorted clothing came as no surprise. Many of them had grabbed an Italian belt or a pair of German boots on the battlefield and wore them proudly as trophies.

The procession was advancing at an uneven pace. From time to time the crowd, which contained a sprinkling of officers and of men on leave from the front, would suppose that it had identified a unit. Whereupon, a cry would go up. The name of a battalion or of a regiment, derived from the history of another country, would be turned by these hoarse throats into some weird and wonderful word that the troops barely recognized. The unintelligible syllables would tumble out in a prolonged roar of love and gratitude: 'Garibaldi', 'Dombrowski', 'Commune de Paris'. Other voices would take up this litany: 'Chapiaev', 'La Marseillaise', 'Edgar André', 'Rakosi', 'Thaelmann'. It wasn't seasoned troops and crack units that Barcelona was acclaiming, but tutelary gods, giants who had raced to the Republic's assistance, just as, in the days of old, St George had plunged into the fray to bolster the courage of other knights. The Cervantes Battalion, made up of the Spanish volunteers who had fought side by side with these foreigners, was jealously cheered.

What is the matter with me? Agustin asked himself. A lump had come into his throat. His eyes were growing misty.

The crowd was now fêting the Brigades by roaring the names of their victories. These familiar names of mountains and rivers, of savagely disputed villages and city suburbs—Lopera, Alfambra, Cerro de Los Angeles, Talavera, Los Quatros Caminos, Las Ventas—these names of remote hamlets in the Sierra Nevada or the Guadalajara plain, now fabled as the scenes of desperate fighting, were becoming the real identity of these men from distant parts, and these syllables were revealing, beneath the soiled uniforms of mercenaries, demi-gods who had decided to exert their influence in the internecine struggles of human beings. It mattered little whether they had taken part in this defeat or that victory, whether they had halted the Nationalist thrust at the gates of Madrid, or tried to save Oviedo, or defended Sagunto and Almaden. The time-sequence of offensives and counter-attacks no longer existed. The same fervour surrounded the defenders of Boadilla del Monte and the victors of Mora del Ebro. As the battalions of the 12th and 13th Brigades went by, a wave of cheering swelled and broke over the same name: Belchite.

At this point, it seemed to Agustin that from the depths of this immoderately blue sky, as from an unsilvered mirror, Luis was smiling, as the dead smile at us, with a pity that disguises a secret contempt for our betrayal of them. But these men from the Old World and the New, marching past in serried ranks, were tearing him away from Luis. They were devoid, now, of nationalities, or homelands, or motives for enlisting, or prestige acquired on this or that battlefield. Spain had chosen them, the way a woman chooses a lover; she had breathed life into them in the days of her might and weakness, of her pride and destitution. Even in Agustin's sharp eyes, these troops were turning into the legendary warriors of a second Romancero.

Emotion was taking hold of him at the sight of their gaunt faces, their rather startled eyes, the eyes of solitary men. There were many fanatics among these volunteers. One day the moody office-worker who never spoke to his colleagues, the high-minded student, the journalist, the shopkeeper, all oppressed by their chains, had woken up with the determination to escape from their lives. Within a week or so, they had drunk their fill of adventure and glory; now they were on their way back to their old hell: everyday existence.

Pale or bronzed, bearded or smooth-cheeked, one row of faces succeeded another.

They are like drug-addicts still under the influence! What are they thinking about? Getting home? Their friends will whisper about them, with a mixture of admiration and embarrassment, as though their escapade had lasted a lifetime, as though they had returned from some unexplored region of the world.

Some bore hideous scars. And the wounded were marching past, as well, displaying their makeshift dressings: they too were entitled to these effusive farewells which resembled the ecstasies of lovers.

You could take them for brigands in some comic opera.

But Agustin could not stop shaking, like those tourists who detest bullfights and faint away when the crowd rises to applaud the matador's cape-work.

These ragged heroes proudly bearing the signs of their ordeal reminded Agustin of the comrades of his youth with whom he had toured Spain, putting on plays. Victims of their own spell, the actors had been unable to recover their normal rate of breathing, their everyday tone, after the fall of the curtain. Their voices had retained the agitated inflections of Hamlet or Caesar. They had gone on suffering from ingratitude like the Cid and Christopher Columbus. They had continued to confront destiny like Philip II or Pizarro. Agustin had loved those hours when his fellow-performers were still fallen kings and valiant knights and conquerors and explorers . . .

Would these troops likewise continue to act the part of liberators, without costumes or props? Would this Englishman with the shy grin put on a chemist's overall in Birmingham, and this heavily scarred Dane spend every hour of every day poring over a ledger in the accounts department of some exclusive store?

Other troops appeared. As he went by, a South American volunteer called out: 'Las Navas!' The words were taken up, in a long, resounding cheer. This had been the latest battle in the attempt to save Madrid. Attacked on all sides, the capital had been resisting for two years. Las Navas! For several days, this name had effaced those of Palacete and Boadilla del Monte and the memory of so many previous bitter engagements aimed at preventing the encirclement of Madrid. A brigade had dug in on a wooded hill: fire had broken out among the tall resinous pines. As though in a blazing cathedral, the troops had fought among the flaring tree-trunks. The acrid smoke had nearly choked them. The splinters emitted by the huge boles had burnt their hands. Under the impact of the bombardment, everything had turned to flame, both the sky above their heads and the earth at their feet, and their lungs had been filled with the stench of an inferno. Sheltering behind these glowing pillars, beneath these sputtering branches, holding on to a difficult position in the face of the enemies' incessant attacks, they had not only been keeping open the road to El Escorial; they were continuing the stand at Brunete, the victory at Belchite, the desperate struggle at Oviedo, which was about to fall . . . In this way, they had postponed the inevitable for another few weeks . . .

Those who were so frenziedly cheering them imagined that every soldier in the parade had taken part in all the offensives, had defended Madrid and Bilbao, had saved Teruel and Almeria. From the coast of Galicia to the shores of the Levante, from the Sierras of Andalusia to the plateaus of Aragon, these men had shared in a single exploit. And in the eyes of these foreigners, forgetting its own divisions, its mistakes, its acts of folly, the Spanish Republic was discovering its own history transformed into legend.

On the point of being carried away by enthusiasm, Agustin was growling to himself: 'Glory to the last-minute warriors! How many of them have experienced anything more than the victorious advance on Gandesa, the arrival in the liberated villages, the flowers, the girls' kisses, the flowing wine . . .?'

A number of very young men had slipped into the front row beside him. They were whispering that the Republican army no longer needed the help of the Brigades and they were glancing at Agustin for confirmation of their views. Did not Juanito think as they did? At this very moment he was supervising the withdrawal of troops and equipment. But even in the midst of that constant stream of men, of that rumble of vehicles which would cause the bridge to shake, his one memory would be of having swum across the Ebro one night in July.

Offensives and counter-attacks, ground won and lost, towns captured and recaptured: it was all in vain. Victories and defeats succeed one another like shadows on a screen. The stakes in this tragic game seemed even more illusory in the midst of this trance that had taken hold of a city. A delirious crowd was applauding the pointless sacrifice of these men—but then, thought Agustin, what else was it that used to carry me away when I read Plutarch and Shakespeare, when I talked to Juanito about the leaders of the '89 Revolution and of the Commune, about Firmin Galan and Garcia Hernandez? A tremendous humility swept through Agustin. What right had he to condemn the ecstatic mood of this crowd?

As soon as the parade marked time, onlookers rushed forward to give the volunteers a drink. It had been a long march for them, all the way through the avenues of Barcelona. Exhausted by the exuberant atmosphere, they threw back their heads and drank, then offered ceremonious thanks.

The crowd was silent now. People were hoarse from shouting so much. Agustin gazed in stupefaction at these legionaries who bore, together with their battle-scars, the names of the provinces and cities and hamlets and rivers of Spain, at the approaches to which they had fought furiously.

The snows of the Asturias, the squalls of the Castilian Sierras, the roasting sunlight of the plateaus of Aragon had given a high colour to the once pallid faces of these northerners. Their lips were blackened, as though they had been nibbling some exotic fruit. And the blast of gunfire during the offensive had absorbed the gentle water of their pale eyes. They were all of them thin, after the manner of the shrubs that withstand the droughts and frosts of the steppes. Their chests and shoulders showed through their tattered shirts, leaner than before and sculpted from a dark clay fresh from the furnace.

Las Navas! These troops were like the trunks of pines whose bark was ablaze, like those bare columns from which burning branches were raining down. Perhaps they could only half-hear the din surrounding them, their ears still deafened by the roar of artillery. Perhaps they had only enough strength to march straight ahead of them, to reach the end of this great avenue, this tunnel of foliage and shouts and flowers which was, like all triumphal arches, a gateway opening on to empty space.

Some of the battalions were parading with their equipment. These obsolete tanks and light armoured cars, with their thin, riddled plating, jolted slowly along like broken toys. But a gunner was standing very erect at his post in each armoured car, and the driver's head projected from the open turret of every tank. With these ramshackle vehicles, purchased from the Soviet Union at excessive cost, with these antiquated and sub-standard weapons, the Republic had withstood every attack; tomorrow, with more equipment, it would triumph. A single, deafening roar, a unanimous cry of confidence and hope filled the avenue, all the way from the Plaza de Cataluña to the sea.

Agustin's heart was going nineteen to the dozen. He had not anticipated that crippled tanks, and armoured cars that were ready to fall to pieces at any moment, would display, for all to see, the audacity and penury of the Republican army. In a final attempt to guard himself against his own feelings, he said to himself: Perhaps Juanito is right: our craziness is our strength! But he could no longer master his emotion at the sight of these relics of unsuccessful offensives, these mementoes of fruitless victories, these guarantees of certain defeat.

The parade seemed to be over. The crowd stood wavering on the pavements, still befuddled by its enthusiasm. Suddenly a quiver of excitement ran through the Ramblas. Regrouped in a happy-go-lucky manner, the foreign troops who had taken part in the offensive on the Ebro were striding down the avenue, confident of the overwhelming reception that they would be given, after their participation in the most momentous breakthrough of the whole war. There was a distant boom of voices: three syllables, clearly rapped out, were accompanying the troops like a fanfare: 'Gandesa!'

Agustin's brain was whirling with the triumphant news of the offensive. He heard himself rejoicing at this bold blow, calculating how much ground had been gained, how many men, guns and vehicles captured. 'A psychological victory, a fantastic haul,' he had said. Today, Gandesa was evacuated, the right bank of the Ebro lost. At headquarters, an elderly officer had whispered in Agustin's ear: 'Gandesa is our army's finest victory . . . It is also its graveyard.'

The strategist's view could not diminish this act of faith on the part of the troops and the crowd: they were all partaking of the certainty of having conquered. They are still living in the early days of the offensive, thought Agustin: at the time, many thought it likely that Gandesa would settle the outcome of the war, one way or the other. But though the experts might reckon up the losses of an offensive into which the Republican army had poured all its resources, nothing could disturb this bright November morning, on which the population of a great city was revelling in all its victories, in a single joyous hour . . .

Agustin was still trying to laugh the thing off. Here come the giants of the Ebro, he said to himself. I can remember when it was the 'giants of Teruel'! But by this time he was inseparably linked to the crowd, and shaking with the same surge of feeling. His thoughts were being drawn into the same whirlpool of love and gratitude.

On each of these men, who no longer had names or destinies, two years of desperate fighting shone like a terrible halo. They were smiling shyly, as though to apologize for the inhuman intensity of the glaring days and icy nights up in the sierras, for those winters and summers which they carried about with them like the torn blankets thrown over their shoulders.

A number of Spanish volunteers had slipped into the column. They could be recognized by the way they were signalling to the crowd, by the spiritedness of their replies and by the warmth of their smiles. They were escorting these foreigners out of the city, like courteous hosts. Setting their jaws, they were savouring the paroxysm of admiration and affection that was sweeping through Barcelona. They were catching some of the flowers that were being tossed at them, and attaching them to their forage caps. Loping along with them was a tall, slim youth with a sullen face. He adjusted the sling of his rifle, and because his eyelids were lowered he looked, for a moment, just like Luis on the eve of his departure for Belchite, packing his belongings with an expression that was at once abstracted and studious. The stranger sensed Agustin's eyes upon him. He looked up again and smiled. Agustin had sagged against the people standing behind him. He could no longer bear the sight of two faces, nor go on marvelling at this double which fate had found for a dead man. When he came to, he was lying on one of the wooden seats in the Rambla. The look of concern on the faces staring down at him filled him with confusion, as though he were hoodwinking these open-hearted people . . . That a staff-officer should faint at the mere sight of the Brigades' farewell parade! he thought. I'm ridiculous. . . . He blurted out a few words of thanks to the men who had lifted him clear of the crowd. He was feeling much better, he said. A short walk would put him right.

He told himself icily: The war is lost. This parade is simply a rehearsal for Franco's arrival in the city in another few days, or another few weeks . . . He had recovered his painful lucidity and returned to his separate existence. Never again would he partake of the blind hope, the total illusion of a population which, on the verge of defeat, was still revelling in its victory.

PART THREE

The Return to Valencia

Not of a woman's tenderness to be,
Requires nor child nor woman's face to see.
I have sat too long.
SHAKESPEARE: *Coriolanus*

40

BARCELONA WAS ON THE POINT OF CAPITULATING. The collusion between the Russians and the Germans was now overt. Yesterday's adversaries were now working hand in glove, with the intention of sharing the world between them. As Agustin bitterly pointed out: 'Hitler can count on Soviet oil to enable him to conquer Europe. We are a useful item in the underhand bargainings of all these tricksters . . . Spain is always good for a swap. These horse-copers keep passing the same weary hack back and forth to one another.'

A powerful army was covering the Levante, but a series of orders given either too early or too late came as perilous jolts to its stability. When a simple manœuvre hurled Franco's units all the way back to Seville, this unexpected victory, unintentionally achieved, was a source of alarm, like those sudden turns for the better that prolong a man's death.

In the plane that was flying them back to Valencia, Agustin quietly summed up the situation to his companion: 'Miaja is loyal, but his staff are waiting for the fall of Barcelona to give them an excuse to surrender. Only cowardice stops them short of actual treason . . . The capitulation of Madrid would spare them any risk or remorse.'

Through the window, Juanito could see El Grao harbour shimmering and Valencia parading its domes and steeples and rooftops. It was enough to put new heart into him.

'Miaja has more than eight hundred thousand men. He controls two-thirds of the country. Do you think Franco can close the net on eight million Spaniards just like that?'

'You are clutching at numbers like a gambler whose system is failing him. Numbers have always been in our favour . . .'

'I'm not clutching at anything: I'm saying that even if

Barcelona surrenders, we still hold Madrid, Murcia, Jaen, Albacete . . .'

'You're a real man of the *huerta*! Don't forget Valencia! And the ports—Alicante, Cartagena, Almeria! And the mines!' Agustin was ironically entering into the spirit of the thing. He went on: 'It boils down to this, Juanito: we have everything that we need to win the war, and we are losing it.'

Juanito's cheeks flushed up in passionate denial. Like a young animal, he was hurling himself against the bars of a cage with all his might.

'You know better than I do how things stand with us. Three hundred and fifty thousand men are storming Barcelona. But the army of Catalonia is about to cross the border into France. Barcelona could safeguard its supplies before it capitulates, and send fuel, guns and food to Valencia . . . The fleet is Republican. We hold the ports along the coast of the Levante.'

Agustin was watching Juanito's expressions out of the corner of his eye. The Valencian was giving the dreary facts the sweep of an epic poem. The Cid himself couldn't get us out of this mess, thought Agustin as his companion continued to work himself up.

'Just think!' he was saying. 'All those resources can be unloaded at El Grao. This time we shall have more rifles than troops, more tanks and planes than men to drive and pilot them. The *huerta* produces enough to feed every army in Spain.'

'Calm down, man! Miaja's staff is eaten up with betrayal . . . Casado's junta is looking for the best way to open the door to Franco, so that his troops can enter the heart of Madrid without firing a shot . . .'

A violent jolt broke in upon their talk. The plane was lurching about inexplicably as it approached the landing field. It was a very old machine. At Barcelona it had been obliged to weave this way and that before it succeeded in taking off. The pilot was looking anxious. For a split second, Agustin confronted the idea that he might just as well die like this as finish up in the hands of the rebels. But there was Juanito to think of. Agustin shot him a sidelong glance. He had stopped talking suddenly.

Was he afraid? No doubt he was praying to some saint who specialized in warding off accidents. The plane gave another lurch, as though it were about to overturn completely. Agustin took Juanito's hand. Once again he made a pact with a nameless demon: I am perfectly willing to die, but don't take him! The pilot regained control of the machine. It touched down smoothly, and Juanito burst out laughing.

'Agustin, I've never been so scared in all my life, but I didn't come back to Valencia to die.'

A staff-car was waiting for them. This clear, glowing December morning was lit like a bonfire above the plain and the rice-fields and the reed-lined canals. Over the outskirts of the city there hung the stench of manure. The smell came as no surprise to Juanito, but his companion held his nose. Deep in its bed, the Turia wound its way along, invisible beneath the vegetation. Juanito returned to their discussion. Obstinate as only a peasant can be, stubborn as a true Valencian, thought Agustin.

'Believe me, Agustin, nothing is lost.'

'I believe you,' conceded Agustin. He averted his eyes from the gaudy ceramic walls of the summer-houses, which drew a whistle of admiration from Juanito. After the mosaics and shiny tiled porches of the country houses came tall, grimy blocks of buildings, bearing the scars of the latest air-raids. But Juanito's face still shone with a sense of wonder: by returning to his city, he was forgetting the Ebro, Campredo, the Sierra Caballs, the victories as disappointing as defeats, and those transports of enthusiasm from which he had awakened with disgust, as from a night of debauchery. Valencia was still intact, the final shield of the Spanish Republic. Powerful, rich and wise, it rejected any thought of capitulation. The anarchists and communists would not dare raise their voices among a people who had served their apprenticeship of freedom centuries before.

The Virgin of the Forsaken had merely left her basilica. An actress grown weary of the indiscreet admiration of the mob, she no longer needed to hold court in this audience chamber of bronze and gold and precious marbles, where she had smiled like a visiting sovereign through the windows of a state coach.

Unseen, she was sharing the ordeals of her people. With both her arms, she was spreading her mantle over the city, above the flowering gardens and the shabby streets and the charred baroque churches and the stucco palaces, which were the colours of faded silk, and the bridges, over which the saints walked, with their haloes taking the place of balancing poles.

The disappearance of her effigy was reminiscent of the earthly peregrinations of the Mother of God. Had she not fled into Egypt with the Infant Jesus? Had she not spent more than one night in a cave and trembled for her Son as today she was trembling for her city? The same conspiracy of demoniacal forces was threatening Valencia. But in the heart of the city, in some inviolable crypt, like a sun concealed in the subterranean darkness, the Madonna was waiting, unharmed, with all her jewels, and her face was like those stars which end their orbits beyond our horizon.

To Juanito, this conviction was as private, as incommunicable, as the memory of Encarnacion's caresses. How could he impart to Agustin a certainty that he derived from his childlike fervour? Police reports claimed that superstition was on the increase again, and that more and more clandestine Masses were being said.

Agustin gently poked fun at him.

'Don't you know where the Madonna is hiding?'

'It's impossible for you to understand . . . When I was fifteen, I carried her statue on my shoulders. I knew that she belonged to me, just as she belongs to all the men of Valencia . . .'

The Madonna no longer rose in a cloud of incense, among a gorgeous display of flowers, but she remained omnipresent in her city. The Valencians reeled off her praises whenever their gaze rested fondly on the crenelated Serranos gateway or the imposing Torres de Cuarte: Gates of Heaven, Tower of David, Tower of Ivory, House of Gold, Ark of the Covenant . . .

As in the early days of the war, Valencia was sheltering the Republican government. It was the last stronghold, impregnable in its resistance. General Miaja's one thought was to husband his resources, but Valencia would raise an army.

Agustin viewed the situation in terms of vast combines, massive overthrows of alliances: 'If the democracies abandoned Spain to Franco, they would by the same act be handing over the Republican government to Moscow. Thus they would be playing into the hands of all their enemies . . .'

From these hypotheses which he had so often turned over in his mind, no flame now spurted. Barcelona was capitulating. Azaña was taking refuge in Paris. Negrín was racing back and forth along the front, like one of those miraculous statues to whom the peasants turn in an attempt to ward off the vagaries of the elements. But Juanito was still dreaming of a sudden desperate resurgence, of a new Dos de Mayo which would re-establish Spain's unity in the face of threats from abroad.

The government had installed itself in the Guild Hall where the silk-manufacturers had grimly defended their authority. Beneath the ogives which opened out like the veins of palm leaves above the slender pillars, the various departments were crowded together. The chaos of desks, typewriters, official files, conjured up impressions of a shipwreck or the sacking of a town. Telephone calls, memoranda, counter-orders, warrants for people's arrests, terrifying news from the front: all these rained down like meteors from outer space. The administrative staff of this or that department would begin to function again like an unaffected organ in a diseased body. A typewriter would start to click. Petitioners were waiting for permission to cross the imaginary antechamber that separated them from a man huddled over his desk. Corruption spread like bindweed. Corps commanders and party secretaries clamoured for more arms. Other, shrewder callers were content to seek safe-conduct passes and profitable licences.

Juanito was entrusted with the security of the Lonja. He knew the names of the political leaders with their weary mouths and puffy eyes, looking older than their portraits in the newspapers. Despite all their differences of age and background, an underlying resemblance was growing between the journalists, tired from working far into the night, and the trade-unionists who carried about with them the stale smell of conference rooms, and the strutting ideologists who were constantly being brought up sharp by reality. Like sleepwalkers startled out of their sleep, they talked of bread and wine and sweat, as though to convince themselves that they had bodies, and mopped their brows, like lawyers devoid of arguments in a trial in which the party both guilty and innocent was the Spanish people.

Plucked from their gloomy meditations, they would gaze at this boy from the *huerta*, so sturdy and plainspoken and bold-eyed. To these men, steeped in allegory and consumed by myths (Freedom, Progress), Juanito was the embodiment of the young Spaniard of tomorrow.

They would question him about the war as though it had been started for him, as though victory and defeat would have meaning for him alone. All prognostications had been proved wrong. The information services were lying, the journalists were merely pulling the wool over people's eyes. But in *his* eyes, which were the colour of the Albufera lake in summer, the future shone with calm radiance. The socialist deputy insisted: 'If Madrid surrendered, do you suppose Valencia would last long?' Juanito held his tongue. How could he explain that a woman was enfolding the city in her mantle of gold, covered with ruby flowers? Juanito did not reply. The deputy, who had been so glad of the opportunity to interview a young officer, was disappointed.

41

IN THE NARROWEST STREETS OF VALENCIA, showers of sparks would leap into the air. A convent, or an unassuming chapel visited by occasional worshippers, or a baroque church whose relics drew a rapt crowd on major feast-days, or a monastery with gilded arcades would turn into a cluster of flames. The old mediaeval terror of arson reawakened obscure superstitions in people's hearts. Rather than as acts of revenge or provocation, Agustin viewed these outbreaks as part of a conspiracy to cause alarm outside Spain. As at the start of the Civil War, tales of looting and torturing, and of the cracking-open of coffins, were travelling round the world. Journalists were mingling stories of priests burned alive in Malaga with reports of the defiling of graves in Gerona. They painted a garish picture of the scenes of carnage, invoking the stake and Goya's engravings, the Inquisition and the Dos de Mayo. As a result, the Republican government would be saddled with the blame for the atrocities of the anarchists, for the systematic slaughtering carried out by the Trotskyists and the communists, for the frenzy of destruction that had misled whole towns, like Murcia, into demolishing their treasures with maniacal joy.

Were not these strange bonfires being lighted by the priests' own hands? Juanito denied it. But Agustin jeered: 'They're meant as a substitute for the old processions! These impostors will rebuild their sacristies and their altars, never fear! The iconoclasts are merely clearing the ground for more cathedrals. In a revolution, the Church always wins . . .'

The steeple of Santa Catalina church was projecting the shifting beam of a lighthouse on to the Plaza de la Reina. The firemen were struggling with all their might to bring the fire under control: if the flames spread to the cathedral, now an ammunition depot, the whole of Valencia would be blown sky-high.

Like an Easter candle planted in the heart of the city, the steeple seemed to be garlanded with fire. But burning brands and long flakes of fire were raining down from the foundering roof. There were shrill screams as the sparks landed on women's shawls. Pathetic shadows and sudden gleams of light played on anxious faces. Men and women alike were celebrating a nocturnal rite, and this initiation was giving them an extraordinary expression of joy and curiosity and terror. The legless, the armless and the deformed, who had for years been begging under the church portal, were infiltrating among the sightseers. In the midst of this Court of Miracles, Juanito thought he recognized Padre

Enrique. The man was already lost in the crowd. Without his soutane, the open neck of his grubby shirt revealing a scraggy neck, the Padre might have been a beggar; but his eyes, full of wisdom and intelligence and love, were sufficient to betray him.

Inside the church, on the walls and beneath the charred vaults, all signs of vandalism had disappeared. The smashed-in shrines with their soiled linings, the trampled cushions, the wax effigies: all were reduced to ashes. A woman surreptitiously picked up a hand of the Infant Jesus, which had once been lifted in a gesture of blessing. She sensed Juanito's eyes upon her and hurled the broken piece of statue to the ground with a look of contempt.

That afternoon, Juanito had been to see his mother again. A groan had escaped her lips.

'Looking after the land is too hard a job for women,' Theresa had said. 'Look at it!'

The *huerta* stretched on and on under a cloudless sky, silent and deserted. The canals glittered in the sunlight, between their reedy banks.

'When will you come back, Juanito?' Theresa asked, with a kind of despair, as though the outcome of this war depended on him.

'Soon, mother . . . Soon.'

He felt ashamed. Was he, too, banking on defeat?

'Are they still setting fire to churches in Valencia?' Theresa asked. 'Are they still hunting priests? Freedom wasn't given us, Juanito, so that we should incur God's wrath and make the Virgin weep . . . How can the aim of freedom be to kill and to burn?'

She had been overjoyed when the radio announced the crossing of the Ebro and the staggering advances of the Republican forces. These illusory successes had prolonged the fratricidal struggle. Today she asked fearfully: 'If they were to win, Juanito, wouldn't men like you have the right to live and to work?'

'I dare say, mother, I dare say.'

Why had the Padre fled? He was the one who could have answered Theresa's questions and solved Juanito's perplexities.

Morning had come. Above the narrow street stretched a radiant sky, like those awnings that are erected in midsummer to help keep out the sunlight. Guards had been posted at the approaches to the church. The semblance of an official inquiry was about to be held. Juanito slipped into a bar. The men sitting at one of the tables, who had been discussing last night's fire, were abruptly silent. The waitress set a cup of coffee in front of him. Agustin will already be in his office, he thought.

'In what does the strength of the Church lie?' Agustin would ask. 'In holy medals, Sunday school, relics? No, in the fact that every priest is up at dawn to say Mass . . . Perhaps the fascists are going to win the war for the same reason.'

The Intelligence Branch had set up its offices in what had formerly been the Archbishop's Palace. Juanito found Agustin already immersed in his files.

'You're an early bird today.'

'I'm following your advice,' said Juanito.

Agustin surveyed him. The Valencian's sleepless night had given him a harder face, the face that he would one day exhibit all the time. I shall not see that face, Agustin said to himself. He felt a sharp stab of pain, as though this familiar thought were occurring to him for the first time.

Juanito described the fire.

'We are a nation addicted to ritual burning,' said Agustin. 'In that way, Spain doesn't change.' He stooped over the table. 'Barcelona has surrendered, Juanito. Why does Madrid make a show of hesitating? To give us time?'

From the adjoining room, through the half-open door, came the regular clicking of a typewriter. A secretary was still pounding away at a memorandum, or a report, or an inventory. The war was over, but for another few days or another few weeks these official documents, together with the press reports and the radio news bulletins, would mask the reality of the situation, would put up a screen of words and lies.

Agustin rose. He had come to the end of inspiring fear, from behind this desk, in wily conspirators, in generals on the look-out for a pronunciamento with no risks attached.

Juanito stood waiting. An enormous silence reigned in this solidly built old house which had something of the quality of both a fortress and a monastery. This silence, which had yesterday spread like a noiseless flood over the depopulated *huerta*, now hung over Valencia before immersing the whole of Spain.

'Weren't you expecting such good news so early in the morning?' Agustin was still trying to be off-hand about it. 'Just think, Juanito . . . We can still get to Algeria . . . I have cousins in Oran . . . For the Republic, all is lost; but there is still time for us to reach safety . . .'

Juanito was silent. He could not live, or even imagine living, anywhere but in Valencia.

'I knew it,' said Agustin. 'For you, the world begins and ends in the *huerta*.'

His voice did not betray the slightest disappointment. He held out his packet of cigarettes. Juanito took one.

'No, keep the packet. It's a decoration for your gallantry on the Santa Catalina front.'

Juanito slipped the packet into his shirt, between the material and his skin. Agustin stared at him. He kept saying to himself: Since I am about to leave him for ever, I have the right to admit everything.

'What are you looking at me like that for, Agustin? When I was a child, a woman gave me a packet of cigarettes; for days I carried it next to my heart. I can still see her smile; I was in love with her for ages afterwards. It was winter, and she had come to shoot duck in our pond. She had a peculiar name which went with her blond hair. She was very beautiful . . .'

Agustin opened the drawer of his desk. His hand impatiently brushed aside letters and photographs and drew out a revolver, followed by a small box of cartridges.

'Juanito, will you load my gun for me? I'll be back in a moment.'

He went out and asked the secretary for a copy of a memorandum. Juanito laid down his cigarette and uncocked the revolver. Then he carefully loaded it and made sure that the safety catch was back in place.

'There,' he said, handing the gun back to Agustin; 'you won't come to any harm while it's set like that.'

All these stories about fire were stimulating Agustin's apocalyptic imagination. Full of sullen impatience, he was longing for some disaster in which the elements would be cast in the role of the agents of retribution in the last act of a drama. Like Sagunto and Numancia, the Republic would be annihilated in an inferno lit by its own hands. For funeral-pyres delight both the gods of the past and those of the future . . .

Without giving much attention to his movements, Agustin placed the revolver at the back of the left-hand drawer. He was dreaming aloud.

'In Greek tragedy, the sacrifice of an individual saves the city, but nowadays it takes the sacrifice of many cities to save a people. Even if he is only a fanatic or an *agent provocateur*, the man who sets fire to a church is obeying implacable forces, the demands of the Immortals, or perhaps the obscure wishes of the dead. He imagines that he is obliterating all trace of his own acts of desecration and abjuration. He seeks to purify and atone . . .'

Juanito fiercely rejected the idea of an end of the world in which his city would perish.

'Valencia has nothing to atone for. Valencia will not burn.'

Agustin shook his head.

'Troy, Rome and Alexandria had nothing to atone for, nor had Moscow in the days of Alexander I, nor had Paris under the Commune . . . But the history of every nation is interspersed with bonfires in which masterpieces go up in smoke, in which libraries, palaces, temples and museums are set ablaze so that a barbaric leader may warm his numb fingers, one night, over a pile of treasures . . .'

'You accuse me of being superstitious, yet you yourself see omens in everything. Simply because some lunatic sets fire to a church, you imagine that the whole of Spain is about to go up in flames!'

The secretary popped his head round the door.

'Captain, fire has broken out in the church of Los Santos Juanes, just across the road from the Lonja . . .'

Jolted out of his prophetic mood, Agustin smiled at Juanito.

'Now the saints are taking a hand . . . Off you go! See how they set about gutting their own churches!'

42

BY THE TIME JUANITO REACHED THE LONJA, smoke and sparks were swirling out of the broken windows of the church. The doors, barricaded from the inside, were withstanding every attempt to break them open.

'There's someone in there,' a woman said. 'An old man . . . I saw him go in by the door at the back of the choir.'

Above the main portal there was a rose window. Juanito managed to hoist himself up to it. Viewed from above, the nave looked very big, with its succession of arches and pillars. Near the high altar, surrounded by a cloud of smoke, Juanito thought he could make out the figure of the Padre. He was reeling about, half-suffocated, clutching a candle. The fire had spread to the altar decorations. The communion rail held the old man imprisoned behind a curtain of fire. Showers of sparks were leaping from the tapestries that still hung in the chancel, and from time to time the wind blowing in through the shattered windows would cause them to settle.

Up on the ledge, Juanito managed to loosen the leaded glass. Before venturing into the church, he shouted to the soldiers to smash the door down. The rose window was set directly above the gallery leading to the choir school. Juanito slid down one of the pillars and landed with a spring. The floor was littered with broken desks and pages from torn-up hymn-books. The organ displayed its burst pipes, its broken pedals. The organist had been at his keyboard when the vandals had broken in. Disappointed, they had contented themselves with hacking away at electric wires, wrenching out light-bulbs, ransacking the doorless cupboards, smashing the empty tabernacles. Juanito raced up the central aisle and vaulted over the communion table. The Padre had collapsed on the altar steps. The candle had rolled away from him.

Juanito lifted the Padre from the steps. When he had been saying Mass in the old days, he had prostrated himself like this, kissing the rustic flagstone floor of the little village church. The Padre opened his eyes. His head was rocking from side to side. His weightless body was like one of those wire dummies, one of those wicker-work skeletons which in springtime the people of Valencia dress up in old clothes and perch on bonfires in the city squares.

He gave the Padre a good shake. 'Padre!' he shouted. 'We've got to be quick!' The fire was consuming the high altar, attacking the gilt reredos, spreading to the choir-screen and invading the side-chapels; the carpets were smouldering and giving off an unbearable stench. The crash of the soldiers' rifle-butts on the steel-clad oak doors was reverberating from one end of the church to the other. The Padre blinked, spotted Juanito's uniform and gave a moan of terror. Juanito was clutching him firmly.

'Padre, it's me—Juanito! Don't you recognize me?'

'I didn't start the fire on purpose,' said the Padre.

He was groping for his candle, to testify to his innocence. He would rather have died in the blaze than be butchered by this soldier. Juanito kicked open the gate of the communion rail and then, without loosening his hold, dragged the Padre to the transept door, at which the soldiers were hammering frenziedly. But it, too, was boarded up; the planks nailed to the oak panels allowed no room for hope.

'Padre,' said Juanito, mopping his brow, 'we've got to do something!'

The side-chapels were fiercely lit up by the blaze. Each of the altars seemed to be garlanded with flames. Poised on their sham clouds, above the holy statues, the cherubim were burning; the saints were threshing about, trapped in their incandescent niches. The sizzling paintwork and varnish were emitting a stifling smell. We shall suffocate, thought Juanito. The hammering on the transept door had ceased. The soldiers had turned their attention to the main portal. One of them clambered up to the rose window. The nave was deserted. Juanito had disappeared. A roar of anger went up. The impotent fury of the crowd turned against the church itself. In Cordoba, the walls of a monastery had been torn open with picks. The obvious thing to do was to blow up the door. But the soldiers had neither grenades nor dynamite.

The Padre was beginning to show signs of life. This soldier was not a killer, but his little Juanito. He reeled about, then clutched at his companion.

'I simply came in to see whether . . .'

'We'll talk later,' said Juanito. 'Wait for me here.'

The Padre leant against one of the pillars in the nave and sagged to the floor, while Juanito vainly exerted all his strength against the other transept door. It was barricaded, on the inside, with enormous planks which had been nailed there to discourage vandals. It was best for them to return to the main portal before the fire reached the front of the church. The chancel and transept, already consumed by the flames, were about to collapse upon them.

The Padre was unconscious. Juanito dragged him over to the font and flung in his face some of the water which was becoming foul. The priest came to; he imagined that he was giving Juanito a Sunday school lesson in the village church.

'You just won't pay attention, Juanito.'

A series of terrifying cracks came from the length and breadth of the gallery. The fire was spreading through the timber-work, attacking the organ-chest. Juanito raced to the staircase. The wooden handrail was collapsing, a flame was spurting from the floor of the gallery. The Padre was still rambling: 'You're setting a bad example, Juanito!'

The lock was resisting every effort to open it. Up in the gallery, the beams were sputtering. Juanito thought despairingly: We are going to be burned alive, waiting here for them to open this door. The Padre was groaning. Just for a moment, his brain was clear.

'Try the sacristy, boy. I have the key.'

Juanito rummaged in the Padre's black, frayed jacket, a manservant's jacket for which he had exchanged his soutane. Beneath the tobacco-pouch he found a large key. Fanned by the draught from the shattered windows, the fire seemed to be sucking in the whole church.

'Padre,' said Juanito, 'be serious, now. Get on to my shoulders.' He pulled the Padre to his feet and, kneeling down, continued: 'Slip your legs over my shoulders and hold on tight, as though I were a horse . . .'

The Padre obeyed, and his hands clutched at Juanito's neck.

'Hold tight, remember!' shouted Juanito.

The panes of glass protecting the holy statues were exploding in the heat, the altar-pieces were crashing down and disintegrating into glowing embers. Juanito made his way up the central aisle again, stooping under the weight of his burden. The Padre was thoroughly enjoying this game. Each side-chapel was a golden honeycomb, a melting beehive, a grotto overgrown with tall, tangled grass, a glowing waterfall.

'What a beautiful sight, boy!'

The Padre could not make out why these pious figures should be gesticulating behind their railings. The saints' haloes were ablaze; their arms, stretched out to work miracles, failed to ward off the fire, which was insinuating itself between the ex-voto offerings, devouring the confraternity flags and emphasizing the baroque curves of the wainscoting.

'For what saint has the church been decorated like this?' the Padre was wondering aloud. The explosions reminded him of the squibs and blank cartridges that the people of Valencia are so addicted to, of that warlike din which on feast-days serves as an act of homage to God and his elect. In their niches, the wax effigies and polychrome wooden Virgins were calling for help. Juanito will not be able to save everyone, the Padre was thinking, only half-conscious. Opposite the high altar, which was now just a pile of smoking debris, Juanito hesitated. The rhythmic hammering of rifle-butts was again coming from the main portal; what battering-ram would ever succeed in breaking down those steel-armoured oak panels? Huge beams were detaching themselves from the circular gallery of the chancel, dragging the balustrade down with them. The canons' pews on either side of the altar were burning away, amid a heavy smell of wax polish and incense. Juanito climbed the steps that led to the sacristy door. It yielded to his touch. The Padre, overcome with fear, was clutching Juanito with all his might.

'Padre, you're strangling me!'

Inside the sacristy there were several cupboards and a half-demolished china wash-hand basin. The oak panelling opposite the basin opened on to another exit, but it was blocked by a processional float representing Jesus being scourged by brutes with enormous muscles and crimson faces.

The sacristy has no other door, thought Juanito. The Padre was wriggling about on his shoulders; his head was sagging forward. Juanito retraced his steps. The door leading to the chancel had caught fire. Juanito kicked it open. The flames devouring the lintel singed his hair. The smell brought the Padre to his senses.

'My son,' he cried, 'we're on fire!'

The fire had not yet spread to the left transept.

'Padre,' said Juanito, 'there is no way out through the sacristy!'

But the priest was delirious again.

'There is no excuse for being late for Mass!' he said.

Amid the crackle of dry wood and the sudden deflagrations when the flames succeeded in investing yet another altar-piece, or in touching off a further empty shrine, a crisp, insistent noise could be heard: the locksmith trying to unfasten the door by inserting a long metal rod. It's best for us to wait here, reflected Juanito. All about them, the church had turned into a hell in which every saint was writhing on the altar like one of the damned.

'Padre, let me get my breath back for a moment.'

He set the old man down against one of the pillars in the left transept.

'You're leaving me!' cried the Padre, starting to weep.

Juanito flung himself down on his knees, facing the side-chapel in which a silver statue of the Virgin normally stood. The Madonna had vanished in the very first days of the Civil War. Juanito gazed at this empty altar with a savage intensity of trust. From the shadows at the back of the niche were emerging the concerned and loving features of the Virgin of the Forsaken. And the divine pity in her expression was like human anguish. So he shouted to her, at the top of his voice: 'Virgin, I am burning! Holy Mother of God, help me out of the fire, help me out of the fire!'

The Padre stopped weeping. Juanito's prayer had restored him to his right mind. He no longer remembered Juanito's attempt to get out by way of the sacristy. He stared about him.

'Juanito, my boy, let's try the Oratory of the Blessed Rosary . . .'

Like swallows' nests, each of them the pride of some powerful confraternity, such oratories clung to the sides of every church in Valencia, the private palaces of popular saints, who held court in them like those influential favourites whom sovereigns install close to their royal persons, and whose doors are always open to the throng. As a child, Juanito had spent hours praying in this oratory; with its ring of side-chapels, it formed another and more intimate church in the heart of the sanctuary and was connected to the street by a long dark corridor.

'Are you quite sure, Padre?'

The church was ablaze from top to bottom. The walls were a mass of tall, rippling flames. Near the intersection of transept and nave, the pulpit was transformed into a pistil of fire. How could I ever have preached in this Elijah's chariot drawn by blazing seraphs? mused the Padre. At regular intervals, an axe struck the oak of the main portal and the wood let out a groan, but by this time the organ-loft was an inferno. Burning hangings were wrapping themselves round the pillars near the entrance.

How could the two men hope to get through this curtain of fire and reach the open air?

Juanito hesitated: they were going to be caught in a trap. The Padre tugged him towards the first of the side-chapels in the left transept, dedicated to SS Justin and Rufina; it led to the oratory, but the blaze in the chancel had spread to the chapel. A confessional was burning. The Padre leapt when he saw that the fire had beaten them to it.

'Juanito,' he asked imploringly, 'where are we going now?'

He tripped on the step that separated the side-chapel from the oratory. Juanito helped him to his feet.

'We mustn't waste another second! This is our last chance!'

The oratory was free of fire. On one of the altars, St James looked as though he was still holding court. Juanito jumped over the rail that separated the saint from the faithful. Behind the altar, a sacristy contained a portable altar, for use on feast-days, together with a velvet canopy and some silver candle-holders. These items reminded the Padre of the open-air ceremonies, during which the saints and the municipal authorities are bound by the same protocol. But the door leading to the market-place was padlocked.

'This time,' said Juanito, 'we are really lost!' He went on silently beseeching Our Lady of the Forsaken: 'Virgin, help us! Get us out of the fire! Virgin of the Forsaken, save the Padre, save us both!'

Light was pouring in from a barless window set almost flush with the ceiling. It was closed. Juanito snatched up a lead crucifix, of the kind which the leaders of processions employ to rap out their orders. Using this cross as a club, he struck out as hard as he could.

'Sacrilege!' cried the Padre.

The window shattered into small pieces. A draught of cool air swept down into the musty atmosphere of the sacristy.

'There,' said Juanito. The sense of danger was giving him the strength of ten. The fire had now spread to the oratory. The Padre swung round to face the connecting door, as though somebody had just come in. On top of an old altar-piece, Juanito dumped the painted wooden altar that must have been used by the Padre in better days. A moment later, the Padre was lurching about on this unstable pyramid. But he managed to straddle himself across the window-ledge.

Juanito hoisted himself up in his turn. The air that they were inhaling already had the flavour of safety. The oratory was crackling away like a pile of deadwood.

'Don't throw me down!' whimpered the Padre. 'I'll break every bone in my body. May St James forgive us!'

Juanito climbed down again and flung open the cupboards, in which some tattered stoles, albs and surplices still hung. He knotted them securely together. Then he rejoined the Padre up on the window-ledge. The old man was shaking with fear.

'Padre, either you jump or you will be burned alive!'

Round the priest's waist he slipped the rope that he had just twined.

'Juanito!' the Padre cried imploringly.

For answer, Juanito pushed him over the side. The Padre swung back and forth beside the wall, dangling at the end of his rope of old lace like one of those light wicker baskets which housewives lower from their balconies in the narrow streets of old Valencia.

'Juanito!' the Padre beseeched him again, terrified by the sight of the drop below him.

Juanito played out the rope between his hands. The whimpering died away; there was a cry of fear, but already the Padre was picking himself up, clutching the wall with both hands. Juanito vaulted over the window-ledge; for a moment he clung on with his hands. Then he let go and found himself, feeling only slightly dazed, standing on the spot where the Padre had landed a few seconds earlier.

'In the nick of time,' observed Juanito, helping the Padre to free himself from his albs and surplices.

The old man hugged him effusively. That wild scamper through the blazing church was effacing itself from his memory like a bad dream. But he sought to justify himself in Juanito's eyes.

'This is my parish church. I have no house, except the house of God. The altar-cloth caught fire . . .'

'Padre,' said Juanito, 'let's hurry. The crowd are in a wild mood at the moment . . . They mustn't see you . . . They might stone you.'

'You are right, my boy.' He glanced at the faded strips of lace on which Juanito was wiping his grazed hands. These bloodied rags looked as though they had been used in a murder.

They walked a few steps down an alley-way which ran alongside the church.

'Let's turn off here,' said the Padre.

Another blind alley confronted them, exhibiting a series of acute angles and abrupt foreshortenings like a backcloth in the theatre. A tremendous silence enveloped this maze of secluded passageways and inner courtyards where the clergy had lived in the old days. Juanito strode along between these two-dimensional houses as though he were in another world; his ears still buzzing with the roar of flames and the crash of beams.

They came to a sudden bend and walked past a row of empty sheds, gaping coach-houses, shadowy cellars from which came nothing but the stale breath of disused tanks. Every house was shuttered up. This was a dead-end.

'We're there,' said the Padre. He gave a series of carefully spaced taps on the wooden shutters of a window. A door opened. They stepped into a darkened room where the vigil lamp cast a ring of yellow light at the feet of Our Lady of the Pillar. A woman rose.

'I was praying,' she said. 'When a church is on fire, you are always among the first on the scene.'

Her voice was severe. Her suspicious eye took stock of Juanito, coming to rest on his singed hair and soot-blackened face.

'My nephew,' said the Padre, by way of introduction. His legs were giving way under him. Juanito picked him up and laid him on the bed. He closed his eyes. Perhaps he had lost consciousness. Yet he groped for Juanito's hand.

'Thank you for bringing him home,' said Angustias. She

spoke of him as though he were an incorrigible child, but the distrustful look had gone from her sleepy face, and she was gazing at this unknown soldier with an expression of placid kindness.

'You had better leave by the other door,' she said. Then, rather drawlingly, she called: 'Isabella!'

A dark girl emerged from an adjoining room.

'The church is on fire,' said Isabella as she came forward.

'So the Padre and this young man noticed,' replied Angustias.

In the dim light, Isabella detected the signs of burning on the soldier's uniform. His shirt had been almost ripped from his shoulder. An extraordinary smell of scorching came from his hair.

'You aren't burnt, are you?'

'No,' said Juanito, 'but we were only just in time.'

Angustias turned to Juanito.

'My daughter will show you out. Do call again, to see how the Padre is.'

I must look like a murderer, thought Juanito. As he walked across the patio, where some evergreen plants were dying a lingering death on the edge of a fountain basin, he hid his blood-smeared hand behind his back.

43

'MADRID!' said the secretary. 'They're complaining because we aren't sending them any more food.'

Agustin took the receiver from him and signalled to him to stay where he was. In the ear-piece, an embarrassed voice was emphasizing the critical nature of the situation. To suspend the already infrequent distributions of rations would give rise to discontent, which in view of the . . .

'So the capital will remain loyal to the Republic only on condition that it receives further supplies from us?' Agustin said icily. 'I see. Madrid is blackmailing Valencia.'

Protestations were blurted out at the other end of the line. The city's morale was magnificent. Madrid would stand firm.

'In that case,' said Agustin, 'there is no need for Madrid to demand what Valencia cannot give her.'

His eye wandered over the notes from which he was in the process of compiling a report. Was it to be his testament? From the series of expedients that had constituted the government's policy, he was trying to draw a lesson. What madness, Agustin said to himself, lending half an ear to his caller's denials. We have gone from failure to failure till we have reached the final disaster. And now, when all is lost, I am laying the foundations for a Committee of Revolutionary Action . . .

'But,' said Agustin, 'seeing that General Franco will soon be responsible for provisioning the Republican army, he will attend to the needs of the civilian population as well! In Madrid, it has been the civilians who have fought hardest.'

The caller's voice was rising. It was essential, he said, to forestall open rebellion by the issue of essential rations.

'What does "essential" mean, when we are supposed to be discussing people who have nothing whatever?' asked Agustin. 'Valencia could send every ounce of food that she possesses, and the appetites of the people of Madrid would still not be satisfied. Franco's troops are better fed than the peasants of the *huerta*.'

The secretary stood listening with shining eyes. He was too closely involved in Agustin's work to feign detachment. He was acknowledging his superior's thrusts with obvious pleasure.

'So that's settled!' concluded Agustin, as though he had just satisfied his caller's demands.

At the other end of the line, the receiver was slammed down. As he himself hung up, Agustin gibed: 'What an extraordinary thing! Here we have a Junta which bargains with Franco but is incapable of keeping the capital supplied with food!'

The secretary, a slender, willowy Andalusian with too high

a colour and too bright a gleam in his eyes, nodded approvingly. Whenever Juanito appeared, the Andalusian would retire instantly. He was so responsive to his superior's slightest shifts of mood that strange suspicions would cross Agustin's mind. In the end, even the most innocent devotion establishes the same connivance between two men as a shared vice.

How could he know? Agustin would ask himself.

For months past, Agustin had been rejecting the easy opportunities which were multiplied by war. Every passion is a deliverance: for petty temptations and passing fancies, for trivial joys and sufferings, for temporary set-backs and gratifications, it substitutes an aspiration that can never be fulfilled. Agustin would look back on his past life with that vague feeling of repugnance, that mixture of boredom and distaste which the converted experience towards their existence as sinners, an existence made up of tiresome expedients and contemptible falls from grace.

Thanks to this new love, Agustin was effortlessly achieving the pared-down purity of lives reduced to their bare essentials and directed towards the Invisible. He would say to himself in amazement: How I have changed! From now on, everything is so simple: the dross is falling from the molten metal . . . What need have I of pleasure-seeking and adventuring? Pleasure-seeking drives a man further into his shell, and adventuring leads only to loneliness. I love: it is enough for me to know that Juanito exists! And for him I have renounced everything, my wisdom and my folly, my preaching and tub-thumping, my pseudo-scientific references, my invocations to evolution and to the Man of the Future: I have shed all that claptrap. It was a small price to pay . . . It is easy to abandon a system, but one cannot give up a human being.

His gaze rested on Joselito's head, bowed over his shorthand pad. What was to become of him?

'I've tried my hand at every job,' he had admitted one day. 'The army has given me the chance to complete my education.'

Agustin had laughed.

'It has been the same with me. I've been a journalist, a

theatre critic, a printer, a schoolmaster, a trade-union leader, an agitator. Now I spend my days nosing out crime: the officers who take money from Franco, the patriots who sell army supplies . . .'

But Agustin was consumed with a secret uneasiness.

'Has anyone seen Lieutenant Sanchez this afternoon?' he asked. 'The story is going round that two men were burnt alive in the church this morning . . .'

'All personnel have returned to barracks,' replied Joselito. 'I telephoned only a few minutes ago.'

He affected ignorance so well that Agustin could not help thinking: What made him telephone? But instead of upbraiding him for this excess of zeal, Agustin sought a little appeasement from this alter ego.

'Was the lieutenant back in barracks too?' How could he keep this tremor of impatience from his voice?

'He was asleep,' Joselito said calmly. 'I saw no point in waking him.'

'Quite right!' The blood was circulating more blithely in Agustin's body. Could he reasonably complain because his feelings were always understood, his wishes constantly anticipated?

'There are more and more of these incidents,' he said. 'We shall have to organize a patrol to defend the churches, since the priests are setting fire to them . . .'

He thrust his notes aside. Madrid is bound to hold out for another few days, he thought. A testament . . .? I'll leave it to the survivors to bury the Republic or save whatever can be saved of it.

'We'll finish the report tomorrow,' said Agustin. 'There are more urgent matters to be dealt with.'

While Joselito rapidly noted down his orders with regard to security precautions on roads and airfields, Agustin allowed his thoughts to roam delightfully. Like a gambler suddenly throwing in his hand, Agustin was flinging aside the grubby cards that went by the name of planning and forecasting. Lying in readiness in the left-hand drawer was the revolver that Juanito had loaded for him. The hours ahead—how many, Agustin did not know—

constituted his stay of execution. Before squeezing the trigger, for a few days or a few weeks, Agustin would be free to gaze upon the guileless face and seaweed-coloured eyes and sunburnt cheeks of a child of the *huerta*.

Nobody can rob me of this share of happiness, this eternity of joy, he thought. I have made a pact. I have paid the price . . .

An orderly announced Juanito.

'Tell him to wait,' said Agustin. Was it to mislead Joselito? Agustin returned to his report. He was deriving a strange pleasure from the thought of Juanito cooling his heels in the antechamber.

'What time is it?' he asked eventually. 'I was forgetting all about the lieutenant . . .'

Agustin relished the control that he was exerting over his own impatience. From where did this sudden happiness spring? And why ever had he been afraid? It was impossible for Juanito to perish in a blaze. He was immortal, as is any being loved passionately by an ephemeral creature.

'I thought you must be in Paradise, surrounded by the virgin-martyrs!' he said aloud. Then his voice failed him. A new love, yet one laden with prodigious experience, had set his heart pounding. What God had moulded this grave and smiling human being in his image? What chance combination of a million circumstances had produced this flower of virile and innocent grace, a boy of the Valencian plain?

Juanito saw this bedazzlement written on Agustin's thin face.

'What is it, Agustin? Are you ill?'

'No, simply exhausted from the task of winding up the Republic's affairs! But in an earthquake, how can we hope to take everything with us?'

He lit a cigarette, then continued: 'How is the fire?'

'The roofing and timberwork were destroyed.'

'Do you mean to tell me you were fool enough to go inside the church?'

'I wanted to find out what had caused the fire.'

'And did you find any clues?'

'I found the man who had started it . . .'

Juanito's voice trailed off.

'What did you do with him?' asked Agustin, pressing him.

'I dragged him out of the church, half-conscious.' Juanito smiled. 'It was an old, ailing priest.'

'Not so ailing,' Agustin said derisively, 'that he couldn't start a fire!' He felt a wave of furious hatred against this fanatic. Juanito had nearly lost his life in the flames. This priest was responsible for all the infernos that had been sparked off since the outbreak of war, for all the destruction of churches and palaces. He would pay for all these acts of arson. Agustin vented his anger on Juanito.

'Instead of playing the knight in shining armour, you'd have done better to get rid of him for us!'

Juanito recalled the faces of the onlookers, their explosion of savage joy at the thought of a priest's being roasted alive in his own church. Theirs had been the cruel satisfaction of peasants drowning a nestful of rats.

'I couldn't have done that,' confessed Juanito.

Agustin was ashamed of his own ferocity.

'Of course not,' he said. 'A son of Don Quixote couldn't finish off an old man or a priest.'

He had difficulty in repressing quite different words—'I trembled for you, Juanito'—but had he uttered them, Juanito would have discovered the true name of an attachment more secret than friendship and more desperate than love.

'He used to be parish priest in my village,' Juanito explained. 'Later, he retired to Valencia. He was merely taking a look at his old church. As he was lighting a candle, he accidentally set fire to the place.'

'Where did you leave him?'

An idea had just flashed through Agustin's mind. Today this old fool would serve as a hostage, tomorrow as a witness.

'I took him home.'

Agustin's face lit up. He rose and opened the window. Down in the ancient courtyard of the Archbishop's Palace, the sentry was marching up and down, up and down, with the regularity of an automaton. Juanito had done well to obey the promptings of his heart. His nonsensical act had been a stroke of genius.

'Man,' said Agustin, 'I have a job to finish. I just wanted to see you for a moment, but keep in touch. Go and see how your fire-bug is. Be a Good Samaritan to the very end.'

Again an absurd conviction set his heart racing. Juanito would not die.

'Juanito, you are like those heroes in the Bible, who walk unscathed in the midst of the fiery furnace. Fire, even more than water, is the sign of a vocation. What have you to fear, after this?'

Fate, which had struck down the Spanish Republic, now took pleasure in prolonging its final convulsions. In Madrid, Negrín was doing his best to breathe fresh life into the last-remaining loyal units, but their heroic efforts looked like a useless repetition.

Following Franco's entry into Barcelona, the city's starving inhabitants had stormed the government warehouses. People had died from overeating; others, so it was whispered, had drowned in the tanks of olive oil. Soon, restrictions had pitched the population back into the worst days of the Civil War. In Madrid, a Junta was being formed—though whether with the aim of carrying on the war to the bitter end, or of capitulating, nobody knew. Some spoke of Kerensky, others of the Committee of Public Safety. Even as such conflicting precedents were being invoked, the communist ministers were installing themselyes close to the airfields. Agustin concluded contemptuously: 'They won't end like the leaders of the Commune.' In Cartagena, Nationalist partisans seized possession of the harbour, but their coup failed. Agustin accorded no importance to these incidents, seeing them as mere vicissitudes of the kind which keep the readers of blood-and-thunder serials breathless with suspense.

In Madrid, at the orders of the Council of Defence, the communist cells were broken up, the party's organs seized and its chief officers arrested—all without a murmur.

'If we had done the same,' Agustin said bitterly, 'we should have put a quite different complexion on things. Casado is taking the vital steps that we didn't even contemplate!'

The secret telegrams from the Kremlin, the coded instructions, all these had been burnt to ashes thanks to the thoroughness and alertness of the Communist Party. At Elda airport, La Pasionaria and Togliatti were buckling the straps of their suitcases. Agustin viewed these preparations ironically.

'Everything is cut-and-dried for me, boy . . . Like a hero in a melodrama, I have turned down my last chance—the chance to be driven out of Spain in a luxury ambulance, with all the respect and consideration due to the dangerously ill. But I don't feel drawn to Gibraltar, or to Algeria, or to Russia . . . I've always been a stay-at-home. Why go so far in search of death?'

'There will be an amnesty,' Juanito protested.

'For you, for those who simply fought! For us commissars, the end will be simpler: a prison yard at dawn . . .' Agustin went through the motions of a dead body pitching into a dug grave. 'So peaceful! In May it will all be over. No more Agustin . . . just a few bones buried at random, with no cross and no gravestone . . . I shall lie mingled with the soil of Spain, as the poets and patriots are so fond of saying . . .

'Where was I? Oh yes! For you, Juanito, the nightmare will be over . . . You will go back to the *huerta* . . . Think of me, when you are there, not as a fanatic but as you will think of Vicente and Esteban and the boy who used to play the guitar. "Agustin?" you will say. "Ah yes, the fellow who knew so many of Lorca's poems by heart."

'No prayers, Juanito. But if you have a moment to spare, recite my epitaph. You know it as well as I do:

Cuando yo me muera,
enterradme si queréis
en una veleta . . .

44

THE BELL WENT UNANSWERED FOR SOME TIME. Finally Isabella's face appeared in the dim light of the patio. She led Juanito over to the old garden chair in which the Padre was dozing. But he opened his eyes.

'Juanito!'

His voice was young and gay.

'Ah, now I recognize him!' said Angustias, who was standing beside the Padre. She answered Juanito's salutation with a sullen, almost vindictive stare. 'The other day he looked like a real incendiary.'

'Angustias,' said the Padre, 'why don't you offer my rescuer a drink, instead of insulting him?'

Angustias smiled. Like torrential floods, her moments of vexation left no permanent trace in her and soon revealed a bruised inherent kindness.

'War spoils everything, Padre, even good manners.'

Angustias set the *anis* and the ice-cool water on the wrought-iron table. There was a silence. About the two women there was the rather sad peacefulness of houses never disturbed by a visitor. For years, mother and daughter had been shoring up one another's loneliness. And Encarnacion? Was she, too, alone in the mayor's house, with the garden full of shade and stars and the honey-suckle which no one now inhaled?

'Of all the children I have taught, Isabella is the only one left to me. And of all those little demons in the *huerta*, Juanito is the only one I have found again . . .'

'In the midst of the flames,' Isabella broke in, 'like your guardian angel.'

Juanito blushed; the Padre was reeling off his memories. After his seminary years in Valencia, he had discovered, in the hamlets of Estremadura and the mining communities of the Asturias, the same faith, the same patience, the same courage. On feast-days, his parishioners would hand him a basketful of eggs, or a scraggy chicken, or a hamper of fruit. As he uttered the names of these villages, the Padre had the impression of seeing their pinched faces and stooping figures parade before him, glowing smiles their only luxury. He loved those souls, fierce and stark as the high plateaus on which wheat and barley have to fight for their lives. Poverty, in those parts, seemed as voluntary as a sacrifice, as inevitable as the winter snows or the blazing skies of summer. By accepting it, men drew closer to Christ.

Later, when he became a priest in a Barcelona suburb, the Padre asked himself whether he were not responsible for the fate of his brethren. Treatises on political economy replaced the poems of St John of the Cross on his bedside table. The successive phases in the lives of the saints, their ecstasies and orisons, struck him as an itinerary reserved for a privileged few. Thereupon, the Padre experienced his great temptation: that communion of suffering and hope which the Marxists invoke. But he rejected solutions based upon hatred. Midnight would find the Padre still grappling with statistics, comparing reforms, setting one theory against another. He was losing his sight; his parishioners revered him, but they were amazed that this saint should work no miracles.

He was taken ill and transferred to Valencia. In this city of plenty, he began to dream of another Reconquest, a crusade directed against human want and hardship.

Isabella and Angustias sat nodding their heads in approval, just like Juanito, readily convinced. The same dogged unrest was at work in the proud minds of the bourgeoisie and in the prickly hearts of the peasants. The Padre had imagined that Valencia would provide Spain with those eloquent lawyers, those exemplars of moral courage, those incorruptible youngsters who had wrought the great Revolution. Angustias was proudly claiming as her ancestors those scholars and privateers and magistrates and merchants and craftsmen whom no power in heaven or earth could intimidate. These bold spirits, free of all prejudice, cleansed of all idolatry, had been the first in Europe to proclaim their fierce independence, in the Constitutions of Aragon and of the Levante. The Cortes of Saragossa and Valencia and Barcelona had revived the senates of antiquity. And along this shore which Rome had sprinkled with the honey-coloured ruins of giant ramparts and aqueducts and temples, the virile imprint and lucid genius of the Eternal City had lingered on in men's minds.

Because of these great memories, the Padre forgave the people of Valencia for their attachment to the richly fertile rice-fields, the impeccably white farmhouses, the thoroughly manured fields, and the cattle-sheds filled with fat livestock, forgave them, too, for the hint of smugness which derived from their regarding themselves as God's Chosen, as though each new harvest came to them as a sign of heaven's approval. In these villages, fruit-picking competed with Sunday school and prayer seemed confined to rainy days. But these peasants, quite inured to toil, adored fiestas: they turned processions into spectacular cavalcades. They heaped flowers at the Virgin's feet. And, poking fun at one another, in springtime they made huge dummies out of wicker and cardboard and set fire to them.

As he sat listening to the Padre, Juanito was carried back through the years. From the hot rice-fields, beneath the radiant blue of the sky, a tranquil breath, a golden vapour, was rising towards the sun. The orange-trees were in blossom and exhaling an intoxicating scent like an impalpable and silky snow. At high noon, in August, the whirr of the cicadas wove the earth's glowing winding-sheet, but in the evenings the poplars shivered from the first touch of coolness. Juanito seemed to hear the shrill cries of the fleeing ducks and the reports from the shot-guns. The Padre's voice was bringing back the flavour of loaves made from new-cut wheat, whose crumb was grey beneath a yellow crust, and the taste of the oily black puddings which in the *barracas* are eaten with cream cheese, and the cloven olives subsiding in the earthenware jars. This world still existed within Juanito's reach, just as the plump haricots and downy scarlet runners and giant cabbages were still ripening in the moist furrows of the orchard. In the sunken paths, other small boys would be trying to snare swallows. The Padre was scolding Juanito for some of his old escapades:

'On the Feast of the Assumption, when you ought to have been carrying the Virgin's float, you disappeared with a couple of other young scamps . . .'

'We were nearly sucked under, in the Alboraya pond,' pleaded Juanito.

The *huerta* was revolving beneath his gaze like a great wheel, with its seasons, its labours, its games and its processions, the men's oaths, the women's laughter and, on the edge of the well, that creak of the chain. It was a very heavy bucket, trembling with innumerable gleams, which Juanito was drawing out of the darkness so that he might plunge his face into it.

The Padre was censuring this thirst for adventure among the men of the *huerta* and smiling at their craze for singing and dancing. Yet they had not betrayed his trust in them. The Republic was lost, but Valencia had fulfilled her mission: she had enabled Madrid and Barcelona to hold out.

The Padre was quite carried away. Señora Angustias interrupted him. He was overtiring himself by talking so much, she said. The señora walked to the door with Juanito while Isabella put the Padre to bed. She shook her head at the priest's childishness.

'My daughter is the only one who can do anything with him.'

Then, with that rather curt authoritativeness which she gave to all her remarks, as though she were even more mistrustful of herself than of others, she said to Juanito: 'I had a son, a fine-looking boy like you. His plane was shot down. For some time afterwards, I used to wake with a start and run to the door. I kept having the same dream. He would arrive home covered with blood, covered with earth. It took me a long time to accept the fact that he died without trace . . .'

Because she was discussing her son with a boy of the same age, Angustias was suffering anew. Now, in every fibre of her body, over and over again, she would be forced to imagine that plane diving in flames. Angustias pulled herself together. She managed a brave smile.

'There are no men here any more. If you don't find the house too dreary, call and see us again.'

As she led him across the patio, she thought: My pain is like a festering abscess. At the sight of this boy who is the same age as Rafaele, my wound begins to bleed again: that is the only solace that I can know. I have no wish for my Rafaele to become a waxwork, as time goes by, or to acquire that resigned, hypocritical expression which the dead all wear in their photographs, so that it seems a family resemblance.

She opened the gate. Juanito did not realize why Angustias had tears in her eyes as she said good-bye to him.

The plane was swooping lower and lower over the city. It was circling widely to encompass an inert prey, to make quite sure that it was asleep or dead. Then, startled by its own temerity, it climbed vertically, vanishing into the glaring midday sky. And again, fascinated by its target, it banked, and the sunlight was glittering on the yellow and red cockade of the Nationalist army, which was like the circular markings on some nocturnal butterflies.

No hail of bullets spurted from the roofs and towers of this city, so openly displayed to the plane's curiosity. The machine wheeled more closely round the Miguelete, then round San Catalina and Los Santos Juanes and all the other charred sanctuaries. Its audacity increased as it gauged the full measure of the city's exhaustion. It was as though it were vainly seeking to provoke anti-aircraft fire. Now, growing more and more confident, it was shaving the rooftops. Sitting beside the pilot, the observer was naming the streets over which they were flying, the squares in which pedestrians were stopping and staring up at the plane without the slightest alarm. There was something unnerving about this all too easy conquest. The observer signalled to the pilot to fly still lower. The manœuvre was a dangerous one. The plane might hit a chimney. It skimmed the city gates, hugged the dried-up bed of the Turia for a few moments, and then described a perfect circle above the bullring. The huge amphitheatre, which could hold eighteen thousand people, was deserted. The midday sunlight was bouncing off the stone seats. Soon, all over Spain, arenas would be buzzing with spectators, and the bullfight would once again be celebrated as though it were a religious service. As the plane headed back towards the city centre and the flower market, the observer noted that on the balconies and rooftops, which had been deserted earlier, men were lifting their hands in welcome. Most of these figures were waving improvised flags of yellow and red.

45

FRANCO'S TROOPS had not yet reached Sagunto when the army of Valencia began to disintegrate. It was not the capitulation of Barcelona or the imminent surrender of Madrid that took the heart out of even the most stalwart. Valencia no longer felt like fighting: after two years of civil war, of looting, of pointless squabbling, of futile butchery, the peasants of the *huerta* had no faith in anything but their farmhouses and their fields. What was the point of killing and destroying when the rice-fields were returning to their primeval state? They longed for their white *barracas*, so thickly coated with limewash that in the midst of the green fields they looked like freshly starched shirts inflated by the wind. The men seemed to catch the smell of the bread-kiln which thrust up its smeary white cupola at the farm gate. They inhaled the aroma of the well, which opened its cool, blue-lipped mouth right beside the house, hidden away behind a plump fig-tree or a spinney. Every *barraca*, with its pigeons, its poultry, its pigs and the horse in the adjoining stable calling for its food by kicking the door with its hoof, was drifting along, like Noah's Ark, wherever the current took it. Even the strictest disciplinary measures could not quell longing of such intensity. In every unit, numbers were dwindling rapidly. Threats and security precautions could not check this haemorrhage, which was robbing the Republican army of the last of its resources. The men of the Levante knew more than one way back to their villages. They avoided the main roads, but the telegraph poles were sufficient to enable them to find their bearings. Every day, lorries would roam the *huerta*, picking up deserters.

Agustin bitterly took stock of the situation. 'There will be no heroic last stand in the city of the Cid,' he said. 'The desperate resistance of Sagunto and Numancia was all very well in the days of the Romans and the Carthaginians. One mustn't be too hard on these men who, when disaster strikes, think of their cattle-sheds and their farmhouses.'

Juanito endeavoured to explain the natural impulse that was driving these peasants, sick of a war that had no end, back to their fields and their ruined harvests and their neglected live-stock.

'You are used to city life, Agustin. To you, one house is the same as another, but they have made the reed-and-mud walls of their *barracas* with their own hands, they have grappled with the soil as they have grappled with their wives. It is not cowardice that is causing them to desert . . . They simply can't bear being parted from the *huerta* any longer . . .' Juanito lowered his eyes as he confessed: 'I'm just the same. When I wake up in the middle of the night in the Granvia barracks, I feel like a prisoner. I ache for the *huerta*, as though it were a woman . . . I can't get to sleep again.'

Agustin gave a sad smile.

'I understand, Juanito . . . The peacefulness, the predictability, the wealth of the soil repaying the sweat of your brow . . .'

'No,' said Juanito, 'you *don't* understand. We are not concerned with wealth: nobody could be more spendthrift than we are. The *barraca* is not simply a comfortable home for well-off peasants. It shelters a whole way of life which is impossible for you to imagine. In the living-room, there is often a corner set aside for prayer, with a statue of the Madonna that is years and years old. You can't see her because she is hidden behind sliding doors, but the people talking and laughing and singing in the room know that she is there, just as they know that the loft over their heads is full of fruit.'

Agustin masked his contempt. 'What else can you expect?' he asked. 'Valencians are not built for hardship, for fighting a war with rags on their backs and on an empty stomach. They need to feel the old propitious influences at work in the very foundations of their lives, the old complicity between heaven and earth.'

Juanito spoke up, as though to exorcise the call of the *huerta:* 'They need to live in harmony with everyone and everything, with heaven and earth alike. Just you wait and see, Agustin: life is beautiful back home. When the war is over, you will bring your books and come and teach in the village. You will live in our house, which is the best-built for miles around . . . Set in the walls are blue *azulejos* depicting St Vincent Ferrier and dating back to the war against the French.'

He was getting quite excited, but Agustin averted his eyes from the boy's rosy face.

'But, Juanito! The war is already over! Didn't you see one of Franco's planes flying over the city in broad daylight, like a dove of peace?'

The Padre lay in a small white bedroom on the first floor, overlooking the patio. As a result of remembering so intensely, he was lapsing into a state of delirium in which scenes from his past life mingled with blurred glimpses of the future. In an interminable monologue, he retraced the flow of his life, moving freely back and forth in time. A moderately bright light was sufficient to cause him to imagine himself back in the heart of the inferno. If he woke up in the night, he screamed at the sight of the slender flame hovering above the oil. Whenever Isabella's household duties brought her close to the bed, the brain behind the closed eyes would sense her presence, and he would reach out for her hand and hold it in his worn fingers.

The night before, he had found himself alone with Angustias;

she had been putting the finishing touches to a piece of embroidery. He pretended to be dozing. Suddenly he spoke aloud. Angustias shuddered. The voice that he adopted was the voice in which he had formerly uttered words of consecration and absolution. Wide open in the dim light, his eyes gave the impression that they did not see the patio, over which night had fallen.

'Angustias, I have been praying hard for Juanito. God will answer my entreaties . . . One night, as on the day of the fire, the boy will come knocking at your door. This time, you will not be afraid; he is the son whom the *huerta* has given me. He will take Isabella by the hand, like those sons of patriarchs who used to travel great distances in quest of their future wives . . .'

Angustias had started crying: this was the first sign that he was weakening.

A warm friendship had quickly established itself between Juanito and the two women. Juanito described Barcelona to them: how its streets were always bustling with parades, and how there were placards demanding every conceivable right, and how the atmosphere of the city combined the elements of a political rally, a military march-past and a religious procession. The anarchists carried their rifles slung over their shoulders, and their women and children followed, clad in the party colours. The city was like a bullring in the middle of a fight. It was just like Valencia at carnival time . . . After the crossing of the Ebro, the war had taken on a different complexion. . . . Isabella voiced her agreement. She had experienced the tremor that had swept through the whole of Spain at the time. She, too, had recited that victorious litany: 'Gandesa, Alcañiz, Mora del Ebro.' Like her mother, she would break off abruptly in mid-sentence. Gazing at her, Juanito recovered a little of his own fervour.

Shady deals were going on in the capital between the rebel Junta and the Republican commanders.

'They are angling for posts in the next government,' Agustin assured Juanito. 'Yet the Junta ought to be on its guard. After five hours of wrangling, the generals and corps commanders have turned their backs on Negrín. It is a sinister parody of Napoleon's betrayal by his Marshals. They have deprived Miaja of his post as commander-in-chief because he alone has had the courage to speak out against capitulation, but nobody has consulted the ordinary people of Madrid or the men from the working-class suburbs, thanks to whose efforts the University City has withstood every assault . . .'

To Agustin, the defeat of the Republicans constituted no more than a harsh interlude, a temporary divergence, in the development of a people. One day this set-back would be effaced. 'Evolution is not a constant advance,' he explained. 'History is marking time, taking the wrong turning at a crossroads; it even seems to be going backwards. Do you see what I mean, Juanito? A road so crooked that it appears to be returning to its starting-point. But if you are on a hill, you can see that it is gradually winding in the right direction.'

Juanito thought about it. Progress, evolution, sense of history: to him these expressions, which Agustin employed so often, remained stumbling-blocks. He still harboured his resentment against the political parties, whose bickerings had played straight into the enemy's hands. The anarchists and the Trotskyists and the communists had discredited and exhausted the Republic by their demagogic slogans, their needless atrocities, their bloody rivalries.

'All the government needed to do was liquidate the anarchists and the followers of Stalin and Trotsky, right at the start. We didn't have the courage: now the generals are betraying us, the ministers bolting, the troops surrendering. We are all alone.'

'We? You are still thinking like a Valencian.'

Agustin leaned closer to him, displaying the warmth of an elder brother towards a younger which carried them back to the early days of their friendship.

'Well, isn't Valencia the last free city in Spain?'

'You're right. Freedom is like the trees which the French planted to commemorate the capture of the Bastille. And here in Spain, it is in Barcelona and Saragossa and Valencia that it can plunge its roots deep into fertile soil. That is why the last free city in Spain is your city.'

Agustin was once again becoming the schoolmaster who had discoursed with greater fire upon the history of the Girondist party than upon the books of Karl Marx.

'Listen, Juanito, when I was young I used to despise the defeated and the soulful, the noble-hearted who allow themselves to be taken in. Today I feel closer in spirit to the sublime simpletons of '89 and '48, and those of the Commune as well . . . Like them, I prefer to await the enemy here! Let Togliatti and La Pasionaria, Stepanov and Hernandez pile into an old crate that will eventually touch down in Moscow: *they* are the bourgeois rushing to save the furniture! They will have earned themselves sinecure appointments as agitators in South America or the Far East.'

'And you?' asked Juanito, uneasily.

'Oh, I've no plans for the future. I'm living in the present. The Russians live in the smoky mists of the future, the Spanish in the mirages of the past. Franco sees himself as one of the Catholic Kings, the Falangists as the Knights of the Reconquest. For my part, I have modestly decided to dwell in my own skin and my own time. Fancy-dress has never appealed to me.'

Agustin smiled. Secret minutes and confidential reports were still piled high on his desk, but what was the point of investigating the activities of a few individuals now that the trial of Republican Spain was about to open? Did Agustin's evenness of temper stem from the serenity of detachment or from a monumental indifference towards his past idols—Freedom, Evolution, Democracy? His ideologist's zeal had vanished, just like his faith in the future. The present sufficed him, since he had Juanito's face to gaze upon.

'You're certainly shaving close these days, Juanito! Even your eyes have changed colour . . . When you go off to see the Padre, you look like a lover hurrying to an assignation!'

'He is getting so weak that I feel each visit will be the last.'

Agustin flung his cigarette-end into the ash-tray. It fell out again, among the bills of indictment and the suspects' statements, producing a number of small round burns. Agustin did not notice. Like a god beyond the realms of time, he was gazing down from a great height on the turmoils of the human race, its neutralizing virtues and vices, its good actions and its bad, interchangeable and insignificant.

'You have put yourself in a bad position by sheltering an incendiary priest, Juanito . . . You could easily be court-martialled . . . Looked at from another point of view, though, that act of folly might well efface the very crimes that you haven't committed. What court could resist your Padre's testimony? Just imagine that human wreck dragging himself in front of your judges and stammering: "This soldier saved my life twice over. He dragged me free of the blaze, which I had started, and he hid me from the mob, which was ready to lynch me . . ." Take great care of the culprit, Juanito! He is a wonderful alibi.'

'I have no need of alibis!'

Juanito recovered the cigarette-end and carefully stubbed it out on the side of the ash-tray. But Agustin grabbed his wrist.

'Do you suppose your valour hasn't been reported to the other side? There is no lack of informers, and spies thrive on war the way rice-shoots thrive on water. Yes, Juanito, the church was destroyed but, thanks to you, the old crank who started the fire is still alive . . . This ludicrous adventure of yours is the shrewdest thing you have ever done . . .'

Agustin pretended to marvel at the unexpected repercussions that an action could have, but Juanito was nettled. His decision to rescue the Padre had been neither calculating nor scatterbrained. He had no wish to be extolled by the Nationalists or condemned by the Republicans. The Padre was practically one of the family. Any boy from the *huerta* would have pulled him out of the flames.

'Do talk sense, Agustin. You are always trying to catch me out. The Padre taught me everything I know. My brothers had no thought for anything but work and girls. The Padre used to lend me books and talk to me—not the way *you* do, to take the wind out of my sails or make me look a fool. He wanted me to be less ignorant. He has done more for me than all the Republic's politicians put together.'

Agustin laughed. He loved this bridling, this galloping of a thoroughbred painfully goaded.

'Juanito, I'm like a cat who cannot play without using its claws . . . Go and call on your Padre! I'm sure there are pages in the catechism that he hasn't yet taught you . . . And perhaps there is a beautiful girl in his house to say the rosary with you.'

On the desk, a fat, cloth-bound book lay among the files: Shakespeare's tragedies.

'Will you teach me English, Agustin?'

Juanito was always eager to learn.

'Why? Are you thinking of going to London? One evening, when things are quiet, I'll read some bits to you. You will find that you are in Roman times or listening to a man of the time of Philip II.'

Agustin opened the well-thumbed volume, softly summoning these vulnerable heroes as though they were visitors hesitating in the doorway: Julius Caesar, Brutus, Cassius, Mark Antony.

'Tell me the plot,' begged Juanito. He had retained a childish thirst for stories of any kind. He was forgetting the Padre and Isabella in favour of these ghosts.

'It would take too long. Imagine a great battle, as embroiled as the whole of our war. Nobody knows who is the victor, or who is the crushed, of who betrayed who, and all these men have blindly loved or hated one another . . . But when the moment comes for them to die, each of them summons his confidant, the man who owes him everything, wishing only to end his life by a trusted hand. Do you remember the anarchists parading with their placards bearing the words "Long live death"? Long live *my* death, Juanito! A death that nobody will have devised for me, a death as unimpeachable as my life, a death that will be well-organized, moving, even a little theatrical (for I have always loved the theatre—actor or prompter, it is all one to me), a grave-featured, clean-handed death . . .'

He broke off, already pricking up his ears for the rumble of lorries, the tramping of feet, all the vast clatter of a victorious army.

'Where was I?' he resumed. 'Oh yes, Brutus and Cassius have each chosen their killer, just as Caesar may have chosen his. They are ready to face death, the way a man is ready for the act of love. And their farewells are imbued with an inexpressible manly tenderness. Listen, Juanito.'

The book opened of its own accord, and in his subdued voice Agustin read:

For ever, and for ever, farewell, Cassius!
If we do meet again, why, we shall smile!
If not, why then, this parting was well made.

On Juanito's face, shadows stirred, like those which clouds cast on mountainsides. He could not capture the meaning of Agustin's words, but their desperate tone moved him.

He said: 'There is no proof that all is lost, Agustin. France and Britain will impose an armistice and prevent us Spanish from slaughtering one another to the bitter end . . .'

Agustin nodded, listening with only half an ear.

'Why not?' he asked. 'Why shouldn't the Non-Intervention Committee become the Intervention Committee and enforce peace?' He was listening to Brutus's and Cassius's farewells, still going on inside him. He was tearing himself away from Juanito for ever.

'I must be on my way to the Padre's,' Juanito said shyly. 'He is expecting me.'

'Off you go, then,' said Agustin. He repeated, with a far-away smile, as though he were already speaking from another world: 'Why then, this parting was well made.'

46

THESE LAST HOPES, these last illusions, were giving the Padre some of his old strength back. He wanted to harangue the Nationalists and the Republicans.

'We could double-lock him in the cellar,' said Isabella, 'he would still break free to confer his blessing on the Moorish "Knights of Christ".'

'Isabella,' said the Padre, 'I long to wear my soutane again, but I have no intention of blessing the Moors.'

'He is determined to get himself shot,' sighed Angustias.

Heartened by the prospect of regaining his liberty, the Padre was throwing caution to the winds.

'I want to be free to move from the sacristy to the altar, from the altar to the confessional nearest the choir: that is my battlefield.'

He was doing his best to joke, in an attempt to dispel the anxiety of these final hours, in which the Republic lay dying like a human being, with sudden peculiar remissions. Valencia was about to experience the tribulations which she had been spared till now: famine, riots, fear, disturbances like those of the early days, which Angustias could not help recalling—despite Isabella's entreaties. Juanito remembered his mother's stories of how the peasants of the *huerta* had been robbed, and their crops piled on to carts, higgledy-piggledy, and the roads covered with trampled maize and corn and mud-soiled rice and barley, while in Valencia 'patriots' with greedy hands had rifled the luxury stores and the smart boutiques.

The two women drew instinctively closer to Juanito. He would defend them, just as he had saved the Padre. His mere presence, his lilting voice, his tranquil gaze brought them reassurance. The hours flowed gently by. The fountain suddenly roused itself, mingling its bluff laugh, its outbursts of grief, with the women's questions and Juanito's artless replies. Franco's troops were nearing Sagunto. But this spring night was brimming over with scattered promises. The rose-bushes were in a hurry to bloom. When midnight struck, Juanito stood up regretfully.

When she opened the front door, which led directly into the square, Angustias found herself face to face with a militiaman. She shuddered, but he only handed her a note, then hurried away without a word. Juanito, who had been chatting to Isabella in the darkness of the patio, stepped forward into the light and ran his eye over this message from Agustin. The women exchanged uneasy stares. Finally Juanito looked up, embarrassed by this order enjoining him not to return to barracks that night but to remain under Angustias's roof pending further instructions.

Isabella consulted her mother. Angustias agreed at once, with a sad smile.

'You will have my brother's room,' said Isabella.

In the vast studio, the soft light of Isabella's oil-lamp strayed across fantastic landscapes populated with enigmatic figures —creatures which were part man, part bird, women still inextricably joined to the barks of trees—as though for Rafaele the Creation had stopped short at this world of half-achieved metamorphoses. Fishermen stood in doorways, casually unwinding huge nets with tremendously wide meshes, nets designed for catching—not fish, but wrecks and monsters, dead bodies and treasures, gods covered all over with shells and flowing seaweed.

'Rafaele called this canvas "Fishing for Dreams": he saw this harbour in a dream, with its green clouds, its pink houses worn like old pebbles, and these men making a show of mending their nets.'

Isabella fell silent. Already they were groping their way towards one another through the dreams of a ghost, in this *trompe l'œil* suffused with the light of the beyond. Then Juanito caught the sound of something pulsating. Its tiny, undeviating beat was filling the room like the scampering of a rodent at night.

'It's his watch,' said Isabella. 'My mother winds it every evening.'

That night, Juanito very soon returned to the fabulous harbour where half-naked men were spreading giant nets like spiders' webs. The harbour resembled El Grao, as it had loomed up in the morning light on Juanito's return from Barcelona. Shivering in the dawn, he was rushing about the deck in search of his companion. Agustin had disappeared . . . A thread of daylight was stealing through the curtain. Waking up lost in a strange house, Juanito imagined that he was still lying beside Encarnacion in that peaceful bedroom invaded by the scent of honeysuckle. But from somewhere in the distance, at lengthy intervals, came a series of rumbling explosions. They are blowing up the ammunition dumps . . . Why has Agustin ordered me to remain here?

His hands shook as he buckled on his belt. He was praying, as he had prayed in the blazing church: 'Virgin, save us!'

He crept out of the sleeping house and quietly shut the front door after him. He strode along in the middle of the road, as though to present an easier target for bullets. The shutters of the houses were hypocritically closed. Yet Juanito had the feeling that he was being spied upon. He glanced round. The street was deserted. Suddenly a militiaman emerged from an alleyway. He saluted Juanito and asked him for a light. Juanito stopped and searched in his uniform for matches. He did not have time to remove his hands from his pockets or cry out. Other men had leapt out of the alleyway, where they had presumably been lying in wait for Juanito. He was bound and gagged before he had a chance to defend himself. This is all a mistake, thought Juanito. He made a violent effort to break free. But he was felled by a blow on the back of the neck. The men carried him off unconscious, as though he were a street casualty.

47

AGUSTIN, with the help of two trusted aides, had spent the whole night burning secret dossiers. They had to turn the papers this way and that to expose them more completely to the flame. Every document that was reduced to ashes might mean the saving of a life. Time weighed heavily on the trio. There was no wind to breathe life into the bonfires scattered beneath the gloomy arcades. Like his companions, Agustin was streaming with sweat. The glow fell on bare arms, making hands look monstrous. Whenever the fire spread to a further heap of signed depositions, Joselito's feverish face would loom out of the shadows, pinched by a curious impatience.

Agustin's fingers felt numb and blistered. He handed the long iron rod, which he had been using as a poker, to Joselito. From a wooden seat on the edge of the narrow strip of lawn, he could silently supervise the destruction of the secret memoranda and the lists of hostages. Abortive battle plans were turning to ashes simultaneously with the codes and names of secret agents. Fire purifies everything, Agustin was thinking: it is the filth of this war that Joselito is stirring like a sorcerer. In this final auto-da-fé, the whole machinery of sabotage was about to be reduced to dust, the entire apparatus erected by human hands for the demolishment of power stations, houses and factories, for the annihilation of a nation's strength and wealth. The faintest pallor showed in the sky. In a strange house, Juanito's fists would be clenched in sleep. Agustin thought: no harm can come to him now, he is back in his city.

The blaze was hypnotizing Agustin. Staring into these flames which danced within a few feet of the ground, he told himself that, together with the archives of the secret police, Joselito was burning the notebooks of a young schoolmaster, commonplace books full of furious underlinings, volumes that were to prepare Agustin for his role as a leader of men: rigorous self-examinations, university curricula, knotty treatises on political economy, collections of maxims, biographies of the illustrious. It was Agustin's days, his hours, spent reading far into the night, which were shrivelling up before his eyes and turning into these charred leaves, and which the overheated air was lifting above the blaze before they were finally deposited, over a wide area, in a fine rain of soot.

Joselito had disappeared. On the first floor, a light appeared in the ante-room, lingered in Agustin's office.

In these final hours, Joselito was still wandering about, on the prowl, devoting himself to unfathomable pursuits, inexplicable tasks.

Agustin called him, without raising his voice.

'What were you doing up there?'

'Looking for my cigarettes.'

'What about the papers concerning the lieutenant? Have you put them in a safe place?'

Joselito roared with laughter.

'The matter has been fully attended to,' he said. 'They must be arresting him at this very moment . . . He will be the first prisoner to be released by Franco.'

Agustin laughed too: 'He will have tasted all the joys of the innocent and of the guilty. Are you sure we can depend on the prison governor?'

'As I would depend on myself!' said Joselito. 'He has a dossier *that* thick on the activities of Juanito Sanchez, protector of incendiary priests, defender of suspects and rebels, deserter . . .'

The sky was gradually blueing over. The last incriminating documents were burning themselves out. The night had lasted a century and a split second. It was ending, but Joselito and Agustin could no longer remember its ever beginning . . .

Joselito was standing beside the seat. He had the lissom spine of a wild cat accustomed to springing from rooftop to rooftop.

'What will you do, Joselito?'

'Oh, I have friends in Valencia.'

In the early-morning light, Agustin sensed a look of defiance on his all too radiant face. He would pull through, right enough. But the Andalusian heaved a sigh.

'If you liked . . .' he began.

The rather agitated entreaty which emerged from his glances and gestures was now taking hold of his voice. They would hide for a few days. Then they would make their way to Almeria. It was Joselito's birthplace. One of his sisters ran a hotel there, and his brothers knew the fishermen. With a bit of luck, it would be easy for them to take to the sea . . .

As Joselito spoke, Agustin indulged in a last day-dream: that of running away with a companion, going absolutely anywhere with him, walking straight ahead and hand in hand. But he had progressed beyond such a temptation. He broke in curtly: 'You're right! We should need a bit of luck, and I'd ruin everything.'

Agustin's other assistant came over to where he was sitting.

'Everything is burnt.'

'Excellent!' Agustin derived satisfaction from the thought that lives would not be lost through incaution.

Joselito still lingered beside the seat. Agustin jerked his head in his direction, as though he were an intruder disturbing this last tête-à-tête with himself.

'Are you waiting for Franco to get here before you make a run for it?'

Suddenly the irritation faded from Agustin's voice.

After a night without sleep, the early morning was shedding a harsh glare on these haggard features. In this irrefutable, apocalyptic light, another Joselito was appearing. This was no longer Agustin's zealous, overbearing and obsequious secretary, no longer his tool, with the capacity to anticipate his every wish: with his compliant and provocative expression, he was an accomplice in lust.

Agustin could no longer withstand the clamourings of his memory. A recollection was pounding away on the other side of oblivion. He pricked up his ears to decode the message which this prisoner was tapping out on the wall of his cell. It was in

Barcelona, a club in the heart of the Barrio Chino. A troupe of Andalusian dancers held the floor, performing furiously amid a swirl of flounced petticoats. Then they yielded before the star of the show.

Sweeping the floor with the long train of her dress, she was like a snake obeying the charmer's summons. She kept coiling and uncoiling. The dark little head which this lovely viper reared and darted in her efforts to bite was adorned with red carnations. She seemed to languish, but her grip was crushing her prey in a slow caress. She was enframed by four male dancers, febrile and quick on their feet. They were taking their tempo, not so much from the playing of the band as from the swell that was straightening the back and arching the breast of this girl from Triana. She was provoking each in turn, in order to lure him into a struggle in which his defeat was a foregone conclusion. She would lie swooning and swaying in his arms, only to dismiss him from the circle of her dance a moment later. These artful dissimulations, these entwinings, these sudden lulls, these renewed outbursts of violence, were simply her means of casting a spell. Bursting forth in these lewd acts of sorcery, in these ferocious coquetries, were an animal cruelty, a delight in destruction through the indulgence of the senses reminiscent of the wedding-flights of insects and the love-battles of snakes . . .

Agustin sat yawning. The same indecent and unvarying eroticism was oozing from all these sevillanas and seguedillas and boleros; it was a show for tourists. He took refuge upstairs. The circular balcony had been fitted with deep boxes, to facilitate the tête-à-têtes of lovers. Each of these private compartments was in half-light, like a box in a theatre. Inside, casual encounters were pursued quite unrestrainedly, as though in an alcove, amid whispers and laughter and kisses interspersed with fainthearted protestations.

Without so much as a glance at the adjoining box through the narrow moucharaby, Agustin sat down by the rail. He leaned well forward, staring down at the dance-floor. A young male dancer was cavorting lightly amid the smell of sweat, scent and alcoholic drink. His slender waist was nipped in by a waistcoat covered with ruby-red spangles, whose gleam gave a lurid colouring to his face. When he threw back his head and spread his arms, he was like the portrait of Lucifer which Agustin had seen in an Italian church. On the smoke-blackened fresco a beautiful and almost naked hermaphrodite, whose arms were adorned with heavy bracelets, was offering a hunk of bread to a Christ on the point of collapse. And this youthful devil was the angel whom God regrets smiting . . .

Once again, to recover his balance between figures, the dancer spread his arms. His expression was that of the Tempter visiting a hermit in order to succour him or lead him astray! Like the Son of Man, Agustin rejected the fruits of the earth and the imaginary kingdoms, but he hungered and thirsted for the faltering gesture of these empty hands. His eye encountered the dancer's. Agustin drew back into the gloom.

The dancer vanished, then returned for the zapateado. The rhythm was flowing through every fibre of his being, as though through the taut string of a guitar. He was the music, the instrument and the contracted fingers of the soloist. He was dancing with his whole body and with ice-cold application; but, while he was stamping out the tempo with crisp fury, his face retained a look of indifference, as though he were not fully involved in the frenzy that had taken hold of his limbs. In the shadows, Agustin was surrendering to the intoxication of the scene and groaning to himself at every click of the young man's heels, though whether from pain or from pleasure he could not have said.

When he had finished his turn, the dancer joined Agustin in his box. The evenly-spaced chinks in the wrought-iron screen provided his face with a flickering mask. Agustin claimed to be an impresario on the look-out for new talent. The light from the dance-floor below gave a softer mould to Joselito's features. His black hair clung in beautiful locks to his damp forehead. He apologized for perspiring. He had ordered an *anis* barely tinged with water. As he set down his glass, he casually laid his hand on Agustin's wrist. After all these years, Agustin could still feel the burning touch of it. Joselito had smiled. He disliked beating about the bush . . .

Now the sun was coming up. Agustin could not take his eyes off the dancer's face.

'We had met before, Captain.'

'Yes,' Agustin said faintly, 'I remember . . . Wait for me, will you?'

He stood up. The other soldier was still stirring the half-calcined leaves. The glowing embers of the braziers were giving off an intolerable heat in the narrow courtyard, designed for the saunterings of a frail old man. Beneath the arcaded gallery, he had to kneel down in order to drink from a tap set very low down on the wall. The water was springing out of the ground, easing the discomfort in his throat, cleansing his feverish face. Its flavour was purer than the morning which was breaking over Valencia, innocent of all the days and nights that had preceded it.

'The coolness of shadows,' Agustin quoted to himself as he straightened up. The words made his head swim and prolonged this sensation of untroubled joy. He had drunk, from this icy spring, a mouthful of peace.

'Joselito!' he called.

Already the Andalusian was standing beneath the portico.

'Joselito,' said Agustin, 'I had forgotten your face.'

'Those boxes were very dark,' Joselito answered calmly.

'I had forgotten your voice.'

'We talked so quietly.' To Joselito, it had been just one adventure among many.

'I wanted to sign you up for a big tour in South America . . .'

Agustin smiled, in retrospect, at these artifices and his own shyness.

'Few of those tours took me any farther than the boxes of the Tabierno Flamenco,' observed Joselito.

They laughed, reconciled beyond pointless lying and pretence.

'Listen,' Agustin said sharply, 'we'll talk about ourselves later. First let us settle the question of Lieutenant Sanchez. Have you taken care of everything?'

'Everything!' affirmed Joselito, with a note of disdain in his voice. He was indignant that he should be suspected of negligence. He hated Juanito, but he was capable of rising above his hatred.

Agustin stared questioningly into those eyes which shone too brightly beneath their excessively long lashes. The whim of memory was all that was needed for the zapateado dancer to reappear in the uniform of a Republican soldier. Agustin ran an amazed glance over Joselito's features; the warm-blooded lips looked as though they had been painted. A very old temptation lay hidden behind this mask . . .

'Meaning what, exactly?'

Joselito gave a shrug and answered: 'At this moment, the lieutenant must be strung up like a chicken. Tomorrow, he will be set free with profuse apologies . . . We can rely on the double-agents.'

The Andalusian's smile contained a hint of smugness and contempt.

'Admirable,' said Agustin, restraining his feeling of joy. Juanito would be saved against his own wishes, saved from and in relation to the rest of the world. Agustin would have liked to see him once more. He blamed himself for this weakness. But what tragic hero had admitted: 'Not of a woman's tenderness to be, requires nor child nor woman's face to see. I have sat too long'? Agustin repeated the last words to himself: 'I have sat too long.' But must I invoke Coriolanus to justify myself? he thought. One morning Juanito will be free; he will gaze at the world through his twenty-year-old eyes. I shall be a little of that immortal dust, a little of that ash which a sharp breeze is sufficient to disperse . . . Yet Agustin felt only a kind of friendship for death. He had chosen it—'a death that will be well-organized, moving, even a little theatrical'. He gazed trustingly at Joselito. He who had struggled so long and hard against loneliness would retain this companion to the very end. He pointed at the courtyard. The soldier was stamping his feet on the last heaps of charred papers.

'Look, Joselito! All burnt, and freedom with it. Forget what you have seen and heard. Find some isolated spot and . . .'

'Don't worry about *me*!' broke in Joselito. The brightness

had gone from his face. Agustin was declining the chance to run away with him. They would not plunge into this adventure together as they had plunged into the shadows of the night-club in the Barrio Chino.

'Yes,' Agustin resumed, 'a port would be best . . . You will tour South America alone. Do you remember how we planned it? Mexico, Rio, Santiago . . . And out there, Joselito, you will dance. Hunger, thirst and pleasure are the same everywhere.'

'What about you?' asked the Andalusian.

'Me?' repeated Agustin, as though he were putting this question to himself for the first time. 'Oh, my arrangements were made a long time ago!'

'No,' Joselito said with a shrug, 'I have emptied the revolver . . .'

'Who gave you the right to do that?' demanded Agustin.

The two men eyed one another challengingly.

'Let's go upstairs,' said Agustin. 'There is nothing more for us to do here.'

They climbed the spaciously winding staircase, built to accommodate the flowing cloaks of prelates. In the office, the gaping shutters afforded a glimpse of untarnished sky above the red-tiled roofs. Over Valencia a morning was rising, as miraculously virginal as all other mornings. The desk was strewn with a jumble of files. Agustin snatched the revolver out of the drawer and extracted the empty loading-clip. He handed the weapon to the Andalusian without a word.

'I can't . . .' protested Joselito.

'Why?' Agustin asked derisively. 'Simply because we met one evening so long ago that when we ran into one another again I didn't even recognize you?'

He broke off. To slow down the advance of the Nationalist forces, bridges, arsenals and ordnance depots were being blown up. Though lost, the war was still giving rise to these explosions and conflagrations. The men were no longer fighting; they were hurriedly destroying everything that they had stocked up for battle.

'We have no time to waste,' said Agustin. 'Reload the revolver. When I'm quite ready, I'll call you.'

Joselito bowed his head submissively.

'You will fire till the gun is empty,' continued Agustin. 'Six bullets are not too many for me. Is it a promise?'

Joselito nodded, fluttering his eyelashes. Agustin smiled gravely.

'You alone could perform this service for me,' he said.

In a choking voice, Joselito repeated: 'I alone.'

Agustin's gaze fell on the book with the worn binding. In any masterpiece there is a prophecy, he reflected. The music of the words, the sense of being carried away in space and time, obscure this judgment delivered centuries ago in another language. He reached out for the battered-looking volume. With his nail he scraped off the label, which was coming unstuck.

Twenty years earlier, the great had been revealed to him in the artificial glare of the footlights. The lives and deaths of heroes, their ambitions and vengeances, their sufferings and acts of forgiveness had been given a manlier and loftier countenance so that they should triumph on the stage. The struggles which each of these men had to endure had become a source of heart-rending gestures, of soul-stirring attitudes. Their destinies had been worked out within the majestic isolation of the drama, within that silence which so enfolds tragedy that the characters' outbursts acquire a new resonance for the breathless audience. For Agustin, conscience had been merely this sublime soliloquy, listened to by a hushed crowd . . . Politics, he thought, weren't Machiavelli or Sorel or Marx. They were the voice of Plutarch, the inspiration of Shakespeare. I was just like that journalist whom I derided to Juanito: so highminded, so determined to model myself on legendary heroes. I saw myself as Caesar or Brutus, Coriolanus or Timon of Athens. And now they are prompting me, putting my closing lines into my mouth, just as actors who are used to performing together will come to the aid of a faltering colleague . . . He read at random, then suddenly stopped at: 'But life, being weary of these worldly bars, never lacks power to dismiss itself.' He was forgetting Joselito, who was handling the revolver with the same calmness with which he would have dusted his typewriter. The Andalusian's movements were going on in a different space and time. 'Cassius from bondage will deliver Cassius': these words, snatched from this or that role, were the substance of his own monologue. Were they a promise, a summons? What voice from the past was proclaiming his salvation? I shall not fall into anyone's hands, he said to himself: I shall bear away my inviolable liberty, like my love, like my secret . . . In the confusion of the battlefield, Shakespeare's heroes sought a reliable hand to administer death. Who dared refuse Brutus this means of escape? 'That's not an office for a friend, my lord.' But Joselito had accepted. There is always some slave prepared to serve as this blade of deliverance . . .

Joselito was extracting the loading-clip. In reality, as on the stage, death calls for detailed rehearsal. Agustin returned to the open book, to these destinies which he had the impression of traversing backwards. He would have liked to dip into this volume and read passages aloud to Juanito, using them as a roundabout way of confiding his secret, as an admission woven with enigmas which the boy would one day understand. Agustin heard his own voice ringing out in the same room: 'Why then, this parting was well made.' A parting between whom? Between two unlucky conspirators, between two generals on the eve of a rout? With a shiver of pride, he said to himself: I used to be a schoolmaster intoxicated with Plutarch's *Lives* and the history of the Girondist party. My end will be the same as Saint-Just's and Fermin Galan's.

The Andalusian had taken the bullets out of his pocket; they lay on a large check handkerchief, just a small pile of gleaming cartridge-cases. He was peacefully reloading the revolver. When each of the smooth-shaped projectiles was in position, he applied the safety-catch. Agustin glanced up. Would Joselito carry out his final order? Everything in Agustin's life had failed. But he was still hoping to make a success of his death. Forgetting Joselito, he searched feverishly for some meaning, for some trace of nobility in this series of coincidences, expedients and substitutions which make up an existence, in this coarse fabric in which pain, disappointment and renunciation are hopelessly entangled. His every chance had been ruined from the outset. This was the bondage of which Cassius spoke, imposed at birth, reinforced by all attempts at escape . . . A nonsensical life, a pointless death. No way out. But the door had opened on that November day when Agustin and Juanito had exchanged glances. Nothing could efface that early morning scene on a barrack square, with the engines of the lorries still ticking over. From that chilly dawn had emerged a round face, fully illumined by the beam of the lamp, and a pair of blue-grey eyes which had not blinked in the presence of the light, in the presence of the stranger.

'Are you from Valencia?'

From that moment, the confession which Agustin had succeeded in repressing had transfigured his life. The arrival of a single human being had been sufficient for this incoherent series of accidents and theories, of misfortunes and setbacks, to cease to be merely the wrong side of a wonderfully woven tapestry. The Republic was in the last stages of collapse, the war was lost, but a boy from the *huerta* was smiling. Agustin averted his gaze, as though Juanito were about to appear.

Un bello niño de junco,
anchos hombros, fino talle,
piel de nocturna manzana,
boca triste y ojos grandes . . .

Agustin sat silently intoning these lines of Lorca's. He no longer felt anything but a wild impatience to immure himself in a final tête-à-tête with a remembered face, to drain these last moments of a life which held all eternity . . . Like a god savouring every moment of his creation, he was embracing, at a single glance, in a single present, all those bygone days: a grey November dawn in Barcelona, the warm nights, with the city emitting a faintly phosphorescent glow in the distance (the moths had danced in the blue beams of the lamp, and Agustin had sat waiting for the sound of footsteps), that exhilarating morning of victory in a village square, and a torrid September afternoon in Gandesa . . . The blazing sky had consumed illusion and deceit. All was lost. Juanito was right: only God and Spain were 'straight'. But the Valencian's despairing cry, and the abusive exchanges between Vicente and Esteban, and Ignacio Sanchez's dirge floating up amid the bullet-slashed vineplants, and the unharvested soil, and the cloudless sky: all these were caught in the imperishable substance of a moment of time. Agustin had stopped pretending, and Juanito had given up hope. Nothing could tarnish this lucidity which was simply the intoxication of being rendered destitute.

That September day, on which everyone had squarely confronted the truth, was now redeeming Agustin's mistakes, expunging his failures, justifying his existence. But a minute would have sufficed, the mere sound of Juanito's breathing as he had lain beside him on the deck of the ship, smiling at the stars . . .

Agustin returned to an awareness of the present. The Andalusian had set the revolver down on the table. Agustin thrust it back towards him.

'Wait in the next room. I'll give you a shout . . .' Agustin could not deny himself this final happiness of gently stirring a few memories, of quietly uttering a Christian name, over and over again.

Joselito nodded his head in agreement. Agustin got up and shook his hand.

'Thanks, man! And good luck!'

He was experiencing an entirely new feeling of comradeship for the killer whom he had chosen, for this slave who, by administering death, would become his equal. The Romans had covered their faces before exposing themselves to the thrusts of their slayers. With Joselito, Agustin said to himself, there is no need for me to be shy or stand on ceremony. He has seen my face naked in lust, naked in sadness. He can see it naked in death. The Andalusian seemed to waver. Agustin tried to put heart into him.

'I know your hand will be steady . . .! Oh, I was forgetting: you will tell Lieutenant Sanchez that I preferred not to say good-bye to him . . . And now, leave me . . .'

The door closed on Joselito. Agustin was at peace with himself. He was soaring above his own existence. On the boat that was bringing them back to Valencia, he was daydreaming among the sleeping figures armoured with moonlight. Tomorrow the sun would rise over El Grao harbour. He would step soundlessly into Juanito's house. For Agustin, dying meant secretly dwelling in the *barraca* from this day forward, invisibly mingling with the talking and laughing and singing and toiling and dreaming of other men, peacefully overthrowing every barrier, effortlessly transgressing every prohibition, overcoming loneliness for all time.

Agustin pricked up his ears. At lengthy intervals, shouts were ringing out. The crowd was welcoming the first victorious detachments. On the mantelpiece, the brandy bottle stood reflected in the mirror. A glass shook in Agustin's hand; all was well. Juanito would be waking in a strange house. He would be holding his head under a tap and sprinkling water in all directions. It would be streaming over his copper-coloured hair and his tanned skin. The nearing of the end was giving rise to a purer tenderness in Agustin, to a marvelling surge of emotion.

'Juanito, you are alive! You will live!'

This face would be impregnated, like fruit, with all the juices of Spain. The shade and sunshine of the *huerta* would wash against this sturdy body. The days, the nights, the seasons would revolve round this human tree . . . Agustin set down the empty brandy glass. He was talking to Juanito in an undertone.

'Remember! This parting was well made! Juanito, the last fishing boats are setting sail from Cartagena and Cadiz. They are sinking under the weight of the fugitives . . . The victors are preparing for the big reckoning: they are laying the blame at certain doors, they are accusing and condemning . . . These waves of cheering at the city gates are going to bring further truths, further lies in their wake . . . Men are going to judge other men . . . Juanito, was I mistaken about the means or about the ends . . .? Was the offensive an act of suicide? I no longer know. Of my whole life, I regret only a few images, Lorca's poems, which make one's head swim like neat spirits, this pristine morning over Valencia, a September night with the stars raining down through the gaping roof of a farmhouse and a boy from the *huerta* whose dreams are entangled with the story of the martyrs of Jaca, and for whom Fermin Galan still draws breath . . . How could I have juggled for so long with theories and ideas? The Revolution? A tattered poster for a show that is no longer running . . . Spain? The passers-by whom one sees through a café window, a flow of indistinct faces. Juanito, I have no past and no future now. My present is this plank thrown over the abyss—but what have I to fear, apart from leaving you? Juanito, I have chosen my killer . . . I should have liked us to take that walk through the countryside which Fermin Galan and Garcia Hernandez took together . . . "Two friends," you said, "who believed in the Republic with all their hearts . . ." Juanito, remember them, remember me, when you kneel before the Madonna of the Forsaken. In the old days, they used to stand her statue on the coffins of executed criminals. She alone remained with the abandoned, the insane and the innocent to the very end. Juanito, do not be angry! She should have pity on me . . .'

Joselito burst into the room, looking very pale. He was holding the revolver tight against his thigh, as though to conceal it.

'Captain, there are three motor-cyclists in the courtyard.'

'Open the window!'

In the morning air, the voices rose almost too clearly; the newcomers were talking in a forced, theatrical manner, to frighten any unseen eavesdroppers or to bolster their own courage.

'There is nobody here,' said one of the motor-cyclists, in a harsh Castilian accent. The blinds were tilted open. Agustin glanced out. The trio were eyeing the building perplexedly, fearing an ambush. Joselito's hand was trembling on the revolver. Now, half-reassured, the men were staring upwards. Sweat was ploughing paler furrows on their dust-blackened faces. They looked like actors with poor make-up, and these victors, pricking up their ears for the slightest sound, were trembling as though they were fugitives. Agustin stepped back and propped himself against the desk. Juanito's features came into his mind with wonderful clarity. His eyelids were fluttering gently over the shadowy pools of his pupils. His mouth was about to open. A boyish smile was quivering on his manly face. Everything was so simple. Agustin soundlessly uttered his name, one last time.

'Well, what are you waiting for?'

A hail of bullets sent him sprawling on the desk.

Out in the corridor, there was a scurry of footsteps. They stopped, prudently, just beyond the door. Joselito swung round. He was still clutching the revolver. He would never be able to let go of it. The boldest of the three men strode up to Joselito and pointed inquiringly at the dead body.

'He was the head of the Intelligence Service,' Joselito said haughtily. 'He was about to make a dash for it.'

The three officers glanced questioningly at one another.

'Where are the secret papers kept?' asked the first.

Joselito shrugged.

'He burnt them all last night.'

The officer plunged an impatient hand into the open drawer. He drew out a jumble of faded photographs.

'Who is this?'

'An infantryman killed at Belchite.'

The officer stared at a small, unpretentious snapshot. Turning it over, he read: 'Mora del Ebro. Juanito.'

'And this?'

'A young lieutenant . . . He harboured priests and incendiaries. The captain had him arrested yesterday.'

'We're wasting time,' said the officer with the harsh voice. 'At this very moment, innocent men are being executed in the prisons.'

His companions nodded, reassured and disappointed. Victory was crumbling in their grasp. Was this body slouched insecurely on the desk really the head of the Intelligence Service? The curtain was being rung down too quickly. They would rather have witnessed the enemy's final death-throes.

For a moment, the Castilian vented his annoyance on Joselito.

'He should have been interrogated!'

The Andalusian gave an imperceptible shrug.

'Dead or alive,' he said, 'he would have told you nothing.'

'Let's not waste time,' reiterated the Castilian.

The leader of the party enveloped Joselito and the dead body in a single contemptuous glance. The motives behind this squaring of accounts could be investigated later.

'You are responsible for everything here,' he said. His expression indicated that the dead body was part of the strange assemblage that he was entrusting to Joselito's safekeeping: the empty offices, the half-destroyed files, the lists of hostages burnt to ashes.

Joselito bowed courteously, as though accepting the most commonplace of instructions. He stood quite still, listening to their footsteps receding down the corridors. The motor-bicycles broke into a roar beneath the window. Joselito drained the brandy bottle before setting about the task of laying out Agustin's body. He cleared the top of the desk with the back of his hand. From among the photographs of Luis which had fallen to the floor, he retrieved the crumpled snapshot of Juanito. He pushed aside a thick, cloth-bound book so that he could spread the body flat on the table. The bullets had hit Agustin throat-high. His shirt was sticky with blood in the region of the heart. He must have died almost instantly. His eyes and brow shone with a strange conviction. When the officers had burst into the room, Agustin had already been in a world in which victory and defeat were devoid of meaning.

With his check handkerchief, Joselito made a chin-bandage to hide the smashed jaw. Before leaving the room, he glanced behind him: on the dark wooden desk, like one of those altars on which a scrawny Christ is exposed during Holy Week, Agustin seemed to be smiling.

48

THE COLONEL called Juanito over to witness the scene.

'Just look at them!' he said.

He leaned out of the window, and over his shoulder Juanito saw a foaming sea of human heads in the barrack square.

These were the troops of the 23rd Corps. To the very end, the government had banked on the loyalty of the Corps's three divisions to bar the way to Valencia and hold off the units from Madrid which had gone over to the side of the Junta. General Menendez, commander-in-chief of the Army of the Levante, had refused to unleash yet another fratricidal struggle, and now this force, the last hope of the Republic, was just a band of would-be deserters. Clearly displayed on all these unshaven faces and in all these human forms, lying sprawled on steps and propped against tree-trunks, were the same, unvarying tiredness and repugnance.

The main gates of the barracks, leading directly into the Gran Via, were closed, but the two side entrances stood wide open. Franco's troops were pouring in through the right-hand gate, in serried ranks, ready for a parade. Their spotless rifles, highly polished belts and glittering helmets were in striking contrast to the dusty uniforms of the Republican soldiers, who were quite prostrate, like refugees waiting for a train.

An invisible line divided the square: on either side of this frontier, the troops were eyeing one another with indifference or hostility. It was luck which had originally placed them on one or other side of this mysterious boundary. Today luck ranged them among the victors or among the vanquished. In this cramped space, feuding brothers were reproaching one another or trying to recognize one another. Those who came from the same part of the country were exchanging news in a hushed and shamefaced

manner. The morning sunlight was beginning to make the sweat stream down their faces. The fountain was on the left of the square, in the Republican 'zone'. Nationalist troops carefully threaded their way through the ranks to kneel and drink. Then there were shy exchanges of lights and cigarettes; a tentative brotherliness was emerging from these time-honoured gestures, which were turning into placatory rites, promises of reconciliation.

'They are in such a hurry to occupy these barracks. We had better take our men to the Plaza de Toros, and demobilize them there.'

Juanito agreed. The bullring, built to hold thirty thousand spectators, was the only place large enough to hold all the troops.

Conversations were being struck up in the square. Andalusians and Catalans were firing questions at one another about Seville and Barcelona, like travellers from the same country mildly surprised at meeting in some remote corner of the world. Dangerous arguments were beginning to break out: the Nationalists had won the right to the final word, and the only revenge now open to the vanquished was to spit in their faces the insults burning on their lips . . .

'We must put a stop to this,' said the colonel. 'The officer who was to have marched at the head of the column is late. Something must have happened to him. Trouble might break out at any moment. Our men are unarmed. Look at Franco's! They are so weighed down with ammunition that they can hardly move.'

They laughed bitterly at this army which bore all the outward signs of victory, at these well-fed and well-equipped warriors. The colonel was anxious to terminate this confrontation of the two armies.

'A word out of place,' he said, 'a drunkard trying to be funny, and it'll be a pitched battle, ending in slaughter. I'm going to look for that lieutenant.'

The colonel turned to a soldier who was sitting at a typewriter, with his back to the light.

'Type out that pass,' he said. 'It may still do the trick.'

The colonel's footsteps receded down the corridor.

'All passes are valid,' observed the secretary, 'since the sentries can't read.'

He had lifted his head and was now clicking away at his machine. In the full light of morning, Joselito was smiling to himself. His eyes shone with a calm impudence, as though he had just played one last trick on the Nationalists and the Republicans, on himself and everyone else.

'Where is Agustin?' entreated Juanito.

The Andalusian evaded this futile question with a shrug of the shoulders. He carefully stamped the pass. Then he examined the clear imprint with an air of satisfaction, before replying with feigned courtesy: 'The captain is out of danger, I imagine . . . Incidentally, lieutenant, I haven't had the pleasure of seeing you for some days . . .'

A bantering smile hovered at the corners of his too finely chiselled mouth. Joselito had been part of this office, the headquarters of the 22nd Corps, since time began. Placid or anguished faces would appear in the doorway and issue feverish demands, orders that met with no response. Joselito viewed with detachment the bustling of these supernumeraries in a play whose text was known to him alone. These officers would nervously crumple papers, producing a smell of dust and ink, and seek instructions or explanations. In Barcelona, in the office of the political commissar, Juanito had witnessed the same untidiness, the same agitation, the same hubbub; but in the heart of that vortex Agustin's intelligence had prevailed, together with his strong will, his crisp yet impassioned voice, his scathing rejoinders, his rather grating irony.

'We are dead,' Joselito concluded, 'but there is no one to bury us: no priest, no altar-boy, no grave-diggers, no relatives.' He burst out laughing. 'We are a corpse that has to bury itself . . .!'

The colonel's anxious voice broke in upon him: 'Lieutenant Sanchez! You will march these men to the Plaza de Toros. There, everything is ready for their demobilization. It will be as well not to dawdle . . . Can I rely on you?'

Juanito nodded.

'Colonel,' he said, 'I should like to know where Captain Benliure is . . .'

The colonel seemed embarrassed.

'The first Nationalist elements to enter Valencia were the police and the Falangist interrogators . . . Our political commissar did not wait to meet them.'

Juanito slowly walked down the stairs. What a strange mission, he thought. I have to prevent these troops from either fraternizing or fighting.

Joselito was following him soundlessly.

In the barrack square, with the eyes of the victors upon him, Juanito felt himself blushing. A few crisp words of command rallied the men who had been sitting on the steps and in doorways. Somehow he had to give this tired-looking column a semblance of discipline and smartness. When the troops had formed up, Juanito placed himself at their head. At that moment, a very tall officer emerged from the Nationalist ranks and marched straight towards him. He was carrying the Nationalist flag in a lordly manner. The untarnished silk trailed over his chest. On the fiery red and bright yellow were quartered the clustered arrows, the yoke and the eagle borrowed from the Catholic Kings.

When he was within a yard of Juanito, the Nationalist officer handed him the flag. A hum of hostility ran through the Republican ranks. Juanito hesitated. Why should he consent to this humiliation? Agustin often derided the weathercock mentality of the people of Valencia. Had Juanito fought throughout all these months of war simply to end up as a Nationalist standard-bearer? A sullen fury was stirring in his blood at this final provocation. He controlled himself, however, and took the flag. The wooden staff was burning his hand. Words of defiance rang out, and there were mutterings of abuse. Juanito shuddered. To whom were these imprecations addressed? Was it the enemy flag or their ignominious capitulation that was giving rise to this convulsion of rage?

The Nationalist officer discreetly turned away. He had no wish to look as if he were finishing off a dying man. These

defeated troops might well have been entitled to the honours of war. Unable to bring himself to scan their faces, so flushed with anger, he pretended to be deep in thought and followed the slow movement of the hands of the great clock in the middle of the façade: the hour soon to strike would solve every problem.

Anxiously, Juanito surveyed the tense faces in search of assistance. He seemed to recognize one of the soldiers and started towards him, meaning to entrust him with the flag. The man stood with his arms stiff at his sides and his lips set tight. Nobody wanted the job.

The Nationalist officer came marching back across the square. An enormous silence hung over these thousands of men, whom hatred was dividing anew.

Leaning out of the window, the colonel made a vague gesture of entreaty or encouragement. Let a single soldier dare to grab and trample on the Nationalist colours, and there would be bloodshed. The Civil War would start all over again.

'Will you trust me with the flag, lieutenant?'

The Andalusian's familiar and obsequious voice made Juanito jump.

Joselito brandished the staff high above him. With the pomp of a conductor about to unleash a tumult of sound from his orchestra, he made the soft, gleaming silk crack in the air. This comic piece of miming drew roars of laughter from his neighbours. He was imitating to perfection the rapt enthusiasm of a standard-bearer. And, lavishing fervent stares on the Nationalist emblem, he was aping the pious zeal of a seminarist in the presence of the Virgin's banner.

The men marched off. At the window of his office, the colonel stood mopping his brow. He had visualized his barrack square, like the square of Montana barracks in Madrid, strewn with bodies lying in pools of blood. Joselito was still acting his part. He was giving sly jerks to the flag, to suggest the powerful momentum of a charge. To cross the Gran Via, he had to step down from the pavement, and then up on to the terrace. At this juncture, clutching his flag for all he was worth, he mimicked the

heroic reeling of a veteran in the moment of victory before returning to the attack.

Jeers and catcalls poured from every mouth, prompted less by hatred for the Nationalist colours than by loathing of any military emblem. Tragedy, thanks to Joselito, was turning into farce.

When they reached the bullring, where a demobilization office had been set up in the open air, Joselito marched all the way round the arena, like a victorious matador, wrapped in the sumptuous folds of his flag.

Outside the open gates of the bull-pen, Joselito started playing the fool again.

'They've let all the bulls loose to celebrate the arrival of the rebels!'

But Juanito pulled him away from the other men, who were jostling one another.

'Now will you tell me where Agustin is?'

Joselito surveyed the bustling amphitheatre. Shouts, calls and laughter were being bandied back and forth. This defeat was mirroring the days of the big fights, the joyous expectancy of the crowd, its impatient rumblings, its curiosity and enthusiasm when, thin and wiry, sheathed in silk and embroidery, the matador emerged in his tight-fitting suit of light.

'Agustin . . .' repeated Joselito, as though searching his memory for the man who bore this name. 'Oh yes, Captain Benliure.' His face took on a vague expression. His gaze seemed to pursue Agustin's puny figure among all these agile bodies clambering over the stone seats and slipping into the ceremonial boxes; then it came to rest on Juanito again, with secret compassion.

'He died the day before yesterday, lieutenant, early in the morning.'

Joselito abandoned his cautious look; his eyes reacquired their cruel gleam beneath the long curling lids.

'I had sworn to shoot him the moment they arrived . . . I have no regrets . . .'

Joselito was reliving those few minutes: the roar of motor-bicycles, the anxious voices of the victors, their upturned faces, which he and Agustin had spied on through the gap in the shutters . . . The whole thing had gone off perfectly.

'I did as he asked, I have no regrets,' Joselito repeated.

But he had an obscure revenge to exact from Juanito. He alone knew the circumstances of Agustin's death, just as he grasped its motives—motives which the open-hearted Valencian would never understand. Joselito consented to give him a few of the details . . . Some soldiers were wrangling noisily beside them. The Army of the Levante could have held out a while longer. . .

'Let's go in here,' said Juanito.

An archway beside the bull-pen led to a small chapel. In the old days, a statue of the Virgin had stood inside: the matadors had fervently crossed themselves in front of her before the fight. Leading off from the chapel was a bare room with a lattice window. Here, emergency treatment used to be given to wounded toreros before they were driven off to a hospital. The two men sat down on the stone bench.

He had to die this way, thought Juanito. What was it he said as he turned the pages of that book? What threat and what promise were concealed beneath his final words: 'This parting was well made . . .'?

'Did the captain know I'd been arrested?' asked Juanito.

Joselito laughed.

'We went to enough trouble to see that you were!'

Juanito gave a start of astonishment.

'Oh yes!' the Andalusian continued mockingly. 'You have only to endorse the alibi we so carefully designed for you. It would be useless to deny it. Nobody would believe you, and there are witnesses ready to testify. On the captain's last night, I was able to set his mind at rest about you, while the papers were burning. I promised him that you would be the last officer to be arrested by the government of Valencia, and the first to be released by Franco . . . I always keep my word . . .'

'I *was* the first prisoner to be let out,' acknowledged Juanito.

'They were in a terrible hurry to give me back my freedom!'

It made him remorseful to think of his preferential treatment, of his few days of captivity during which the gaolers had vied with one another in attentiveness. They had kept a solicitous eye on these last-minute prisoners, while a constant flow of refugees poured along the road to Almeria, night and day, dragging their hastily packed belongings. This throng, seized with panic time and again, was composed of political 'militants' and anyone else in fear of reprisals. Meanwhile other men and women had gone to Sagunto to meet Franco's army. The first priests, clad in their soutanes, appeared at the gates of the city, and women went down on their knees to them, craving their blessing. Never had the violent conflict of emotions been more clearly displayed in Valencia. Thanks to his spell in prison, Juanito escaped this spectacle: the capitulation of a city, the end of a régime, correspond to the deathbed scenes of human beings, with their false remissions, their moments of childishness, their whims, their flashes of despair and resignation, their sudden changes of heart dictated by caution, their conversions inspired by fear. Juanito learnt only through his gaolers of the preparations for the victors' triumphal entry into the last city to fall. Anxious to soften these final days of captivity, the warders acted as messengers to the outside world, bought tobacco and newspapers, passed on news, posted letters. Their one role now, it seemed, was to safeguard their prisoners from the last undercurrents of civil war, from pointless escapes, from the final reckonings between partisans.

The Andalusian dwelt with a curious mixture of smugness and bitterness on the perfect timing and planning of Juanito's arrest and imprisonment.

'No complaints, now! We allowed for everything.'

Juanito had seen himself as combatant and prisoner, hero and victim. He had been nothing but the unwitting accessory to a fraud. He recalled how he had been summoned by the prison governor. The room was a small one, like the chief inspector's office in a local police station. On one of the walls hung an old photograph of Azaña, which nobody had thought to remove.

The Nationalist officer congratulated him on his courage. Juanito replied falteringly that he had known the Padre for as long as he could remember. The prison governor gazed with deep emotion at this Republican soldier who had risked his life for an incendiary priest.

Joselito was right: one cannot demolish an alibi which has links with the truth.

'Why did the captain do all that?'

Juanito was endeavouring to wrest a quiver of emotion from that impassive face, to disarm his enemy.

'Did he leave any message for me?' he asked. 'A letter, a short note . . .?'

Joselito smiled disdainfully.

'Nothing whatever . . . The captain counted on your prayers . . .'

The Andalusian's lips twisted ironically; he was enjoying an incommunicable feeling of revenge.

'I shall pray for him,' said Juanito.

He broke off abruptly. An argument had broken out in the arena. Juanito leapt to his feet; two soldiers withdrew hurriedly as he ran past them, as though they had been caught eavesdropping. The men who lived farthest from Valencia were demanding that they should be demobilized first. Soldiers who came from the same districts, the same villages, were congregating in groups. Parties no longer existed, but old rivalries, ancestral hatreds, were taking their place. The Catalans were scoffing at the men from the Levante. Galicians and Aragonese, Andalusians and Castilians were already sizing one another up. Demobilization was giving rise to a kind of competitiveness. This rush of young animals set at liberty was threatening to turn into a bloody battle.

'Each province will have its own demobilization desk,' said Juanito. 'If you want a scrap, you can fight with men from the same part of the country as yourselves.'

These words of arbitration restored their tempers. The colonel appeared. He had just handed over his barracks in the Gran Via to the impatient Nationalists. He was completely at

a loss, like a sea-captain who has seen his ship go down. He ran an astonished eye over this arena, which stood ready for other activities. He turned to Juanito.

'I was on tenterhooks back there,' he said. 'That business with the flag . . . You handled it splendidly.'

But Juanito had no wish to hark back to the surrender of the barracks; he wanted urgently to return to Joselito and question him. He abandoned the colonel in the middle of the arena and made his way back to the bull-pen. The same sickly, cattleshed smell enveloped him. A whiff of fresh sawdust was unsuccessful in concealing the stench of slaughter. After each series of fights, the bodies of the bulls were cut up, still warm, within these walls, so that pieces of the sacred meat could be distributed among the poor.

The moment he set foot in the chapel, Juanito saw the Andalusian lying on the stone bench. The white walls were splashed with blood. Joselito was in the throes of death. His eyes were closed. On the flagstone floor lay a knife with a long thin blade. When Juanito had rushed out into the arena to stop the quarrel, two men had hurriedly made themselves scarce. He had caught a look of consternation on their faces. Had they been spying on Joselito? One of them, a militant communist from Murcia, had saluted Juanito.

'The man from Murcia?' asked Juanito.

Joselito's eyelids fluttered. Some soldiers helped Juanito to rip off the torn and bloody remains of his shirt. The doctor did his best to stop the haemorrhage. How could this long thin body, which the soldiers were lifting with such clumsy care, how could this trunk, whose ribs showed through the skin, have harboured so much blood?

Juanito knelt down; the Andalusian's head was so close to his face that they could talk as though they were alone. Joselito seemed to recover a little life. The doctor stepped back.

'We ought to get him to hospital,' he said, as though to himself, 'but there is a danger of his dying on the way.'

Joselito lifted his head. A hint of bravado shone in his eyes; for a moment, impudence bloomed on his face again.

'Don't bother, doctor! I would rather die in here like a fashionable matador!'

'Who said anything about dying?' cried Juanito. 'Just you lie still. The doctor will put you right.'

Joselito stared at him. His hatred for Juanito had vanished. He could not understand why the lieutenant was frenziedly helping the doctor to open his bag.

'It's all over,' he said softly. 'I'm on my way to join Agustin . . .'

There were beads of sweat on his forehead. He had turned very pale and, lying there with his body stripped to the waist, he was shivering.

'Lieutenant, if there is a hell, the captain and I will burn together.'

'You mustn't blaspheme,' said Juanito. 'You have done enough today to earn your place in heaven. Nobody else would have shown such courage.'

'What courage?' asked Joselito. He thought he was accounting for his actions to Agustin. 'I had given you my word . . .'

He recognized Juanito.

'Lieutenant, you have seen more than one man die . . . The world isn't losing much in losing me.' Must he be silent to the very end? He made a final effort; the blood was rushing to his face, giving it a mysterious radiance. He smiled at Juanito as he confided his secret: 'Remember, lieutenant . . . Hunger, thirst and pleasure are the same everywhere.'

His head fell back on to the hard stone bench. The doctor, who had been stooping over him, straightened up. He stood examining the sharp, rusty knife as though it were a surgical instrument.

'It would take a peasant to use it as skilfully as that.'

Joselito reopened his eyes. The doctor was handling the Murcian's dagger with considerable care. Joselito was stirred to a final act of defiance.

'Doctor, give me back the knife . . . Where I come from, there is a saying:

I am the dried-up spring,
I am the forest without trees,
I am the corpse without a dagger.

He was unable to give distinct utterance to this *copla* which he had sung in the old days, accompanying himself on the guitar. Only Juanito could catch the closing words as they came hissing out between his lips. They spread an old blanket over him, as though he were a wounded matador. But, lying on the stone bench, Joselito thought he was back in the Tabierno Flamenco. He was in the centre of the floor, dancing . . . His life was merging with this trance, with this bluish ring in which the spotlights were enclosing his steps. The earth was moving at the same time as he, drawing him along in its field of gravitation. The Andalusian's high heels were thudding on the resonant floor. With his chest thrust out, his belly drawn in, his narrow hips sheathed in his high-waisted trousers, he was planted like a quivering knife in the souls of his audience. He was suffocating in his waistcoat, with its covering of ruby-red spangles. The silk and metal 'points' of his jacket were whirling round his chest. The tiny area that he was bestriding, traversing and retraversing enclosed past and future, reality and illusion. From the semi-darkness of their tables, the customers were intently following the frenzied rhythm of the zapateado, as though they were witnessing some ferocious sport or the cape-work of a matador.

Joselito was dancing, the musicians were huddling over their guitars in their efforts to keep up with him. Was it his unerring steps that were giving birth to the music? Nobody dared to lift a glass, or drink, or speak. They were all waiting, petrified, for Joselito himself to break the evil spell that he was in process of weaving. But Joselito would never unspring the trap in which these men were caught. What trap? Tenderness, music, beauty, happiness, or a vague longing for all these fleeting paradises, a desperate ache to return to a weightless body, an angelic or demoniac form propelled by unflagging energy?

Joselito was dancing with all his youthfulness, all his strength. And his dance was becoming increasingly furious and concerted,

bolder than a caress, more savage and swifter than a murder, lewder than an evil possession. Caught up in this whirl, Joselito no longer had any desire but to dance to the very end, to dance till it killed him.

The whites of his eyes were showing: he was an exhausted horseman, quivering in time with his steed. A trace of pink foam appeared at the corner of his gasping mouth. Lying motionless on the stone bench, he was devising his finest dance. For no one else would ever dance with such rage and vehemence, with such calculation and vigour. He was casting a spell over the audience merely by laying out a labyrinth before their eyes, a labyrinth that was effaced at every step, reconstructed at every step. He was binding these defenceless victims with every tremor of his muscles, with every jerk of his body. If Joselito were to stop, the customers of the Tabierno Flamenco would waken from their dream. They would become idle rich again, mere loungers on the look-out for amusement. They would raise their voices to joke, to call out to one another, to demand a drink, a dancing girl, a tune. Joselito was preventing them from returning to that simulacrum of living, to that simulacrum of freedom. He was riveting them to this piece of floor-board; he was nailing them down with every click of his heels, within the narrow orbit of his dance. Were Joselito to slow down the furious rhythm of the zapateado, were he to stop quivering from head to foot and pounding the floor, were he to give them time to cry mercy, they would break free from the magic circle, they would escape.

But giddiness was taking hold of the dancer and plucking him from his imaginary gyrations. Joselito let out a groan. He was beaten. Juanito's face was close to his.

'Don't be afraid, lieutenant,' he whispered. 'Remember . . . Hunger, thirst and pleasure . . .'

49

DOWNSTAIRS, a hand was patiently rattling the shutters.

Their regular creaking sounded like a signal. Without switching on the light, Encarnacion tiptoed to her bedroom window.

The moon shone down on the tranquil garden. A kneeling figure was exerting the same gentle pressure outside each of the ground-floor rooms, one after another. Was it a looter, a deserter? All that Encarnacion could see was a powerful pair of shoulders, a bulky body . . .

Franco's forces had entered Madrid, but improbable and sublime instances of heroism were going round by word of mouth. Those who circulated these tales of stubborn resistance were deriving a sly feeling of revenge from them, an absurd hope that all was not over. In the Paseo de San Vicente, a single officer, with a handful of men about him, had refused to give up his arms and ammunition. It had taken a regular siege to dislodge him . . .

But most of the troops were deserting in the hope of slipping across the frontier. Others were hiding out in the sierras or taking to the forests. Recklessly, they would prowl at night near farmhouses and villages. Evading every trap, they would try to steal back into their homes, into their former lives, trembling with curiosity, love and longing. They had hurled their rifles over the nearest hedge, but they still wore army tunics, belts and puttees. And these ghostly figures looked as though they had dressed in a hurry, by robbing corpses on a battlefield.

Whenever they came knocking at Encarnacion's door, she questioned them, in the hope that one of these vagrants would be the bearer of a message from Pablo or Juanito. The stranger who was now trying to get into the house did not frighten her. This hunted human being was merely begging for a roof over

his head and a peaceful night's sleep. Resting her weight on the banister, Encarnacion started down the stairs. The polished wood glided by beneath her hand. The steps did not creak under her bare feet. When she reached the bottom, she paused for a few seconds.

The faint scraping of the catch on its iron ring was filing away at the night silence. The man was making a desperate effort to open the window of the sitting-room which led into the passage-way adjoining Encarnacion's old bedroom. After Juanito left, she had abandoned that ground-floor room which had been a party to the long sleepless nights when another, happier woman had been roused by the caresses and declarations of a young lover. The noise ceased. The man had lost heart. Or had he sensed someone standing there in the dark? Holding her breath, she stepped forward, meaning to peer through the chink in the shutters. She thought she heard her name, as though someone were calling her without moving his lips. Syllables were being formed one by one, in a barely modulated whisper . . . She still hesitated. The toneless voice was breathing, directly against the shutters: 'En-car-na-cion.'

She threw caution to the winds.

'I'm here,' she said. 'Who is it?'

The voice broke, letting out a brief groan.

'Pablo!'

Encarnacion burst open the latches. Pablo stepped over the iron rail. She made to clasp him in her arms, but he barely brushed his lips against her forehead. His movements were sluggish and unsteady, like those of a drunk. She lit the lamp that stood on a low table while he carefully closed the shutters and drew the curtains. He was reeling about. Almost ashamedly, he stammered out: 'Encarnacion, I'm so tired. I want to sleep, I want to eat . . .'

She smiled at him.

'Lie down on the divan, Pablo. I shall only be gone a moment . . .'

For days he had been roaming the countryside, starting at even the most distant barking of a dog, trembling when, hiding

behind a hedge, he recognized a farmer's voice. He had not dared to venture into a village to buy bread. I'm not going to be caught through carelessness, he had said to himself. He had temporarily allayed his hunger by stealing some fruit, but lack of food had given him long dizzy spells during which he imagined that he was already back in Santa Creus. He would stand knocking at the door in vain. Encarnacion had gone. He would rouse himself from this nightmare only to sink into another. The house would be just a mass of charred ruins. He was vainly trying to extricate a dead body from the debris. The exertion would wake him up. He would find himself hiding in a muddy ditch. Then he would again fall into this faint, in which fear, tiredness and hunger composed a dream more incoherent than the dreams of the living. Pablo was already dreaming like a ghost: nothing now distinguished the tattered remains of his existence from other imaginary episodes. He would be sitting at Enrico's bedside in Tarragona hospital. His son was dictating that short note of farewell, penned by an unknown hand, which Pablo had been carrying in his pocket for days. Enrico entrusted Encarnacion to him, as though Pablo were capable of experiencing with her the happiness that he would have liked to give to his son. Pablo was trying to get him to enlarge on these few words, with their marvellous tone of detachment. Why was Enrico claiming that, after his death, Encarnacion and Pablo would be united forever? Why was he promising them, whatever their future, this mysterious reconciliation, this spiritual joy, to which he was already lending his approval . . .? But, with a smile, the dying man refused to explain himself further. He was apologizing for not lingering among the living. Like his mother, he was discreetly slipping away from a brilliant, chaotic party into which he had strayed unawares. He was already making his bow. Streaming with sweat, Pablo would open his eyes to find the same bough hanging over him. Hunger was gnawing again, impelling him to bite into a rotten apple thrown away by a child, or chew a dry ear of corn which had fallen off a cart. And now, back in his own house, Pablo imagined that he was still the victim of an illusion. Why was he alone? Hadn't Encarnacion opened the shutters just

now? His hand clawed at the material of the sofa, recognized its rather coarse texture. Reassured, he closed his eyes . . . When she returned, he was asleep, shielding his head with his forearm: he looked like a harvester overcome with fatigue in the middle of a field. There was a dark stain on his sleeve. She was afraid that he might be wounded, but when she made to touch his arm, he shrank away.

She dared not rouse him from this exhausted sleep, so much like a tramp's. She returned to the kitchen with the tray, on which a bowl of soup lay steaming beside the carafe of dark red wine, the sliced ham and the whole-meal bread. A wonderful feeling of peace came over her. She had only a few hours more to spend within these walls, but she had already taken her leave of persons and of objects, of her past and of herself.

Pablo was threshing about in his sleep; he was protesting his innocence. Perhaps he was continuing the waking dream which they had shared, one summer night. Were they strolling through the Paris of his youth, poor as exiles, tremulous as an engaged couple?

Encarnacion stood hesitating. I ought to wake him, she thought, get him to eat something, pack his case. The pallor of dawn showed through the slats. What was the safest way of getting to France? But before going into the question of routes and hiding-places, Encarnacion would have to confess everything: 'Pablo, I am no longer frustrated, a woman divided against herself. Loneliness and bitterness, folly and deceit—everything has ripened within me, everything has turned to sap, gentleness and strength within my breast . . . Now my life is nourishing another life . . . Pablo, it was privation that made me give myself to Juanito; the love of that twenty-year-old boy was the miracle of a scorching summer, the miracle of a short-lived victory. It was a mirage appearing at high noon above the desert of my life . . .'

But when Pablo woke, when he stood blinking as though dazzled by the sun, he would ask no questions. Encarnacion would say nothing. She would go wherever he led her. She was a boat run aground, which the tide was about to carry out to sea

again. There was nothing more for her to resolve, nothing more for her to decide. She was left with just a few moments of solitude in which to say good-bye to Juanito.

She sat down at the little desk on which, as a young woman, she had recorded the entries in her personal diary, trying to allay her disappointment by stooping over this mirror. 'You are free now,' Enrico had murmured. No one is ever free, thought Encarnacion. Juanito's love had been merely loaned to her; now, with Pablo, she was returning to her old state of bondage. All the motives that she invoked would wound Juanito. Slowly, on the smooth writing paper, she wrote the words which would set Juanito free, which would restore him to his youth. She told him that she would never return to the house in which she had known his love . . .

'Darling Juanito, Pablo came back last night. He has managed to break out of prison. At the moment he is sleeping as though he had months of sleep to catch up on. We shall be making an early start today, but with me I shall take your caresses and your kisses, your words and your glances, all twined together like the sprig of honeysuckle which I picked from the garden for you, that first day . . .'

Words did not seem simple enough, pure enough, strong enough for this farewell. She did not have the heart to write any more. Her soul was bursting open, like a wound . . . Pablo stirred. She pulled herself together and quickly sealed the letter. Everything was settled. Without impatience or anxiety, she was waiting for Pablo to rouse himself so that she could start a new life with him: in the same way, our souls will one day wait to acquire bodily shape again, so that they may love and suffer afresh, and more deeply.

From his dream he called: 'Encarnacion!'

'I'm here, Pablo.'

She reassured him as though he were an anxious child. Was he striving to reach her in his gaol-accustomed dreams? Had captivity freed him of other restraints? Was he at last daring to perform the motions which he had never performed when he was free? With racing heart, Encarnacion stooped over him.

A maternal pity, a desperate need to succour him, were causing her hands to shake. She longed to rest that massive head in her lap, to entangle her fingers with those locks of black and grey, to efface the deeply scored lines in that weary brow . . . But Pablo was still shielding his face with his arm. Was he defending himself against the early-morning light, or against the horror of waking in a prison cell? Enrico was dead, Juanito gone. Pablo had come back to her: no one would ever again attempt to break the mysterious bond between them. Encarnacion was discovering the love that flowed, fierce and taciturn, within her. Throughout the months of absence, it had been hollowing out its bed in the depths of her being. Juanito's confidences and embraces were powerless against a passion which had always avoided pledges, always eschewed kisses. Encarnacion knelt listening to this cry from a love walled up alive in her, as overwhelming as a cry of resurrection. Her hand brushed lightly, in a slow caress, over this cheek grimed with stubble. Pablo's breath was playing between her fingers. Very softly and shamefacedly, she confessed: 'Pablo, you know I have never really loved anyone but you.'

He opened his eyes, as though he had heard these barely articulated words. The prohibitions of society, the scruples of the proud-spirited, the conventions fabricated by human beings, the obstacles which hearts with a gift for self-torture invent for themselves—all these had vanished while Pablo was asleep, and now Encarnacion's face shone with assent alone . . .

Pablo strode into the room looking jubilant and young. He had changed his clothes and shaved with care.

'For a prisoner, how perplexing to have to choose between a variety of suits and shirts and ties!'

There was a long gash on his cheek.

'I had difficulty with that old razor which somebody has left in my dressing-room.'

'I had an officer billeted on me soon after the offensive was launched.' Encarnacion set the cups and the steaming coffee-pot on the table. There was a gentle, far-away look on her face. 'He was from Valencia,' she went on. 'He talked on and on

about the *huerta*, and the games they play there, and the carnival, and the processions. In his eyes, the Madonna was a young bride being led through a battle of flowers.' She slowly filled a cup and handed it to Pablo. 'I think you would have liked the boy. He was full of laughter and zest and fire . . . Even when the Republicans evacuated the village, he was still certain of victory . . .'

But Pablo was staring at Encarnacion, without listening. There was a glorious slowness to her every movement. She had something of the look of those beautiful figures of the seasons, the goddesses of abundance and fertility who gaze down in triumph from the ceilings of Venetian palaces. Her lowered eyelids, her shut lips quivered with a mysterious voluptuousness. Her skin was of a mat colour beside the blue-black hair.

'I had forgotten how beautiful you are, Encarnacion,' Pablo said, with something not far short of amazement.

She accepted these words of praise with a smile.

'I hadn't forgotten how flattering *you* are, Pablo.'

She threw open the french windows which led into the garden. The sunlight came flooding in, glittering on the cup in her hand. Pablo inhaled, with a kind of greed, this spring morning air which melted in the mouth like the tart pulp of a young fruit. Both of them looked as though they were about to embark, not on a journey into exile, but on an early ramble.

'Let me take a quick look at my books.'

Pablo thrust open the door of his library. In the dim light, he ran his hand mechanically over the polished spines and, turning to Encarnacion, said: 'Privation has made me possessive. How happy I am to see all these books again, even though I haven't time even to dip into them!' To stifle this childish regret, he said to himself: What need have I today of books, pictures, *objets d'art*, of anything that rouses and fosters the covetousness of the poor? I am rich now . . . I possess the human being of whom alone my life was in need.

Encarnacion stepped closer to him. For her too, these books were bringing back memories of the long winter evenings spent alone together. The logs were crackling in the fireplace. Above

them, they could hear the soft tread of a ghost. Pablo would glance up from his book to swap impressions with his daughter-in-law. They had called these oblique confidences, this counterpoint of confessions and silences, a conversation . . .

'I too am beginning to grow attached to things, Pablo, because we are about to leave them.'

She was smiling bravely. He averted his head slightly.

'We shan't miss any of them, Encarnacion.' Over the years, while they had been building up the decor of their lives together, they had perpetuated a fiction. They had tried to be a couple just like other couples, with their mutual attentiveness, their divergences of taste, their quarrels and their concessions. Now they were throwing off this chrysalis woven from old subterfuges, habits, feelings of deference, lies: they no longer needed this simulacrum of intimacy, since they loved one another.

Very softly, Pablo continued: 'I have no feelings of regret, Encarnacion—quite the reverse, in fact . . . I wanted to see this house again, the garden, my books, just as one wishes to see a friend alive and kicking on the eve of a critical operation. But one is anxious not to spend too long in a hospital ward. One quickly garners his everyday smile, his everyday expression. One mentally takes a cast of a face still full of life . . . But after that, one leaves . . .'

He pointed to the suitcase lying open on the living-room table in which Encarnacion was assembling a few clothes, some papers, some jewellery and a small photograph of Enrico taken at the time of their engagement. Encarnacion nodded, fluttering her eyelashes. Within her were being wrought this shedding of the cocoon, this uprooting, this rebirth . . . One last worry occurred to her: 'No one saw you come in?'

Pablo hesitated.

'No one!' he said. One of his tenant-farmers had brought him nearly as far as the village in his cart and set him down under cover of darkness. This morning, the same man was to pick them up and drive them to Barcelona. Pablo would be over the frontier before the police were alerted. Encarnacion had finished packing the few things that they were taking with them. She

closed the shutters. People would suppose that she had gone away for a few days. There was something wonderfully soothing about covering their tracks like this, about stealing out of this house which had for so long been a party to their love.

They crept along the gravel drive as though for fear of waking an invalid. The flower-beds had run wild, but the trees were in full bloom. The pink snow of the almond blossom quivered in the light breeze, making intricate gestures of welcome and farewell. Pomegranates hung almost ripe from the low branches. A single gulp of this morning air, laden with pollen and the impatient darting of bees, contained the whole blossoming of spring. Water was murmuring along in an irrigation channel. The olive trees were dancing on the spot, convulsed with happiness from their roots to their topmost leaves.

Near the little gate which led into the fields, Encarnacion noticed that a rose-bush had been trampled down. The flower-beds were mangled, as though as a result of a fierce struggle. But she was thinking of the Valencian flinging open this gate at night, traversing the garden with a few rapid strides, sprinting towards her with a marvellous, boyish avidity. She said to herself: It isn't possible. Very close, as though pressed to her lips, she saw the golden face, the lagoon-coloured pupils, of a twenty-year-old boy. Why have they taken Juanito away from me? It's unfair, it's monstrous! A furious wave of rebellion was sweeping through her heart, dispelling a precarious self-control, a precarious renunciation. From the honeysuckle plant growing beside the hedge, she plucked a sprig of flowers and pressed them to her face. Their scent, miraculously like the scent of so many other growths of honeysuckle, had a pacifying effect on her. In the ditch bordering the garden, a man was lying face downwards. It was Javier.

The night before, Pablo had encountered a threatening figure, barring the way to his house. There had been an embroiled tussle. In the violent affray, they had each gasped for breath, trembling at the thought of being denounced by this voiceless enemy. I'm done for, Pablo had thought. He had managed to free himself from the stranger's grasp. He had fired, at point-blank range.

The roar of the gun had gone echoing over the countryside. For a moment, Pablo and his adversary had stood motionless, like a pair of wrestlers exerting equal force. Then, quite suddenly, Javier had pitched forward. Had he recognized his killer? Pablo had flattened himself against his victim. There had been no sign of life from the house. The village had given the impression of being fast asleep. Javier's blood had soaked into Pablo's sleeve. To be on the safe side, he had flung away the revolver and dragged the corpse over to the ditch . . .

In the implacable brightness of morning, Pablo could make out all the traces of the previous night's struggle. At the bottom of the ditch, with his face buried in the grass, a man seemed to be sleeping off the after-effects of drink. Pablo felt an urge to kiss that icy cheek, to say: 'Forgive me, Javier; I had no hatred for you.'

But he had to step over the dead body to rejoin Encarnacion.

'It's Javier,' she whispered. 'Night after night he is out here, prowling by the gate. He will denounce us.'

'Don't worry,' said Pablo. 'He's asleep.'

The path was wet with early-morning dew, and Encarnacion found herself slipping. Pablo supported her with his free arm. It seemed to him, without his really being aware of it, that Encarnacion had a slower gait than before, the gait of a woman, and that her body itself had a secret fullness. They were walking along, arm in arm, like the world's first couple being expelled from the garden of Eden; but they felt no temptation to retrace their steps.

They came to the road. Through the trees, Pablo could see the roofs of the schoolhouse and the maternity hospital. They had not had time to turn this village into a Future City. No feeling of regret troubled the limpidity of this spring morning, on which their love, it seemed, was being born.

When the cart drew up, Pablo asked the farmer for the latest news.

'They have just entered Valencia,' the man answered, helping Encarnacion into the back of the cart, where she would be hidden among the harnesses, straps, tools and sacks of corn.

Pablo did not answer. Encarnacion sat watching the roadway glide past at their feet and stretch out behind them. Like staring at the fall of snow, there was something hypnotic about gazing intently at this road rolling by, ever replenishing itself, at this growing distance, at this parting—increased by every turn of the wheel—between Encarnacion and herself . . .

50

THE GRAN VIA WAS BUZZING WITH LIFE. With cars and pedestrians milling round him, Juanito was walking along stirred by a strange feeling of giddiness. The morning coolness lingered in the narrow streets. The war had only been a nightmare. Unconnected images—some recent, others very old—were flashing through Juanito's brain: the ostentatious handshake with which the Nationalist officer had set him free; the hospital in Barcelona where Ramon had lain dying; getting up before first light in Encarnacion's house. In the victorious dawn at Gandesa, Agustin's voice was proclaiming: 'Son of the *huerta*!'

What about the shop assistants raising the iron shutters, and the women giving their doorsteps a thorough soaking? Were they, too, visited by this fleeting revelation in which yesterday merged with tomorrow? Were they the disincarnate spectators of their own destinies? Were they imagining their future lives or rediscovering, like a language which one thinks one has forgotten, the existences that lay behind them? He saw the colonel appearing suddenly at Joselito's deathbed. A dancer from the Barrio Chino was becoming a hero. His dying words were just one more enigma: 'Hunger, thirst and pleasure are the same everywhere . . .' It all had the jumbled and inescapable progression, the unaccountable changeability, the jerkiness and circuitousness of a dream. Were other people likewise waking from a

confused and bloody dream? Wasn't their awakening turning out to be another dream? Wasn't Juanito really asleep in the shade of the puny vine-plants, devastated by the blaze of the sky and the man-made blaze of gunfire?

Everyone he passed wore the anxious look of a convalescent taking his first few steps. A young woman, with a sleeping child wrapped in her shawl, brushed against Juanito. She stood hesitating on the pavement of the boulevard and, before disappearing down a side-street, shot a hunted look at this officer who seemed to be following her. She had the same gait as Encarnacion, and the same pliant, delicate neck beneath the abundant black hair. Juanito pictured her walking straight ahead along a road in Catalonia, waiting at the frontier for the train or lorry which would carry her to safety.

For her, the nightmare continued. Yet, when he had released Juanito, the Nationalist officer had claimed that the war was over. That was true for Agustin, for Joselito who had died with a smile of defiance, a mysterious message, on his lips. Everyone had lied, but everyone was the plaything of a different illusion, the victim of a different imposture. At Guadalajara, at Brunete, at Teruel, at Belchite, the dead, buried at random, were fraternizing at last in the same soil. Impossible for armies to recognize their heroes, for parties to count and identify their martyrs. Who was right? Agustin, who had chosen death? Encarnacion, who preferred exile? Joselito, concocting that ludicrous grand finale which had cost him his life?

Who was the victor in the eyes of God? Would Fernando, the first man to die in the offensive on the Ebro, meet the dancer from the Barrio Chino? Would heaven open to admit Ramon—like the living circle of the *sardana*, flowing in and out, like the tide, to the rhythm of the *cobla*? Would Agustin take his place within the ring of prophets clad in the skins of wild animals, who stone sinners with words that are harder than pebbles?

Phrases and ideas were all jumbled together in Juanito's brain. He was besieged by a whirl of longings, fears and hopes. Why was he not, even now, in the midst of the rice-fields, which the rising sun turns into a lake of gold? He would speed

along behind his horse, driving the invisible plough which turns the warm mud. But before returning to the *huerta*, Juanito was seeking the aid of an incorruptible witness, the encouragement of a familiar face. In the distance, a bullet ricocheted off a wall. From the crowd there came an indignant roar of abuse against this sniper: would the slaughtering never end . . .?

Juanito was walking along in a trance: images were succeeding one another too rapidly beneath his brow. Events were contradicting one another and cancelling one another out; person was replacing person at dizzying speed. Faces were slipping off like masks, masks were turning into faces. The façade of the city hall, decked with the Nationalist colours, was disappearing beneath the banners and streamers borne aloft by the wind. Juanito nearly fell: the paving-stones were slippery with trampled flowers. The prison warders had told him how, when Franco's forces had entered the city, petals had snowed from the balconies as though for a procession. The people's joyous faces had simply been acclaiming, with the end of bloodshed, the right to work and laze, to laugh and love, to live.

The door of San Martino church stood open. Gone were the vehicles and munitions which, for two years, had taken the place of altars. A supply of uniforms was piled insecurely beside the smashed stoop. A sour smell of cooking still hung in the air, for the church had been put to every kind of use.

After crossing the Plaza de la Reina, Juanito walked up the street, more secluded than a cul-de-sac, which runs alongside the cathedral. This road, which bends like an arm round a sleeping head, divides the House of God from the Virgin's basilica; but an arcaded gallery bestrides it in mid-air, so that the Mother may visit her Son privily.

Juanito stopped beside the grating which enables the devout to call upon the Madonna at any hour of the day or night. In the old days, a curtain had been lowered in front of the altar every evening, bearing a painting of the Virgin of the Forsaken. Kneeling in the roadway, passers-by had caught a glimpse of her through the bars of the spy-hole. Thus they had respected the repose and the dreams of the Mother of God. But, when the time

came for the first Mass of the new day, the priest raised the curtain. The Virgin stood there, open-eyed, waiting to receive the entreaties of sinners. To her, the darkness of the ages was merely a long vigil, for when the candles burnt out in front of her statue, human anguish and hope blazed more intensely in the heart of the Madonna.

Juanito lowered his head till he could see through the grating. Figures were flitting about in the semi-darkness. Hands were sheltering a pistil of flame. The candle lit up a nunlike face. Tongues of fire were leaping up all over the Lady-chapel, like a new Pentecost. Facing the altar, with their arms spread to form a cross, men and women were praying in this flickering light: they might have been in the catacombs. Each of them was conversing with Our Lady of the Forsaken as though he or she were alone. Juanito ran to the main door. The uneven flagstones seemed to subside under his feet. The sacred grotto enclosed him in the warm darkness of a mother's heart. Juanito knelt down. Motionless and attentive, behind the burning bush of the candles, the Madonna was listening to him.

'You are back! A bullet has grazed your cheek, but the shadows conceal your scar. Where did you hide with your Son? Despite all the sacking of churches, you are still wearing your gold-embroidered mantle, like a sun. You have preserved your shimmering breastplate of jewels, but there is not a trace of blood on your pale hands.

'You are back . . . The gardens of the *huerta* will blossom for you, despite the war, and one Sunday in May, amid the stench of gunpowder, the handsomest men of Valencia will abduct you in broad daylight.

'Mother of Christ, you belong to us. You defended the peasants and tradesmen of Valencia when they rose up against the kings. You will defend their sons, too, for a taste for freedom flows in their veins, mixed with the pleasure of being alive!

'Between you and the men of Valencia there exists a contract which nobody can break, a bond more inviolable than marriage, an oath inscribed in body and soul.

'And I too have the right to speak to you as a son speaks to his mother, as a husband speaks to his wife, using words crude and tender, words that are a caress and a quarrel.

'Our Lady of the Forsaken, of the mad and of the innocent, you prefer the vanquished to the victors, the weak to the strong! Shelter the Republicans! Preserve Agustin from hell, just as you helped me out of the burning church. He did not want me to share his death as Garcia Hernandez shared Fermin Galan's. Blessed Virgin, he loved the poor and the humble. He knew poems more beautiful than any hymn . . . Save him, and his thanksgiving will carry to you like the scent of a huge rose-bush in blossom. Deliver Joselito from the flames, too: he shot Agustin out of obedience to his promise, just as he snatched from my hands the flag which no one else would carry. He took upon himself the crime, the deceit and the shame of us all . . . In the old days, he used to dance in the Barrio Chino, with whores and thieves, but in a church in Barcelona I saw a jester sleeping beside your altar with his cap and bells. Hide Agustin and Joselito under your mantle, as you hid the Holy Innocents when the soldiers were after them!

'Mother of the Forsaken, do not forget Fernando, whose death prompts a smile as though it were a blunder, nor the man at Campredo who got himself killed through obstinacy, nor the little Falangist who refused to change sides, nor the airman who *did* change sides! I entrust to your safekeeping those who wanted to live at any price and those who preferred not to survive: in your Paradise, make room for the cowards who for a moment saw themselves as heroes, and for the heroes who for a moment were cowards . . .

'Render unto each his share of worldly happiness, his share of the crops and the wine-harvests . . . Let Ramon, in your heaven, come sailing home from his night-time fishing. It is then that the lamps dazzle the fish, and the boat is fully laden, and the oars weigh heavily on the sailors' arms; but, from the shore, the wind carries the grave and triumphant summons of the *sardanas*. Let Felix and Carlos have long warm evenings under the arcades of their little towns, and endless card-games amid the smell of *anis*,

and the plucking of guitars, and the laughter of the girls as they dance.

'Gather my brother Federico in your nets, so that we may build him a house of gleaming marble at the gates of Valencia, a house with transparent windows. He will no longer be a drowned sailor without a grave: among the flowers, he will look like the best man at a wedding, waiting for the bridal procession to enter the church.

'Take care of Encarnacion: she has followed Pablo on the road to France. She had drunk a love-potion: nothing could free her from it, not even this child ripening in her womb. But whenever I speak her name, it is as though I were crushing a spray of jasmine in my fingers. Is that a sin? Blessed Virgin, I still love Encarnacion. It was a summer night. She was as lonely as night, as glowing as summer . . .

'Forgive my sacrilege, Virgin of the Forsaken: she looked like you! But all women have your sad eyes and your sealed lips. Their words set us dreaming of your silence, their promises turn our thoughts to your refusal, their confessions make us thirst for your seclusion, when your black hair trails on to your shoulders and you gently incline your head to listen to us . . .'